events, it becomes necessary for one

the Laws of Nature and of Natu

————— We hold these truths

the pursuit of Happiness.———

rnment becomes destructive of th

powers in such form, as to then

ght and transient causes; and a

ich they are accustomed. But

t, it is their duty, to throw off suc

which constrains them to alter th

object the establishment of an

holesome and necessary for the p

nt should be obtained; and whe

e people would relinquish the rig

HONOUR AMONG THIEVES

By the same author

Novels

NOT A PENNY MORE, NOT A PENNY LESS
SHALL WE TELL THE PRESIDENT?
KANE AND ABEL
THE PRODIGAL DAUGHTER
FIRST AMONG EQUALS
A MATTER OF HONOUR
AS THE CROW FLIES

Short stories

A QUIVER FULL OF ARROWS
A TWIST IN THE TALE

Plays

BEYOND REASONABLE DOUBT
EXECUTIVE

JEFFREY ARCHER

HONOUR AMONG THIEVES

BCA

LONDON NEW YORK SYDNEY TORONTO

This edition published 1993
by BCA
by arrangement with HarperCollins Ltd.

Copyright © Jeffrey Archer 1993

CN 1469

Set in Janson

Printed and bound in Germany
by Graphischer Großbetrieb Pößneck GmbH
A member of the Mohndruck printing group

To Geoffrey and Babs

PART ONE

'*When in the Course of human events...*'

1

ANTONIO CAVALLI stared intently at the Arab, who he considered looked far too young to be a Deputy Ambassador.

'One hundred million dollars,' Cavalli said, pronouncing each word slowly and deliberately, giving them almost reverential respect.

Hamid Al Obaydi flicked a worry bead across the top of his well-manicured thumb, making a click that was beginning to irritate Cavalli.

'One hundred million is quite acceptable,' the Deputy Ambassador replied in a clipped English accent.

Cavalli nodded. The only thing that worried him about the deal was that Al Obaydi had made no attempt to bargain, especially as the figure the American had proposed was double that which he had expected to get. Cavalli had learned from painful experience not to trust anyone who didn't bargain. It inevitably meant that they had no intention of paying in the first place.

'If the figure is agreed,' he said, 'all that is left to discuss is how and when the payments will be made.'

The Deputy Ambassador flicked another worry bead before he nodded.

'Ten million dollars to be paid in cash immediately,' said Cavalli, 'the remaining ninety million to be deposited in a Swiss bank account as soon as the contract has been carried out.'

'But what do I get for my first ten million?' asked the Deputy Ambassador, looking fixedly at the man whose origins were as hard to hide as his own.

'Nothing,' replied Cavalli, although he acknowledged that the Arab had every right to ask. After all, if Cavalli didn't honour his side of the bargain, the Deputy Ambassador had far more to lose than just his government's money.

Al Obaydi moved another worry bead, aware that he had little choice – it had taken him two years just to get an interview with Antonio Cavalli. Meanwhile, President Clinton had settled into the White House, while his own leader was growing more and more impatient for revenge. If he didn't accept Cavalli's terms, Al Obaydi knew that the chances of finding anyone else capable of carrying out the task before July the fourth were about as promising as zero coming up on a roulette wheel with only one spin left.

Cavalli looked up at the vast portrait that dominated the wall behind the Deputy Ambassador's desk. His first contact with Al Obaydi had been only days after the war had been concluded. At the time the American had refused to deal with the Arab, as few people were convinced that the Deputy Ambassador's leader would still be alive by the time a preliminary meeting could be arranged.

As the months passed, however, it began to look to Cavalli as if his potential client might survive longer than President Bush. So an exploratory meeting was arranged.

The venue selected was the Deputy Ambassador's office in New York, on East 79th Street. Despite being a little too public for Cavalli's taste, it had the virtue of proving the credentials of the party claiming to be willing to invest one hundred million dollars in such a daring enterprise.

'How would you expect the first ten million to be paid?' enquired Al Obaydi, as if he were asking a real estate agent about a down-payment on a small house on the wrong side of the Brooklyn Bridge.

'The entire amount must be handed over in used, unmarked

hundred-dollar bills and deposited with our bankers in Newark, New Jersey,' said the American, his eyes narrowing. 'And Mr Obaydi,' Cavalli added, 'I don't have to remind you that we have machines that can verify . . .'

'You need have no anxiety about us keeping to our side of the bargain,' interrupted Al Obaydi. 'The money is, as your Western cliché suggests, a mere drop in the ocean. The only concern I have is whether you are capable of delivering your part of the agreement.'

'You wouldn't have pressed so hard for this meeting if you doubted we were the right people for the job,' retorted Cavalli. 'But can I be as confident about you putting together such a large amount of cash at such short notice?'

'It may interest you to know, Mr Cavalli,' replied the Deputy Ambassador, 'that the money is already lodged in a safe in the basement of the United Nations building. After all, no one would expect to find such a vast sum deposited in the vaults of a bankrupt body.'

The smile that remained on Al Obaydi's face indicated that the Arab was pleased with his little witticism, despite the fact that Cavalli's lips hadn't moved.

'The ten million will be delivered to your bank by midday tomorrow,' continued Al Obaydi as he rose from the table to indicate that, as far he was concerned, the meeting was concluded. The Deputy Ambassador stretched out his hand and his visitor reluctantly shook it.

Cavalli glanced up once again at the portrait of Saddam Hussein, turned, and quickly left.

When Scott Bradley entered the room there was a hush of expectancy.

He placed his notes on the table in front of him, allowing his eyes to sweep around the lecture hall. The room was packed with eager young students holding pens and pencils poised above yellow legal pads.

'My name is Scott Bradley,' said the youngest Professor in the Law School, 'and this is to be the first of fourteen lectures on Constitutional Law.' Seventy-four faces stared down at the tall, somewhat dishevelled man who obviously hadn't noticed that the top button of his shirt was missing and who couldn't have made up his mind which side to part his hair that morning.

'I'd like to begin this first lecture with a personal statement,' he announced. Some of the pens and pencils were laid to rest. 'There are many reasons to practise law in this country,' he began, 'but only one which is worthy of you, and certainly only one that interests me. It applies to every facet of the law that you might be interested in pursuing, and it has never been better expressed than in the engrossed parchment of The Unanimous Declaration of the Thirteen United States of America.

' "We hold these truths to be self-evident, that all men are created equal, that they are endowed by their Creator with certain inalienable Rights, that among these are Life, Liberty and the pursuit of Happiness." That one sentence is what distinguishes America from every other country on earth.

'In some aspects, our nation has progressed mightily since 1776,' continued the Professor, still not having referred to his notes as he walked up and down tugging the lapels of his well-worn Harris tweed jacket, 'while in others we have moved rapidly backwards. Each of you in this hall can be part of the next generation of law makers or law breakers –' he paused, surveying the silent gathering, '– and you have been granted the greatest gift of all with which to help make that choice, a first-class mind. When my colleagues and I have finished with you, you can if you wish go out into the real world and ignore the Declaration of Independence as if it were worth no more than the parchment it was written on, outdated and irrelevant in this modern age. Or,' he continued, 'you may choose to benefit society by upholding the law. That is the course great lawyers take. Bad lawyers, and I do not mean stupid ones, are those who begin to bend the law, which, I submit, is only a step away from breaking it. To those of you in this class who wish to pursue such a course I must advise that I have nothing to teach you, because you are beyond learning. You are still free to attend my lectures, but "attending" is all you will be doing.'

The room was so silent that Scott looked up to check they hadn't all crept out. 'Not my words,' he continued as he stared at the intent faces, 'but those of Dean Thomas W. Swan, who lectured in this theatre for the first twenty-seven years of this century. I see no reason not to repeat his philosophy whenever I address an incoming class of the Yale Law School.'

The Professor opened the file in front of him for the first time. 'Logic,' he began, 'is the science and art of reasoning correctly. No more than common sense, I hear you say. And nothing so uncommon, Voltaire reminds us. But those who cry "common sense" are often the same people who are too lazy to train their minds.

'Oliver Wendell Holmes once wrote: "The life of the law has not been logic, it has been experience." ' The pens and pencils began to scratch furiously across the yellow pages, and continued to do so for the next fifty minutes.

When Scott Bradley had come to the end of his lecture, he closed his file, picked up his notes and marched quickly out of the room. He did not care to indulge himself by remaining for the sustained applause that had followed his opening lecture for the past ten years.

Hannah Kopec had been considered an outsider as well as a loner from the start, although the latter was often thought by those in authority to be an advantage.

Hannah had been told that her chances of qualifying were slim, but she had now come through the toughest part, the twelve-month physical, and although, despite her background, she had never killed anyone – six of the last eight applicants had – those in authority were now convinced she was capable of doing so. Hannah knew she could.

As the plane lifted off from Tel Aviv's Ben Gurion airport for Heathrow, Hannah pondered once again what had caused a twenty-five-year-old woman at the height of her career as a model to want to apply to join the Institute for Intelligence and Special Tasks – better known as Mossad – when she could have had her pick of a score of rich husbands in a dozen capitals.

Thirty-nine Scuds had landed on Tel Aviv and Haifa during the Gulf War. Thirteen people had been killed. Despite much wailing and beating of breasts, no revenge had been sought by the Israeli Government because of some tough political bargaining by James Baker, who had assured them that the Coalition forces would finish the job. The American Secretary of State had failed to fulfil his promise. But then, as Hannah often reflected, Baker had not lost his entire family in one night.

The day she was discharged from hospital, Hannah had immediately applied to join Mossad. They had been dismissive of her request, assuming she would, in time, find that the wound healed. Hannah visited the Mossad headquarters every day for the next two weeks, by which time even they acknowledged that the wound remained open and, more importantly, was still festering.

In the third week they reluctantly allowed her to join a course for trainees, confident that she couldn't hope to survive for more than a few days, and would then return to her career as a model. They were wrong a second time. Revenge for Hannah Kopec was a far more potent drug than ambition. For the next twelve months she worked hours that began before the sun rose and ended long after it had set. She ate food that would have been rejected by a tramp and forgot what it was like to sleep on a mattress. They tried everything to break her, and they failed. To begin with the instructors had treated her gently, fooled by her graceful body and captivating looks, until one of them ended up with a broken leg. He simply didn't believe Hannah could move that fast. In the classroom the sharpness of her mind was less of a surprise to her instructors, though once again she gave them little time to rest.

But now they'd come onto her own ground.

Hannah had always, from a young age, taken it for granted that she could speak several languages. She had been born in Leningrad in 1968, and when fourteen years later her father died, her mother immediately applied for an emigration permit to Israel. The new liberal wind that was blowing across the Baltics made it possible for her request to be granted.

Hannah's family did not remain in a kibbutz for long: her mother, still an attractive, sparkling woman, received several proposals of marriage, one of which came from a wealthy widower. She accepted.

When Hannah, her sister Ruth and brother David took up their new residence in the fashionable district of Haifa, their whole world changed. Their new stepfather doted on Hannah's mother and lavished gifts on the family he had never had.

After Hannah had completed her schooling she applied to universities in America and England to study languages. Mama didn't approve, and had often suggested that with such a figure, glorious long black hair and looks that turned the heads of men from seventeen to seventy, she should consider a career in modelling. Hannah laughed and explained that she had better things to do with her life.

A few weeks later, after Hannah had returned from an interview at Vasser, she joined her family in Paris for their summer holiday. She also planned to visit Rome and London, but she received so many invitations from attentive Parisians that when the three weeks were over she found she hadn't once left the French capital. It was on the last Thursday of their holiday that the Mode Rivoli Agency offered her a contract that no amount of university degrees could have obtained for her. She handed her return ticket to Tel Aviv back to her mother and remained in Paris for her first job. While she settled down in Paris her sister Ruth was sent to finishing school in Zurich, and her brother David took up a place at the London School of Economics.

In January 1991, the children all returned to Israel to celebrate their mother's fiftieth birthday. Ruth was now a student at the Slade School of Art; David was completing his studies for a PhD; and Hannah was appearing once again on the cover of *Elle*.

At the same time the Americans were massing on the Kuwaiti border, and many Israelis were becoming anxious about a war, but Hannah's stepfather assured them that Israel would not get involved. In any case, their home was on the north side of the city and therefore immune to any attack.

A week later, on the night of their mother's fiftieth birthday, they all ate and drank a little too much, and then slept a little too soundly. When Hannah eventually woke, she found herself strapped down in a hospital bed. It was to be days before they told her that her mother, brother and sister had been killed instantly by a stray Scud, and only her stepfather had survived.

For weeks Hannah lay in that hospital bed planning her revenge. When she was eventually discharged her stepfather told her that he hoped she would return to modelling, but that he would support her in whatever she wanted to do.

Hannah informed him that she was going to join Mossad.

It was ironic that she now found herself on a plane to London that, under different circumstances, her brother might have been taking to complete his studies at the LSE. She was one of eight trainee agents being despatched to the British capital for an advanced course in Arabic. Hannah had already completed a year of night classes in Tel Aviv. Another six months and the Iraqis would believe she'd been born in Baghdad. She could now think in Arabic, even if she didn't always think like an Arab.

Once the 757 had broken through the clouds, Hannah stared down at the winding River Thames through the little porthole window. When she had lived in Paris she had often flown over to spend her mornings working in Bond Street or Chelsea, her afternoons at Ascot or Wimbledon, her evenings at Covent

Garden or the Barbican. But on this occasion she felt no joy at returning to a city she had come to know so well.

Now, she was only interested in an obscure sub-faculty of London University and a terraced house in a place called Chalk Farm.

2

ON THE JOURNEY BACK to his office on Wall Street, Antonio Cavalli began to think more seriously about Al Obaydi and how they had come to meet. The file on his new client supplied by their London office, and updated by his secretary Debbie, revealed that although the Deputy Ambassador had been born in Baghdad, he had been educated in England.

When Cavalli leaned back, closed his eyes and recalled the clipped accent and staccato delivery, he felt he might have been in the presence of a British Army officer. The explanation could be found in Al Obaydi's file under Education: The King's School, Wimbledon, followed by three years at London University reading law. Al Obaydi had also eaten his dinners at Lincoln's Inn, whatever that meant.

On returning to Baghdad, Al Obaydi had been recruited by the Ministry of Foreign Affairs. He had risen rapidly, despite the self-appointment of Saddam Hussein as President and the regular placement of Ba'ath Party apparatchiks in posts they were patently unqualified to fill.

As Cavalli turned another page of the file, it became obvious that Al Obaydi was a man well capable of adapting himself to unusual circumstances. To be fair, that was something Cavalli also prided himself on. Like Al Obaydi he had studied law, but in his case at Columbia University in New York. When that time of the year came round for graduates to fill out their applications to join leading law firms, Cavalli was always shortlisted when the partners saw his grades, but once they realised who his father was, he was never interviewed.

After working fourteen hours a day for five years in one of Manhattan's less prestigious legal establishments, the young Cavalli began to realise that it would be at least another ten years before he could hope to see his name embossed on the firm's masthead, despite having married one of the senior partners' daughters. Tony Cavalli didn't have ten years to waste, so he decided to set up his own law practice and divorce his wife.

In January 1982 Cavalli and Co. was incorporated, and ten years later, on April 15th 1992, the company declared a profit of $157,000, paying its tax demand in full. What the company books did not reveal was that a subsidiary had also been formed in 1982, but not incorporated. A firm that showed no tax returns, and despite its profits mounting year on year, could not be checked up on by phoning Dun & Bradstreet and requesting a complete VIP business report. This subsidiary was known to a small group of insiders as 'Skills' – a company that specialised in solving problems that could not be taken care of by thumbing through the Yellow Pages.

With his father's contacts, and Cavalli's driving ambition, the unlisted company soon made a reputation for handling problems that their unnamed clients had previously considered insoluble. Among Cavalli's latest assignments had been the recovery of taped conversations between Sinatra and Nancy Reagan that were due to be published in *Rolling Stone* and the theft of a Vermeer from Ireland for an eccentric South American collector. These coups were discreetly referred to in the company of potential clients.

The clients themselves were vetted as carefully as if they were applying to be members of the New York Yacht Club because, as Tony's father had often pointed out, it would only take one mistake to ensure that he would spend the rest of his life in less pleasing surroundings than 23 East 75th Street, or their villa in Lyford Cay.

Over the past decade, Tony had built up a small network of representatives across the globe who supplied him with clients requiring a little help with a more 'imaginative' proposition. It was his Lebanese contact who had been responsible for introducing the man from Baghdad, whose proposal unquestionably fell into this category.

When Tony's father was first briefed on the outline of Operation 'Desert Calm' he recommended that his son demand a fee of one hundred million dollars to compensate for the fact that the whole of Washington would be at liberty to observe him going about his business.

'One mistake,' the old man warned him, licking his lips, 'and you'll make more front pages than the second coming of Elvis.'

Once he had left the lecture theatre, Scott Bradley hurried across Grove Street Cemetery, hoping that he might reach his apartment in St Ronan Street before being accosted by a pursuing student. He loved them all – well, almost all – and he was sure that in time he would allow the more serious among them to stroll back to his rooms in the evenings for a drink and to talk long into the night. But not until they were well into their second year.

Scott managed to reach the staircase before a single would-be lawyer had caught up with him. But then, few of them knew that he had once covered four hundred metres in 48.1 seconds when he'd anchored the Georgetown varsity relay team. Confident he was out of reach, Scott leapt up the staircase, not stopping until he reached his apartment on the third floor.

He pushed open the unlocked door. It was always unlocked. There was nothing in his apartment worth stealing – even the television didn't work. The one file that would have revealed that the law was not the only field in which he was an expert had been carefully secreted on his bookshelf between Tax and Torts. He failed to notice the books that were piled up everywhere or the fact that he could have written his name in the dust on the sideboard.

Scott closed the door behind him and glanced, as he always did, at the picture of his mother on the sideboard. He dumped the pile of notes he was carrying by her side and retrieved the mail poking out from under the door. Scott walked across the room and sank into an old leather chair, wondering how many of those bright, attentive faces would still be attending his lectures in two years' time. Forty per cent would be good – thirty per cent more likely. Those would be the ones for whom fourteen hours' work a day became the norm, and not just for the last month before exams. And of them, how many would live up to the standards of the late Dean Thomas W. Swan? Five per cent, if he was lucky.

The Professor of Constitutional Law turned his attention to the bundle of mail he held in his lap. One from American Express – a bill with the inevitable hundred free offers which would cost him even more money if he took any of them up; an invitation from Brown to give the Charles Evans Hughes Lecture on the Constitution; a letter from Carol reminding him she hadn't seen him for some time; a circular from a firm of stockbrokers who didn't promise to double his money but . . .; and finally a plain buff envelope postmarked Virginia, with a typeface he recognised immediately.

He tore open the buff envelope and extracted the single sheet of paper which gave him his latest instructions.

Al Obaydi strolled onto the floor of the General Assembly and slipped into a chair directly behind his Head of Mission. The Ambassador had his earphones on and was pretending to be deeply interested in a speech being delivered by the Head of the Brazilian Mission. Al Obaydi's boss always preferred to have confidential talks on the floor of the General Assembly: he suspected it was the only room in the United Nations building that wasn't bugged by the CIA.

Al Obaydi waited patiently until the older man flicked one of the earpieces aside and leaned slightly back.

'They've agreed to our terms,' murmured Al Obaydi, as if it was he who had suggested the figure. The Ambassador's upper lip protruded over his lower lip, the recognised sign among his colleagues that he required more details.

'One hundred million,' Al Obaydi whispered. 'Ten million to be paid immediately. The final ninety on delivery.'

' "Immediately"?' said the Ambassador. 'What does "immediately" mean?'

'By midday tomorrow,' whispered Al Obaydi.

'At least Sayedi anticipated that eventuality,' said the Ambassador thoughtfully.

Al Obaydi admired the way his superior could always make the term 'my master' sound both deferential and insolent at the same time.

'I must send a message to Baghdad to acquaint the Foreign Minister with the details of your triumph,' added the Ambassador with a smile.

Al Obaydi would also have smiled, but he realised the Ambassador would not admit to any personal involvement with the project while it was still in its formative stage. As long as he distanced himself from his younger colleague for the time being, the Ambassador could continue his undisturbed existence in New York until his retirement fell due in three years' time. By following such a course he had survived almost fourteen years of Saddam Hussein's reign while many of his colleagues had conspicuously failed to become eligible for their state pension. To his knowledge one had been shot in front of his family, two hanged and several others posted as 'missing', whatever that meant.

The Iraqi Ambassador smiled as his British counterpart walked past him, but he received no response for his trouble.

'Stuck-up snob,' the Arab muttered under his breath.

The Ambassador pulled the earpiece back over his ear to indicate that he had heard quite enough from his number two.

He continued to listen to the problems of trying to preserve the rainforests of Brazil, coupled with a request for a further grant from the UN of a hundred million dollars.

Not something he felt Sayedi would be interested in.

Hannah would have knocked on the front door of the little terraced house, but it was opened even before she had closed the broken gate at the end of the pathway. A dark-haired, slightly overweight lady, heavily made-up and with a beaming smile came bustling out to greet her. Hannah supposed she would have been about the same age as her mother, had Mama still been alive.

'Welcome to England, my dear. I'm Ethel Rubin,' she announced in gushing tones. 'I'm sorry my husband's not here to meet you, but I don't expect him back from his chambers for another hour.' Hannah was about to speak when Ethel added, 'But first let me show you your room, and then you can tell me all your plans.' She picked up one of Hannah's bags and led her inside. 'It must be such fun seeing London for the first time,' she said as they climbed the stairs, 'and there will be so many exciting things for you to do during the next six months.'

As each sentence poured out Hannah became aware that Ethel Rubin had no idea why she was in London.

After she had unpacked and taken a shower Hannah joined her hostess in the sitting room. Mrs Rubin chatted on, barely listening to Hannah's intermittent replies.

'Do you know where the nearest gym is?' Hannah had asked.

'My husband should be back at any moment,' Mrs Rubin replied. But before she could get the next sentence out, the front door swung open and a man of about five foot three with dark, wiry hair and even darker eyes almost ran into the room. Once Peter Rubin had introduced himself and asked how her flight had been he didn't waste any words suggesting that Hannah might have come to London to enjoy the social life of the metropolis. Hannah quickly learned that Peter Rubin didn't ask any questions he realised she couldn't answer truthfully. Although Hannah felt sure Mr Rubin knew no details of her mission, he was obviously aware that she hadn't come to London on a package holiday.

Mrs Rubin, however, didn't allow Hannah to get to bed until well after midnight, by which time she was exhausted. Once her head had touched the pillow she slept soundly, unaware of Peter Rubin explaining to his wife in the kitchen that in future their guest must be left in peace.

3

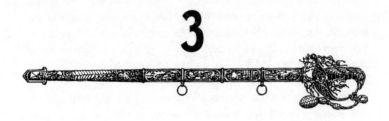

THE DEPUTY AMBASSADOR'S chauffeur slipped out of the UN's private garage and headed west through the Lincoln Tunnel under the Hudson in the direction of New Jersey. Neither Al Obaydi nor he spoke for several minutes while the driver continually checked his rear-view mirror. Once they were on the New Jersey Turnpike he confirmed that no one was following them.

'Good,' was all Al Obaydi offered. He began to relax for the first time that day, and started to fantasise about what he might do if the ten million dollars were suddenly his. When they had passed a branch of the Midlantic National Bank earlier, he had asked himself for the thousandth time why he didn't just stop the car and deposit the money in a false name. He could be halfway across the globe by the following morning. That would certainly make his Ambassador sweat. And, with an ounce of luck, Saddam would be dead long before they caught up with him. And then who would care?

After all, Al Obaydi didn't believe, not even for one moment, that the great leader's outrageous plan was feasible. He had been hoping to report back to Baghdad after a reasonable period of time that no one reliable or efficient enough could be found to carry out such a bold coup. And then the Lebanese gentleman had flown into New York.

There were two reasons why Al Obaydi knew he could not touch one dollar of the money stuffed into the golf bag that rested on the seat beside him. First, there were his mother and younger sister, who resided in Baghdad in relative comfort and who, if the money suddenly disappeared, would be arrested, raped, tortured and hanged – the only explanation being that they had collaborated with a traitor. Not that Saddam ever needed an excuse to kill anyone, especially someone he suspected might have betrayed him.

Secondly, Al Obaydi – who fell on his knees five times daily, faced east and prayed that Saddam would eventually die a traitor's death – could not help observing that Gorbachev, Thatcher and Bush had found it considerably more difficult than the great Sayedi to cling on to power.

Al Obaydi had accepted from the moment he had been handed this assignment by the Ambassador that Saddam would undoubtedly die peacefully in his bed while his own chances of survival – the Ambassador's favourite word – were slim. And once the money had been paid over, if Antonio Cavalli failed to carry out his side of the bargain, it would be Al Obaydi who was called back to Baghdad on some diplomatic pretext, arrested, summarily tried and found guilty. Then all those fine words his law professor at London University had uttered would turn out to be so much sand in the desert.

The driver swung off the turnpike and headed for the centre of Newark as Al Obaydi's thoughts returned to what the money was being used for. The idea had all the hallmarks of his President. It was original, required daring, raw courage, nerve and a fair degree of luck. Al Obaydi still gave the plan no more than a one per cent chance of even reaching the starting blocks, let alone the finishing tape. But then, some people in the State Department had only given Saddam a one per cent chance of surviving Operation Desert Storm. And if the great Sayedi could pull this off, the United States would become a laughing stock and Saddam would have guaranteed himself a place in Arab history alongside Saladin.

Although Al Obaydi had already checked the exact location of the building, he instructed the driver to stop two blocks west of his final destination. An Iraqi getting out of a large black limousine right in front of the bank would be enough of an excuse for Cavalli to pocket the money and cancel the deal. Once the car had stopped, Al Obaydi climbed over the golf bag and out onto the pavement on the curb side. Although he only had to cover a couple of hundred yards to the bank, this was the one part of the journey that he considered was a calculated risk. He checked up and down the street. Satisfied, he dragged the golf bag out onto the pavement and humped it up onto his shoulder.

The Deputy Ambassador felt he must have looked an incongruous sight as he marched down Martin Luther King Drive in a Saks Fifth Avenue suit with a golf bag slung over his shoulder.

Although it took less than two minutes to cover the short distance to the bank, Al Obaydi was sweating profusely by the time he reached the front entrance. He climbed up the well-worn steps and walked through the revolving door. He was met by two armed men who looked more like sumo wrestlers than bank clerks. The Deputy Ambassador was quickly guided to a waiting lift that closed the moment he stepped inside. The door slid open only when he reached the basement. As Al Obaydi stepped out he came face to face with another man, bigger, if anything, than the two who had originally greeted him. The giant nodded and led him towards a door at the end of a carpeted corridor. As he approached, the door swung open and Al Obaydi entered a room to find twelve men waiting expectantly round a large table. Although conservatively dressed and silent, none of them looked like bank tellers. The door closed behind him and he heard a lock turning. The man at the head of the table stood up and greeted him.

'Good morning, Mr Al Obaydi. I believe you have something to deposit for one of our customers.'

The Deputy Ambassador nodded and handed over the golf bag without a word. The man showed no surprise. He had seen valuables transported in everything from a crocodile to a condom.

He was, however, surprised by the weight of the bag as he humped it up onto the table, spilled out the contents and divided the spoils among the other eleven men. The tellers began counting furiously, making up neat piles of ten thousands. No one offered Al Obaydi a seat, so he remained standing for the next forty minutes, with nothing to do but watch them go about their task.

When the counting had been completed, the chief teller double-checked the number of piles. One thousand exactly. He smiled, a smile that was not directed at Al Obaydi but at the money, then looked up in the direction of the Arab and gave him a curt nod, acknowledging that the man from Baghdad had made the down-payment.

The golf bag was then handed back to the Deputy Ambassador, as it had not been part of the deal. Al Obaydi felt slightly stupid as he slung it over his shoulder. The chief teller touched a buzzer under the table and the door behind him was unlocked.

One of the men who had first met Al Obaydi when he had entered the bank was standing waiting to escort him back to the ground floor. By the time the Deputy Ambassador stepped out onto the street, his guide had already disappeared.

With an enormous sigh of relief, Al Obaydi began to stroll the two blocks back to his waiting car. He allowed himself a small smile of satisfaction at the professional way he had carried out the whole exercise. He felt sure the Ambassador would be pleased to learn that there had been no mishaps. He would undoubtedly take most of the praise when the message was relayed back to Baghdad that 'Operation Desert Calm' had begun.

Al Obaydi collapsed on the sidewalk before he realised what had hit him: the golf bag had been wrenched from his shoulder before he could react. He looked up to see two youths moving swiftly down the street, one of them clutching their prize.

The Deputy Ambassador had been wondering how he was going to dispose of it.

*　　　*　　　*

Tony Cavalli joined his father for breakfast a few minutes after seven the following morning. He had moved back into their brownstone on 75th and Park soon after his divorce. Since his retirement, Tony's father spent most of his time pursuing his lifelong hobby of collecting rare books, manuscripts and historical documents. He had also spent many hours passing on to his son everything he'd learned as a lawyer, concentrating on how to avoid wasting too many years in one of the state's penitentiaries.

Coffee and toast were served by the butler as the two men went about their business.

'Nine million dollars has been placed in forty-seven banks across the country,' Tony told his father. 'Another million has been deposited in a numbered account with Franchard et cie in Geneva, in the name of Hamid Al Obaydi,' he added, buttering a piece of toast.

The father smiled at the thought of his son using an old ploy he had taught him so many years before.

'But what will you tell Al Obaydi when he asks how his ten million is being spent?' the unofficial chairman of Skills enquired.

For the next hour, Tony took his father through Operation Desert Calm in great detail, interrupted only by the occasional question or suggestion from the older man.

'Can the actor be trusted?' he asked before taking another sip of coffee.

'Lloyd Adams still owes us a little over thirty thousand dollars,' Tony replied. 'He hasn't been offered many scripts lately – a few commercials . . .'

'Good,' said Cavalli's father. 'But what about Rex Butterworth?'

'Sitting in the White House waiting for his instructions.'

His father nodded. 'But why Columbus, Ohio?' he asked.

'The surgical facilities there are exactly what we require, and the Dean of the Medical School has the ideal qualifications. We've had his office and home bugged from top to bottom.'

'And his daughter?'

'We've got her under twenty-four-hour surveillance.'

The chairman licked his lips. 'So when do you press the button?'

'Next Tuesday, when the Dean is due to make a keynote speech at his daughter's school.'

The butler entered the room and began to clear the table.

'And how about Dollar Bill?' asked Cavalli's father.

'Angelo is on his way to San Francisco to try and convince him. If we're going to pull this off we'll need Dollar Bill. He's the best. In fact no one else comes close,' added Cavalli.

'As long as he's sober,' was all the chairman said.

4

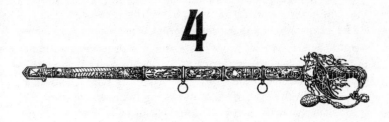

THE TALL, ATHLETIC MAN stepped off the plane into the US Air terminal at Washington National Airport. He carried only hand luggage, so he didn't have to wait at the baggage carousel where someone might recognise him. He needed just one person to recognise him – the driver who was picking him up. At six foot one, his fair hair tousled and with almost chiselled fine features, and dressed in light blue jeans, cream shirt and a dark blue blazer, he made many women rather hope that he would recognise them.

The back door of an anonymous black Ford was opened as soon as he came through the automatic doors into the bright morning sunlight.

He climbed into the back of the car without a word and made no conversation during the twenty-five-minute journey that took him in the opposite direction to the capital. The forty-minute flight always gave him a chance to compose his thoughts and prepare his new persona. Twelve times a year he made the same journey.

It had all begun when Scott was a child back in his home town of Denver, and he had discovered his father was not a respectable lawyer but a criminal in a Brooks Brothers suit, a man who, if the price was right, could always find a way round the law. His mother had spent years protecting her only child from the truth, but when her husband was arrested, indicted and finally sentenced to seven years, the old excuse 'there must

31

have been some misunderstanding' no longer carried any
conviction.

His father survived three years in prison before dying of what
was described in the coroner's report as a heart attack, without
any explanation being given for the marks around his throat. A
few weeks later, his mother did die of a heart attack, while he
was coming to the end of his third year at Georgetown studying
law. Once the body had been lowered into the grave and the
sods of earth hurled on top of the coffin, he left the cemetery
and never spoke of his family again.

When the final rankings were announced, Scott Bradley was
placed first in the graduating class, and several universities and
leading law firms contacted him to ask about his plans for the
future. To the surprise of his contemporaries, Scott applied for
an obscure professorship at Beirut University. He didn't explain
to anyone why he needed a clean break with the past.

Appalled by the low standard of the students at the university
and bored by the social life, Scott began to fill his hours by
attending courses on everything from the Islamic religions to
the history of the Middle East. When three years later the
university offered him the Chair of American Law, he knew it
was time to return to the United States.

A letter from the Dean of the Law Faculty at Georgetown
suggested he should apply for a vacant professorship at Yale. He
wrote the following day and packed his bags when he received
their reply.

Once he had taken up his new post, whenever he was asked
the casual question, 'What do your parents do?' he would
simply reply, 'They're both dead and I'm an only child.' There
was a certain type of girl who delighted in this knowledge – they
assumed he would need mothering. Several of them entered his
bed, but none of them became part of his life.

But he hid nothing from the people he was summoned to
see twelve times a year. They couldn't tolerate deception of
any kind, and were highly suspicious of his real motives when
they learned of his father's criminal record. He told them

simply that he wished to make amends for his father's disgrace, and refused to discuss the subject any further.

At first they didn't believe him. After a time they took him on his own terms, but it was still to be years before they trusted him with any classified information. It was when he started coming up with solutions for problems in the Middle East that the computer couldn't handle that they began to stop doubting his motives. When the Clinton Administration was sworn in, the new team welcomed Scott's particular expertise.

Twice recently he had penetrated the State Department itself to advise Warren Christopher. He had been amused to see Mr Christopher suggest on the early-evening news a solution to the problem of sanctions-busting by Saddam that he had put to him earlier that afternoon.

The car turned off Route 123 and drew to a halt outside a pair of massive steel gates. A guard came out to check on the passenger. Although the two men had seen each other regularly over the past nine years, the guard still asked to see his credentials.

'Welcome back, Professor,' the uniformed man finally offered before saluting.

The driver proceeded down the road and stopped outside an anonymous office block. The passenger climbed out of the car and entered the building through a turnstile. His papers were checked once again, followed by another salute. He walked down a long corridor with cream walls until he reached an unmarked oak door. He gave a gentle knock and entered before waiting for a reply.

A secretary was sitting behind a desk on the far side of the room. She looked up and smiled. 'Go right in, Professor Bradley, the Deputy Director is expecting you.'

Columbus School for Girls, Columbus, Ohio, is one of those establishments that prides itself on discipline and scholarship, in that order. The headmistress would often explain to parents that it was impossible to have the second without the first.

Breaking school rules could, in the headmistress's opinion, only be considered in rare circumstances. The request that she had just received fell into such a category.

That night, the graduating class of '93 was to be addressed by one of Columbus's favourite sons, T. Hamilton McKenzie, Dean of the Medical School at Ohio State University. His Nobel Prize for Medicine had been awarded for the advances he had made in the field of plastic and reconstructive surgery. T. Hamilton McKenzie's work on war veterans from Vietnam and the Gulf had been chronicled from coast to coast, and there were men in every city who, thanks to his genius, had been able to return to normal lives. Some lesser mortals who had trained under the Nobel Laureate used their skills to help women of a certain age appear more beautiful than their maker had originally intended. The headmistress of Columbus felt confident that the girls would only be interested in the work T. Hamilton McKenzie had done for 'our gallant war heroes', as she referred to them.

The school rule that the headmistress had allowed to be waived on this occasion was one of dress. She had agreed that Sally McKenzie, head of student government and captain of lacrosse, could go home one hour early from afternoon class and change into clothes of a casual but suitable nature to accompany her father when he addressed the class later that evening. After all, the headmistress had learned the previous week that Sally had won an endowed national scholarship to Oberlin College to study chemistry.

A car service had been called with instructions to pick Sally up at four o'clock. She would miss one hour of school, but the driver had confirmed that he would deliver father and daughter back by six.

As four chimed on the chapel clock, Sally looked up from her desk. A teacher nodded and the student gathered up her books. She placed them in her bag, and left the building to walk down the long drive in search of the car. When Sally reached the old iron gates at the entrance to the drive, she was surprised to find the only car in sight was a Lincoln Continental stretch limousine. A chauffeur wearing a grey uniform and a peaked cap stood by the driver's door. Such extravagance, she knew only too well, was not the style of her father, and certainly not that of the headmistress.

The man touched the peak of his hat with his right hand and enquired, 'Miss McKenzie?'

'Yes,' Sally replied, disappointed that the long winding drive prevented her classmates from observing the whole scene.

The back door was opened for her. Sally climbed in and sank into the luxurious leather upholstery.

The driver jumped into the front, pressed a button and the window that divided the passenger from the driver slid silently up. Sally heard the safety lock click into place.

She allowed her mind to drift as she glanced out of the misty windows, imagining for a moment that this was the sort of lifestyle she might expect once she left Columbus.

It was some time before the seventeen-year-old girl realised the car wasn't actually heading in the direction of her home.

Had the problem been posed in textbook form, T. Hamilton McKenzie would have known the exact course of action to be taken. After all, he lived 'by the book', as he so often told his students. But when it happened in real life, he behaved completely out of character.

Had he consulted one of the senior psychiatrists at the university, they would have explained that many of the anxieties he'd kept suppressed over a long period of time had, in his new circumstances, been forced to the surface.

The fact that he adored his only child, Sally, was clear for all to see. So was the fact that for many years he had become bored with, almost completely uninterested in, his wife Joni. But the discovery that he was not good under pressure once he was outside the operating theatre – his own little empire – was something he could never have accepted.

T. Hamilton McKenzie became at first irritated, then exasperated, and finally downright angry when his daughter failed to return home that Tuesday evening. Sally was never late, or at least not for him. The journey by car from Columbus should have taken no more than thirty minutes, even in the rush-hour traffic. Joni would have picked Sally up if she hadn't fixed her hair appointment so late. 'It's the only time Julian could fit me in,' she explained. She always left everything to the last minute. At 4.50 T. Hamilton McKenzie phoned Columbus School for Girls to check there had been no late change of plan.

Columbus doesn't change its plans, the headmistress would have liked to tell the Nobel Laureate, but satisfied herself with the confirmation that Sally had left school at four o'clock, and that the limousine company had phoned an hour before to confirm that they would be waiting for her at the end of the drive by the main school gates.

Joni kept repeating in that Southern accent he had once found so attractive, 'She'll be here at any minute, jus' you wait. You can always rely on our Sally.'

Another man, who was sitting in a hotel room on the other side of town and listening to every word they exchanged, poured himself a beer.

By five o'clock, T. Hamilton McKenzie had taken to looking out of the bedroom window every few moments, but the path to their front door lay obstinately unbeaten.

He had hoped to leave at 5.20 p.m., allowing himself enough time to arrive at the school with ten or fifteen minutes to spare. If his daughter did not appear soon, he would have to go without her. He warned his wife that nothing would stop him leaving at 5.20 p.m.

At 5.20 p.m. T. Hamilton McKenzie placed the notes for his speech on the hall table and began pacing up and down the front path as he waited for his wife and daughter to come from opposite directions. By 5.25 p.m., neither of them was at his side and his famous 'cool' was beginning to show distinct signs of steaming.

Joni had taken some considerable time to select an appropriate outfit for the occasion, and was disappointed when she appeared in the hall that her husband didn't even seem to notice.

'We'll have to go without her,' was all he said. 'If Sally hopes to be a doctor one day, she'll have to learn that people have a tendency to die when you keep them waiting.'

'Shouldn't we give her just a li'l longer, honey?' asked Joni.

'No,' he barked, and without even looking back set off for the garage. Joni spotted her husband's notes on the hall table and stuffed them into her handbag before she pulled the front door closed and double-locked it. By the time she reached the road, her husband was already waiting behind the wheel of his car, drumming his fingers on the gear lever.

They drove in silence towards Columbus School for Girls. T. Hamilton McKenzie checked every car heading towards Upper Arlington to see if his daughter was in the back seat.

A small reception party, led by the headmistress, was waiting for them at the foot of the stone steps at the school's main entrance. The headmistress walked forward to shake hands with the distinguished surgeon as he stepped out of the car, followed by Joni McKenzie. Her eyes searched beyond them for Sally. She raised an eyebrow.

'Sally never came home,' Dr McKenzie explained.

'She'll probably join us in a few minutes, if she's not already here,' suggested his wife. The headmistress knew Sally was not on the school premises, but did not consider it courteous to correct the guest of honour's wife, especially as she had just received a call from the car service that required an explanation.

At fourteen minutes to six they walked into the headmistress's study, where a young lady of Sally's age offered the guests a choice of dry sherry or orange juice. McKenzie suddenly remembered that in the anxiety of waiting for his daughter he had left his notes on the hall table. He checked his watch and realised that there wasn't enough time to send his wife back for them. In any case, he was unwilling to admit such an oversight in front of this particular gathering. Damn it, he thought. Teenagers are never an easy audience, and girls are always the worst. He tried to marshal his thoughts into some sort of order.

At three minutes to six, despite there still being no sign of Sally, the headmistress suggested they should all make their way to the Great Hall.

'Can't keep the girls waiting,' she explained. 'It would set a bad example.'

Just as they were leaving the room, Joni took her husband's notes out of her handbag and passed them over to him. He looked relieved for the first time since 4.50.

At one minute to six, the headmistress led the guest of honour onto the stage. He watched the four hundred girls rise and applaud him in what the headmistress would have described as a 'ladylike' manner.

When the applause had faded away, the headmistress raised and lowered her hands to indicate that the girls should be seated again, which they did with the minimum of noise. She then walked over to the lectern and gave an unscripted eulogy on T. Hamilton McKenzie that would have surely impressed the Nobel Committee. She talked of Edward Zeir, the founder of modern plastic surgery, of J.R. Wolte and Wilhelm Krause, and reminded her pupils that T. Hamilton McKenzie had followed in their great tradition by advancing the still-burgeoning science. She said nothing about Sally and her many achievements while at the school, although it had been in her original script. It was still possible to be punished for breaking school rules even if you had just won an endowed national scholarship.

When the headmistress returned to her place in the centre of the stage, T. Hamilton McKenzie made his way to the lectern. He looked down at his notes, coughed, and then began his dissertation.

'Most of you in the audience, I should imagine, think plastic surgery is about straightening noses, removing double chins and getting rid of bags from under your eyes. That, I can assure you, is not plastic but cosmetic surgery. Plastic surgery,' he continued – to the disappointment, his wife suspected, of most of those seated in front of him – 'is something else.' He then lectured for forty minutes on z-plasty, homograting, congenital malformation and third-degree burns without once raising his head.

When he finally sat down, the applause was not quite as loud as it had been when he had entered the room. T. Hamilton McKenzie assumed that was because showing their true feelings would have been considered 'unladylike'.

On returning to the headmistress's study, Joni asked the secretary if there had been any news of Sally.

'Not that I am aware of,' replied the secretary, 'but she might have been seated in the hall.'

During the lecture, versions of which Joni had heard a hundred times before, she had scanned every face in the room, and knew that her daughter was not among them.

More sherry was poured, and after a decent interval T. Hamilton McKenzie announced that they ought to be getting back. The headmistress nodded her agreement and accompanied her guests to their car. She thanked the surgeon for a lecture of great insight, and waited at the bottom of the steps until the car had disappeared from view.

'I have never known such behaviour in all my days,' she declared to her secretary. 'Tell Miss McKenzie to report to me before chapel tomorrow. The first thing I want to know is why she cancelled the car I arranged for her.'

Scott Bradley also gave a lecture that evening, but in his case only sixteen students attended, and none of them was under the age of thirty-five. Each was a senior CIA field officer, and as fit as any quarterback in America. When they talked of logic, it had a more practical application than the one suggested when Scott lectured his younger students at Yale.

These men were all operating in the front line, stationed

right across the globe. Often Professor Bradley pressed them to go over, detail by detail, decisions they had made under pressure, and whether those decisions had achieved the result they'd originally hoped for.

They were quick to admit their mistakes. There was no room for personal pride – only pride in the service was considered acceptable. When Scott had first heard this sentiment he thought they were being corny, but after nine years of working with them in the classroom and in the gym, he'd learned otherwise.

For over an hour Bradley threw test cases at them, at the same time suggesting ways of how to think logically, always weighing known facts with subjective judgement before reaching any firm conclusion.

Over the past nine years, Scott had learned as much from them as they had from him, but he still enjoyed helping them put his knowledge to practical use. Scott had often felt he too would like to be tested in the field, and not simply in the lecture theatre.

When the session was over, Scott joined them in the gym for another workout. He climbed ropes, pumped iron and practised karate exercises, and they never once treated him as anything other than a full member of the team. Anyone who patronised the visiting professor from Yale often ended up with more than their egos bruised.

Over dinner that night – no alcohol, just Quibel – Scott asked the Deputy Director if he was ever going to be allowed to gain some field experience.

'It's not a vacation job, you know,' came back Dexter Hutchins' reply as he lit up a cigar. 'Give up Yale and join us full time and then perhaps we'll consider the merits of allowing you out of the classroom.'

'I'm due for a sabbatical next year,' Bradley reminded his superior.

'Then take that trip to Italy you've always been promising yourself. After dining with you for the last seven years, I think I know as much about Bellini as ballistics.'

'I'm not going to give up trying for a field job – you realise that, Dexter, don't you?'

'You'll have to when you're fifty, because that's when we'll retire you.'

'But I'm only thirty-six . . .'

'You rise too easily to make a good field officer,' said the Deputy Director, puffing away at his cigar.

When T. Hamilton McKenzie opened the front door of his house, he ignored the ringing phone as he shouted, 'Sally? Sally?' at the top of his voice, but he received no response.

He finally snatched the phone, assuming it would be his daughter. 'Sally?' he repeated.

'Dr McKenzie?' asked a calmer voice.

'Yes, it is,' he said.

'If you're wondering where your daughter is, I can assure you that she's safe and well.'

'Who is this?' demanded McKenzie.

'I'll call later this evening, Dr McKenzie, when you've had time to calm down,' said the quiet voice. 'Meanwhile, do not, under any circumstances, contact the police or any private agency. If you do, we'll know immediately, and will be left with no choice but to return your lovely daughter –' he paused '– in a coffin.' The phone went dead.

T. Hamilton McKenzie turned white, and in seconds was covered in sweat.

'What's the matter, honey?' asked Joni, as she watched her husband collapse onto the sofa.

'Sally's kidnapped,' he said, aghast. 'They said not to contact the police. They're going to call again later this evening.' He stared at the phone.

'Sally's been kidnapped?' repeated Joni in disbelief.

'Yes,' snapped her husband.

'Then we ought to tell the police right away,' Joni said, jumping up. 'After all, honey, that's what they're paid for.'

41

'No, we mustn't. They said they'd know immediately if we did, and would send her back in a coffin.'

'A coffin? Are you sure that's what they said?' Joni asked quietly.

'Damn it, of course I'm sure, but they told me she'll be just fine as long as we don't talk to the police. I don't understand it. I'm not a rich man.'

'I still think we ought to call the police. After all, Chief Dixon's a personal friend.'

'No, no!' shouted McKenzie. 'Don't you understand? If we do that they'll kill her.'

'All I understand,' replied his wife, 'is that you're out of your depth and our daughter is in great danger.' She paused. 'You should call Chief Dixon right now.'

'No!' repeated her husband at the top of his voice. 'You just don't begin to understand.'

'I understand only too well,' said Joni, her voice remarkably calm. 'You intend to play Chief of Police for Columbus as well as Dean of the Medical School, despite the fact that you're quite unqualified to do so. How would you react if a State Trooper marched into your operating theatre, leaned over one of your patients and demanded a scalpel?'

T. Hamilton McKenzie stared coldly at his wife, and assumed it was the strain that had caused her to react so irrationally.

The two men listening to the conversation on the other side of town glanced at each other. The man with earphones said, 'I'm glad it's him and not her we're going to have to deal with.'

When the phone rang again an hour later both T. Hamilton McKenzie and his wife jumped as if they had been touched by an electric wire.

McKenzie waited for several rings as he tried to compose himself. Then he picked up the phone. 'McKenzie,' he said.

'Listen to me carefully,' said the quiet voice, 'and don't interrupt. Answer only when instructed to do so. Understood?'

'Yes,' said McKenzie.

'You did well not to contact the police as your wife suggested,' continued the quiet voice. 'Your judgement is better than hers.'

'I want to talk to my daughter,' interjected McKenzie.

'You've been watching too many late-night movies, Dr McKenzie. There are no heroines in real life – or heroes, for that matter. So get that into your head. Do I make myself clear?'

'Yes,' said McKenzie.

'You've wasted too much of my time already,' said the quiet voice. The line went dead.

It was over an hour before the phone rang again, during which time Joni tried once more to convince her husband that they should contact the police. This time T. Hamilton McKenzie picked up the receiver without waiting. 'Hello? Hello?'

'Calm down, Dr McKenzie,' said the quiet voice. 'And this time, listen. Tomorrow morning at 8.30 you'll leave home and drive to the hospital as usual. On the way you'll stop at the Olentangy Inn and take any table in the corner of the coffee shop that is not already occupied. Make sure it can only seat two. Once we're confident that no one has followed you, you'll be joined by one of my colleagues and given your instructions. Understood?'

'Yes.'

'One false move, Doctor, and you will never see your daughter again. Try to remember, it's you who are in the business of extending life. We're in the business of ending it.'

The phone went dead.

5

HANNAH WAS SURE that she could carry it off. After all, if she couldn't deceive them in London, what hope was there that she could do so in Baghdad?

She chose a Tuesday morning for the experiment, having spent several hours reconnoitring the area the previous day. She decided not to discuss her plan with anyone, fearing that one of the Mossad team might become suspicious if she were to ask one question too many.

She checked herself in the hall mirror. A clean white T-shirt and baggy sweater, well-worn jeans, sneakers, tennis socks and her hair looking just a little untidy.

She packed her small, battered suitcase – the one family possession they'd allowed her to keep – and left the little terraced house a few minutes after ten o'clock. Mrs Rubin had gone earlier to do what she called her 'big shop', an attempt to stock up at Sainsbury's for a fortnight.

Hannah walked slowly down the road, knowing that if she were caught they'd put her on the next flight home. She disappeared into the tube station, showed her travelcard to the ticket collector, went down in the lift and walked to the far end of the brightly-lit platform as the train rumbled into the station.

At Leicester Square she changed to the Piccadilly line, and when the train pulled in to South Kensington, Hannah was among the first to reach the escalator. She didn't run up the steps, which would have been her natural inclination, because running attracted attention. She stood quietly on the escalator, studying the advertisements on the wall so that no one could see her face. The new fuel-injected Rover 200, Johnnie Walker whisky, a warning against AIDS, and Andrew Lloyd Webber's *Sunset Boulevard* at the Adelphi glared back at her. Once she'd emerged into the sunlight, Hannah quickly checked left and right before she crossed Harrington Road and walked towards the Norfolk Hotel, an inconspicuous medium-sized hostelry that she had carefully selected. She had checked it out the day before, and could walk straight to the ladies' rest room without having to ask for directions.

Hannah pushed the door open, and after quickly checking to confirm she was alone, chose the end cubicle, locked the door, and flicked open the catch of the battered suitcase. She began the slow process of changing identity.

Two sets of footsteps entered and left while she was undressing. During that time, Hannah sat hunched up on the lavatory seat, continuing only when she was confident she was alone.

The exercise took her nearly twenty minutes. When she emerged, she checked herself in the mirror and made a few minor adjustments.

And then she prayed, but not to their God.

Hannah left the ladies' room and made her way slowly up the stairs and back into the lobby of the hotel. She handed over her little case to the hall porter, telling him she'd collect it again in a couple of hours. She pushed a pound coin across the counter, and in return she received a little red ticket. She followed a tour party through the revolving doors and seconds later was back on the pavement.

She knew exactly where she was going and how long it would take to reach the front door, as she'd carried out a dry-run the previous day. She only hoped her Mossad instructor was right about the internal layout of the building. After all, no other agent had ever been inside before.

Hannah walked slowly along the pavement towards the Brompton Road.

She knew she couldn't afford to hesitate once she reached the front door. With twenty yards to go, she nearly decided to walk straight past the building. But once she reached the steps she found herself climbing them and then boldly knocking on the door. A few moments later, the door was opened by a bull of a man who towered a full six inches over her. Hannah marched in, and to her relief the guard stepped to one side, looked up and down the road and then slammed the door closed.

She walked down the corridor towards the dimly lit staircase without ever looking back. Once she reached the end of the fading carpet, she slowly climbed the wooden staircase. They'd assured her that it was the second door on the left on the first floor, and when she reached the landing she saw a door to the left of her, with peeling brown paint and a brass handle that hadn't been polished for months. She turned the handle slowly and pushed the door open. As she entered, she was greeted by a babble of noise that suddenly ceased. The occupants of the room all turned to stare at her.

How could they know that Hannah had never been there before, when all they could see were her eyes?

Then one of them began talking again, and Hannah quietly took a seat in the circle. She listened carefully, and found that even when three or four of them were speaking at once she could understand almost every word. But the tougher test came when she decided to join in the conversation herself. She volunteered that her name was Sheka and that her husband had just arrived in London, but had only been allowed to bring one wife. They nodded their understanding and expressed their disbelief at British Immigration's inability to accept polygamy.

For the next hour, she listened to and discussed with them their problems. How dirty the English were, how decadent, all dying of AIDS. They couldn't wait to go home and eat proper food, drink proper water. And would it ever stop raining? Without warning, one of the black-clad women rose and bade her friends farewell. When a second got up to join her, Hannah realised this was her chance to leave. She followed the two women silently down the stairs, remaining a few paces behind. The massive man who guarded the entrance opened the door to let the three of them out. Two of them climbed into the back of a large black Mercedes and were whisked away, while Hannah turned west and began to retrace her steps to the Norfolk Hotel.

T. Hamilton McKenzie spent most of the night trying to work out what the man with the quiet voice could possibly want. He had checked his bank statements. He only had about $230,000 in cash and securities, and the house was probably worth another quarter of a million once the mortgage had been paid off – and this certainly wasn't a sellers' market, so that might take months to realise. All together, he could just about scrape up half a million. He doubted if the bank would advance him another cent beyond that.

Why had they selected him? There were countless fathers at Columbus School who were worth ten or twenty times what he was – Joe Ruggiero, who never stopped reminding everybody that he owned the biggest liquor chain in Columbus, must have been a millionaire several times over. For a moment, McKenzie wondered if he was dealing with a gang that had simply picked the wrong man, amateurs even. But he dismissed that idea when he considered the way they'd carried out the kidnap and the follow-up. No, he had to accept that he was dealing with professionals who knew exactly what they wanted.

He slipped out of bed at a few minutes past six and, staring out of the window, discovered there was no sign of the morning sun. He tried to be as quiet as he could, although he knew that his motionless wife must surely be awake – she probably hadn't slept a wink all night. He took a warm shower, shaved, and for reasons he couldn't explain to himself, put on a brand new shirt, the suit he only wore when he went to church, and a flowered Liberty tie Sally had given him two Christmases before and which he had never had the courage to wear.

He then went down to the kitchen and made coffee for his

wife for the first time in fifteen years. He took the tray back to the bedroom where he found Joni sitting upright in her pink nightgown rubbing her tired eyes.

McKenzie sat on the end of the bed and they drank black coffee together in silence. During the previous eleven hours they had exhausted everything there was to say.

He cleared the tray away and returned downstairs, taking as long as he could to wash and tidy up in the kitchen. The next sound he heard was the thud of the paper landing on the porch outside the front door.

He dropped the dishcloth, rushed out to get his copy of the *Dispatch* and quickly checked the front page, wondering if the press could have somehow got hold of the story. Clinton dominated the headlines, with trouble in Iraq flaring up again. The President was promising to send in more troops to guard the Kuwaiti border if it proved necessary.

'They should have finished off the job in the first place,' McKenzie muttered as he closed the front door. 'Saddam is not a man who works by the book.'

He tried to take in the details of the story but couldn't concentrate on the words. He gathered from the editorial that the *Dispatch* thought Clinton was facing his first real crisis. The President doesn't begin to know what a crisis is, thought T. Hamilton McKenzie. After all, his daughter had slept safely in the White House the previous night.

He almost cheered when the clock in the hall eventually struck eight. Joni appeared at the bottom of the stairs, fully dressed. She checked his collar and brushed some dandruff off his shoulder, as if he were about to leave for a normal day's work at the university. She didn't comment on his choice of tie.

'Come straight home,' she added, as she always did.

'Of course I will,' he said, kissing his wife on the cheek and leaving without another word.

As soon as the garage door swung up, he saw the flickering headlights and swore out loud. He must have forgotten to turn them off the previous night when he had been so cross with his daughter. This time he directed his anger at himself, and swore again.

He climbed in behind the wheel, put the key in the ignition and prayed. He switched the lights off and, after a short pause, turned the key. First quickly, then slowly, he tried to coax the engine into action, but it barely clicked as he pumped the accelerator pedal up and down.

'Not today!' he screamed, banging the steering wheel with the palms of his hands. He tried a couple more times and then jumped out and ran back to the house. He didn't take his thumb off the bell until Joni opened the door with a questioning look on her face.

'My battery's flat. I need your car, quickly, quickly!'

'It's being serviced. You've been telling me for weeks to have it attended to.' T. Hamilton McKenzie didn't wait to offer an opinion. He turned his back on his wife, ran down the drive into the road and began searching the tree-lined avenue for the familiar yellow colour with a sign reading 444 4444 attached to the roof. But he realised there was a hundred to one chance of finding a cab driving around looking for a fare that early in the morning. All he could see was a bus heading towards him. He knew the stop was a hundred yards away, so he began running in the same direction as the bus. Although he was still a good twenty or thirty yards short of the stop when it passed him, the bus pulled in and waited.

McKenzie climbed up the steps, panting. 'Thank you,' he said. 'Does this bus go to Olentangy River Road?'

'Gets real close, man.'

'Then let's get going,' said T. Hamilton McKenzie. He checked his watch. It was 8.17 a.m. With a bit of luck he might still make the meeting on time. He began to look for a seat.

'That'll be a dollar,' said the driver, staring at his retreating back.

T. Hamilton McKenzie rummaged in his Sunday suit.

'Oh, my God,' he said. 'I've left . . .'

'Don't try that one, man,' said the driver. 'No cash, no dash.'

McKenzie turned to face him once again. 'You don't understand, I have an important appointment. A matter of life and death.'

'So is keeping my job, man. I gotta stick by the book. If you can't pay, you've gotta debus 'cause that's what the regulations say.'

'But –' spluttered McKenzie.

'I'll give you a dollar for that watch,' said a young man seated in the second row who'd been enjoying the confrontation.

T. Hamilton McKenzie looked at the gold Rolex that had been presented to him for twenty-five years' service to the Ohio State University Hospital. He whipped it off his wrist and handed it over to the young man.

'It *must* be a matter of life and death,' said the young man as he exchanged the prize for a dollar. He slipped the watch onto his wrist. T. Hamilton McKenzie handed the dollar on to the driver.

'You didn't strike a good bargain there, man,' he said, shaking his head. 'You could have had a week in a stretch limo for a Rolex.'

'Come on, let's get going!' shouted McKenzie.

'It's not me who's been holding us up, man,' said the driver as he moved slowly away from the curb.

T. Hamilton McKenzie sat in the front seat wishing it were he who was driving. He looked at his watch. It wasn't there. He turned round and asked the youth, 'What's the time?' The young man looked proudly at his new acquisition, which he hadn't taken his eyes off for one moment.

'Twenty-six minutes after eight and twenty seconds.'

McKenzie stared out of the window, willing the bus to go faster. It stopped seven times to drop and pick up passengers before they finally reached the corner of Independence, by which time the driver feared the watchless man was about to have a heart attack. As T. Hamilton McKenzie jumped off the steps of the bus, he heard the clock on the town hall strike 8.45 a.m.

'Oh God, let them still be there,' he said as he ran towards the Olentangy Inn, hoping no one would recognise him. He stopped running only when he had reached the path that led up to reception. He tried to compose himself, aware that he was badly out of breath and sweating from head to toe.

He pushed through the swing door of the coffee shop and peered around the room, having no idea who or what he was looking for. He imagined that everyone was staring back at him.

The coffee shop had about sixty café tables in twos and fours, and he would have guessed it was about half full. Two of the corner tables were already taken, so McKenzie headed to the one that gave him the best view of the door.

He sat and waited, praying that they hadn't given up on him.

It was when Hannah arrived back at the crossing on the corner of Thurloe Place that she first had the feeling someone was following her. By the time she had reached the pavement on the South Kensington side, she was convinced of it.

A tall man, young, evidently not very experienced at shadowing, bobbed rather obviously in and out of doorways. Perhaps he thought she wasn't the type who would ever be suspicious. Hannah had about a quarter of a mile in which to plan her next move. By the time the Norfolk came in sight, she knew exactly what needed to be done. If she could get into the building well ahead of him, she estimated she only needed about thirty, perhaps forty-five, seconds at most, unless the porters were both fully occupied. She paused at the front window of a chemist's shop and stared at the array of beauty products that filled the shelves. She turned to look towards the lipsticks in the corner and saw his reflection in the brightly polished window. He was standing by a newspaper stand at the entrance to South Kensington tube station. He picked up a copy of the *Daily Mail* – amateur, she thought – which gave her the chance to cross the road before he could collect his change. She had reached the front door of the hotel by the time he had passed the chemist. Hannah didn't run up the steps, as it would have acknowledged his existence, but mistakenly pushed the revolving door so sharply that she sent an unsuspecting old lady tumbling onto the pavement much sooner than she'd intended.

The two porters were chatting as she shot across the lobby. The red ticket and another pound were already in her hand before she reached the porters' desk. Hannah slammed the coin down on the counter, which immediately attracted the older man's attention. When he spotted the pound, he quickly took the ticket, retrieved Hannah's little case and returned it to her just as her pursuer was coming through the revolving doors. She headed in the direction of the staircase at the end of the corridor, clutching the little case close to her stomach so the man following her would be unaware that she was carrying anything. When she reached the second step of the staircase she did run, as there was no one else in sight. Once down the staircase she bolted across the corridor and into the comparative safety of the ladies' room.

This time she was not alone. A middle-aged woman was leaning over a washbasin to check her lipstick. She didn't give Hannah so much as a glance when she disappeared into one of the cubicles. Hannah sat on the top of the lavatory, her knees tucked under her chin as she waited for the woman to finish her handiwork. It was two or three minutes before she finally left. Once Hannah heard the door close, she lowered her feet onto the cold marble floor, opened the battered suitcase to check everything was there and, satisfied that it was, changed back into her T-shirt, baggy sweater and jeans as quickly as she could.

She'd just managed to get her sneakers on when the door opened again, and she watched the lower part of two stockinged legs cross the floor and enter the cubicle next to hers. Hannah shot out, and buttoned up her jeans, before checking herself quickly in the mirror. She ruffled her hair a little and then began checking round the room. There was a large receptacle in the corner for depositing dirty towels. Hannah removed the plastic lid, took out all the towels that were there and forced her little case to the bottom, then quickly covered it with the towels and put the lid back in place. She tried to forget she had carried the bag from Leningrad to Tel Aviv to London – halfway across the world. She cursed in her native tongue before checking her hair in the mirror again. Then she strolled out of the ladies' room, attempting to appear calm, even casual.

The first thing Hannah saw when she stepped into the corridor was the young man sitting at the far end reading the *Daily Mail*. With luck, he wouldn't even give her a second thought. She had reached the bottom of the stairs when he glanced up. Rather good-looking, she thought, staring back at him for a second too long. She turned and began to climb the staircase. She was away; she'd made it.

'Excuse me, miss,' said a voice from behind her. Don't panic, don't run, act normally. She turned and smiled. He smiled back, almost flirting with her, and then blushed.

'Did you by any chance see an Arab lady when you were in the rest room?'

'Yes, I did,' replied Hannah. 'But why do you ask?' she demanded. Always put the enemy on the defensive whenever possible was the standard rule.

'Oh, it's not important. Sorry to have bothered you,' he said, and disappeared back around the corner.

Hannah climbed the stairs, returned to the lobby and headed straight for the revolving doors.

Pity, she thought once she was back on the pavement. He looked rather sexy. She wondered how long he would sit there, who he was working for, and to whom he would eventually be reporting.

Hannah began to retrace her steps home, regretting that she couldn't drop into Dino's for a quick spaghetti bolognese and then take in Frank Marshall's latest film, which was showing at the Cannon. There were still times when she yearned to be just a young woman in London. And then she thought of her mother, her brother, her sister, and once again told herself all of that would have to wait.

She sat alone for the first part of the tube journey, and was beginning to believe that if they sent her to Baghdad – as long as no one wanted to go to bed with her – she could surely now pass herself off as an Iraqi.

When the train pulled in to Green Park two youths hopped on. Hannah ignored them. But as the doors clamped shut she became aware that there was no one else in the carriage.

After a few moments, one of them sauntered over towards her and grinned vacantly. He was dressed in a black bomber jacket with the collar covered in studs, and his jeans were so tight they made him look like a ballet dancer. His spiky black hair stood up so straight that it looked as if he had just received convulsive shock therapy. Hannah thought he was probably in his early twenties. She glanced down at his feet to see that he was wearing heavy-duty army boots. Although he was a little overweight, she suspected from his movements that he was quite fit. His friend stood a few paces away, leaning against the railing by the door.

'So what do you say to my mate's suggestion of a quick strip?' he asked, removing a flick-knife from his pocket.

'Get lost,' Hannah replied evenly.

'Oh, a member of the upper classes, eh?' he said, offering the same vacant grin. 'Fancy a gang bang, do we?'

'Fancy a thick lip, do you?' she countered.

'Don't get clever with me, lady,' he said as the train pulled in to Piccadilly Circus.

His friend stood in the doorway so that anyone who might have considered entering the end carriage thought better of it.

Never seek attention, never cause a scene: the accepted rule if you work for any branch of the secret service, especially when you're stationed abroad. Only break the rules in extreme circumstances.

'My friend Marv fancies you. Did you know that, Sloane?'

Hannah smiled at him as she began planning the route she would have to take out of the carriage once the train pulled in to the next station.

'Quite like you myself,' he said. 'But I prefer black birds. It's their big bums, you know. They turn me on.'

'Then you'll like your friend,' said Hannah, regretting her words the moment she had said them. Never provoke.

She heard the click as a long thin blade shot out and flashed in the brightly lit carriage.

'Now there are two ways we can go about this, Sloane – quietly or noisily. It's your choice. But if you don't feel like co-operating, I might have to make a few etchings in that pretty face of yours.' The youth by the door began laughing. Hannah rose and faced her tormentor. She paused before slowly undoing the top button of her jeans.

'She's all yours, Marv,' said the young man as he turned to face his friend. He never saw the foot fly through the air as Hannah swivelled 180 degrees. The knife went flying out of his hand and shot across the floor to the far end of the carriage. A flat arm came down across his neck and he slumped to the ground in a heap, looking like a sack of potatoes. She stepped over his body and headed towards Marv.

'No, no, miss. Not me. Owen's always been the trouble-maker. I wouldn't have done nothin', not me, nothin'.'

'Take off your jeans, Marvin.'

'What?'

She straightened the fingers of her right hand.

'Anything you say, miss.' Marvin quickly undid his zip and pulled off his jeans to reveal a grubby pair of navy Y-fronts and a tattoo on his thigh that read 'Mum'.

'I do hope your mother doesn't have to see you like that too often, Marvin,' Hannah said as she picked up his jeans. 'Now the pants.'

'What?'

'You heard me, Marvin.'

Marvin slowly pulled off his Y-fronts.

'How disappointing,' said Hannah as the train pulled in to Leicester Square.

As the doors squelched closed behind her Hannah thought she heard, 'You filthy bitch, I'll . . .'

As she walked down the passage to the Northern line, Hannah couldn't find a litter bin in which to dispose of Marvin's grubby clothing. They had all been removed some time before after a sudden outbreak of IRA bombs in the London Underground. She had to carry the jeans and pants all the way to Chalk Farm, where she finally deposited them in a skip on the corner of Adelaide Road, then strolled quietly back home.

As she opened the front door, a cheery voice called from the kitchen, 'Lunch is on the table, my dear.' Mrs Rubin walked through to join Hannah and declared, 'I've had the most fascinating morning. You wouldn't believe what happened to me at Sainsbury's.'

'What will it be, honey?' asked a waitress who wore a red skirt and a black apron and held a pad in her hand.

'Just black coffee, please,' said T. Hamilton McKenzie.

'Coming right up,' she said cheerfully.

He was about to check the time when he was reminded once again that his watch was on the wrist of a young man who was now probably miles away. McKenzie looked up at the clock above the counter. Eight fifty-six. He began to check everyone as they came through the door.

A tall, well-dressed man was the first to walk in, and as he scanned the room McKenzie became quite hopeful and willed him to look in his direction. But the man walked towards the counter and took a seat on a stool, with his back to the restaurant. The waitress returned and poured the nervous doctor a steaming black coffee.

Next to enter the room was a young woman, carrying a shopping bag with a long rope handle. She was followed a moment later by another smartly-dressed man who also searched the

56

room with his eyes. Once again, T. Hamilton McKenzie's hopes were raised, only to be dashed when a smile of recognition flickered across the man's face. He too headed for the counter and took the stool next to the man who had come in a few moments earlier.

The girl with the shopping bag slipped into the place opposite him. 'That seat's taken,' said T. Hamilton McKenzie, his voice rising with every word.

'I know, Dr McKenzie,' said the girl. 'It's been taken by me.'

T. Hamilton McKenzie began to perspire.

'Coffee, honey?' asked the waitress who appeared by their side.

'Yes, black,' was all she said, not glancing up.

McKenzie looked at the young woman more carefully. She must have been around thirty – still at an age when she didn't require his professional services. From her accent, she was undoubtedly a native of New York, though with her dark hair, dark eyes and olive skin her family must surely have emigrated from southern Europe. She was slight, almost frail, and her neatly-patterned Laura Ashley dress of autumn browns, which could have been purchased in any one of a thousand stores across the country, made certain she would be forgettable in any crowd. She didn't touch the coffee that was placed in front of her.

McKenzie decided to go on the attack. 'I want to know how Sally is.'

'She's fine, just fine,' said the woman calmly. She reached down and with a gloved hand removed a single sheet of paper from her bag. She passed it over to him. He unfolded the anonymous-looking sheet:

Dear Daddy
They are treating me well but please agree to whatever they want.
Love Sal.

It was her writing, no question of that, but she would never have signed herself 'Sal'. The coded message only made him more anxious.

The woman leaned across and snatched the letter back.

'You bastards. You won't get away with it,' he said, staring across at her.

'Calm down, Dr McKenzie. No amount of threats or rhetoric is going to influence us. It's not the first time we've carried out this sort of operation. So, if you hope to see your daughter again . . .'

'What do you expect me to do?'

The waitress returned to the table with a fresh pot of coffee, but when she saw that neither party had taken a sip she said, 'Coffee's getting cold, folks,' and moved on.

'I've only got about $200,000 to my name. You must have made some mistake.'

'It's not your money we're after, Dr McKenzie.'

'Then what *do* you want? I'll do anything to get my daughter back safely.'

'The company I represent specialises in gathering skills, and one of our clients is in need of your particular expertise.'

'But you could have called and made an appointment like anyone else,' he said in disbelief.

'Not for what we have in mind, I suspect. And, in any case, we have a time problem, and we felt Sally might help us get to the front of the queue.'

'I don't understand.'

'That's why I'm here,' said the woman. Twenty minutes later, when both cups of coffee were stone cold, T. Hamilton McKenzie understood exactly what was expected of him. He was silent for some time before he said, 'I'm not sure if I can do it. To begin with, it's professionally unethical. And do you realise just how hard –'

The woman leaned down and removed something else from her bag. She tossed a small gold earring over to his side of the table. 'Perhaps this will make it a little easier for you.'

T. Hamilton McKenzie picked up his daughter's earring. 'Tomorrow you get the other earring,' the woman continued. 'On Friday the first ear. On Saturday the other ear. If you keep on worrying about your ethics, Dr McKenzie, there won't be much of your daughter left by this time next week.'

'You wouldn't . . .'

'Ask John Paul Getty III if we wouldn't.'

T. Hamilton McKenzie rose from the table and leaned across.

'We can speed the whole process up if that's the way you want it,' she added, displaying not the slightest sign of fear.

McKenzie slumped back into his seat and tried to compose himself.

'Good,' she said. 'That's better. At least we now seem to understand each other.'

'So what happens next?' he asked.

'We'll be back in touch with you sometime later today. So make sure you're in. Because I feel confident that by then you'll have come to terms with your professional ethics.'

McKenzie was about to protest when the woman stood up, took a five-dollar bill out of her bag and placed it on the table.

'Can't have Columbus's leading surgeon washing up the dishes, can we?' She turned to leave and had reached the door before it struck McKenzie that they even knew he had left the house without his wallet.

T. Hamilton McKenzie began to consider her proposition, not certain if he had been left with any alternative.

But he was certain of one thing. If he carried out their demands, then President Clinton was going to end up with an even bigger problem.

6

SCOTT HEARD THE PHONE ringing when he was at the foot of the stairs. His mind was still going over the morning lecture he had just given, but he leaped up the stairs three at a time, pushed open the door of his apartment and grabbed the phone, knocking his mother to the floor.

'Scott Bradley,' he said as he picked up the photograph and replaced it on the sideboard.

'I need you in Washington tomorrow. My office, nine o'clock sharp.'

Scott was always impressed by the way Dexter Hutchins never introduced himself, and always assumed that the work he did for the CIA was more important than his commitment to Yale.

It took Scott most of the afternoon to rearrange his teaching schedule with two understanding colleagues. He couldn't use the excuse of not feeling well, as everyone on campus knew he hadn't missed a day's work through illness in nine years. So he fell back on 'woman trouble', which always elicited sympathy from the older professors, but didn't lead them to ask too many questions.

Dexter Hutchins never gave any details over the phone as to why Scott was needed, but as all the morning papers had carried pictures of Yitzhak Rabin arriving in Washington for his first meeting with President Clinton, he made the obvious assumption.

Scott removed the file that was lodged between Tax and Torts and extracted everything he had about the new Israeli Prime Minister. His policy towards America didn't seem to differ greatly from that of his predecessor. He was better educated than Shamir, more conciliatory and gentler in his approach, but Scott suspected that if it came to a knife fight in a downtown bar, Rabin was the one who would come out unmarked.

He leaned back and started thinking about a blonde named Susan Anderson who had been present at the last briefing he had been asked to attend with the new Secretary of State. If she was at the meeting, the trip to Washington might prove worthwhile.

A quiet man sat on a stool at the end of the bar emptying the final drops in his glass. The glass had been almost empty of Guinness for some time, but the Irishman always hoped that the movement would arouse some sympathy in the barman, and he might just be kind enough to pour a drop more into the empty glass. But not this particular barman.

'Bastard,' he said under his breath. It was always the young ones who had no heart.

The barman didn't know the customer's real name. For that matter, few people did except the FBI and the San Francisco Police Department.

The file at the SFPD gave William Sean O'Reilly's age as fifty-two. A casual onlooker might have judged him to be nearer sixty-five, not just because of his well-worn clothes, but from the pronounced lines on his forehead, the wrinkled bags under his eyes and the extra inches around his waist. O'Reilly blamed it on three alimonies, four jail sentences and going too many rounds in his youth as an amateur boxer. He never blamed it on the Guinness.

The problem had begun at school when O'Reilly discovered by sheer chance that he could copy his classmates' signatures when they signed chits to withdraw pocket money from the school bank. By the time he had completed his first year at

Trinity College, Dublin, he could forge the signatures of the provost and the bursar so well that even they believed that they had awarded him a bursary.

While at St Patrick's Institution for Offenders, Bill was introduced to the banknote by Liam the Counterfeiter. When they opened the gates to let him out, the young apprentice had nothing left to learn from the master. Bill discovered that his mother was unwilling to allow him to return to the bosom of the family, so he forged the signature of the American Consul in Dublin and departed for the brave new world.

By the age of thirty, he had etched his first dollar plate. The work was so good that, during the trial that followed its discovery, the FBI acknowledged that the counterfeit was a masterpiece which would never have been detected without the help of an informer. O'Reilly was sentenced to six years and the crime desk of the *San Francisco Chronicle* dubbed him 'Dollar Bill'.

When Dollar Bill was released from jail, he moved on to tens, twenties and later fifties, and his sentences increased in direct proportion. In between sentences he managed three wives and three divorces. Something else his mother wouldn't have approved of.

His third wife did her best to keep him on the straight and narrow, and Bill responded by producing documents only when he couldn't get any other work – the odd passport, the occasional driver's licence or social security claim – nothing really criminal, he assured the judge. The judge didn't agree and sent him back down for another five years.

When Dollar Bill was released this time, nobody would touch him, so he had to resort to doing tattoos at fairgrounds and, in desperation, pavement paintings which, when it didn't rain, just about kept him in Guinness.

Bill lifted the empty glass and stared once again at the barman, who returned a look of stony indifference. He failed to notice the smartly-dressed young man who took a seat on the other side of him.

'What can I get you to drink, Mr O'Reilly?' said a voice he

didn't recognise. Bill looked round suspiciously. 'I'm retired,' he declared, fearing that it was another of those young plain-clothes detectives from the San Francisco Police Department who hadn't made his quota of arrests for the month.

'Then you won't mind having a drink with an old con, will you?' said the younger man, revealing a slight Bronx accent.

Bill hesitated, but the thirst won.

'A pint of draught Guinness,' he said hopefully.

The young man raised his hand and this time the barman responded immediately.

'So what do you want?' asked Bill, once he'd taken a swig and was sure the barman was out of earshot.

'Your skill.'

'But I'm retired. I already told you.'

'And I heard you the first time. But what I require isn't criminal.'

'So what are you hoping I'll knock up for you? A copy of the *Mona Lisa*, or is it to be the Magna Carta?'

'Nearer home than that,' said the young man.

'Buy me another,' said Bill, staring at the empty glass that stood on the counter in front of him, 'and I'll listen to your proposition. But I warn you, I'm still retired.'

After the barman had filled Bill's glass a second time, the young man introduced himself as Angelo Santini, and began to explain to Dollar Bill exactly what he had in mind. Angelo was grateful that at four in the afternoon there was no one else around to overhear them.

'But there are already thousands of those in circulation,' said Dollar Bill. 'You can find them all over the place. You could buy a good reproduction from any decent tourist shop.'

'Maybe, but not a perfect copy,' insisted the young man.

Dollar Bill put down his drink and thought about the statement.

'Who wants one?'

'It's for a client who's a collector of rare manuscripts,' Angelo said. 'And he'll pay a good price.'

Not a bad lie, as lies go, thought Bill. He took another sip of Guinness. 'But it would take me weeks,' he said, almost under his breath. 'In any case, I'd have to move to Washington.'

'We've already found a suitable place for you in Georgetown, and I'm sure we can lay our hands on all the materials you'd need.'

Dollar Bill considered this claim for a moment, before taking another gulp and declaring, 'Forget it – it sounds too much like hard work. As I explained, it would take me weeks and, worse, I'd have to stop drinking,' he added, placing his empty glass back on the counter. 'You must understand, I'm a perfectionist.'

'That's exactly why I've travelled from one side of the country to the other to find you,' said Angelo quietly. Dollar Bill hesitated and looked at the young man more carefully.

'I'd want $25,000 down and $25,000 on completion, with all expenses paid,' said the Irishman.

The young man couldn't believe his luck. Cavalli had authorised him to spend up to $100,000 if he could guarantee the finished article. But then he remembered that his boss never trusted anyone who didn't bargain.

'$10,000 when we reach Washington and another $20,000 on completion.'

Dollar Bill toyed with his empty glass.

'$30,000 on completion if you can't tell the difference between mine and the original.'

'But we'll need to tell the difference,' said Angelo. 'You'll get your $30,000 if no one else can.'

The following morning a black limousine with smoked windows pulled up outside Ohio State University Hospital. The chauffeur parked in the space reserved for T. Hamilton McKenzie, as he had been instructed to do.

His only other orders were to pick up a patient at ten o'clock and drive him to the University of Cincinnati and Homes Hospital.

At 10.10, two white-coated orderlies wheeled a tall, well-built man in a chair out through the swing doors and, seeing the car parked in the Dean's space, guided him towards it. The driver jumped out and quickly opened the back door. Poor man, he thought, his head all covered in bandages and only a small crack left for his lips and nostrils. He wondered if it had been burns.

The stockily-built man clambered from the wheelchair into the back, sank into the luxurious upholstery and stretched out his legs. The driver told him, 'I'm going to put on your seat-belt,' and received a curt nod in response.

He returned to his seat in the front and lowered his window to say goodbye to the two orderlies and an older, rather distinguished-looking man who stood behind them. The driver had never seen such a drained face.

The limousine moved off at a sedate pace. The chauffeur had been warned not, under any circumstances, to break the speed limit.

T. Hamilton McKenzie was overcome with relief as he watched the car disappear down the hospital drive. He hoped the nightmare was at last coming to an end. The operation had taken him seven hours, and the previous night had been the first time he had slept soundly for the past week. The last order he had received was to go home and wait for Sally's release.

When the demand had been put to him by the woman who left five dollars on the table at the Olentangy Inn, he had considered it impossible. Not, as he had suggested, on ethical grounds, but because he had thought he could never achieve a true likeness. He had wanted to explain to her about autografting, the external epithelium and the deeper corium, and how unlikely it was that . . . But when he saw the unnamed man in his private office, he immediately realised why they had chosen him. He was almost the right height, perhaps a shade short – an inch, no more – and he might have been five to ten pounds too light. But shoe lifts and a few Big Macs would sort out both of those problems.

The skull and features were remarkable and bore a stunning resemblance to the original. In fact in the end it had only proved necessary to perform rhinoplasty and a partial thickness graft. The results were good, very good. The surgeon assumed that the man's red hair was irrelevant because they could shave his head and use a wig. With a new set of teeth and good make-up, only his immediate family would be able to tell the difference.

McKenzie had had several different teams working with him during the seven hours in the operating theatre. He'd told them he needed fresh help whenever he began to tire. No one ever questioned T. Hamilton McKenzie inside the hospital, and only he had seen the final result. He had kept his side of the bargain.

She parked the Ford Taurus – America's most popular car – a hundred yards from the house, but not before she'd swung it round to face the direction in which she would be leaving.

She changed her shoes in the car. The only time she had nearly been caught was when some mud had stuck to the soles of her shoes and the FBI had traced it to within yards of a spot she had visited a few days before.

She swung her bag over her shoulder and stepped out onto the road. She began to walk slowly towards the house.

They had chosen the location well. The farmhouse was several miles from the nearest building – and that was an empty barn – at the end of a track that even desperate lovers would have thought twice about.

There was no sign of anyone being in the house, but she knew they were there, waiting, watching her every move. She opened the door without knocking and immediately saw one of them in the hall.

'Upstairs,' he said, pointing. She did not reply as she walked past him and began to climb the stairs.

She went straight into the bedroom and found the young girl

sitting on the end of the bed reading a book. Sally turned and smiled at the slim woman in the green Laura Ashley dress, hoping that she had brought another book with her.

The woman placed a hand in her bag and smiled shyly, before pulling out a paperback and passing it over to the young girl.

'Thank you,' said Sally, who took the book, checked the cover and then quickly turned it over to study the plot summary.

While Sally became engrossed by the promised story, the woman unclipped the long plaited rope that was attached to the two sides of her shopping bag.

Sally opened the book at the first chapter, having already decided she would have to read every page very slowly. After all, she couldn't be sure when the next offering might come.

The movement was so fast that she didn't even feel the rope go round her neck. Sally's head jerked back and with one flick her vertebra was broken. Her chin slumped onto her chest.

Blood began to trickle out of her mouth, down her chin and onto the cover of *A Time to Love and a Time to . . .*

The driver of the limousine was surprised to be flagged down by a traffic cop just as he was about to take the exit ramp onto the freeway. He felt sure he hadn't broken the speed limit. Then he spotted the ambulance in his rear-view mirror, and wondered if they simply wanted to pass him. He looked to the front again to see the motorcycle cop was firmly waving him onto the hard shoulder.

He immediately obeyed the order and brought the car to a standstill, puzzled as to what was going on. The ambulance drew in and stopped behind him. The cop dismounted from his motorcycle, walked up to the driver's door and tapped on the window. The chauffeur touched a button in the armrest and the window slid silently down.

'Is there a problem, officer?'

'Yes, sir, we have an emergency on our hands,' the policeman said without raising his visor. 'Your patient has to return to the

Ohio State University Hospital immediately. There have been unforeseen complications. You're to transfer him to the ambulance and I will escort them back into the city.'

The wide-eyed driver agreed with a series of consenting nods. 'Should I go back to the hospital as well?' he asked.

'No, sir, you're to continue to Cincinnati and report to your office.'

The driver turned his head to see two paramedics dressed in white overalls standing by the side of the car. The policeman nodded and one of them opened the back door while the other released the seatbelt so that he could help the patient out.

The driver glanced in the rear-view mirror and watched the paramedics guide the well-built man towards the ambulance. The siren on the motorcycle brought his attention back to the policeman who was now directing the ambulance up the exit ramp so that it could cross the bridge over the highway and begin its journey back into the city.

The whole changeover had taken less than five minutes, leaving the driver in the limousine feeling somewhat dazed. He then did what he felt he should have done the moment he saw the policeman, and telephoned his headquarters in Cincinnati.

'We were just about to call you,' said the girl on the switchboard. 'They don't need the car any longer, so you may as well come straight back.'

'Suits me,' said the driver. 'I just hope the client pays the bill.'

'They paid cash in advance last Thursday,' she replied. The driver clicked the phone back on its cradle and began his journey to Cincinnati. But something was nagging in the back of his mind. Why had the policeman stood so close to the door that he couldn't get out, and why hadn't he raised his visor? He dismissed such thoughts. As long as the company had been paid, it wasn't his problem.

He drove up onto the freeway, and didn't see the ambulance ignore the signpost to the city centre and join the stream of traffic going in the opposite direction. The man behind the wheel was also contacting his headquarters.

'It went as planned, boss,' was all he replied to the first question.

'Good,' replied Cavalli. 'And the chauffeur?'

'On his way back to Cincinnati, none the wiser.'

'Good,' Cavalli repeated. 'And the patient?'

'Fine, as far as I can tell,' said the driver, glancing in the rear-view mirror.

'And the police escort?'

'Mario took a detour down a side road so he could get changed into his Federal Express uniform. He should catch up with us within the hour.'

'How long before the next switch?'

The driver checked the milometer. 'Must be about another ninety miles, just after we cross the state line.'

'And then?'

'Four more changes between there and the Big Apple. Fresh drivers and a different car each time. The patient should be with you around midnight tomorrow, though he may have to stop off at a rest room or two along the way.'

'No rest rooms,' said Cavalli. 'Just take him off the highway and hide him behind a tree.'

7

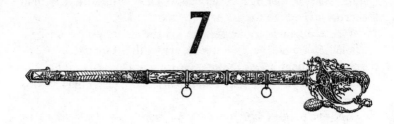

DOLLAR BILL'S NEW HOME turned out to be the basement of a house in Georgetown, formerly an artist's studio. The room where he worked was well lit without glare and, at his request, the temperature was kept at sixty-six degrees with a constant humidity.

Bill attempted several 'dry runs' as he called them, but he couldn't get started on the final document until he had all the materials he needed. 'Nothing but perfection will do,' he kept reminding Angelo. He would not have his name associated with anything that might later be denounced as a forgery. After all, he had his reputation to consider.

For days they searched in vain for the right pen nibs. Dollar Bill rejected them all until he was shown a picture of some in a small museum in Virginia. He nodded his approval and they were in his hands the following afternoon.

The curator of the museum told a reporter from the *Richmond Times Dispatch* that she was puzzled by the theft. The pens were not of any historic importance or particularly valuable. There were far more irreplaceable objects in the next display case.

'Depends who needs them,' said Dollar Bill when he was shown the press cutting.

The ink was a little easier once Bill had found the right shade of black. When it was on the paper he knew exactly how to control the viscosity by temperature and evaporation to give the impression of old age. Several pots were tested until he had more than enough to carry out the job.

While others were searching for the materials he needed, Dollar Bill read several books from the Library of Congress and spent a few minutes every day in the National Archives until he discovered the one mistake he could afford to make.

But the toughest requirement proved to be the parchment itself, because Dollar Bill wouldn't consider anything that was less than two hundred years old. He tried to explain to Angelo about carbon dating.

Samples were flown in from Paris, Amsterdam, Vienna, Montreal and Athens, but the forger rejected them all. It was only when a package arrived from Bremen with a selection dated 1781 that Dollar Bill gave a smile which only Guinness normally brought to his lips.

He touched, caressed and fondled the parchment as a young man might a new lover but, unlike a lover, he pressed, rolled and flattened the object of his attentions until he was confident it was ready to receive the baptism of ink. He then prepared ten sheets of exactly the same size, knowing that only one would eventually be used.

Bill studied the ten parchments for several hours. Two were dismissed within a moment, and four more by the end of the day. Using one of the four remaining sheets, the craftsman worked on a rough copy that Angelo, when he first saw it, considered perfect.

'Perfect to the amateur eye, possibly,' Bill said, 'but a professional would spot the seventeen mistakes I've made within moments. Destroy it.'

During the next week three copies of the text were executed in the basement of Dollar Bill's new home in Georgetown. No one was allowed to enter the room while he was working, and the door remained locked whenever he took a break. He worked in two-hour shifts and then rested for two hours. Light meals were brought to him twice a day and he drank nothing but water, even in the evening. At night, exhausted, he would often sleep for eight hours without stirring.

Once he had completed the three copies of the forty-six-line text, Dollar Bill declared himself satisfied with two of them. The third was destroyed.

Angelo reported back to Cavalli, who seemed pleased with Dollar Bill's progress, although neither of them had been allowed to see the two final copies.

'Now comes the hard part,' Bill told Angelo. 'Fifty-six signatures, every one requiring a different nib, a different pressure, a different shade of ink, and every one a work of art in itself.'

Angelo accepted this analysis, but was less happy to learn that Dollar Bill insisted on a day off before he began to work on the names because he needed to get paralytically drunk.

Professor Bradley flew into Washington on Tuesday evening and booked himself into the Ritz Carlton – the one luxury the CIA allowed the schizophrenic agent/professor. After a light dinner in the Jockey Club, accompanied only by a book, Scott retired to his room on the fifth floor. He flicked channels from one bad movie to another before falling asleep thinking about Susan Anderson.

He woke at six-thirty the next morning, rose, and read the *Washington Post* from cover to cover, concentrating on the articles dealing with Rabin's visit. He got dressed watching a CNN report on the Israeli Prime Minister's speech at a White House dinner that had taken place the previous evening. Rabin assured the new President he wanted the same warm relationship with America that his predecessor had enjoyed.

After a light breakfast, Scott strolled out of the hotel to find a company car waiting for him.

'Good morning, sir,' were the only words his driver spoke on the entire journey. It was a pleasant trip out of the city that Wednesday morning, but Scott smiled wryly as he watched commuters blocking all three lanes going in the opposite direction.

When he arrived at Dexter Hutchins' office ten minutes before his appointment, Tess, the Deputy Director's secretary, waved him straight through.

Dexter greeted Scott with a firm handshake and a cursory attempt at an apology.

'Sorry to pull you in at such short notice,' he said, removing the butt of a cigar from his mouth, 'but the Secretary of State wants you to be present for his working meeting with the Israeli Prime Minister. They're having one of the usual official lunches, rack of lamb and irrelevant small talk, and they expect to start the working session around three.'

'But why would Christopher want me there?' asked Scott.

'Our man in Tel Aviv says Rabin is going to come up with something that isn't officially on the agenda. That's all he could find out. No details. You know as much about the Middle East as anyone in the department, so Christopher wants you around. I've had Tess put the latest data together so that you'll be right up to date by the time we get to this afternoon's meeting.' Dexter Hutchins picked up a pile of files from the corner of his desk and handed them to Scott. The inevitable 'Top Secret' was stamped on each of them, despite the fact that most of the information they contained could be found strewn across the Foreign Desk of the *Washington Post*.

'The first file is on the man himself and Labour Party policy; the others are on the PLO, Lebanon, Iran, Iraq, Syria, Saudi Arabia and Jordan, all in reference to our current defence policy. If Rabin's hoping to get more money out of us, he can think again, especially after Clinton's speech last week on domestic policy. There's a copy in the bottom file.'

'Marked "Top Secret", no doubt,' said Scott.

Dexter Hutchins raised his eyebrows as Scott bundled up the files and left without another word. Tess unlocked a door that led to a small empty office next to her own. 'I'll make sure you're not disturbed, Professor,' she promised.

As Scott turned the pages of the PLO file, he read little that he didn't already know. When it came to the file on the Iraq–Iran conflict there was a whole section he'd written himself only two weeks before.

At twelve o'clock, Tess brought in a plate of sandwiches and a glass of milk as he began to read the reports on no-fly zones beyond the 36th and 32nd parallels in Iraq. When he had finished reading the President's speech, Scott spent another hour trying to puzzle out what change of course or surprise the new Prime Minister of Israel might have in mind. He was still deep in thought when Dexter Hutchins stuck his head round the door and said, 'Five minutes.'

In the car on the way to the State Department, Dexter asked Scott if he had any theories about what the Israeli leader might be going to surprise them with.

'Several, but I need to observe the man in action before I try to second guess. After all, I've only seen him once before, and on that occasion he still thought Bush might win the election.'

When they arrived at the C Street entrance it took almost as long for the two men from the CIA to reach the seventh floor as it always did for Scott to penetrate the inner sanctum of Langley.

At 2.53 they were ushered into an empty conference room. Scott selected a chair against the wall, just behind where Warren Christopher would be seated but slightly to his left so he would have a clear view of Prime Minister Rabin across the table. Dexter sat on Scott's right.

At one minute to three, five senior staffers entered the room, and Scott was pleased to see that Susan Anderson was among them. Her fine fair hair was done up in a coil, making her look rather austere, and she wore a tailored blue suit that accentuated her slim figure. The spotted white blouse with the little bow at the neck would have frightened off most men; it appealed to Scott.

'Good afternoon, Professor Bradley,' she said when Scott stood up. But she took a seat on the other side of Dexter

Hutchins, and informed him that the Secretary of State would be joining them in a few moments.

'So how are the Orioles doing?' Scott asked, leaning forward and looking straight across at Susan, trying not to stare at her slim shapely legs. Susan blushed. From some file, Scott had recalled that she was a baseball fan, and when she wasn't accompanying the Secretary of State abroad, she never missed a game. Scott knew only too well that they had lost their last three matches.

'Doing about as well as Georgetown did in the NCAAs,' came back her immediate reply.

Scott could think of no suitable reply. Georgetown had failed to make the national tournament for the first time in years.

'Fifteen all,' said Dexter, who was obviously enjoying sitting on the high stool between them.

The door suddenly swung open and Warren Christopher entered the room accompanied by the Prime Minister of Israel, and followed by officials from both countries. They split down each side of the long table, taking their places according to seniority.

When the Secretary of State reached his seat in the centre of the table, in front of the American flag, he spotted Scott for the first time, and nodded an acknowledgement of his presence.

Once everyone was settled, the Secretary of State opened the meeting with a predictably banal speech of welcome, most of which could have been used for anyone from Yeltsin to Mitterrand. The Prime Minister of Israel responded in kind.

Then for the next hour they discussed the problems of the Middle East, and Scott could find few differences, other than those of emphasis, between the two men and their predecessors. Both were perhaps a tiny bit more conciliatory, but still every bit as cautious as Shamir and Baker had been before them. During the second hour, Scott began to wonder why they had dragged him away from Yale when any decent CIA Middle East operative could have handled this particular meeting.

It was during 'any other business' that Rabin raised the subject no one had anticipated. The Prime Minister circled around the problem for a few minutes, but Scott could see exactly where he was heading. Christopher was obviously being given the opportunity, if he wanted it, to kill any discussion stone dead before Rabin raised it officially.

Scott scribbled a note on a piece of paper and passed it over to Susan. She read his words, nodded, leaned across and placed the note on the blotting pad in front of the Secretary of State. He unfolded the single sheet, glanced at the contents but showed no sign of surprise. Scott assumed that Christopher had also worked out the size of the bombshell that was about to be dropped.

The Prime Minister had switched the discussion to the role of Israel in relation to Iraq, and reminded the Secretary of State three times that they had gone along with the Allied policy on Operation Desert Storm, when it was Tel Aviv and Haifa that were being hit by Scuds, not New York or Little Rock. It amused Scott that at the last meeting Rabin had said 'New York or Kennebunkport'.

He went on to say he had every reason to believe that Saddam was, once again, developing a nuclear weapon, and Tel Aviv and Haifa still had to be the first candidates for any warhead.

'Try not to forget, Mr Secretary, that we've already had to take out their nuclear reactors once in the past decade,' the Prime Minister said. 'And if necessary, we'll do so again.'

Christopher nodded, but made no comment.

'And were the Iraqis to succeed in developing a nuclear weapon,' continued Rabin, 'no amount of compensation or sympathy would help us this time. And I'm not willing to risk the consequences of that happening to the Israeli people while I'm Prime Minister.'

Christopher still offered no opinion.

'For over two years since the Gulf War ended, we have waited for the downfall of Saddam Hussein, either at the hands of his own people or, at least, by some outside influence encouraged by you. As each month goes by, the Israeli people are increasingly wondering if Operation Desert Storm was ever a victory in the first place.'

Christopher still didn't interrupt the Israeli Prime Minister's flow.

'The Israeli Government feels it has waited long enough for others to finish the job. We have therefore prepared a plan to assassinate Saddam Hussein.' He paused to allow the implications of his statement to sink in. 'We have at last found a way of breaching Saddam's security, and possibly of being invited into his bunker. Even so, this will still be a more difficult operation than those which led to the capture of Eichmann and the rescue of the hostages at Entebbe.'

The Secretary of State looked up. 'And are you willing to share this knowledge with us?' he asked quietly.

Scott knew what the reply would be even before the Prime Minister spoke, and so, he suspected, did Christopher.

'No, sir, I am not,' replied Rabin, looking down at the page in front of him. 'The only purpose of my statement is to ensure we do not clash with your colleagues from the CIA, as we have information which suggests that they are currently considering such a plan themselves.'

Dexter Hutchins thumped his knee with a clenched fist. Scott hastily wrote a two-word note and passed it across to Susan. She removed her glasses, read the message and looked back at him. Scott nodded firmly, so she once again leaned forward and placed the note in front of the Secretary of State. He glanced at Scott's words, and this time he reacted immediately.

'We have no such plan,' said Christopher. 'I can assure you, Prime Minister, that your information is not correct.' Rabin looked surprised. 'And may I add that we naturally hope you will not consider any such action yourselves without keeping President Clinton fully informed.'

It was the first time the President's name had been brought into play, and Scott admired the way the Secretary of State had applied pressure without any suggestion of a threat.

'I hear your request,' replied the Prime Minister, 'but I must tell you, sir, that if Saddam is allowed to continue developing his nuclear arsenal, I cannot expect my people to sit by and watch.'

Christopher had reached the compromise he needed, and perhaps even gained a little time. For the next twenty minutes the Secretary of State tried to steer the conversation onto more friendly territory, but everyone in that room knew that once their guests had departed only one subject would come under discussion.

When the meeting was concluded the Secretary instructed his own staff to wait in the conference room while he accompanied the Prime Minister to his limousine. He returned a few minutes later with only one question for Scott.

'How can you be so sure Rabin was bluffing when he suggested we were also preparing a plan to eliminate Saddam? I watched his eyes and he gave away nothing,' said Christopher.

'I agree, sir,' replied Scott. 'But it was the one sentence he delivered in two hours that he read word for word. I don't even think he had written it himself. Some adviser had prepared the statement. And, more important, Rabin didn't believe it.'

'Do you believe the Israelis have a plan to assassinate Saddam Hussein?'

'Yes, I do,' said Scott. 'And what's more, despite what Rabin says about restraining his people, I suspect it was his idea in the first place. I think he knows every detail, including the likely date and place.'

'Do you have any theories on how they might go about it?'

'No, sir, I don't,' replied Scott.

Christopher turned to Susan. 'I want to meet with Ed Djerijian and his senior Middle Eastern people in my office in one hour, and I must see the President before he departs for Houston.'

Christopher turned to leave, but before he reached the door, he glanced back. 'Thank you, Scott. I'm glad you were able to get away from Yale. It looks as if we're going to be seeing a lot more of you over the next few weeks.' The Secretary of State disappeared out of the room.

'May I add my thanks, too,' said Susan as she gathered up her papers and scurried after her master.

'My pleasure,' said Scott, before adding, 'Care to join me for dinner tonight? Jockey Club, eight o'clock?'

Susan stopped in her tracks. 'You must do your research more thoroughly, Professor Bradley. I've been living with the same man for the past six years and . . .'

'. . . and I heard it wasn't going that well lately,' interjected Scott. 'In any case, he's away at a conference in Seattle, isn't he?'

She scribbled a note and passed it over to Dexter Hutchins. Dexter read the two words and laughed before passing it on to Scott: 'He's bluffing.'

When the two of them had been left alone, Dexter Hutchins also had one question that he needed answering.

'How could you be so sure that we aren't planning to take Saddam out?'

'I'm not,' admitted Scott. 'But I am certain that the Israelis don't have any information to suggest we are.'

Dexter smiled and said, 'Thanks for coming down from Connecticut, Scott. I'll be in touch. I've got a hunch the plane to Washington is going to feel like a shuttle for you over the next few months.' Scott nodded, relieved that the term was just about to end and no one would expect to see him around for several weeks.

Scott took a cab back to the Ritz Carlton, returned to his room and began to pack his overnight case. During the past year he'd considered a hundred ways that the Israelis might plan to assassinate Saddam Hussein, but all of them had flaws because of the massive protection that always surrounded the Iraqi President wherever he went. Scott felt certain also that Prime Minister Rabin would never sanction such an operation unless there was a good chance that his operatives would get home alive. Israel didn't need that sort of humiliation on top of all its other problems.

Scott flicked on the evening news. The President was heading to Houston to carry out a fund-raiser for Senator Bob Krueger, who was defending Lloyd Bentsen's seat in the special May elections. His plane had been late taking off from Andrews. There was no explanation as to why he was behind schedule – the new President was quickly gaining a reputation for working by Clinton Standard Time. All the White House correspondent was willing to say was that he had been locked in talks with the Secretary of State. Scott switched off the news and checked his watch. It was a little after seven, and his flight wasn't scheduled until 9.40. Just enough time to grab a bite before he left for the airport. He had only been offered sandwiches and a glass of milk all day, and considered that the CIA at least owed him a decent meal.

Scott went downstairs to the Jockey Club and was taken to a seat in the corner. A noisy congressman was telling a blonde half his age that the President had been locked in a meeting with Warren Christopher because 'they were discussing my amendment to the defence budget'. The blonde looked suitably impressed, even if the maître d' didn't.

Scott ordered the smoked salmon, a sirloin steak and a half bottle of Mouton Cadet before once again going over everything the Israeli Prime Minister had said at the meeting. But he concluded that the shrewd politician had given no clues as to how or when – or even whether – the Israelis would carry out their threat.

On the recommendation of the maître d', he agreed to try the house special, a chocolate soufflé. He convinced himself that he wasn't going to be fed like this again for some time and, in any case, he could work it off in the gym the next day. When he had finished the last mouthful, Scott checked his watch: three minutes past eight – just enough time for a coffee before grabbing a taxi to the airport.

Scott decided against a second cup, raised his hand and

scribbled in the air to indicate that he'd like the check. When the maître d' returned, he had his MasterCard ready.

'Your guest has just arrived,' said the maître d', without indicating the slightest surprise.

'My guest . . .?' began Scott.

'Hello, Scott. I'm sorry I'm a little late, but the President just went on and on asking questions.'

Scott stood up and slipped his MasterCard back into his pocket before kissing Susan on the cheek.

'You did say eight o'clock, didn't you?' she asked.

'Yes, I did,' said Scott, as if he had simply been waiting for her.

The maître d' reappeared with two large menus and handed them to her customers.

'I can recommend the smoked salmon and the steak,' she said without even a flicker of a smile.

'No, that sounds a bit too much for me,' said Susan. 'But don't let me stop you, Scott.'

'No, President Clinton's not the only one dieting,' said Scott. 'The consommé and the house salad will suit me just fine.' Scott looked at Susan as she studied the menu, her glasses propped on the end of her nose. She had changed from her well-cut dark blue suit into a calf-length pink dress that emphasised her slim figure even more. Her blonde hair now fell loosely on to her shoulders and for the first time in his memory she was wearing lipstick. She looked up and smiled.

'I'll have the crab cakes,' she told the maître d'.

'What did the President have to say?' asked Scott, as if they were still in a State Department briefing.

'Not a lot,' she said, lowering her voice. 'Except that if Saddam were to be assassinated he feels that he would become the Iraqis' number-one target.'

'A human enough response,' suggested Scott.

'Let's not talk politics,' said Susan. 'Let's talk about more interesting things. Why do you feel Ciseri is underrated and Bellini overrated?' she enquired. Scott realised Susan must have also read his internal file from cover to cover.

'So that's why you came. You're an art freak.'

For the next hour they discussed Bellini, Ciseri, Caravaggio, Florence and Venice, which kept them fully occupied until the maître d' reappeared by their side.

She recommended the chocolate soufflé, and seemed disappointed that they both rejected the suggestion.

Over coffee, Scott told his guest about his life at Yale, and Susan admitted that she sometimes regretted she had not taken up an offer to teach at Stanford.

'One of the five universities you've honoured with your scholarship.'

'But never Yale, Professor Bradley,' she said before folding her napkin. Scott smiled. 'Thank you for a lovely evening,' she added as the maître d' returned with the check.

Scott signed it quickly, hoping she couldn't see, and that the CIA accounts department wouldn't query why it was a bill for three people.

When Susan went to the ladies' room Scott checked his watch. Ten twenty-five. The last plane had taken off nearly an hour before. He walked down to the front desk and asked if they could book him in for another night. The receptionist pressed a few keys on the computer, studied the result and said, 'Yes, that will be fine, Professor Bradley. Continental breakfast at seven and the *Washington Post* as usual?'

'Thank you,' he said as Susan reappeared by his side.

She linked her arm in his as they walked towards the taxis parked in the cobblestone driveway. The doorman opened the back door of the first taxi as Scott once again kissed Susan on the cheek.

'See you soon, I hope.'

'That will depend on the Secretary of State,' said Susan with a grin as she stepped into the back of the taxi. The doorman closed the door behind her and Scott waved as the car disappeared down Massachusetts Avenue.

Scott took a deep breath of Washington air and felt that after two meals a walk round the block wouldn't do him any harm.

His mind switched constantly between Saddam and Susan, neither of whom he felt he had the full measure of.

He strolled back into the Ritz Carlton about twenty minutes later, but before going up to his room he returned to the restaurant and handed the maître d' a twenty-dollar bill.

'Thank you, sir,' she said. 'I hope you enjoyed both meals.'

'If you ever need a day job,' Scott said, 'I know an outfit in Virginia that could make good use of your particular talents.' The maître d' bowed. Scott left the restaurant, took the lift to the fifth floor and strolled down the corridor to room 505.

When he removed his key from the lock and pushed the door open he was surprised to find he'd left a light on. He took his jacket off and walked down the short passageway into the bedroom. He stopped and stared at the sight that met him. Susan was sitting up in bed in a rather sheer negligee, reading his notes on the afternoon's meeting, her glasses propped on the end of her nose. She looked up and gave Scott a disarming smile.

'The Secretary of State told me that I was to find out as much as I possibly could about you before our next meeting.'

'When's your next meeting?'

'Tomorrow morning, nine sharp.'

8

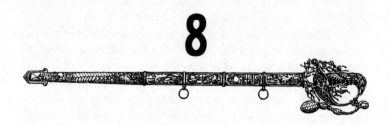

BUTTON GWINNETT WAS PROVING to be a problem. The writing was spidery and small, and the *G* sloped forward. It was several hours before Dollar Bill was willing to transfer the signature onto the two remaining parchments. In the days that followed, he used fifty-six different shades of ink and subtle changes of pressure on the dozen nibs he tried out before he felt happy with Lewis Morris, Abraham Clark, Richard Stockton and Caesar Rodney. But he felt his masterpiece was undoubtedly John Hancock, in size, accuracy, shade and pressure.

The Irishman completed two copies of the Declaration of Independence forty-eight days after he had accepted a drink from Angelo Santini at a downtown bar in San Francisco.

'One is a perfect copy,' he told Angelo, 'while the other has a tiny flaw.'

Angelo stood looking at the two documents in amazement, unable to think of the words that would adequately express his admiration.

'When William J. Stone was asked to make a copy back in 1820, it took him nearly three years,' said Dollar Bill. 'And, more important, he had the blessing of Congress.'

'Are you going to tell me the one difference between the final copy you've chosen and the original?'

'No, but I will tell you it was William J. Stone who pointed me in the right direction.'

'So what's next?' asked Angelo.

'Patience,' said the craftsman, 'because our little soufflé needs time to rise.'

Angelo watched as Dollar Bill transferred the two parchments carefully onto a table in the centre of the room where he had rigged up a water-cooled Xenon lamp. 'This gives out a light similar to daylight, but of much greater intensity,' he explained. He flicked the switch on and the room lit up like a television studio. 'If I've got my calculations right,' said Bill, 'that should achieve in thirty hours what nature took over two hundred years to do for the original.' He smiled. 'Certainly enough time to get drunk.'

'Not yet,' said Angelo, hesitating. 'Mr Cavalli has one more request.'

'And what might that be?' asked Dollar Bill in his warm Irish brogue.

He listened to Mr Cavalli's latest whim with interest. 'I feel I ought to be paid double in the circumstances,' was the forger's only response.

'Mr Cavalli has agreed to pay you another ten thousand,' said Angelo.

Dollar Bill looked down at the two copies, shrugged his shoulders and nodded.

Thirty-six hours later, the chairman and the chief executive of Skills boarded a shuttle for Washington.

They had two assessments to make before flying back to New York. If both came out positively, they could then arrange a meeting of the executive team they hoped would carry out the contract.

If, however, they came away unconvinced, Cavalli would return to Wall Street and make two phone calls. One to Mr Al Obaydi, explaining why it would be impossible to fulfil his request, and the second to their contact in the Lebanon to tell him that they could not deal with a man who had demanded that ten per cent of the money be lodged in a Swiss bank account in his name. Cavalli would even supply the number of the account they had opened in Al Obaydi's name in Geneva, and thus the blame for failure would be shifted from the Cavallis to the Deputy Ambassador from Iraq.

When the two men stepped out of the main terminal, a car was waiting to ferry them into Washington. Crossing the 14th Street bridge they proceeded east on Constitution Avenue where they were dropped outside the National Gallery, a building that neither of them had ever visited before.

Once inside the East Wing, they took a seat on a little bench against the wall just below the vast Calder mobile and waited.

It was the clapping that first attracted their attention. When they looked up to see what was causing the commotion, they watched as flocks of tourists quickly stood to one side, trying to make a clearing.

When they saw him for the first time, the Cavallis automatically stood. A group of bodyguards, two of whom Antonio recognised, was leading the man through a human passage while he shook hands with as many people as possible.

The chairman and the chief executive took a few paces forward to get a better view of what was taking place. It was remarkable: the broad smile, the gait and walk, even the same turn of the head. When he stopped in front of them and bent down to speak to a little boy for a moment they might, if they hadn't known the truth, have believed it themselves.

When the man reached the front of the building, the bodyguards led him towards the third limousine in a line of six. In moments he had been whisked away, the sound of sirens fading into the distance.

'That two-minute exercise cost us one hundred thousand dollars,' said Tony as they made their way back towards the entrance. As he pushed through the revolving door a little boy rushed past him shouting at the top of his voice, 'I've just seen the President! I've just seen the President!'

'Worth every penny,' said Tony's father. 'Now all we need to know is whether Dollar Bill also lives up to his reputation.'

Hannah received an urgent call asking her to attend a meeting at the embassy when there was still another four months of her course to complete. She assumed the worst.

In the exams which were conducted every other Friday, Hannah had consistently scored higher marks than the other five trainee agents who were still in London. She was damned if she was going to be told at this late stage that she wasn't up to it.

The unscheduled appointment with the Councillor for Cultural Affairs, a euphemistic title for Colonel Kratz, Mossad's top man in London, was for six that evening.

At her morning tutorial, Hannah failed to concentrate on the works of the Prophet Mohammed, and during the afternoon she had an even tougher time with The British Occupation and Mandate in Iraq, 1917–32. She was glad to escape at five o'clock without being set any extra work.

The Israeli Embassy had, for the past two months, been forbidden territory for all the trainee agents unless specifically invited. If you were summoned you knew it was simply to collect your return ticket home: we no longer have any use for you. 'Goodbye,' and, if you were lucky, 'Thank you.' Two of the trainees had already taken that route during the past month.

Hannah had only seen the embassy once, as she was driven quickly past it on her first day back in the capital. She wasn't even sure of its exact location. After consulting an A–Z map of London, she discovered it was in Palace Green, Kensington, slightly back from the road.

Hannah stepped out of the South Kensington underground station a few minutes before six. She strolled up the wide pavement into Palace Green and on as far as the Philippine Embassy before turning back to reach the Israeli Mission just before the appointed hour. She smiled at the policeman as she climbed the steps up to the front door.

Hannah announced her name to the receptionist, and explained she had an appointment with the Councillor for Cultural Affairs. 'First floor. Once you reach the top of the stairs, it's the green door straight in front of you.'

Hannah climbed the wide staircase slowly, trying to gather her thoughts. She felt a rush of apprehension as she knocked on the door. It was immediately opened with a flourish.

'A pleasure to meet you, Hannah,' said a young man she had never seen before. 'My name is Kratz. Sorry to call you in at such short notice, but we have a problem. Please take a seat,' he added, pointing to a comfortable chair on the other side of a large desk. Not a man given to small talk, was Hannah's first conclusion.

Hannah sat bolt upright in the chair and stared at the man opposite her, who looked far too young to be the Councillor for Cultural Affairs. But then she recalled the real reason for the Colonel's posting to London. Kratz had a warm, open face, and if he hadn't been going prematurely bald at the front, he might even have been described as handsome.

His massive hands rested on the desk in front of him as he looked across at Hannah. His eyes never left her and she began to feel unnerved by such concentration.

Hannah clenched her fist. If she was to be sent home she would at least state her case, which she had already prepared and rehearsed.

The Councillor hesitated as if he were deciding how to express what needed to be said. Hannah wished he would get on with it. It was worse than waiting for the result of an exam you knew you had failed.

'How are you settling in with the Rubins?' Kratz enquired.

'Very well, thank you,' said Hannah, without offering any details. She was determined not to hold him up from the real purpose of their meeting.

'And how's the course working out?'

Hannah nodded and shrugged her shoulders.

'And are you looking forward to going back to Israel?' asked Kratz.

'Only if I've got a worthwhile job to go back to,' Hannah replied, annoyed that she had lowered her guard. She wished Kratz would look away for just a moment.

'Well, it's possible you may not be going back to Israel,' said Kratz.

Hannah shifted her position in the chair.

'At least, not immediately,' added Kratz. 'Perhaps I ought to explain. Although you have four more months of your course to complete' – he opened a file that lay on the desk in front of him – 'your tutor has informed us that you are likely to perform better in the final exams than any of the other five remaining agents, as I'm sure you know.'

It was the first time she had ever been described as an agent.

'We have already decided you'll be part of the final team,' Kratz said, as if anticipating her question. 'But, as so often happens in our business, an opportunity has arisen which we feel you are the best-qualified person to exploit at short notice.'

Hannah leaned forward in her chair. 'But I thought I was being trained to go to Baghdad.'

'You are, and in good time you will go to Baghdad, but right now we want to drop you into a different enemy territory. No better way of finding out how you'll handle yourself under pressure.'

'Where do you have in mind?' asked Hannah, unable to disguise her delight.

'Paris.'

'Paris?' repeated Hannah in disbelief.

'Yes. We have picked up information that the head of the Iraqi Interest Section has asked his government to supply him with a second secretary. The girl has been selected and will leave Baghdad for Paris in ten days' time. If you are willing to take her place, she will never reach Charles de Gaulle airport.'

'But they'd know I was the wrong person within minutes.'

'Unlikely,' said Kratz, taking out a thicker file from a drawer of his desk and turning a few pages. 'The girl in question was educated at Putney High School and then went on to Durham University to study English, both on Iraqi government grants. She wanted to remain in England but was forced to return to

Baghdad when student visas were rescinded just over two years ago.'

'But her family . . .'

'Father was killed in the war with Iran and the mother has gone to live with her sister, just outside Karbala.'

'Brothers and sisters?'

'A brother in the Republican Guard, no sisters. It's all in the file. You'll be given a few days to study the background before you have to make up your mind. Tel Aviv is convinced we've a good chance of dropping you in her place. Your detailed knowledge of Paris is an obvious bonus. We would only leave you there for three to six months at the most.'

'And then?'

'Back to Israel in final preparation for Baghdad. By the way, if you decide to take on this assignment, our primary purpose is not to use you as a spy. We already have several agents in Paris. We simply want you to assimilate everything around you and get used to living with Arabs and thinking like them. You must not keep any records, or even make notes. Commit everything to memory. You will be debriefed when we take you out. Never forget that your final assignment is far more important to the state of Israel than this could ever be.' He smiled for the first time. 'Perhaps you'd like a few days to think it over.'

'No, thank you,' said Hannah. This time it was Kratz who looked anxious. 'I'm happy to take on the job, but I have a problem.'

'What's that?' asked Kratz.

'I can't type, and certainly not in Arabic.'

The young man laughed. 'Then we'll have to lay on a crash course for you. You'd better leave the Rubins' immediately and get yourself moved into the embassy by tomorrow night. They won't ask you for an explanation, and don't offer any. Meanwhile, study this.' He passed over a manila folder with the name 'Karima Saib' written across the top in bold letters. 'Within ten days you must know its contents by heart. The knowledge you retain may save your life.'

Kratz rose from his side of the desk and walked round to accompany Hannah to the door. 'Just one more thing,' he said as he opened the door for her. 'I believe this is yours.'

The Councillor for Cultural Affairs handed Hannah a small, battered suitcase.

In a car on the way to Georgetown, Cavalli explained to his father that within a hundred yards of the gallery the sirens would have been turned off and the limousines would peel away one after another as they reached the next six intersections, losing themselves in the normal morning traffic.

'And the actor?'

'With his wig removed and wearing dark glasses, no one would give Lloyd Adams a second look. He'll be taking the Metroliner back to New York this afternoon.'

'Clever.'

'Once their licence plates have been switched, the six limos will return to the city in a couple of days with their original New York plates.'

'You've done a highly professional job,' said his father.

'Yes, but that was only the dress rehearsal of a single scene. What we're planning in four weeks' time is to put on a three-act opera with the whole of Washington as our invited audience.'

'Try not to forget that we're being paid one hundred million for our troubles,' the old man reminded him.

'If we deliver, it will be good value for money,' said Cavalli as the car drove past the Four Seasons Hotel. The chauffeur turned left down a side street and came to a halt outside a quaint old wooden house. Angelo was waiting by a little iron gate at the top of a small flight of stone steps. The Chairman and Chief Executive got out of the car and followed Angelo down the steps at a brisk pace, without speaking.

The door at the bottom was already open. Once they were inside, Angelo introduced them to Bill O'Reilly. Bill led them down the corridor to his room. When he reached the locked door he turned the key as if they were about to enter Aladdin's cave. He opened the door and paused for just a moment before switching on the lights, then led his little party to the centre of the room, where the two manuscripts awaited their inspection. He explained to his visitors that only one was a perfect copy of the original.

Bill passed both men a magnifying glass, then took a pace backwards to await their judgement. Tony and his father were not quite sure where to start, and began studying both documents for several minutes without uttering a word. Tony took his time as he went over the opening paragraph, 'When in the course of human events . . .', while his father became fascinated by the signatures of Francis Lightfoot Lee and Carter Braxton, whose colleagues from Virginia had left them so little room at the foot of the parchment to affix their names.

After some time, Tony's father stood up to his full height, turned towards the little Irishman and handed back the magnifying glass, and said, 'Maestro, all I can say is that William J. Stone would have been proud to know you.'

Dollar Bill bowed, acknowledging the ultimate forger's compliment.

'But which one is the perfect copy and which one has the mistake?' asked Cavalli.

'Ah,' said the forger. 'It was also William J. Stone who pointed me in the right direction for solving that little conundrum.'

The Cavallis waited patiently for Dollar Bill to continue his explanation. 'You see, when Timothy Matlock engrossed the original in 1776, he made three mistakes. Two he was able to correct by simple insertions.' Dollar Bill pointed to the word 'represtative', where the letters *e* and *n* were missing, and then to the word 'only', which had been omitted a few lines further down. Both of the corrections had been inserted with a ∧.

'But,' continued Dollar Bill, 'Mr Matlock also made one spelling mistake which he did not correct. On one of the copies, you will find, I *have*.'

9

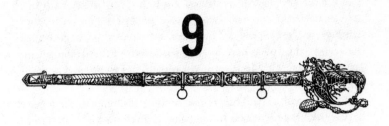

HANNAH LANDED AT Beirut airport the night before she was due to fly to Paris. No one from Mossad accompanied the new agent, to avoid the risk of compromising her. Any Israeli found in the Lebanon is automatically arrested on sight.

Hannah had taken over an hour to be cleared by customs, but she finally emerged carrying a British passport, hand luggage and a few Lebanese pounds. Twenty minutes later she booked herself into the airport Hilton. She explained to the receptionist that she would only be staying one night and paid her bill in advance with the Lebanese pounds. She went straight to her room on the ninth floor and did not venture out again that evening.

She received just one phone call, at 7.20. To Kratz's question she simply replied 'Yes,' and the line went dead.

She climbed into bed at 10.40, but couldn't sleep for more than an hour at a time. She occasionally flicked on the television to watch spaghetti Westerns dubbed into Lebanese. In between she managed to catch moments of restless sleep. She rose at ten to seven the following morning, ate a slab of chocolate she found in the tiny fridge, cleaned her teeth and took a cold shower.

She dressed in clothes taken from her hand luggage of a type which the file had indicated Karima favoured, and sat on the corner of the bed staring at herself in the mirror. She didn't like what she saw. Kratz had insisted that she crop her hair so that she looked like the one blurred photograph of Miss Saib they had in their possession. They also expected her to wear steel-rimmed spectacles, even if the glass in them didn't magnify. She had worn the spectacles for the past week but still hadn't got used to them, and often simply forgot to put them on or, worse, mislaid them.

At 8.19 a.m. she received a second phone call to let her know the plane had taken off from Amman with the 'cargo' on board.

When Hannah heard the morning cleaners chatting in the corridor a few moments later, she opened the door and quickly switched the sign on the knob outside to 'Do Not Disturb'. She waited impatiently in her room for a call saying either 'Your baggage has been mislaid,' which meant she was to return to London because they had failed to kidnap the girl, or 'Your baggage has been retrieved,' the code to show they had succeeded. If it was the second message she was to leave the room immediately, take the hotel minibus to the airport and go to the bookshop on the ground floor, where she was to browse until she was contacted.

A courier would then arrive at Hannah's side and leave a small package containing Saib's passport with the photograph changed, the airline ticket in Saib's name and any baggage tickets and personal items that had been found on her.

Hannah was then to board the flight to Paris as quickly as possible with only the one piece of hand luggage she had brought with her from London. Once she had landed at Charles de Gaulle she was to pick up Karima Saib's luggage from the carousel and get herself to the VIP carpark. She would be met by the Iraqi Ambassador's chauffeur, who would take her to the Jordanian Embassy, where the Iraqi Interest Section was currently located, the Iraqi Embassy in Paris being officially closed. From that moment, Hannah would be on her own, and at all times she was to obey the instructions given by the embassy staff, particularly remembering that in direct contrast to Jewish women, Arab women were subservient to men. She must never contact the Israeli Embassy or attempt to find out who the Mossad agent in Paris was. If it ever became necessary, he would contact her.

'What do I do about clothes if Saib's don't fit?' she had asked Kratz. 'We know I'm taller than she is.'

'You must carry enough in your overnight bag to last for the first few days,' he had told her, 'and then purchase what you will need for six months in Paris.' Two thousand French francs had been supplied for this purpose.

'It must be some time since you've been shopping in Paris,' she had told him. 'That's just about enough for a pair of jeans and a couple of T-shirts.' Kratz had reluctantly handed over another five thousand francs.

At 9.27 the phone rang.

When Tony Cavalli and his father entered the boardroom, they took the remaining chairs at each end of the table, as the chairman and chief executive of any distinguished company might. Cavalli always used the oak-panelled room in the basement of his father's house on 75th Street for such meetings, but no one present believed they were there to conduct a normal board meeting. They knew there would be no agenda and no minutes.

In front of each of the six places where the board members were seated was a notepad, pencil and a glass of water, as there would have been at a thousand such meetings across America that morning. But at this particular gathering, in front of every place were also two long envelopes, one thin and one bulky, neither giving any clue as to its contents.

Tony's eyes swept the faces of the men seated round the table. All of them had two things in common: they had reached the top of their professions, and they were willing to break the law. Two of them had served jail sentences, albeit some years before, while three of the others would have done so had they not been able to afford the finest lawyers available. The sixth was himself a lawyer.

'Gentlemen,' Cavalli began, 'I've invited you to join me this evening to discuss a business proposition that might be described as a little unusual.' He paused before continuing, 'We have been requested by an interested party to steal the Declaration of Independence from the National Archives.'

Tony paused for a moment as uproar broke out immediately and the guests tried to outdo each other with one-liners.

'Just roll it up and take it away.'

'I suppose we could bribe *every* member of the staff.'

'Set the White House on fire. That would at least cause a diversion.'

'Write in and tell them that you won it on a game show.'

Tony was content to wait for his colleagues to run out of wisecracks before he spoke again.

'Exactly my reaction when we were first approached,' he admitted. 'But after several weeks of research and preparation, I hope you will at least grant me an opportunity to present my case.'

They quickly came to order and began concentrating on Tony's every word, though 'scepticism' would have best described the expression on their faces.

'During the past weeks, my father and I have been working on a draft plan to steal the Declaration of Independence. We are now ready to share that knowledge with you, because I must admit that we have reached a point where we cannot advance further on this project without the professional abilities of everyone seated around this table. Let me assure you, gentlemen, that your selection has not been a random exercise.

'But first I would like you all to see the Declaration of Independence for yourself.' Tony pressed a button underneath the table and the doors behind him swung open. The butler entered the room carrying two thin sheets of glass, a parchment held between them. He placed the glass frame on the centre of the table. The six sceptics leaned forward to study the masterpiece. It was several moments before anyone offered an opinion.

'Bill O'Reilly's work, would be my guess,' said Frank Piemonte, the lawyer, as he leaned over to admire the fine detail of the signatures below the text. 'He once offered to pay me in forged bills, and I would have accepted if I'd got him off.'

Tony nodded, and after they had all spent a little more time studying the parchment, he said, 'So, allow me to reword my earlier statement. We are not so much planning to steal the Declaration of Independence as to replace the original with this copy.' A smile settled on the lips of two of the previously sceptical guests.

'You will now be aware,' said Tony, 'of the amount of preparation that has gone into this exercise so far, and, indeed, the expense my father and I have been put to. But the reason we have continued is because we feel the rewards if we are successful far outweigh the risk of being caught. If you will open the thin envelopes in front of you, I believe the contents will make my point more clearly. Inside each envelope you will find a piece of paper on which is written the sum of money you will receive if you decide to become a member of the executive team.'

While the six men tore open the thinner of their two envelopes, Tony continued, 'If you feel, on discovering the amount involved, that the reward does *not* warrant the risk, now is the time to leave. I trust that those of us who remain may have confidence in your discretion because, as you will be only too aware, our lives will be in your hands.'

'And theirs in ours,' said the chairman, speaking for the first time.

A ripple of nervous laughter broke out around the table as each of the six men eyed the unsigned cheque in front of him.

'That figure,' said Tony, 'is the payment you will receive should we fail. If we succeed, the amount will be tripled.'

'So will the jail sentence if we get caught,' said Bruno Morelli, speaking for the first time.

'Summing up, gentlemen,' said Cavalli, ignoring the comment, 'if you decide to join the executive team, you will receive ten per cent of that payment in advance when you leave tonight, and the remaining sum within seven days of the contract being completed. This would be paid into any bank of your choice in any country of your choosing.

'Before you make your decision, there's one further thing I'd like you all to see.' Once again Tony pressed a button under the table, and this time the doors opened at the far end of the room. The sight that greeted them caused two of the guests to immediately stand, one to gasp and the remaining three to simply stare in disbelief.

'Gentlemen, I am happy that you were able to join me today. I wanted to assure you all of my commitment to this project, and I hope you'll feel able to be part of the executive team. I'll have to leave you now, gentlemen,' said the man standing next to the chairman in the Ozark accent that had become so familiar to the American people during the past few months, 'so that you can study Mr Cavalli's proposition in greater detail. You can be confident that I'll do everything I can to help make the change this country needs. But for now, I have one or two pressing engagements. I feel sure you'll understand.' The actor smiled, and shook hands warmly with everyone around the table before strolling out of the boardroom.

Spontaneous applause broke out after the door had closed behind him. Tony allowed himself a smile of satisfaction.

'Gentlemen, my father and I will now leave you for a few minutes to consider your decision.'

The chairman and chief executive rose without another word and left the room.

'What do you think?' asked Tony as he poured his father a whisky and water from the cabinet in his study.

'A lot of water,' he replied. 'I have a feeling we may be in for a long night.'

'But did they buy it?'

'Can't be certain,' replied the old man. 'I was watching their faces while you were giving the presentation, and sure as hell, they didn't doubt the work you've put in. They were all impressed by the parchment and Lloyd Adams' performance, but other than Bruno and Frank they didn't give much away.'

'Let's start with Frank,' said Tony.

'First in then out, as Frank always is, but he likes money far too much to walk away from an offer as good as this.'

'You're that confident?' said Tony.

'It's not just the money,' replied his father. 'Frank's not going to have to be there on the day, is he? So he'll get his share whatever happens. I've never yet met a lawyer who would make a good field commander. They're too used to being paid whether they win or lose.'

'If you're right, Al Calabrese may turn out to be a problem. He's got the most to lose.'

'As our trade union leader, he'll certainly have to be out there on centre stage most of the day, but I suspect he won't be able to resist the challenge.'

'And what about Bruno? If –' began the chief executive, but he was cut short as the doors swung open and Al Calabrese walked into the room. 'We were just talking about you, Al.'

'Not too politely, I hope.'

'Well, that depends on . . .' said Tony.

'On whether I'm in?'

'Or out,' said the chairman.

'I'm in up to my neck is the answer,' said Al, smiling. 'So you'd better have a foolproof plan to present to us.' He turned to face Tony. 'Because I don't want to spend the rest of my life on top of America's most wanted list.'

'And the others?' asked the chairman, as Bruno brushed past them without even saying goodnight.

10

HANNAH NERVOUSLY GRABBED the ringing phone. 'This is Reception, madam. We were just wondering if you'll be checking out before midday, or do you require the room for an extra night?'

'No, thank you,' said Hannah. 'I'll have left by twelve, one way or the other.'

Two minutes later, the phone rang again. It was Colonel Kratz. 'Who were you speaking to a moment ago?'

'Reception were asking me when I would be checking out.'

'I see,' said Kratz. 'Your baggage has been retrieved,' was all he added.

Hannah replaced the phone and stood up. She felt a shot of adrenalin go through her body as she prepared for her first real test. She picked up her overnight bag and left the room, switching the sign on the door to 'Clean Me Please'.

Once she had reached the foyer, she had to wait only a few minutes before the hotel minibus returned from the airport on its circular journey. She sat alone in the back for the short trip to the departure area, then headed straight for the bookshop as instructed. She began to browse among the hardbacks, struck by how many American and British authors were obviously read by the Lebanese.

'Do you know where I can get some money changed, miss?' Hannah turned to find a priest smiling at her, who had spoken in Arabic with a slight mid-Atlantic accent. Hannah apologised and replied in Arabic that she didn't know where the currency exchange was, but perhaps the girl at the counter could help him.

As she turned back, Hannah became aware of someone else standing by her side. He removed a copy of *A Suitable Boy* from the shelf and replaced it with a small package. 'Good luck,' he whispered, and was gone even before she had seen his face. Hannah removed the package from the shelf and strolled slowly out of the bookshop. She began to search for the check-in counter for Paris. It turned out to be the one with the longest queue.

When she reached the front, Hannah requested a non-smoking seat.

The girl behind the counter checked her ticket and then began tapping away on her computer terminal. She looked puzzled. 'Were you unhappy with the seat previously allocated to you, Miss Saib?'

'No, it's just fine,' said Hannah, cursing herself for having made such a simple mistake. 'Sorry to have bothered you.'

'The flight will be boarding at Gate 17 in about fifteen minutes,' the girl added with a smile.

A man pretending to read the Vikram Seth novel he had just purchased watched as the plane took off. Satisfied he had carried out his instructions, he went to the nearest phone booth and rang first Paris and then Colonel Kratz to confirm that 'The bird has flown.'

The man in the priest's surplice also watched Miss Saib board her plane, and he too made a phone call. Not to Paris or London, but to Dexter Hutchins in Langley, Virginia.

Cavalli and his father walked back into the room and once again resumed their places at each end of the table. One seat was empty.

'Too bad about Bruno,' said the chairman, licking his lips. 'We'll just have to find someone else to make the sword.'

Cavalli opened one of the six files in front of him. It was marked 'Transport'. He passed a copy to Al Calabrese.

'Let's start with the Presidential motorcade, Al. I'm going to need at least four limo's, six motorcycle cops, two or three staff cars, two vans with surveillance cameras and a counter-assault team in a black Chevy Suburban – all of them able to pass the most eagle eye. I'll also want an additional van that would normally carry the White House media pool – the death-watch. Don't forget, the motorcade will be under far more scrutiny than last week, when we only had to turn on the sirens at the last moment, and then for just a few seconds. There's bound to be someone in the crowd who either works in government or is a White House junkie. It's often children who spot the most elementary mistakes and then tell their parents.'

Al Calabrese opened his file to find dozens of photographs of the President's motorcade leaving the White House on its way to the Hill. The photographs were accompanied by as many pages of notes.

'How long will it take you to have everything in place?' asked Cavalli.

'Three weeks, maybe four. I've got a couple of big ones in stock that would pass muster, and a bulletproof limo that the government often hires when minor heads of state are visiting the capital. I think the last crest we had to paint on the door was Uruguay, and the poor guy never even got to see the President – he ended up just getting twenty-five minutes with Warren Christopher.'

'But now for the hard part, Al. I need six outriders, riding police motorcycles, and all wearing the correct uniform.'

Al paused. 'That could take longer.'

'We haven't got any longer, Al. A month's going to be the outside for all of us.'

'It's not that easy, Tony. I can't exactly put an ad in the *Washington Post* asking for police –'

'Yes you can, Al. In a moment you'll all see why. Most of you round this table must be wondering why we've been honoured by the presence of Johnny Scasiatore, a man nominated for an Oscar for his direction of *The Honest Lawyer*.' What Cavalli didn't add was that since the police had found Johnny in bed with a twelve-year-old girl, the studios hadn't been in touch quite as frequently as in the past.

'I was beginning to wonder myself,' admitted Johnny.

The chief executive smiled. 'The truth is, you're the reason we'll be able to pull this whole plan off. Because you're going to direct the entire operation.'

'You're going to steal the Declaration of Independence and make a movie of it at the same time?' asked Johnny in disbelief. Cavalli waited for the laughter that broke out around the table to die down.

'Not exactly. But everyone in Washington on that day is going to believe that you are making a movie, not of us stealing the Declaration of Independence, but of the President visiting Congress. The fact that he drops into the National Archives on the way to the Capitol is something they won't ever need to know.'

'I'm lost already,' said Frank Piemonte, the team's lawyer. 'Can you take it a little slower?'

'Sure, Frank, because this is where you come in. I need a city permit to close down the route between the White House and Congress for one hour on any day I choose in the last week in May. Deal direct with the city's motion picture and television office.'

'What reason do I give?' asked Piemonte.

'That Johnny Scasiatore, the distinguished director, wants to film the President of the United States on his way to the Senate to address a joint session of Congress.' Piemonte looked doubtful. 'Clint Eastwood managed it last year, so there's no reason why you shouldn't.'

'Then you'd better put $250,000 into the Fraternal Order of Police, Lodge No. 1,' suggested Piemonte. 'And the Mayor will probably expect the same amount for her re-election fund.'

'You can bribe any city official you know,' continued Tony,

JEFFREY ARCHER

'and I also want every member of the City Police Force on our books squared for the day – all they have to believe is that we're making a movie about the new President.'

'Do you have any idea what mounting an operation like this is likely to cost?' asked Johnny Scasiatore.

'Looking at the budget of your last film, and the return we made on our investment, I'd say yes,' replied Tony. 'And by the way, Al,' he added, turning his attention back to the old Teamster Union boss, 'sixty cops are due for retirement from the DCPD in April. You can employ as many of them as you need. Tell them it's a crowd scene and pay them double.' Al Calabrese added a note to his file.

'Now, the key to the operation's success,' continued Tony, 'is the half-block from the intersection of 7th Street and Pennsylvania Avenue to the delivery entrance of the National Archives.' He unfolded a large map of Washington and placed it in the centre of the table, then ran his finger along Constitution Avenue. 'Once they leave you, Johnny, it's for real.'

'But how do we get in and out of the Archives?'

'That's not your problem, Johnny. Your contribution ends when the six motorcycles and the Presidential motorcade turn right onto 7th Street. From then on, it's up to Gino.'

Until that moment, Gino Sartori, an ex-Marine who ran the best protection racket on the West Side, had not spoken. His lawyer had told him many times: 'Don't speak unless I tell you to.' His lawyer wasn't present, so he hadn't opened his mouth.

'Gino, you're going to supply me with the heavy brigade. I need eight Secret Service agents to act as the counter-assault team, preferably government-trained and well-educated. I only plan to be in the building for about twenty minutes, but we're going to have to be thinking on our feet for every second of that time. Debbie will continue to act as a secretary and Angelo will be dressed in naval uniform and carrying a small black case. I'll be there as the President's assistant, along with Dollar Bill as the President's physician.'

His father looked up, frowning. 'You're going to be inside

104

the National Archives building when the document is switched?'

'Yes,' replied Tony firmly. 'I'll be the only person who knows every part of the plan, and I'm sure not watching this one from the sidewalk.'

'A question,' said Gino. 'If, and I only say if, I am able to supply the twenty or so people you need, tell me this: when we reach the National Archives, are they just going to open the doors, invite us in, and then hand over the Declaration of Independence?'

'Something like that,' replied Cavalli. 'My father taught me that the successful conclusion of any enterprise is always in the preparation. I still have one more surprise for you.' Once again he had their undivided attention. 'We have our own Special Assistant to the President in the White House. His name is Rex Butterworth, and he's on temporary assignment from the Department of Commerce for six months. He returns to his old job when the Clinton nominee has completed his contract in Little Rock and joins the President's staff. That's another reason why we have to go in May.'

'Convenient,' said Frank.

'Not particularly,' said Cavalli. 'It turns out that the President has forty-six Special Assistants at any one time, and when Clinton made his interest in commerce clear, Butterworth volunteered for the job. He's fixed a few overseas contracts for us in the past, but this will be the biggest thing he's done for us yet. For obvious reasons, it will also have to be his last assignment.'

'Can he be trusted?' asked Frank.

'He's been on the payroll for fifteen years, and his third wife is proving rather expensive.'

'Show me one who isn't,' said Al.

'Butterworth's looking for a big payday to get himself out of trouble, and this is it. And that brings me on to you, Mr Vicente, as a close friend of my father's and one of the biggest tour operators in Manhattan.'

'That's the legit side of my business,' replied the elderly man who sat on the right of the chairman, as befitted his oldest friend.

'Not for what I have in mind,' promised Tony. 'Once we have the Declaration in our possession, we'll need it kept out of sight for a few days and then smuggled abroad.'

'As long as no one realises it's been removed and I'm told well in advance where you want it delivered, that should be simple.'

'You'll get a week,' said Cavalli.

'I'd prefer two,' said Vicente, raising an eyebrow.

'No, Nick, you get a week,' the chief executive repeated.

'Can you give me a clue what distance it will have to travel?' Vicente asked, turning the pages of the file Tony had passed across to him.

'Several thousand miles. And as far as you're concerned it's COD, because if you fail to deliver, none of us gets paid.'

'That figures. But I'll still need to know how it has to be transported. For starters, will I have to keep the Declaration between two sheets of glass the whole time?'

'I don't know myself yet,' replied Cavalli, 'but I'm hoping you'll be able to roll it up and deposit it in a cylindrical tube of some kind. I'm having one specially made.'

'Does that explain why I've got several sheets of blank paper in my file?' asked Nick.

'Yes,' said Tony. 'Except those sheets aren't paper but parchment, each one of them 29¾ inches by 24¼ inches, the exact size of the Declaration of Independence.'

'So now all I've got to hope is that every customs agent and coastguard patrol won't be looking for it.'

'I want you to assume the whole world will be looking for it,' replied Cavalli. 'You aren't being paid this sort of money for doing a job I could handle with one call to Federal Express.'

'I thought you might say something like that,' said Nick. 'Still, I had the same problem when you wanted the Vermeer of Russborough stolen, and Irish Customs still haven't worked out how I got the painting out of the country.'

Cavalli smiled. 'So now we all know what's expected of us. And I think in future we should meet at least twice a week to start with, every Sunday at three o'clock and every Thursday at six, to make sure none of us falls behind schedule. One person out of synch and nobody else will be able to move.' Tony looked up and was greeted by nods of agreement.

It always fascinated Cavalli that organised crime needed to be as efficiently run as any public company if it hoped to show a dividend. 'So we'll meet again next Thursday at six?'

All five men nodded and made notes in their diaries.

'Gentlemen, you may now open the second of your two envelopes.' Once again, the five men ripped open their envelopes, and each pulled out a thick wad of thousand-dollar bills.

The lawyer began to count each note.

'Your down-payment,' Tony explained. 'Expenses will be met at the end of every week, receipts whenever possible. And, Johnny,' said Tony, turning to the director, 'this is not *Heaven's Gate* we're financing.' Scasiatore managed a smile.

'Thank you, gentlemen,' said Tony, rising. 'I look forward to seeing you all next Thursday at six o'clock.'

The five men rose and made their way to the door, each stopping to shake hands with Tony's father before he left. Tony accompanied them to their cars. When the last one had been driven away, he returned to find his father had moved to the study and was toying with a whisky while staring at the perfect copy of the Declaration that Dollar Bill had intended to destroy.

'CALDER MARSHALL, PLEASE.'

'The Archivist can't be interrupted right now. He's in a meeting. May I ask who's calling?'

'It's Rex Butterworth, Special Assistant to the President. Perhaps the Archivist would be kind enough to call me back when he's free. He'll find me at the White House.'

Rex Butterworth put the phone down without waiting to hear what usually happened once it was known the call had come from the White House: 'Oh, I feel sure I can interrupt him, Mr Butterworth, can you hold on for a moment?'

But that wasn't what Butterworth wanted. No, the Special Assistant needed Calder Marshall to phone back himself, because once he had gone through the White House switchboard, Marshall would be hooked. Butterworth also realised that, as one of forty-six Special Assistants to the President, and in his case only on temporary assignment, the switchboard might not even recognise his name. A quick visit to the little room that housed the White House telephone operators had dealt with that problem.

He drummed his fingers on the desk and gazed down with satisfaction at the file in front of him. One of the President's two schedulers had been able to supply him with the information he needed. The file revealed that the Archivist had invited each of the last three Presidents – Bush, Reagan and Carter – to visit the National Archives, but due to 'pressing commitments' none of them had been able to find the time.

Butterworth was well aware that the President received, on average, 1,700 requests every week to attend some function or other. The latest letter from Mr Marshall, dated January 22nd 1993, had evoked the reply that although it was not possible for the President to accept his kind invitation at the present time, Mr Clinton hoped to have the opportunity to do so at some date in the future – the standard reply that about 1,699 requests in the weekly postbag were likely to receive.

But on this occasion, Mr Marshall's wish was about to be granted. Butterworth continued to drum his fingers on the desk as he wondered how long it would take Marshall to return his call. Less than two minutes would have been his guess. He allowed his mind to wander back over the events of the past week.

When Cavalli had first put the idea to him, he had laughed more loudly than any of the six men who had gathered round the table at 75th Street. But after studying the parchment for over an hour and still not being able to identify the mistake, and then later meeting with Lloyd Adams, he began to believe, like the other sceptics, that switching the Declaration might just be possible.

As he lay awake that night thinking about the proposition, he also came to the conclusion that Cavalli couldn't take the next step without him, and more important, his role in the deception would probably be obvious within minutes of the theft being discovered, in which case he could end up spending the rest of his life in Leavenworth. Against that possibility he had to weigh the fact that he was fifty-seven years old, had only three years to go before retirement, and a third wife who was suing him for a divorce he couldn't afford. Butterworth no longer dreamed of promotion. He was now simply trying to come to terms with the fact that he was probably going to have to spend the rest of his life alone, eking out some sort of existence on a meagre government pension.

Cavalli was also aware of these facts, and the offer of a million dollars – a hundred thousand the day he signed up, a further nine hundred thousand on the day the exchange took place – and a first-class ticket to any country on earth, almost convinced Butterworth that he should agree to Cavalli's proposition.

But it was Maria who tilted the balance in Cavalli's favour.

At a trade conference in Brazil the previous year, Butterworth had met a local girl who answered most of his questions during the day and the rest of them at night. He'd phoned her the morning after Cavalli's first approach. Maria seemed pleased to hear from him, a pleasure which became more vocal when she learned that he'd be leaving the service and, having come into 'a reasonable inheritance', was thinking of settling down somewhere abroad.

The President's Special Assistant joined the team the following day.

He had spent most of the hundred thousand dollars by the end of the week, clearing his debts and getting up to date with his first two wives' alimony. With only a few thousand left, there was now nothing to do but commit himself wholeheartedly to the plan. He didn't give a moment's thought to changing his mind, because he knew he could never hope to repay the money. He hadn't forgotten that the man he had replaced on Cavalli's payroll *had* once neglected to repay a far smaller sum after making certain promises. Once had been enough: Cavalli's father had had him buried under the World Trade Center when he'd failed to secure the promised contract for the building. A similar departure did not appeal to Butterworth.

Over the years, Butterworth had served the Cavalli family well. Meetings had been arranged with politicians at a moment's notice, words were dropped in the ears of trade officials from someone thought to be well placed in Washington, and the odd piece of inside information had been passed on, ensuring that Butterworth's income was commensurate with his own high opinion of his true worth.

The phone rang on Butterworth's desk, as he had predicted, in under two minutes, but he allowed it to continue ringing for some time before he picked it up. His temporary secretary announced that there was a Mr Marshall on the line and asked if he wanted to take the call.

'Yes, thank you, Miss Daniels.'

'Mr Butterworth?' enquired a voice.

'Speaking.'

'This is Calder Marshall over at the National Archives. I understand you phoned while I was in a meeting. Sorry I wasn't available.'

'No problem, Mr Marshall. It's just that I wondered if it would be possible for you to drop by to the White House. There's a private matter I'd like to discuss with you.'

'Of course, Mr Butterworth. What time would be convenient?'

'I'm up to my eyes the rest of this week,' Butterworth said, looking down at the blank pages in his diary, 'but the President's away at the beginning of next week, so perhaps we could schedule something for then?'

There was a pause which Butterworth assumed meant Marshall was checking his diary. 'Would Tuesday, 10 a.m. suit you?' the Archivist eventually asked.

'Let me check my other diary,' said Butterworth, staring into space. 'Yes, that looks fine. I have another appointment at 10.30, but I'm confident we'll have covered everything I need to go over with you by then. Perhaps you would be kind enough to come to the Pennsylvania Avenue entrance of the Old Executive Office building. There'll be someone there to meet you and after you've cleared security they'll bring you up to my office.'

'The Pennsylvania Avenue entrance,' said Marshall. 'Of course.'

'Thank you, Mr Marshall. I look forward to seeing you next Tuesday at ten o'clock,' said Butterworth before replacing the receiver.

The President's Special Assistant smiled as he dialled Cavalli's private number.

*   *   *

Scott promised Dexter Hutchins he would be around when Dexter's son came to Yale for his admission interview.

'He's allowing me to tag along,' said Dexter, 'which will give me a chance to bring you up to date on our little problem with the Israelis. And I may even have found something to tempt you.'

'Dexter, if you're hoping that I'll get your son into Yale in exchange for a field job, I think I ought to let you know I have absolutely no influence with the Admissions Office.' Dexter's laugh crackled down the phone. 'But I'll still be happy to show you both over the place and give the boy any help I can.'

Dexter Jr could not have turned out to be more like his father: five foot ten, heavily built, a perpetual five o'clock shadow and the same habit of calling everything that moved 'sir'. When, after an hour strolling round the grounds, he left his father for his interview with the head of the Admissions Office, the Professor of Constitutional Law took the Deputy Director of the CIA back to his rooms.

Even before the door was closed, Dexter had lit up a cigar. After a few puffs he said, 'Have you been able to make any sense of the coded message sent by our operative in Beirut?'

'Only that everyone who joins the intelligence community has some strange personal reason for wanting to do so. In my case, it's because of my father and a Boy Scout determination to balance the books morally. In the case of Hannah Kopec, Saddam Hussein wipes out her family, so she immediately offers her talents to Mossad. With that powerful a motive, I wouldn't want to cross her path.'

'But that's exactly what I'm hoping you will do,' said Dexter. 'You're always saying you want to be tested in the field. Well, this could be your opportunity.'

'Am I hearing you properly?'

'Yale's spring term is about to end, right?'

'Yes. But that doesn't mean I don't have a lot of work to do.'

'Oh, I see. A happy amateur, twelve times a year when it suits you, but the moment you might have to get your hands dirty . . .'

'I didn't say that.'

'Well then, hear me out. First, we know Hannah Kopec was one of eight girls selected from a hundred to go to London for six months to study Arabic. This followed a year's intensive physical course at Herzliyah, where they covered the usual self-defence, fieldcraft and surveillance work. The reports on her were excellent. Second, a chat with her host's wife at Sainsbury's in Camden Town, wherever the hell that is, and we discover that she left suddenly, despite the fact that she was almost certainly meant to return to Israel as part of the team that was working on the assassination of Saddam. That's when we lose sight of her. Then we get one of those breaks that only come from good detective work. One of our agents who works at Heathrow spots her in duty free, when she's buying some cheap perfume.

'After she boards a plane for the Lebanon he phones our man in Beirut, who shadows her from the moment she arrives. Not that easy, I might add. We lost her for several hours. Then, out of nowhere, up she pops again, but this time as Karima Saib, who Baghdad are under the impression is on her way to Paris as second secretary to the Ambassador. Meanwhile, the real Miss Saib is abducted at Beirut airport and is now being held at a safe house somewhere across the border on the outskirts of Tel Aviv.'

'Where's all this leading, Dexter?'

'Patience, Professor,' he said, relighting the stub of his cigar, which hadn't been glowing for several minutes. 'Not all of us are born with your academic acuity.'

'Get on with it,' said Scott with a smile, 'because my academic acuity hasn't been stretched yet.'

'Now I come to a bit you're going to enjoy. Hannah Kopec has not been placed in the Iraqi Interest Section of the Jordanian Embassy in Paris to spy.'

'Then why bother to put her there in the first place? In any case, how can you be certain?' asked Scott.

'Because the Mossad agent in Paris – how shall I put it? –

does a little work for us on the side, and he hasn't even been informed of her existence.'

Scott scowled. 'So why *has* the girl been placed in the embassy?'

'We don't know, but we sure as hell would like to find out. We think Rabin can't give the go-ahead to strike Saddam while Kopec is still in France, so the least we need to know is when she's expected back in Israel. And that's where you come in.'

'But we must have a man in Paris already.'

'Several, actually, but every one of them is known by Mossad at a hundred paces, and, I suspect, even by the Iraqis at ten. So, if Hannah Kopec is in Paris without the Mossad sleeper knowing, I'd like you to be in Paris without our people knowing. That is, if you feel you can spare the time away from Susan Anderson.'

'She broke away from me the day her boyfriend returned from his conference. I don't know what it is I do to women. She called me last week to tell me they're getting married next month.'

'All the more reason for you to go to Paris.'

'On a wild goose chase.'

'This goose may just be about to lay us a golden egg, and in any case, I don't want to read about another brilliant Israeli coup on the front page of the *New York Times* and then have to explain to the President why the CIA knew nothing about it.'

'But where would I even start?'

'In your own time, you try to make contact with her. Tell her you're the Mossad agent in Paris.'

'But she would never believe –'

'Why not? She doesn't know who the agent is, only that there is one. Scott, I need to know –'

The door swung open and Dexter Jr came in.

'How did it go?' asked his father. The young man walked across the room and slumped into an armchair, but did not utter a word.

'That bad, eh son?'

*   *   *

'Mr Marshall, how nice to meet you,' said Butterworth, thrusting out his hand to greet the Archivist of the United States.

'It's nice to meet you, too, Mr Butterworth,' Calder Marshall replied nervously.

'Good of you to find the time to come over,' said Butterworth. 'Do have a seat.'

Butterworth had booked the Roosevelt Room in the West Wing for their meeting. It had taken a lot of persuading of a particularly officious secretary who knew Mr Butterworth's station in life only too well. She reluctantly agreed to release the room for thirty minutes, and then only because he was seeing the Archivist of the United States. She also agreed to his second request, as the President would be out of town that day. The Special Assistant had placed himself at the top of a table that usually seated twenty-four, and beckoned Mr Marshall to be seated on his right, facing Tade Stykal's portrait of *Theodore Roosevelt on Horseback*.

The Archivist must have been a shade over six foot, and as thin as most women half his age would have liked to be. He was almost bald except for a semicircle of grey tufts around the base of his skull. He wore an ill-fitting suit that looked as if it normally experienced outings only on a Sunday morning. From his file, Butterworth knew the Archivist was younger than himself, but he vainly felt that if they had been seen together, no one would have believed it.

He must have been born middle-aged, thought Butterworth, but the Special Assistant had no such disparaging thoughts about the quality of the man's mind. After a *magna cum laude* at Duke University, Marshall had written a book on the history of the Bill of Rights that was now considered to be the standard text for every undergraduate studying American history. It had made him a small fortune – not that one could have guessed it by the way he dressed, thought Butterworth.

On the table in front of him was a file stamped 'Confidential', and above that the name 'Calder Marshall' in bold letters. Despite the fact that the Archivist was wearing horn-rimmed glasses with thick lenses, Butterworth felt he could hardly have missed it.

Butterworth paused before he began a speech he'd prepared every bit as assiduously as the President had his inauguration address. Marshall sat, fingers intertwined, nervously waiting for Butterworth to proceed.

'You have, over the past sixteen years,' began the Special Assistant, 'made several requests for the President to visit the National Archives.' Butterworth was pleased to observe that Marshall was looking hopeful. 'And, indeed, this particular President wishes to accept your invitation.' Mr Marshall's smile broadened. 'To that end, in our weekly meeting, President Clinton asked me to convey a private message to you, which he hoped you would understand must be in the strictest confidence.'

'In the strictest confidence. Of course.'

'The President felt sure he could rely on your discretion, Mr Marshall. So, I feel I can let you know that we're trying to clear some time during the last week of this month for him to visit the Archives, but nothing, as yet, has been scheduled.'

'Nothing, as yet, has been scheduled. Of course.'

'President Clinton has also requested that it be a strictly private visit, which would not be open to the public or the press.'

'Not be open to the press. Of course.'

'After the explosion at the World Trade Center, one can't be too careful.'

'Can't be too careful. Of course.'

'And I would be obliged if you did not discuss any aspect of the visit with your staff, however senior, until we are able to confirm a definite date. These things have a habit of getting out and then, for security reasons, the visit might have to be cancelled.'

'Have to be cancelled. Of course. But if it's to be a private visit,' said the Archivist, 'is there anything the President particularly wants to see, or will it just be the standard tour of the building?'

'I'm glad you asked that question,' said Mr Butterworth, opening the file in front of him. 'The President has made one particular request, apart from which he will be in your hands.'

'In my hands. Of course.'

'He wants to see the Declaration of Independence.'

'The Declaration of Independence. That's easy enough.'

'That is not the request,' said Butterworth.

'Not the request?'

'No. The President wishes to see the Declaration, but not as he saw it when he was a freshman at Georgetown, under a thick pane of glass. He wishes the frame to be removed so he can study the parchment itself. He hopes you will grant this request, if only for a few moments.'

This time the Archivist did not immediately say 'Of course.' Instead he said, 'Most unusual,' and added, 'Hopes I would grant him this request, if only for a few moments.' There was a long pause before he said, 'I'm sure that will be possible, of course.'

'Thank you,' said Mr Butterworth, trying not to sound too relieved. 'I know the President will be most appreciative. And, if I could impress on you again, not a word until we've been able to confirm the date.'

Butterworth rose and glanced at the long-case clock at the far end of the room. The meeting had taken twenty-two minutes. He would still be able to escape from the conference room before he was thrown out by the officious woman from Scheduling.

The Special Assistant to the President guided his guest towards the door.

'The President wondered if you would like to see the Oval Office while you're here?'

'The Oval Office. Of course, of course.'

12

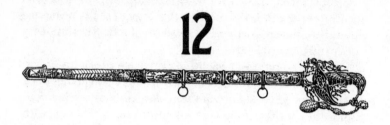

HAMID AL OBAYDI was left alone in the centre of the room. After two of the four guards had stripped him naked, the other two had expertly checked every stitch of his clothing for anything that might endanger the life of their President.

On a nod from the man who appeared to be the chief guard, a side door opened and a doctor entered the room, followed by an orderly who carried a chair in one hand and a rubber glove in the other. The chair was placed behind Al Obaydi, and he was invited to sit. He did so. The doctor first checked his nails and ears before instructing him to open his mouth wide while he tapped every tooth with a spatula. He then placed a clamp in his jaw so that it opened even wider, which allowed him slowly to check every crevice. Satisfied, he removed the clamp. He then asked Al Obaydi to stand up, turn round, place his legs straight and wide while bending over until his hands touched the seat of the chair. Al Obaydi heard the rubber glove being placed on the doctor's hand and felt a sudden burst of pain as two fingers were thrust up his rectum. He cried out and the guards facing him began to laugh. The fingers were extracted just as abruptly, repeating the jab of pain a second time.

'Thank you, Deputy Ambassador,' said the doctor, as if he had just checked Al Obaydi's temperature for a mild dose of 'flu. 'You can get dressed now.' Al Obaydi knelt down and picked up his pants as the doctor and the orderly left the room.

As he dressed, Al Obaydi couldn't help wondering if each member of the Security Council went through the same humiliation every time Saddam called a meeting of the Revolutionary Command Council.

The order to return to Baghdad to give Sayedi an update on the latest position, as the Ambassador to the UN had described the summons, filled Al Obaydi with considerable apprehension, despite the fact that following his most recent meeting with Cavalli he felt he had the answers to any questions the President might put to him.

Once Al Obaydi had reached Baghdad after a seemingly endless journey through Jordan – direct flights having been suspended as part of the UN sanctions – he hadn't been allowed to rest or even given the chance to change his clothes. He'd been driven direct to Ba'ath headquarters in a black Mercedes.

When Al Obaydi had finished dressing, he checked himself in a small mirror on the wall. His apparel was, on this occasion, modest compared with the outfits he'd left in his apartment in New York: Saks Fifth Avenue suits, Valentino sweaters, Church's shoes and a solid gold Cartier watch. All this had been rejected in favour of the one set of cheap Arab clothing he retained in the bottom drawer of his wardrobe in Manhattan.

When Al Obaydi turned away from the mirror, one of the guards beckoned him to follow as the door at the end of the room opened for the first time. The contrast to the bare, almost barrack-room surroundings of the examination room took him by surprise. A thickly carpeted, ornately painted corridor was well lit by chandeliers that hung every few paces.

The Deputy Ambassador followed the guard down the corridor, becoming more aware with each step of the massive gold-painted door that loomed up ahead of him. But when he was only a few paces away, the guard opened a side door and ushered him into an ante-room that echoed the opulence of the corridor.

Al Obaydi was left alone in the room, but no sooner had he taken a seat on the large sofa than the door opened again. Al

Obaydi jumped to his feet only to see a girl enter carrying a tray, in the centre of which was a small cup of Turkish coffee.

She placed the coffee on a table beside the sofa, bowed and left as silently as she had come. Al Obaydi toyed with the cup, aware that he had fallen into the Western habit of preferring cappuccino. He drank the muddy black liquid simply out of a nervous desire to be doing something.

An hour passed slowly: he became increasingly nervous, with nothing in the room to read and only a massive portrait of Saddam Hussein to stare at. Al Obaydi spent the time going over every detail of what Cavalli had told him, wishing he could refer to the file in his small attaché case, which the guards had whisked away long before he'd reached the examination room.

During the second hour, his confidence began to drain away. During the third, he started to wonder if he would ever get out of the building alive.

Then suddenly the door swung open and Al Obaydi recognised the red-and-yellow flash on the uniform of one of Saddam's Presidential Guards: the Hemaya.

'The President will see you now,' was all the young officer said, and Al Obaydi rose and followed him quickly down the corridor towards the gold-painted door.

The officer knocked, opened the massive door and stood on one side to allow the Deputy Ambassador to join a full meeting of the Revolutionary Command Council.

Al Obaydi stood and waited, like a prisoner in the dock hoping to be told by the judge that he might at least be allowed to sit. He remained standing, well aware that no one ever shook hands with the President unless invited to do so. He stared round at the twelve-man council, noticing that only two, the Prime Minister, Tariq Aziz, and the State Prosecutor, Nakir Farrar, were wearing suits. The other ten members were dressed in full military uniform but did not wear sidearms. The only hand gun, other than those worn by General Hamil, the Commander of the Presidential Guard, and the two armed soldiers directly behind Saddam, was on the table in front of the President, placed where other heads of state would have had a memo pad.

Al Obaydi became painfully aware that the President's eyes had never left him from the moment he had entered the room. Saddam waved his Coheba cigar at the Deputy Ambassador to indicate that he should take the vacant seat at the opposite end of the table.

The Foreign Minister looked towards the President, who nodded. He then turned his attention to the man who sat nervously in the far chair.

'This, Mr President, as you know, is Hamid Al Obaydi, our Deputy Ambassador at the United Nations, whom you honoured with the responsibility of carrying out your orders to steal the Declaration of Independence from the American infidels. On your instructions, he has returned to Baghdad to inform you, in person, of what progress he has made. I have not had an opportunity to speak to him, Mr President, so you will forgive me if I appear, like yourself, to be a seeker after information.'

Saddam waved his cigar again to let the Foreign Minister know that he should get on with it.

'Perhaps I could start, Deputy Ambassador' – Al Obaydi was surprised by such a formal address, as their two families had known each other for generations, but he accepted that to show friendship of any kind in front of Saddam was tantamount to an admission of conspiracy – 'by asking you to bring us all up to date on the President's imaginative scheme.'

'Thank you, Foreign Minister,' replied Al Obaydi, as if he had never met the man before. He turned back to face Saddam, whose black eyes remained fixed on him.

'May I begin, Mr President, by saying what an honour it has been to be entrusted with this task, especially remembering the idea had emanated from Your Excellency personally.' Every member of the Council was now concentrating his attention on the Deputy Ambassador, but Al Obaydi noticed that from time to time each of them would glance in Saddam's direction to see how he was reacting.

'I am happy to be able to report that the team led by Mr Antonio Cavalli . . .'

Saddam raised a hand and looked towards the State Prosecutor, who opened a thick file in front of him.

Nakir Farrar, the State Prosecutor, was feared second only to Saddam in the Iraqi regime. Everyone knew of his reputation. A first-class honours degree in jurisprudence at Oxford, President of the Union, and a bencher at Lincoln's Inn. That was where Al Obaydi had first come across him. Not that Farrar had ever acknowledged his existence. He had been tipped to be the first QC Iraq had ever produced. But then came the invasion of the Nineteenth Province and the British expelled the high-flyer, despite several appeals from people in high places. Farrar returned to a city he had deserted at the age of eleven, and immediately offered his remarkable talent for Saddam Hussein's personal use. Within a year Saddam had appointed him State Prosecutor. A title, it was rumoured, he had selected himself.

'Cavalli is a New York criminal, Mr President, who, because he has a law degree and heads a private legal practice, creates a legitimate front for such an operation.' Saddam nodded and turned his attention back to Al Obaydi.

'Mr Cavalli has completed the preparation stage and his team is now ready to carry out the President's orders.'

'Do we have a date yet?' asked Farrar.

'Yes, State Prosecutor. May 25th. Clinton has a full day's schedule at the White House, with his speechwriters in the morning, and his wife's health-policy task unit in the afternoon, and he' – the Iraqi Ambassador to the UN had warned Al Obaydi never to refer to Clinton as 'the President' – 'will therefore not be involved in any public engagements that day, which would have made our task impossible.'

'And tell me, Deputy Ambassador,' said the State Prosecutor, 'did Mr Cavalli's lawyer succeed in getting a permit to close down the road between the White House and the National Archives during the time when Clinton will be involved in these internal meetings?'

'No, State Prosecutor, he did not,' came back Al Obaydi's reply. 'The Mayor's Office did, however, grant a permit for filming to take place on Pennsylvania Avenue from 13th Street east. But the road can only be closed for forty-five minutes. It seems this Mayor was not as easy to convince as her predecessor.'

A few members of the Council looked puzzled. 'Not as easy to convince?' asked the Foreign Minister.

'Perhaps "persuade" would be a better word.'

'And what form did this persuasion take?' asked General Hamil, who sat on the right of the President and knew only one form of persuasion.

'A $250,000 contribution to her re-election fund.'

Saddam began to laugh, so the others round the table followed suit.

'And the Archivist, is he still convinced it's Clinton who will be visiting him?' asked the State Prosecutor.

'Yes, he is,' said Al Obaydi. 'Just before I flew out Cavalli had taken eight of his own men over the building posing as a Secret Service preliminary reconnaissance team, carrying out a site survey. The Archivist could not have been more co-operative, and Cavalli was given enough time to check out everything. That exercise should make the switching of the Declaration on May 25th far easier for him.'

'But if, and I only say if, they succeed in getting the original out, have they made arrangements for passing the document over to you?' asked the State Prosecutor.

'Yes,' replied Al Obaydi confidently. 'I understand that the President wants the document to be delivered to Barazan Al-Tikriti, our venerated Ambassador to the United Nations in Geneva. When he has received the parchment, and not before, I will authorise the final payment.'

The President nodded his approval. After all, the venerated

Ambassador in Geneva was his half-brother. The State Prosecutor continued his questioning.

'But how can we be sure that what is handed to us will be the original, and not just a first-class copy?' he demanded. 'What's to prevent them from making a show of walking in and out of the National Archives, but not actually switching the documents?'

A smile appeared on Al Obaydi's lips for the first time. 'I took the precaution, State Prosecutor, of demanding such proof,' he replied. 'When the fake replaces the original, it will continue to be displayed for the general public to view. You can be assured that I shall be among the general public.'

'But you have not answered my question,' said the State Prosecutor sharply. 'How will you know ours is the original?'

'Because on the original document penned by Timothy Matlock, there is a simple spelling mistake, which has been corrected on the copy executed by Bill O'Reilly.'

The State Prosecutor reluctantly sat back in his chair when his master raised a hand.

'Another criminal, Excellency,' explained the Foreign Minister. 'This time a forger, who has been responsible for making the copy of the document.'

'So,' said the State Prosecutor, leaning forward once again, 'if the incorrect spelling is still on the document displayed in the National Archives on May 25th, you will know we have a fake and will not pay out another cent. Is that right?'

'Yes, State Prosecutor,' said Al Obaydi.

'Which word on the original has been incorrectly spelt?' demanded the State Prosecutor.

When the Deputy Ambassador told him, all Nakir Farrar said was, 'How appropriate,' and then closed the file in front of him.

'However, it will still be necessary for me to have the final payment to hand,' continued Al Obaydi, 'should I be satisfied that they have carried out their part of the bargain, and that we are in possession of the original parchment.'

The Foreign Minister looked towards Saddam who, again, nodded.

'It will be in place by May 25th,' said the Foreign Minister. 'I would like the opportunity to go over some of the details with you before your return to New York. As long as that meets with the President's approval?'

Saddam waved a hand to indicate that such a request was not important to him. His eyes remained fixed on Al Obaydi. The Deputy Ambassador wasn't sure if he was meant to leave or await further questioning. He favoured caution, and remained seated and silent. It was some time before anyone spoke.

'You must be curious, Hamid, about why I place such importance on this scrap of useless paper.' As the Deputy Ambassador had never met the President before, he was surprised to be called by his first name.

'It is not for me to question Your Excellency's reasoning,' replied Al Obaydi.

'Nevertheless,' continued Saddam, 'you would be less than human not to wonder why I am willing to spend one hundred million dollars and at the same time risk international embarrassment should you fail.'

Al Obaydi noted the word 'you' with some discomfort.

'I would be fascinated to know, Sayedi, if you felt able to confide in such an unworthy soul.'

Twelve members of the Council looked towards the President to gauge his reaction to the Deputy Ambassador's comment. Al Obaydi felt immediately that he had gone too far. He sat, terrified, during what felt like the longest silence in his life.

'Then I shall let you share my secret, Hamid,' said Saddam, his black eyes boring into the Deputy Ambassador. 'When I captured the Nineteenth Province for my beloved people, I found myself at war not with the traitors we had invaded, but the combined strength of the Western world – and that despite an agreement previously reached with the American Ambassador. "Why?" I had to ask, when everyone knew that Kuwait was run by a few corrupt families who had little interest in the welfare of their own people. I'll tell you why. In one word, oil. Had it been coffee beans that the Nineteenth Province was exporting, you would never have seen as much as an American rowing boat armed with a catapult enter the Gulf.'

The Foreign Minister smiled and nodded.

'And who were the leaders who ganged up against me? Thatcher, Gorbachev and Bush. That was less than three years ago. And what has happened to them since? Thatcher was removed by a coup carried out by her own supporters; Gorbachev was deposed by a man he himself had sacked only a year before and whose own position now looks unstable; Bush suffered a humiliating defeat at the hands of the American people. While I remain the Supreme Leader and President of my country.'

There followed a burst of applause which died instantly when Saddam began speaking again.

'That, of course, would be ample reward for most people. But not me, Hamid. Because Bush's place has been taken by this man Clinton, who has learned nothing from his predecessor's mistakes, and who now also wishes to challenge my supremacy. But this time it is my intention to humiliate him along with the American infidels long before they are given the opportunity to do so. And I shall go about this in such a way that will make it impossible for Clinton to recover any credibility in his lifetime. I intend to make Clinton and the American people the laughing stock of the world.'

The heads continued nodding.

'You have already witnessed my ability to turn the greed of their own people into a willingness to steal the most cherished document in their nation's history. And you, Hamid, are the chosen vessel to ensure that my genius will be acknowledged.'
Al Obaydi lowered his head.

'Once I am in possession of the Declaration I shall wait patiently until the fourth of July, when the whole of America will be spending a peaceful Sunday celebrating Independence

Day.' No one in the room uttered a word while the President paused.

'I shall also celebrate Independence Day, not in Washington or New York, but in Tahrir Square, surrounded by my beloved people. When I, Saddam Hussein, President of Iraq, will in front of the entire world's media burn to a cinder the American Declaration of Independence.'

Hannah lay awake in her barrack-room bed, feeling not unlike the child she had been some thirteen years before when she had spent her first night at boarding school.

She had collected Karima Saib's cases from the carousel at Charles de Gaulle airport, dreading what she might find inside them.

A driver had picked her up as promised, but as he had been unwilling to make any attempt at conversation she had no idea what to expect when they pulled up outside the Jordanian Embassy. Hannah was surprised by its size.

The beautiful old house which was set back from the boulevard Maurice Barrès was formerly the home of the late Aga Khan. The Iraqi annexe had been allocated two complete floors, tangible proof that the Jordanians did not wish to get on the wrong side of Saddam.

On entering the annexe to the embassy, the first person she met was Abdul Kanuk, the Chief Administrator. He certainly didn't look like a diplomat, and when he opened his mouth she realised he wasn't. Kanuk informed her that the Ambassador and his senior secretary Muna Ahmed were tied up in meetings and that she was to unpack and then wait in her room until called for.

The cramped accommodation was just about large enough for a bed and two suitcases, and might, she thought, have been a store room before the Iraqi delegation moved in. When she eventually forced open Karima Saib's suitcase she quickly discovered that the only things that fitted from her wardrobe were her shoes. Hannah didn't know whether to be relieved, because of Saib's taste, or anxious about how little of her own she had to wear.

Muna Ahmed, the senior secretary, joined her in the kitchen for dinner later that evening. It seemed that secretaries in the embassy were treated on the same level as servants. Hannah managed to convince Muna that it was better than she had expected, especially since they were only able to use the annexe to the Jordanian Embassy. Muna explained that as far as the Corps Diplomatique of France was concerned, the Iraqi Ambassador was to be treated only as a Head of Interest Section, although they were to address him at all times as 'Your Excellency' or 'Ambassador'.

During the first few days in her new job, Hannah sat in the room next to the Ambassador's on the other side of Muna's desk. She spent most of her time twiddling her fingers. Hannah quickly discovered that no one took much interest in her as long as she completed any work the Ambassador had left for her on his dictating machine. In fact that soon became Hannah's biggest problem, as she had to slow down in order to make Muna look more efficient. The only thing Hannah ever forgot was to keep wearing her see-through glasses.

In the evenings, over supper in the kitchen, Hannah learned from Muna everything that was expected of an Iraqi woman abroad, including how to avoid the advances of Abdul Kanuk, the Chief Administrator. By the second week, her learning curve had already slowed down, and increasingly Hannah found the Ambassador was relying on her skills. She tried not to show too much initiative.

Once they had finished their work, Hannah and Muna were expected to remain indoors, and were not allowed to leave the building at night unless accompanied by the Chief Administrator, a prospect that didn't tempt either of them. As Muna had no interest in music, the theatre or even going to cafés, she was happy to pass the time in her room reading the speeches of Saddam Hussein.

As the days slowly passed Hannah began to hope that the Mossad agent in Paris would contact her so that she could be pulled out and sent back to Israel to prepare for her mission – not that she had any clue who the Mossad agent was. She wondered if they had one in the embassy. Alone in her room, she often speculated. The driver? Too slow. The gardener? Too dumb. The cook? Certainly possible – the food was bad enough to believe it was her second job. Abdul Kanuk, the Chief Administrator? Hardly, since, as he pointed out at least three times a day, he was a cousin of Barazan Al-Tikriti, Saddam Hussein's half-brother and the UN Ambassador in Geneva. Kanuk was also the biggest gossip in the embassy, and supplied Hannah with more information about Saddam Hussein and his entourage in one night than the Ambassador managed in a week. In truth, the Ambassador rarely spoke of Sayedi in her presence, and when he did he was always guarded and respectful.

It was during the second week that Hannah was introduced to the Ambassador's wife. Hannah quickly discovered that she was fiercely independent, partly because she was half Turkish, and didn't consider that it was necessarily her duty always to stay inside the embassy compound. She did things that were thought extreme by Iraqi standards, like accompanying her husband to cocktail parties, and she had even been known to pour herself a drink without waiting to be asked. She also went – which was more important for Hannah – twice a week to swim at the nearby public baths in the boulevard Lannes. The Ambassador agreed, after a little persuasion, that it would be acceptable for the new secretary to accompany his wife.

Scott arrived in Paris on a Sunday. He had been given a key to a small flat on the avenue de Messine, and they had opened an account for him at the Société Générale on boulevard Haussmann in the name of Simon Rosenthal.

He was to telephone or fax Langley only after he had located the Mossad agent. No other operative had been informed of his existence, and he had been told not to make contact with any field agent he had worked with in the past who was now stationed in Europe.

Scott spent the first two days discovering the nine places from which he could observe the front door of the Jordanian Embassy without being seen by anyone in the building.

By the end of a week he had begun to realise for the first time what agents really meant by the expression 'hours of solitude'. He even started to miss some of his students.

He developed a routine. Every morning before breakfast he would run for five miles in the Parc Monceau, before he began the morning shift. Every evening he would spend two hours in a gym on rue de Berne before cooking supper, which he ate alone in his flat.

Scott began to despair of the Mossad agent ever leaving the embassy compound, and to wonder if Miss Kopec was even in there. The Ambassador's wife seemed to be the only woman to come and go as she pleased.

And then without warning, on the Tuesday of his second week, someone else left the building accompanying the Ambassador's wife. Was it Hannah Kopec? He only caught a fleeting glimpse as the car sped away.

He followed the chauffeur-driven Mercedes, always remaining at an angle that would make it difficult for the Ambassador's driver to spot him in his rear-view mirror. The two women were dropped outside the swimming pool on the boulevard Lannes. He watched them get out of the car. In the photographs he had been shown at Langley, Hannah Kopec had had long black hair. The hair was now cropped, but it was unquestionably her.

Scott drove a hundred yards further down the road, turned right and parked the car. He walked back, entered the building and purchased a spectator's ticket at a cost of two francs. He strolled up to the balcony which overlooked the pool. By the time he had selected an obscure seat in the gallery the Mossad agent was already swimming up and down. It only took moments for Scott to realise how fit she was, even if the Iraqi version of a swimsuit wasn't all that alluring. Her pace only slowed when the Ambassador's wife appeared at the edge of the pool, after which Kopec ventured only an occasional dog-paddle from one side to the other.

Some forty minutes later, when the Ambassador's wife left the pool, Kopec immediately quickened her pace, covering each length in under a minute. When she had swum ten lengths she pulled herself out of the water and disappeared towards the changing room.

Scott returned to his car, and when the two women re-appeared he allowed the Mercedes to overtake him before following them back to the embassy.

Later that night he faxed Dexter Hutchins at Langley to let him know he seen her, and would now try to make contact.

The following morning, he bought a pair of swimming trunks.

It was on the Thursday that Hannah first noticed him. He was doing the crawl at a steady rate, completing each length in about forty seconds, and looked as if he might once have been a useful athlete. She tried to keep up with his pace but could only manage five lengths before he stretched away. She watched him pull himself out of the water after another dozen lengths and head off in the direction of the men's changing room.

On Monday morning the following week, the Ambassador's wife informed Hannah that she wouldn't be able to go for their usual swim the next day as she would be accompanying the Ambassador on his visit to Saddam Hussein's half-brother in Geneva. Hannah had already been told about the trip by the Chief Administrator, who seemed to know even the finest details.

'I can't think why you haven't been invited to accompany the Ambassador as well,' said the cook that evening. The Chief Administrator was silenced for about two minutes until Muna left the kitchen to go to her room. Then he revealed a piece of information that disturbed Hannah.

The following day Hannah was given permission to go swimming by herself. She was glad to have an excuse to get out of the building, especially as Kanuk was in charge of the delegation in the Ambassador's absence. He had taken the Mercedes for himself, so she made her own way to the boulevard Lannes by Métro. She was disappointed to find that the man who swam so well was nowhere to be seen when she started off on her thirty lengths. Once she had completed her exercise she clung onto the side, tired and slightly out of breath. Suddenly, she was aware that he was swimming towards her in the outside lane. When he touched the end he turned smoothly and said distinctly, 'Don't move, Hannah, I'll be back.'

Hannah assumed he must be someone who remembered her from her days as a model, and her immediate reaction was to make a run for it. But she continued to tread water as she waited for him to return, thinking he might perhaps be the Mossad agent Kratz had referred to.

She watched him swimming towards her, and became more apprehensive with each stroke. When he touched the edge he came to a sudden halt and asked, 'Are you alone?'

'Yes,' she replied.

'I thought I couldn't see the Ambassador's wife. She usually displaces a great deal of water without much forward motion. By the way, I'm Simon Rosenthal. Colonel Kratz instructed me to make contact. I have a message for you.'

Hannah felt stupid shaking hands with the man while they were both clinging onto the edge of the pool.

'Do you know the avenue Bugeaud?'

'Yes,' she replied.

'Good. See you at the Bar de la Porte Dauphine in fifteen minutes.'

He pulled himself out of the pool in one movement and disappeared in the direction of the men's changing room before she had a chance to reply.

A little over fifteen minutes later Hannah walked into the Bar de la Porte Dauphine. She searched around the room and almost missed him perched behind one of the high-backed wooden chairs directly below a large, colourful mural.

He rose to greet her and then ordered another coffee. He warned her that they must spend only a few minutes together, because she ought to return to the embassy without delay. As she sipped the first real coffee she had tasted in weeks, Hannah took a closer look at him, and began to recall what it was like just to enjoy a drink with someone interesting. His next sentence snapped her back into the real world.

'Kratz plans to pull you out of Paris in the near future.'

'Any particular reason?' she asked.

'The date of the Baghdad operation has been settled.'

'Thank God,' said Hannah.

'Why do you say that?' asked Scott, risking his first question.

'The Ambassador expects be called back to Baghdad to take up a new post. He intends to ask me to go with him,' replied Hannah. 'Or that's what the Chief Administrator is telling everyone, except Muna.'

'I'll warn Kratz.'

'By the way, Simon, I've picked up two or three scraps of information that Kratz might find useful.'

He nodded and listened as Hannah began to give him details of the internal organisation of the embassy, and of the comings and goings of diplomats and businessmen who publicly spoke out against Saddam while at the same time trying to close deals with him. After a few minutes he stopped her and said, 'You'd better leave now. They might begin to miss you. I'll try and arrange another meeting whenever it's possible,' he found himself adding.

She smiled, rose from the table and left, without looking back.

Later that evening, Scott sent a coded message to Dexter Hutchins in Virginia to let him know that he had made contact with Hannah Kopec.

A fax came back an hour later with only one instruction.

13

ON MAY 25TH 1993, the sun rose over the Capitol a few minutes after five. Its rays crept along the White House lawn and minutes later seeped unnoticed into the Oval Office. A few hundred yards away, Cavalli was slapping his hands behind his back.

Cavalli had spent the previous day in Washington, checking the finer details for what felt like the hundredth time. He had to assume that something must go wrong and, whatever it turned out to be, it would automatically become his responsibility.

Johnny Scasiatore walked over and handed Cavalli a steaming mug of coffee.

'I had no idea it could be this cold in Washington,' Cavalli said to Johnny, who was wearing a sheepskin jacket.

'It's cold at this time of the morning almost everywhere in the world,' replied Johnny. 'Ask any film director.'

'And do you really need six hours to get ready for three minutes of filming?' Cavalli asked incredulously.

'Two hours' preparation for a minute's work is the standard rule. And don't forget, we'll have to run through this particular scene twice, in somewhat unusual circumstances.'

Cavalli stood on the corner of 13th Street and Pennsylvania Avenue and eyed the fifty or so people who came under Johnny's direction. Some were preparing a track along the pavement that would allow a camera to follow the six cars as they travelled slowly down Pennsylvania Avenue. Others were

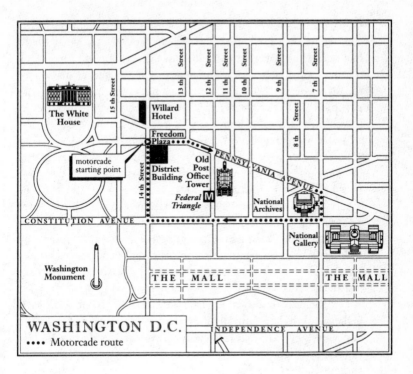

fixing up massive IK arc lights along the seven hundred yards that would eventually be powered by a 200kw generator which had been transported into the heart of the capital at four o'clock that morning. Sound equipment was being tested to make sure that it would pick up every kind of noise – feet walking on a pavement, car doors slamming, the rumble of the subway, even the chimes of the clock on the Old Post Office Tower.

'Is all this expense really necessary?' asked Cavalli.

'If you want everyone except us to believe they're taking part in a motion picture, you can't afford to risk any short-cuts. I'm going to shoot a film that anybody watching us, professional or amateur, could expect to see one day in a movie theatre. I'm even paying full equity rates for all of the extras.'

'Thank God none of my people have a union,' commented Cavalli. The sun was now full on his face, twenty-one minutes after the President would have enjoyed its warmth over breakfast in the White House.

Cavalli looked down at the checklist on his clipboard. Al Calabrese already had all his twelve vehicles in place on the curbside, and the drivers were standing around in a huddle drinking coffee, sheltered from the wind by one of the walls of Freedom Plaza. The six limousines glistened in the morning sun as passers-by, cleaners and janitors leaving offices and early-morning commuters coming up from the Federal Triangle Metro stop slowed to admire the spectacle. A painter was just touching up the Presidential Seal on the third car while a girl was unfurling a flag on the right-hand fender.

Cavalli turned to see a police truck, tailboard down, parked in front of the District Building. Barriers were being lifted off and carried onto the pavement to make sure innocent passers-by did not stray onto the set during those crucial three minutes when the filming would be taking place.

Lloyd Adams had spent the previous day going over his lines one last time and dipping into yet another book on the history of the Declaration of Independence. That night he had sat in bed replaying again and again a video of Bill Clinton on his

Georgia Avenue walk, noting the tilt of the head, the Razorback accent, the way he subconsciously bit his lower lip. The Monday before, Adams had purchased a suit that was identical to the one the President had worn to welcome the British Prime Minister in February – straight off the rack from Dillard's Department Store. He chose a red, white and blue tie, a rip-off of the one Clinton wore on the cover of the March issue of *Vanity Fair*. A Timex Ironman had been the final addition to his wardrobe. During the past week a second wig had been made, this time a little greyer, which Adams felt more comfortable with. The director and Cavalli had taken him through a dress rehearsal the previous evening: word perfect – though Johnny had commented that his collapse at the end of the scene was a bad case of overacting. Cavalli felt the Archivist would be far too overwhelmed to notice.

Cavalli asked Al Calabrese to go over the breakdown of his staff yet again. Al tried not to sound exasperated, as he had gone over it in great detail during their last three board meetings: 'Twelve drivers, six outriders,' he rattled off. 'Four of them are ex-cops or military police and all of them have worked with me before. But as none of them are going into the National Archives, they've simply been told they're involved in a movie. Only those working directly under Gino Sartori know what we're really up to.'

'But are they fully briefed on what's expected of them once they reach the Archives?'

'You'd better believe it,' replied Al. 'We went over it at least half a dozen times yesterday, first on a map in my office, and then we came down here in the afternoon and walked the route. They drive down Pennsylvania Avenue at ten miles an hour while they're being filmed and continue east until they reach 7th Street. Then they take a sharp right, when they'll be out of sight of everyone involved in the filming, not to mention the police. Then they turn right again at the delivery entrance of the National Archives, where they'll come to a halt in front of the loading dock. Angelo, Dollar Bill, Debbie, you and the counter-assault team leave their vehicles and accompany the actor into the building, where they'll be met by Calder Marshall.

'Once your party has entered the building the cars will go back up the ramp and take a right on 7th Street, another right on Constitution Avenue and then right on 14th Street before returning to the location where the filming began. By then, Johnny will be ready for a second take. On the signal from you that the Declaration of Independence has been exchanged for a fake, the second take will begin immediately, except this time we'll be picking up the thirteen operatives we dropped outside the National Archives.'

'And, if all goes to plan, the Declaration of Independence as well,' said Cavalli. 'Then what happens?' he asked, wanting to be sure that nothing had changed since their final board meeting in New York.

'The limos leave Washington by six separate routes,' continued Al. 'Three of them return to the capital during the afternoon, but not until they've changed their licence plates; two others go on to New York, and one drives to a destination known only to you; that will be the vehicle carrying the Declaration.'

'If it all runs as smoothly as that, Al, you'll have earned your money. But it won't, and that's when we'll really find out how good you are.' He nodded as Al left to grab a mug of coffee and rejoin his men.

Cavalli checked his watch: 7.22. When he looked up he saw Johnny heading towards him, red in the face. Thank God I don't have to work in Hollywood, thought Cavalli.

'I'm having trouble with a cop who says I can't put my lighting equipment on the sidewalk until 9.30 a.m. That means I won't be able to begin filming until after ten, and if I've only got forty-five minutes to start with –'

'Calm down, Johnny,' said Cavalli, and checked his list of personnel. He looked up and began to search the crowd of workers that was flowing off Freedom Plaza onto the pavement.

He spotted the man he needed. 'You see the tall guy with grey hair practising his charm on Debbie?' he said, pointing.

'Yeah,' said Johnny.

'That's Tom Newbolt, ex-Deputy Chief of the DCPD, now a security consultant. We've hired him for the day. So go and tell him what your problem is, and then we'll find out if he's worth the five thousand dollars his company is charging me.'

Cavalli smiled as Johnny stormed off in Newbolt's direction.

Angelo stood over the slumbering body. He leaned across, grabbed Dollar Bill's shoulders, and began to shake him furiously.

The little Irishman was belching out a snore that sounded more like an old tractor than a human being. Angelo leaned closer, only to find Dollar Bill smelt as if he had spent a night in the local brewery.

Angelo realised that he should never have left Bill the previous evening, even for a moment. If he didn't get the bastard to the Archives on time, Cavalli would kill them both. He even knew who'd carry out the job, and the method she would use. He went on shaking, but Dollar Bill's eyes remained determinedly closed.

At eight o'clock a klaxon sounded and the film crew took a break for breakfast.

'Thirty minutes. Union regulations,' explained Johnny when Cavalli looked exasperated. The crew surrounded a parked trailer – another expensive import – on the pavement, where they were served eggs, ham and hash browns. Cavalli had to admit that the crowds gathered behind the police barriers and the passers-by lingering on the pavement never seemed to doubt for a moment that this was a film crew getting ready for a shoot.

Cavalli decided to use the thirty-minute break to check for

himself that, once the cars had turned right on 7th Street, they could not be seen by anyone involved in the filming back on Pennsylvania Avenue.

He strode briskly away from the commotion, and when he reached the corner of 7th Street he turned right. It was as if he'd entered a different world. He joined a group of people who were quite unaware of what was taking place less than half a mile away. It was just like Washington on a normal Tuesday morning. He was pleased to spot Andy Borzello sitting on the bench in the bus shelter near the loading dock entrance to the National Archives, reading the *Washington Post*.

By the time Cavalli had returned, the film crew were beginning to move back and start their final checks; no one wanted to be the person responsible for a retake.

The crowds at the barriers were growing thicker by the minute, and the police spent a considerable amount of their time explaining that a film was going to be shot, but not for at least another couple of hours. Several people looked disappointed at this information and moved on, only to allow others to take up the places they had vacated.

Cavalli's cellular phone began ringing. He pressed the talk button and was greeted by the sound of his father's Brooklyn vowels. The chairman was cautious over the phone, and simply asked if there were any problems.

'Several,' admitted Tony. 'But none so far that we hadn't anticipated or can't overcome.'

'Don't forget, cancel the entire operation if you're not satisfied with the response to your nine o'clock phone call. Either way, he mustn't be allowed to return to the White House.' The line went dead. Cavalli knew that his father was right on both counts.

Cavalli checked his watch again: 8.43. He strolled over to Johnny.

'I'm going across to the Willard. I don't expect to be too long, so just keep things rolling. By the way, I see you got all your equipment on the sidewalk.'

'Sure thing,' said Johnny. 'Once Newbolt talked to that cop, he even helped us carry the damn stuff.'

Cavalli smiled and began walking towards the National Theater on the way to the Willard Hotel. Gino Sartori was coming in the opposite direction.

'Gino,' Cavalli said, stopping to face the ex-Marine. 'Are all your men ready?'

'Every one of the bastards.'

'And can you guarantee their silence?'

'Like the grave. That is, if they don't want to end up digging their own.'

'So where are they now?'

'Coming from eight different directions. All of them are due to report me by nine-thirty. Smart dark suits, sober ties, and holsters that aren't too obvious.'

'Let me know the moment they're all signed in.'

'Will do,' said Gino.

Cavalli continued his journey to the Willard Hotel, and after checking his watch again began to lengthen his stride.

He strolled into the lobby, and found Rex Butterworth marching nervously up and down the centre of the hall as if his sole aim in life was to wear out the blue-and-gold carpet. He looked relieved when he saw Cavalli, and joined him as he strode towards the elevator.

'I told you to sit in the corner and wait, not parade up and down in front of every freelance journalist looking for a story.'

Butterworth mumbled an apology as they stepped into the elevator and Cavalli pressed button eleven. Neither of them spoke again until they were safely inside 1137, the room in which Cavalli had spent the previous night.

Cavalli looked more carefully at Rex Butterworth now they were alone. He was sweating as if he had just finished a five-mile jog, not travelled up eleven floors in an elevator.

'Calm down,' said Cavalli. 'You've played your part well so far. Only one more phone call and you're through. You'll be on your flight to Rio before the first outrider even reaches the National Archives. Now, are you clear about what you have to say to Marshall?'

Butterworth took out some handwritten notes, mouthed a few words and said, 'Yes, I'm clear and I'm ready.' He was shaking like a jelly.

Cavalli dialled the private number of the Archivist's office half a mile away, and when he heard the first ring, passed the receiver over to Butterworth. They both listened to the continuing ringing. Eventually Cavalli put his hand out to take back the receiver. They would have to try again in a few minutes' time. Suddenly there was a click and a voice said, 'Calder Marshall speaking.'

Cavalli went into the bathroom and picked up the extension. 'Good morning, Mr Marshall. It's Rex Butterworth at the White House, just checking everything's all set up and ready your end.'

'It certainly is, Mr Butterworth. Every member of my staff has been instructed to be at their desks by nine o'clock sharp. In fact, I've seen most of them already, but only my deputy and the Senior Conservator know the real reason I've asked them all not to be late this morning.'

'Well done,' said Butterworth. 'The President is running on time and we anticipate he will be with you around ten, but I'm afraid he still has to be back at the White House by eleven.'

'By eleven, of course,' said the Archivist. 'I only hope we can get him round the whole building in fifty minutes, because I expect there are many of my staff who would like to meet him.'

'We'll just have to hope that fifty minutes is enough time to fit them all in,' said Butterworth. 'Can I assume that there are still no problems with the President's personal request?'

'None that I'm aware of,' said Marshall. 'The Conservator is quite happy to remove the glass so that the President can study the parchment in its original form. We'll keep the Declaration in the vault until the President has left the building. I hope to

142

have the document back on view to the general public a few minutes after he's left.'

'It sounds to me as if you have everything under control, Mr Marshall,' said Butterworth, the sweat pouring off his forehead. 'I'm just off to see the President, so I'm afraid I'll be out of contact for the rest of the morning, but let's talk again this afternoon and you can tell me how it all went.'

Cavalli placed the phone on the side of the bath and bolted back into the bedroom, coming to a halt in front of the President's Special Assistant. Butterworth looked terrified. Cavalli shook his head frantically from side to side.

'Actually, now that I look at my schedule, Mr Marshall, I see you won't be able to reach me again today because I promised my wife I'd leave the office a little earlier than usual to prepare for our annual vacation which begins tomorrow.'

'Oh. Where are you going?' asked Marshall, innocently.

'Off to see my mother in Charleston. But I feel confident that the President's visit to the Archives will be a great success. Why don't we get together as soon as I'm back?'

'I would enjoy that,' said Marshall. 'And I do hope you have a pleasant break in South Carolina; the azaleas should still be blooming.'

'Yes, I suppose they will,' said Butterworth as he watched Cavalli pulling a finger across his throat. 'My other line is ringing,' he added, and without another word put the phone down.

'You said too much, you fool. We don't ever want him trying to contact you again.'

Butterworth looked apprehensive.

'How long will it be before the White House wonders where you are?' asked Cavalli.

'At least a week,' replied Butterworth. 'I really am due for my annual leave, and even my boss thinks I'm going to Charleston.'

'Well, that's something you did right,' said Cavalli, as he handed Butterworth a one-way ticket to Rio de Janeiro and a letter of confirmation that the sum of nine hundred thousand dollars had been deposited in the Banco do Brazil.

'I have to get back to the set,' said Cavalli. 'You stay put for ten minutes and then take a taxi to Dulles airport. And when you get to Brazil, don't spend all the money on a girl. And Rex, don't even think about coming back. If you do, it won't just be the Feds who are waiting for you at the airport.'

Angelo had somehow managed to get Dollar Bill dressed, but he still stank of Guinness, and he certainly didn't look like the President's personal physician – or anybody else's physician for that matter.

'Sorry, lad. Sorry, lad,' Dollar Bill kept repeating. 'I hope this won't get you into any trouble.'

'It will if you don't sober up in time to play your part and see that the parchment is transferred into the special cylinder. Because if Cavalli ever finds out I wasn't with you last night, you're dead, and more important, so am I.'

'Settle down, lad, and just make me a Bloody Mary. Two parts tomato juice and one part vodka. I'll be as right as rain in no time, you'll see.' Angelo looked doubtful as the little man's head fell back on the pillow.

As Cavalli closed the door of room 1137, a woman pushing a large laundry basket passed him in the corridor.

He took the lift to the ground floor and walked straight out of the hotel. The first thing he saw as he left the Willard and crossed the plaza that divided the hotel from Pennsylvania Avenue was that the morning traffic was backed up for half a mile down 15th Street.

Al and Johnny came running towards him from different directions. 'What's going on?' were Cavalli's first words.

'Normal morning traffic coming in from Virginia, the police assure us, except we're blocking a lane and a half with our twelve vehicles and six outriders.'

'Damn, my mistake,' said Cavalli. 'I should have anticipated it. So what do you suggest, Al?'

'I send my boys over to Atlantic Garage on 13th and F until the police get the traffic on the move again, and then bring them back nearer the starting time.'

'It's a hell of a risk,' said Johnny. 'That permit only allows me to film for forty-five minutes, and they aren't going to stretch it by a second.'

'But if my cars stay put you might never get started at all,' said Al.

'OK, Al, you get moving, but make sure you're back on the grid by 9.50.' Cavalli checked his watch. 'That's twenty-seven minutes.' Al began running towards the parked cars.

Cavalli turned his attention to the director. 'What time are you bringing the actor out?'

'Nine-fifty, or the moment the last car is back in place. He's being made up in that trailer over there,' said Johnny, pointing.

Cavalli watched as the sixth limousine pulled away, and was relieved to see the traffic start to flow again.

'And Gino's Secret Service agents, what will happen to them now that the cars have gone?'

'Most of them are hanging around with the extras, but they aren't looking too convincing.'

Cavalli's cellular phone began to ring. 'I have to get back or you won't have a film, real or otherwise,' said Johnny. Cavalli nodded and said 'Yes,' into the mouthpiece as the director rushed away. Something caught Cavalli's eye as he tried to concentrate on the voice on the other end of the line.

'The helicopter is all set to take off at ten o'clock sharp, boss; but it loses its slot at seven minutes past. The traffic cops won't let it go up after that, however much you gave to the Fraternal Order of Police.'

'We're still running to schedule, despite some problems,' said Cavalli, 'so take her up at ten and just hover over the route. Marshall and his staff must be able to see and hear you when we arrive at the Archives. That's all I care about.'

'OK, boss. Understood.'

Cavalli checked his watch again. It was 9.36 and the traffic was now flowing smoothly. He walked over to the officer co-ordinating the shoot for the city's motion picture and television office.

'Don't worry,' said the Lieutenant even before Cavalli had opened his mouth. 'The traffic will be stopped and the detour signs in place by 9.59. We'll have you moving on time, I promise.'

'Thank you, officer,' said Cavalli, and quickly dialled Al Calabrese.

'I think you'd better start getting your boys back . . .'

'Number one has already left with two outriders. Number two's just about to go; after that, they leave at twenty-second intervals.'

'You should have been an army general,' said Cavalli.

'You can blame the government for that. I just didn't get the right education.'

Suddenly, Pennsylvania Avenue was ablaze with lights. Cavalli, like everyone else, shielded his eyes and then, just as suddenly, the lights were switched off, making the morning sun appear like a dim lightbulb.

'Good sparks,' Cavalli heard the director shout. 'I could only spot one that didn't function. The seventh on the right.'

Cavalli stood on the pavement and looked towards the corner of 13th Street, where he could see the first of Al's limousines with two outriders edging its way back through the traffic. The sight of the shining black limo made him feel nervous for the first time.

A tall, well-built, bald man wearing dark glasses, a dark blue suit, white shirt and a red, white and blue striped tie was walking towards him. He stopped by Cavalli's side as the first of the two outriders and the leading police car drew in to the curb.

'How are you feeling?' asked Cavalli.

'Like all first nights,' said Lloyd Adams. 'I'll be just fine once the curtain goes up.'

'Well, you sure knew your lines word perfect last night.'

'My lines aren't the problem,' said Adams. 'It's Marshall's I'm worried about.'

'What do you mean?' asked Cavalli.

'He's not been able to attend any of our rehearsals, has he?' replied the actor. 'So he doesn't know his cues.'

The second car drew into line, accompanied by two more outriders, as Al Calabrese came running across the pavement and Lloyd Adams strode off in the direction of the trailer.

'Can you still do it in nine minutes?' asked Cavalli, looking at his watch.

'As long as Chief Thomas's finest don't foul things up like they do every other morning,' said Al. He headed on towards the cars and immediately began to organise the unfurling of the Presidential flag on the front of the third car before checking on any specks of dirt that might have appeared on the bodywork after one trip round the block.

The staff van drew up in line. Scasiatore immediately swung round on his high stool and, through a megaphone, told the actor, the secretary, the Lieutenant and the physician to be ready to climb into the third and fourth cars.

When the director asked for the Lieutenant and the physician, Cavalli suddenly realised that he hadn't seen Dollar Bill or Angelo all morning. Perhaps they'd been waiting in the trailer.

The fourth limousine drew up as Cavalli's eyes swept the horizon, searching for Angelo.

The klaxon sounded again for several seconds, this time to warn the film crew that they had ten minutes left before shooting. The noise almost prevented Cavalli from hearing his phone ringing.

'It's Andy reporting in, boss. I'm still outside the National Archives. Just to let you know it's no busier than when you checked up an hour ago.'

'At least someone's awake,' said Cavalli.

'There can't be more than twenty or thirty people around at the moment.'

'Glad to hear it. But don't call me again unless something goes wrong.' Cavalli flicked off the phone and tried to remember what it was that had been worrying him before it rang. Eleven vehicles and six outriders were now in place. One vehicle was still missing. But something else was nagging at the back of Cavalli's mind. He became distracted when an officer standing in the middle of Pennsylvania Avenue began shouting at the top of his voice that he was ready to stop the traffic whenever the director gave the word. Johnny stood up on his chair and pointed frantically to the twelfth car, which remained obstinately stuck in traffic a couple of hundred yards away.

'If you divert the traffic now,' shouted Johnny, 'that one's never going to end up in the motorcade.'

The officer remained in the middle of the road and waved the traffic through as fast as he could in the hope of getting the limousine there quicker, but it didn't make a lot of difference.

'Extras on the street!' shouted Johnny, and several people who Cavalli had supposed were members of the public strolled onto the pavement and began walking up and down professionally.

Johnny stood up on his chair again and this time turned to face the crowd huddled behind the barriers. An aide handed him a megaphone so that he could address them.

'Ladies and gentlemen,' he began. 'This is a short cut for a movie about the President going to the Hill to address a joint session of Congress. I'd be grateful if you could wave, clap and cheer as if it were the real President. Thank you.' Spontaneous applause broke out, which made Cavalli laugh for the first time that morning. He hadn't noticed that the former Deputy Police Chief had crept up behind him during the director's address. He whispered in his ear, 'This is going to cost you a whole lot of money if you don't pull it off first time.'

Cavalli turned to face the ex-policeman and tried not to show how anxious he felt.

'The hold-up, I mean. If you don't get the shoot done this

morning, the authorities aren't going to let you go through this charade again for one hell of a time.'

'I don't need to be reminded of that,' snapped Cavalli. He turned his attention back to Johnny, who had climbed down from his chair and was walking over to take his seat on the tracking dolly, ready to move as soon as the twelfth vehicle was in place. Once again, the aide passed Johnny the megaphone. 'This is a final check. Check your positions, please. This is a final check. Everyone ready in car one?' There was a sharp honk in reply. 'Car two?' Another honk. 'Car three?' Another sharp honk from the driver of Lloyd Adams' car. Cavalli stared in through the window as the bald actor removed the top of his wig box. 'Car four?' Not a sound came from car four.

'Is everyone in car four who should be in car four?' barked the director.

It was then that Cavalli remembered what had been nagging at him: he still hadn't seen Angelo or Dollar Bill all morning. He should have checked earlier. He hurried towards the direc-tor as a naval Lieutenant jumped out of a car which he'd left stranded in the middle of the road. He was six foot tall, with short-cropped hair, wearing a white uniform with a sword swinging by his side and medals for service in Panama and the Gulf on his chest. In his right hand he carried a black box. A policeman began chasing after him while Dollar Bill, carrying a small leather bag, followed a few yards behind at a slower pace. When Cavalli saw what had happened he changed direction and walked calmly out into the middle of the road, and the naval officer came to a halt by his side.

'What the hell do you think you're playing at?' barked Cavalli.

'We got held up in the traffic,' said Angelo lamely.

'If this whole operation fails because of you . . .'

Angelo turned the colour of his uniform as he thought about what had happened to Bruno Morelli.

'And the sword?' snapped Cavalli.

'A perfect fit.'

'And our physician. Is *he* fit?'

'He'll be able to do his job, I promise you,' Angelo said, looking over his shoulder.

'Which car are you both in?'

'Number four. Directly behind the President.'

'Then get in, and right now.'

'Sorry, sorry,' Dollar Bill said, as he arrived panting. 'My fault, not Angelo's. Sorry, sorry,' he repeated as the back door of car four was held open for him by the Lieutenant, who was gripping his sword. Once Dollar Bill was safely in, Angelo joined the would-be physician and slammed the door behind him.

The policeman who'd been chasing Angelo took his notebook out as Cavalli turned round looking for Tom Newbolt. Tom was already running across the road.

'Leave him to me,' was all he said.

The second van with surveillance cameras on board screeched to a halt to complete the line. The front window purred down. 'Sorry, boss,' said the driver. 'Some jerk just dumped his car right in front of me.' The clock on the Old Post Office Tower struck ten. At that moment, on a signal from the co-ordinating officer, several policemen walked out into the road. Some held up the traffic coming down Pennsylvania Avenue while others placed diversion signs to direct the cars away from where the filming was taking place.

Cavalli turned his attention to the other end of Pennsylvania Avenue, a mere seven hundred yards away. It was once again bumper to bumper with slow-moving traffic.

'Come on, come on!' he shouted out loud as he checked his watch and waited impatiently for the all clear.

'Any moment now,' shouted back the officer, who was standing in the middle of the road.

Cavalli looked up to see the blue-and-white police helicopter hovering noisily overhead.

Neither he nor the officer spoke again until a couple of minutes later when they heard a sharp whistle blow three times from the far end of Pennsylvania Avenue. Cavalli checked his watch. They'd lost six precious minutes.

'I'll kill Angelo,' he said. 'If –'

'All clear!' shouted the co-ordinating officer. He turned to face Cavalli, who gave the director a thumbs-up sign.

'You've still got thirty-nine minutes,' bellowed the officer. 'That should easily be enough time to complete the shoot twice.' But Cavalli didn't hear the last few words as he ran to the second car, pulled open the door and jumped into the seat next to the driver.

And then a nagging thought hit him. Looking out of the side window, Cavalli began to scan the crowd once again.

'Lights!' screamed the director, and Pennsylvania Avenue lit up like Christmas Eve at Macy's.

'OK, everybody, we're going to shoot in sixty seconds.'

The limousines and motorcycles switched on their engines and began revving up. The extras strolled up and down while the police continued to divert commuters away from the scene. The director leaned back over his chair to check the lights and see if the seventh in line was working.

'Thirty seconds.' Johnny looked at the driver of the first car and said through the megaphone, 'Don't forget to take it easy. My tracking dolly can only manage ten miles an hour going backwards. And walkers,' – the director checked up and down the pavement – 'please look as if you're walking, not auditioning for *Hamlet*.'

The director turned his attention to the crowd. 'Now, don't let me down behind the barriers. Clap, cheer and wave, and please remember we're going to do the whole exercise again in about twenty minutes, so stick around if you possibly can.

'Fifteen seconds,' said the director as he swung back to face the first car in line. 'Good luck, everybody.'

Tony stared at Scasiatore, willing him to get on with it. They were now eight minutes late – which with this particular President, he had to admit, added an air of authenticity.

'Ten seconds. Rolling. Nine, eight, seven, six, five, four, three, two, one – action!'

The woman pushing the laundry basket down the corridor ignored the 'Do Not Disturb' sign on Room 1137 and walked straight in.

A rather overweight man, sweating profusely, was seated on the edge of the bed. He was jabbing out some numbers on the phone when he looked round and saw her.

'Get out, you dumb bitch,' he said, and turned back to concentrate on redialling the numbers.

In three silent paces she was behind him. He turned a second time just as she leaned over, took the phone cord in both hands and pulled it round his neck. He raised an arm to protest as she flicked her wrists in one sharp movement. He slumped forward and fell off the bed onto the carpet, just as the voice on the phone said, 'Thank you for using AT & T.'

She realised that she shouldn't have used the phone cord. Most unprofessional – but nobody called her a dumb bitch.

She replaced the phone on the hook and bent down, deftly hoisting the Special Assistant to the President onto her shoulder. She dropped him into the laundry basket. No one would have believed such a frail woman could have lifted such a heavy weight. In truth the only use she had ever made of a degree in physics was to apply the principles of fulcrums, pivots and levers to her chosen profession.

She opened the door and checked the passageway. At this hour it was unlikely there'd be many people around. She wheeled the basket down the corridor until she reached the house-keepers' elevator, faced the wall and waited patiently. When the lift arrived she pressed the button that would take her to the garage.

When the lift came to a halt on the lower ground floor she wheeled the basket out and over to the back of a Honda Accord, the second-most popular car in America.

Shielded by a pillar, she quickly transferred the Special Assistant from the basket into the boot of the car. She then wheeled the basket back to the lift, took off her baggy black uniform, dropped it into the laundry basket, removed her bag with the long cord handle and despatched the laundry basket to the twenty-fifth floor.

She straightened up her Laura Ashley dress before climbing into the car and placing her carrier bag under the front seat. She drove out of the car park onto F Street, and had only travelled a short distance before she was stopped by a traffic cop.

She wound the window down.

'Follow the diversion sign,' he said, without even looking at her.

She glanced at the clock on her dashboard. It was 10.07.

14

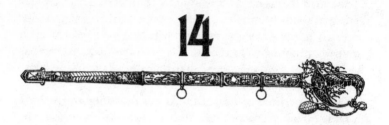

AS THE LEAD POLICE CAR moved slowly away from the curb, the director's tracking dolly began running backwards at the same pace along its rails. The crowds behind the barriers started to cheer and wave. If they had been making a real film the director would have called 'Cut' after twenty seconds because that fool of a co-ordinating officer was still standing in the middle of the road, hands on hips, oblivious to the fact that he wasn't the star of the film.

Cavalli didn't notice the officer as he concentrated on the road ahead of him. He phoned through to Andy, who he knew would still be seated on the bench on 7th Street reading the *Washington Post*.

'Not much action this end, boss. A little activity at the bottom of the ramp, but no one on the street is showing any real interest. Is everything all right your end? You're running late.'

'Yes, I know, but we should be with you in about sixty seconds,' said Cavalli, as the director reached the end of his private railroad track and put one thumb in the air to indicate that the cars could now accelerate to twenty-five miles per hour. Johnny Scasiatore jumped off the dolly and walked slowly back down Pennsylvania Avenue so he could prepare himself for the second take.

Cavalli flicked the phone off and took a deep intake of breath as the motorcade passed 9th Street; he stared at the FDR

Monument that was set back on a grass plot in front of the main entrance of the Archives. The first car turned right on 7th Street; a mere half-block remained before they would reach the driveway into the loading dock. The lead motorcycles speeded up and when they were opposite Andy standing on the pavement, they swung right and drove down the ramp.

The rest of the motorcade formed a line directly opposite the delivery entrance, while the third limousine drove down the ramp to the loading dock.

The counter-assault team were the first onto the street, and eight of them quickly formed a circle facing outwards around the third car.

After the eight men had stared in every direction for a few seconds, Cavalli jumped out of the second car, ran across to join them and opened the back door of the third car so that Lloyd Adams could get out.

Calder Marshall was waiting on the loading dock, and walked forward to greet the President.

'Nice to meet you, Mr Marshall,' said the actor, thrusting out his hand. 'I've been looking forward to this occasion for some time.'

'As, indeed, have we, Mr President. May I on behalf of my staff welcome you to the National Archives of the United States. Will you please follow me.'

Lloyd Adams and his entourage dutifully followed Marshall straight into the spartan freight elevator. As one of the Secret Service agents kept his finger on the 'open' button, Cavalli gave the order for the motorcade to return to its starting point. Six motorcycles and the twelve vehicles moved off and began the journey back to rejoin the director and prepare for the second shoot.

The whole exercise of getting the actor into the building and the motorcade started on its return journey had taken less than two minutes, but Cavalli was dismayed to see that a small crowd had already gathered on the far side of the road by the Federal Trade Commission, obviously sensing something important was taking place. He only hoped Andy could deal with the problem.

Cavalli quickly slipped into the elevator, wedging himself behind Adams. Marshall had begun a short history of how the Declaration of Independence had ended up in the National Archives.

'Most people know that John Adams and Thomas Jefferson drafted the Declaration that was approved by Congress on July 4th 1776. Few, however, know that the second and third Presidents died on the same day, July 4th 1826 – fifty years to the day after the official signing.' The elevator doors opened on the ground floor and Marshall stepped out into a marble corridor and led them in the direction of his office.

'The Declaration had a long and turbulent journey, Mr President, before it ended up safely in this building.'

When they reached the fifth door on the left, Marshall guided the President and his staff into his office, where coffee awaited them. Two of the Secret Service agents stepped inside while the other six remained in the corridor.

Lloyd Adams sipped his coffee as Marshall ignored his in favour of continuing the history lesson. 'After the signing ceremony, on August 2nd 1776, the Declaration was filed in Philadelphia, but because of the danger of the document being captured by the British, the engrossed parchment was taken to Baltimore in a covered wagon.'

'Fascinating,' said Adams in a soft drawl. 'But had it been captured by the British infantry, copies would still have been in existence, no doubt?'

'Oh certainly, Mr President. Indeed, we have a good example of one in this building executed by William J. Stone. However, the original remained in Baltimore until 1777, when it was returned to the relative safety of Philadelphia.'

'In another wagon?' asked the President.

'Indeed,' said Marshall, not realising his guest was joking. 'We even know the name of the man who drove it, a Mr Samuel Smith. Then, in 1800, by direction of President Adams, the

Declaration was moved to Washington, where it first found a home in the Treasury Department, but between 1800 and 1814 it was moved all over the city, eventually ending up in the old War Office building on 17th Street.'

'And, of course, we were still at war with Britain at that time,' said the actor.

Cavalli admired the way Adams had not only learned his lines, but done his research so thoroughly.

'That is correct, Mr President,' said the Archivist. 'And when the British fleet appeared in Chesapeake Bay, the Secretary of State, James Monroe, ordered that the document be moved once again. Because, as I am sure you know, Mr President, it is the Secretary of State who is responsible for the safety of the parchment, not the President.'

Lloyd Adams did know, but wasn't sure if the President would have, so he decided to play safe. 'Is that right, Mr Marshall? Then perhaps it should be Warren Christopher who is here today to view the Declaration, and not me.'

'The Secretary of State was kind enough to visit us soon after he took office,' Marshall replied.

'But he didn't want the document moved again,' said the actor. Marshall, Cavalli, the Lieutenant and the physician dutifully laughed before the Archivist continued.

'Monroe, having spotted the British advancing on Washington, despatched the Declaration on a journey up the Potomac to Leesburg, Virginia.'

'August 24th,' said Adams, 'when they razed the White House to the ground.'

'Precisely,' said Marshall. 'You are well informed, sir.'

'To be fair,' said the actor, 'I've been well briefed by my Special Assistant, Rex Butterworth.'

Marshall showed his recognition of the name, but Cavalli wondered if the actor was being just a little too clever.

'That night,' continued Marshall, 'while the White House was ablaze, thanks to Monroe's foresight the Declaration was stored safely in Leesburg.'

'So when did they bring the parchment back to Washington?' asked Adams, who could have told the Archivist the exact date.

'Not for several weeks, sir. On September 17th 1814, to be precise. With the exception of a trip to Philadelphia for the centennial celebrations and its time in Fort Knox during World War II, the Declaration has remained in the capital ever since.'

'But not in this building,' said Adams.

'No, Mr President, you are right again. It has had several other homes before ending up here, the worst being the Patent Office, where it hung opposite a window and was for years exposed to sunlight, causing the parchment irreparable damage.'

Bill O'Reilly stood in the corner, thinking how many hours of work he had had to do and how many copies he had had to destroy during the preparation stage because of that particular piece of stupidity. He cursed all those who had ever worked in the Patent Office.

'How long did it hang there?' asked Adams.

'For thirty-five years,' said Marshall, with a sigh that showed he was every bit as annoyed as Dollar Bill that his predecessors had been so irresponsible. 'In 1877 the Declaration was moved to the State Department library. Not only was smoking common at the time, but there was also an open fireplace in the room. And, I might add, the building was damaged by fire only months after the parchment had been moved.'

'That was a close one,' said Adams.

'After the war was over,' continued Marshall, 'the Declaration was taken from Fort Knox and brought back to Washington in a Pullman carriage before it was housed in the Library of Congress.'

'I hope it wasn't exposed to the light once again,' said Adams as Cavalli's phone rang.

Cavalli slipped into the corner and listened to the director tell him, 'We're back on the starting line, ready to go whenever you are.'

'I'll call when I need you,' was all Cavalli said. He switched his phone off and returned to listen to the Archivist's disquisition.

' . . . in a Thermapane case equipped with a filter to screen out damaging ultra-violet light.'

'Fascinating. But when did the document finally reach this building?' asked Adams.

'On December 13th 1952. It was transported from the Library of Congress to the National Archives in a tank under the armed escort of the US Marine Corps.'

'First a covered wagon, and finally a tank,' said the actor, who noticed that Cavalli kept glancing at his watch. 'Perhaps the time has come for me to see the Declaration in its full glory.'

'Of course, Mr President,' said the Archivist.

Marshall led the way back into the corridor, followed by the actor and his entourage.

'The Declaration can normally be seen by the public in the rotunda on the ground floor, but we shall view it in the vault where it is stored at night.' When they reached the end of the corridor the Archivist led the President down a flight of stairs while Cavalli kept checking over the route that would allow them the swiftest exit if any trouble arose. He was delighted to find that the Archivist had followed his instructions and kept the corridors clear of any staff.

At the bottom of the steps, they came to a halt outside a vast steel door at which an elderly man in a long white coat stood waiting. His eyes lit up when he saw the actor.

'This is Mr Mendelssohn,' said Marshall. 'Mr Mendelssohn is the Senior Conservator and, I confess, the real expert on anything to do with the parchment. He will be your guide for the next few minutes before we visit the rest of the building.'

The actor stepped forward, and once again thrust out his hand. 'Good to meet you, Mr Mendelssohn.'

The elderly man bowed, shook the actor's hand, and pushed the steel door open.

'Please follow me, Mr President,' he said in a mid-European

accent. Once inside the tiny vault, Cavalli watched his men spread out in a small circle, their eyes checking everything except the President. Bill O'Reilly, Angelo and Debbie also took their places as they had rehearsed the previous evening.

Cavalli quickly glanced at Dollar Bill, who looked as if it was he who might be in need of a physician.

Mendelssohn guided the actor towards a massive block of concrete that took up a large area of the far wall.

He patted the slab of concrete and explained that the protective shell had been built at a time when the nation's greatest fear had been a nuclear attack.

'The Declaration is covered in five tons of interlocking leaves of metal, embedded in the fifty-five-ton concrete and steel vault you see before you. I can assure you, Mr President,' Mendelssohn added, 'if Washington was razed to the ground, the Declaration of Independence would still be in one piece.'

'Impressive,' said Adams, 'most impressive.'

Cavalli checked his watch; it was 10.24, and they'd already been inside the building for seventeen minutes. Although the limousines were waiting, he had no choice but to allow the Conservator to carry on at his own pace. After all, their hosts were aware of the limitations on the President's time if they were still hoping to show him round the rest of the building.

'The entire system, Mr President,' continued the Conservator enthusiastically, 'is worked electronically. At the press of a button, the Declaration, which is always exhibited and stored in an upright position, travels up from this level through interlocking doors which open before the document finally comes to rest in a case of solid bronze, protected by ballistically tested glass and plastic laminate. Ultra-violet filters in the laminate give the inner layer a slightly greenish hue.' The actor looked lost, but Mr Mendelssohn continued, quite unconcerned. 'We are presently standing some twenty-two feet below the exhibit hall, and as the mechanics can be worked manually, I am able to stop the machinery at any time. With your permission, Mr Marshall.'

The Archivist nodded, and the Conservator touched a button that neither the actor nor Cavalli had spotted until that moment. The five-ton leaves began to slide apart above their heads, and a sudden whirling and clanking sounded as the massive brass frame that housed the parchment began its daily journey towards the ceiling. When the frame had reached desk height, Mr Mendelssohn pressed a second button, and the whirling sound instantly ceased. He then raised an open palm in the direction of the casing.

Lloyd Adams took a pace forward and stared across at the historic document.

'Now, remembering your personal wish, Mr President, we in turn have a small request of you.'

The actor seemed uncertain what his lines were meant to be, and glanced towards Cavalli in the wings.

'And what might that request be?' prompted Cavalli, apprehensive of any change of plan at this late stage.

'Simply,' said Mr Mendelssohn, 'that while the Archivist and I are removing the outer casing of the Declaration, your men will be kind enough to turn and face the wall.'

Cavalli hesitated, aware that the Secret Service would never allow a situation to arise where they could not see the President at all times.

'Let me make it easier for you, Mr Mendelssohn,' said Adams. 'I'll be the first to comply with your request.' The actor turned away from the document, and the rest of the team followed suit.

In the brief space of time that the team were unable to see what was going on behind them, Cavalli heard twelve distinct clicks and the exaggerated sighs of two men not used to moving heavy weights.

'Thank you, Mr President,' said Calder Marshall. 'I hope that didn't put you to too much inconvenience.'

The thirteen intruders turned round to face the massive frame. The bronze casing had been lifted over to leave the impression of an open book.

Lloyd Adams, with Cavalli and Dollar Bill a pace behind, stepped forward to admire the original while Marshall and the Conservator continued to stare at the old parchment. Suddenly, without warning, the actor reeled back, clutching his throat, and collapsed to the ground. Four of the Secret Service agents immediately surrounded Adams while the other four bundled the Archivist and the Conservator out of the vault and into the corridor before they could utter a word. Tony had to admit Johnny was right – it had been a bad case of overacting.

Once the door was closed, Cavalli turned to see Dollar Bill already staring at the parchment, his eyes alight with excitement, the Lieutenant by his side.

'Time for us to get to work, Angelo,' said the Irishman. He stretched his fingers out straight. The Lieutenant removed a pair of thin rubber gloves from the doctor's bag and pulled them over his hands. Dollar Bill wiggled his fingers like a concert pianist about to begin a recital. Once the gloves were in place, Angelo bent down again and lifted a long, thin knife out of the bag, placing the handle firmly in Dollar Bill's right hand.

While these preparations were being carried out, Dollar Bill's eyes had never once left the document. Those who remained in the room were so silent that it felt like a tomb as the forger leaned over towards the parchment and placed the blade of the knife gently under the top right-hand corner. It peeled slowly back, and he transferred the knife to the left-hand corner, and that too came cleanly away. Dollar Bill passed the knife back to Angelo before he began rolling the parchment up slowly and as tightly as he could without harming it.

At the same time, Angelo flicked back the handle of his dress sword and held the long shaft out in front of him. Cavalli took a pace forward and slowly pulled out Dollar Bill's counterfeit copy from the specially constructed chamber where the sword's blade would normally have lodged.

Cavalli and Dollar Bill exchanged their prizes and reversed the process. While Cavalli slid the original Declaration inch by inch down the scabbard of the dress sword, Dollar Bill began to unroll his fake carefully onto the backplate of the laminated glass, the moist chemical mixture helping the document to remain in place. The counterfeiter sniffed loudly. The strong smell suggested thymol to his sensitive nose. Dollar Bill gave his copy one more long look, checked the spelling correction and then took a pace backward, reluctantly leaving his masterpiece to the tender care of the National Archives and its concrete prison.

Once he had completed his task Dollar Bill walked quickly over to the side of Lloyd Adams. Debbie had already undone his collar, loosened his tie and applied a little pale foundation to his face. The forger bent down on one knee, took off the rubber gloves and threw them into a physician's bag full of make-up as Cavalli dialled a number on his cellphone.

It was answered even before he heard a ring, but Cavalli could only just make out a faint voice.

'Take two,' said Cavalli firmly, and rang off before pointing at the door. One of the Secret Service agents swung the steel grid wide open and Cavalli watched carefully as Mr Mendelssohn came charging through the gap and headed straight to the brass encasement, while Marshall, who was pale and quivering, went immediately to the side of the President.

Cavalli was relieved to see a smile come across the lips of the Conservator as he leaned over the fake Declaration. With the help of Angelo, he pulled the brass casing across and gave the manuscript a loving stare before fixing the lid back into place, then quickly tightened the twelve locks around the outside of the casing. He pressed one of the buttons and the whirling and clanking noise began again as the massive brass frame slowly disappeared back into the ground.

Cavalli turned his attention to the actor and watched as two of the Secret Service agents helped him to his feet, while Dollar Bill fastened his physician's bag.

'What chemical is it that protects the parchment?' asked Dollar Bill.

'Thymol,' replied the Archivist.

'Of course, I should have guessed. With the President's allergy problem, I might have expected this reaction. Don't panic. As long as we get him out in the fresh air as quickly as possible, he'll be back to normal in no time.'

'Thank God for that,' said Marshall, who hadn't stopped shaking.

'Amen,' said the little Irishman as the actor was helped towards the door.

Marshall quickly rushed to the front and led them back up the stairs, with the Secret Service agents following as close behind as possible.

Cavalli left Lloyd Adams stumbling behind him while he caught up with the Archivist. 'No one, I repeat, no one, must hear about this incident,' he said, running by Marshall's side. 'Nothing could be more damaging to the President when he has only been in office for such a short time, especially remembering what Mr Bush went through after his trip to Japan.'

'After his trip to Japan. Of course, of course.'

'If any of your staff should ask why the President didn't complete his tour of the building, stick to the line that he was called back to the White House on urgent business.'

'Called back on urgent business. Of course,' said Marshall, who was now whiter than the actor.

Cavalli was relieved to find his earlier orders about no staff being allowed in the lower corridor while the President was in the building still remained in force.

Once they had reached the freight elevator, and all the group were inside, they descended to the level of the loading dock. Cavalli sprinted out ahead of them and up the ramp onto 7th Street.

He was annoyed to find that there was still a small crowd on the far pavement, and no sign of the motorcade. He looked anxiously to his right, where Andy was now standing on the bench, pointing towards Pennsylvania Avenue. Cavalli turned to look in the same direction and saw the first motorcycle escort turning right into 7th Street.

He ran back down the ramp to find Lloyd Adams next to a Federal Express pick-up box, being propped up by two Secret Service agents.

'Let's make it snappy,' said Cavalli. 'There's a small crowd out there and they're beginning to wonder what's going on.' He turned to face the Archivist, who was standing next to the Conservator on the loading dock.

'Please remember, the President was called back to the White House on urgent business.' They both nodded vigorously as Cavalli ran back up the ramp. Four of the Secret Service agents rushed forward just as the third car, engine running, pulled up to the loading dock at the bottom of the ramp.

Cavalli opened the door of the third limousine and frantically waved the actor in. The lead riders on the motorcycles held up the traffic as the final car came to a halt at the mouth of the delivery entrance. As Lloyd Adams was assisted into the limousine, the small crowd on the other side of the road began pointing and clapping.

One of the Secret Service agents nodded back in the direction of the building. Angelo jumped into the second car, still clinging onto the sword, while Dollar Bill and the secretary piled into the fourth. By the time Cavalli had joined Angelo in the back of the second car and given the signal to move, the motorcycle escort was already in the middle of 7th Street holding up the traffic to allow the motorcade to proceed towards Constitution Avenue.

As the sirens blared and the limousines began their journey down 7th Street, Cavalli looked back and was relieved to see there was no longer any sign of Marshall or Mendelssohn.

He quickly switched his attention to the east side of 7th Street, where Andy was explaining to the crowd that it had not been the President but simply a rehearsal for a movie, nothing more. Most of the onlookers showed their obvious disappointment and quickly began to disperse.

Then he thought he saw him again.

As Cavalli's car sped down Constitution Avenue, the lead police car was already turning right into 14th Street, accompanied by two of the outriders. The sirens had been turned off, and the rest of the motorcade peeled off one by one as they reached their allotted intersections.

The first car swung right on 9th Street and right again back onto Pennsylvania Avenue before heading away in the direction of the Capitol. The third continued on down Constitution Avenue, keeping to the centre lane, while the fourth turned left onto 12th Street and the sixth right at 13th.

The fifth turned left on 23rd Street, crossing Memorial Bridge and following the signs to Old Town, while the second car turned left at 14th Street and headed towards the Jefferson Memorial and onto the George Washington Parkway.

Cavalli, who was seated in the back of the second car, dialled the director. When Johnny answered the phone, the only words he heard were, 'It's a wrap.'

15

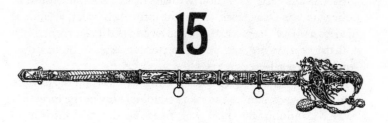

SCOTT PRAYED THAT the Ambassador's wife would be unable to get away on Thursday, or might still be in Geneva. He remembered Dexter Hutchins saying, 'Patience is not a virtue when you work for the CIA, it's nine-tenths of the job.'

When he stopped at the end of the pool Hannah told him that the Ambassador's wife hadn't returned from Switzerland. They didn't bother to swim another length, but agreed to meet later at the amusement park in the bois de Vincennes.

The moment he saw her walking across the road he wanted to touch her. There were no instructions in any of the CIA handbooks on how to deal with such a situation, and no agent had ever raised the problem with him during the past nine years.

Hannah briefed him on everything that was happening at the embassy, including 'something big' taking place in Geneva that she didn't yet know the details of. Scott told her in reply to her question that he had reported back to Kratz, and that it wouldn't be long before she was taken out. She seemed pleased.

Once they began to talk of other things, Scott's training warned him that he ought to insist she return to the embassy. But this time he left Hannah to make the decision as to when she should leave. She seemed to relax for the first time, and even laughed at Scott's stories about the macho Parisians he met up with in the gym every evening.

As they strolled around the amusement park, Scott discovered it was Hannah who won the teddy bears at the shooting gallery and didn't feel sick on the big dipper.

'Why are you buying cotton candy?' he asked.

'Because then no one will think we're agents,' she replied. 'They'll assume we're lovers.'

When they parted two hours later he kissed her on the cheek. Two professionals behaving like amateurs. He apologised. She laughed and disappeared.

Shortly after ten o'clock, Hamid Al Obaydi joined a small crowd that had formed on the pavement opposite a side entrance of the National Archives. He had to wait some twenty minutes before the door opened again and Cavalli came running up the ramp just as the motorcade reappeared on the corner of 7th Street. Cavalli gave a signal and they all came rushing out to the waiting cars. Al Obaydi couldn't believe his eyes. The deception completely fooled the small crowd, who began waving and cheering.

As the first car disappeared around the corner, a man who had been there all the time explained that it was not the President but simply the rehearsal for a film.

Al Obaydi smiled at this double deception while the disappointed crowd drifted away. He crossed 7th Street and joined a long line of tourists, schoolchildren and the simply curious who had formed a queue to see the Declaration of Independence.

The thirty-nine steps of the National Archives took as many minutes to ascend, and by the time the Deputy Ambassador entered the rotunda the river of people had thinned to a tributary which flowed on across the marble hall to a single line up a further nine steps, ending in a trickle under the gaze of Thomas Jefferson and John Hancock. Before him stood the massive brass frame that housed the Declaration of Independence.

Al Obaydi noted that when a person reached the parchment, they were only able to spend a few moments gazing at the historic document. As his foot touched the first of the steps his heart started beating faster, but for a different reason from everyone else waiting in the queue. He removed from his inside pocket a pair of spectacles whose glass could magnify the smallest writing by a degree of four.

The Deputy Ambassador walked across to the centre of the top step and stared at the Declaration of Independence. His immediate reaction was one of horror. The document was so perfect it must surely be the original. Cavalli had fooled him. Worse, he had succeeded in stealing ten million dollars by a clever deception. Al Obaydi checked that the guards on each side of the encasement were showing no particular interest in him before putting on the spectacles.

He leaned over so that his nose was only an inch from the glass as he searched for the one word that had to be spelt correctly if they expected to be paid another cent.

His eyes widened in disbelief when he came to the sentence: 'Nor have We been wanting in attentions to our British brethren.'

The Ambassador's wife returned from Geneva with her husband the following Friday. Hannah and Scott had managed to steal a few hours together that morning.

It had been less than three weeks since he had first seen her in the public baths in the boulevard Lannes. Little more than a fortnight since that first hastily arranged meeting at the café on the avenue Bugeaud. That was when the lies had begun; small ones to start with, that grew larger until they had spun themselves into an intricate web of deceit. Now Scott longed to tell her the truth, but as each day passed it became more and more impossible.

Langley had been delighted with the coded messages, and Dexter had congratulated him on doing such a first-class job. 'As good a junior field officer as I can remember,' Dexter admitted. But Scott had discovered no code to let the Deputy Director know he was falling in love.

He had read Hannah's file from cover to cover, but it gave no clue as to her real character. The way she laughed – a smile that could make you smile however sad or angry you were. A mind that was always fascinating and fascinated by what was happening around her. But most of all a warmth and gentleness that made their time apart seem like an eternity.

And whenever he was with her, he was suddenly no more mature than his students. Their clandestine meetings had rarely been for more than an hour, perhaps two, but it made each occasion all the more intense.

She continued to tell him everything about herself with a frankness and honesty that belied his deceit, while he told her nothing but a string of lies about being a Mossad agent whose front, while he was stationed in Paris, was writing a book, a travel book, which would never be published. That was the trouble with lies – each one created the next in a never-ending spiral. And that was the trouble with trust; she believed his every word.

When he returned home that evening, he made a decision he knew Langley would not approve of.

As the car edged its way into the outside lane of the George Washington Memorial Parkway bound for the airport the driver checked the rear-view mirror and confirmed no one was following them. Cavalli breathed a deep sigh of relief, though he had two alternative plans worked out if they were caught with the Declaration. He'd realised early on that it would be necessary to get as far away from the scene of the crime as quickly as possible. It had always been a crucial part of the plan that he would hand over the document to Nick Vicente within two hours of its leaving the National Archives.

'So let's get on with it,' said Cavalli, turning his attention to Angelo, who was seated opposite him. Angelo unbuckled the sword that hung from the belt around his waist. The two men then faced each other like Japanese sumo wrestlers, each waiting for the other to make the first move. Angelo placed the sword firmly between his legs, the handle pointing towards his boss. Cavalli leaned over and snapped the top back. Then, with the nail of his right thumb and forefinger, he began extracting the thin black plastic cylinder from its casing. Angelo pressed the handle back in place and hitched the sword onto his belt.

Cavalli held the twenty-six-inch-long slim plastic cylinder in his hands.

'It must be tempting to have a look,' said Angelo.

'There are more important things to do at the moment,' said Cavalli, placing the cylinder on the seat next to him. He picked up the carphone, pressed a single digit followed by 'Send', and waited for a response.

'Yes?' said a recognisable voice.

'I'm on my way, and I'll have something to export when I arrive.' There was a long silence, and Cavalli wondered if he had lost the connection.

'You've done well,' came back the eventual reply. 'But are you running to schedule?'

Cavalli looked out of the window. The exit sign for Route 395 South flashed past. 'I'd say we're about a couple of minutes from the airport. As long as we make our allocated time slot, I still hope to be with you around one o'clock.'

'Good, then I'll have Nick join us so that the contract can be picked up and sent on to our client. We'll expect you around one.'

Cavalli replaced the phone and was amused to find Angelo was dressed only in a vest and underpants. He smiled and was about to comment when the phone rang. Cavalli picked it up.

'Yes,' he said.

'It's Andy. I thought you'd like to know it's back on display to the general public and the queues are as long as ever. By the way, an Arab stood around in the crowd the whole time you were in the building, and then joined the line to see the Declaration.'

'Well done, Andy. Get yourself back to New York. You can fill me in on the details tomorrow.'

Cavalli put the phone down and considered Andy's new piece of information as Angelo was completing a Windsor knot on a tie no lieutenant would have been seen dead in. He still didn't have his trousers on.

The smoked glass between the driver and the passengers slid down.

'We're just coming up to the terminal, sir. No one has followed us at any point.'

'Good,' said Cavalli as Angelo hurriedly pulled on his trousers. 'Once you've changed your licence plates, drive back to New York.'

The driver nodded as the limousine came to a halt outside Signature Flight Support.

Cavalli grabbed the plastic tube, jumped out of the car, ran through the terminal and out onto the tarmac. His eyes searched for the white Learjet. Then he saw it. A door opened and the steps were lowered to the ground. Cavalli ran towards them as Angelo followed, trying to pull on his jacket in the high wind.

The Captain was waiting for them on the top step. 'You've just made it in time for us to keep our slot,' he told them. Cavalli smiled, and once they had both clicked on their seat-belts, the Captain pressed a button to allow the steps to swing back into place.

The plane lifted off seventeen minutes later, banking over the Kennedy Center, but not before the steward had served them each a glass of champagne. Cavalli rejected the offer of a second glass as he concentrated on what still needed to be done before he could consider his role in the operation was finished. His thoughts turned once again to Al Obaydi, and he began to wonder if he'd underestimated him.

When the Learjet landed at La Guardia fifty-seven minutes later, Cavalli's driver was waiting by his car, ready to whisk them into the city.

As the driver continually switched lanes and changed direction on the highway that would eventually take them west over the Triborough Bridge, Cavalli checked his watch. They were now lost in a sea of traffic heading into Manhattan, only eighty-seven minutes after leaving Calder Marshall outside the delivery entrance of the National Archives. Roughly the time it would take a Wall Street banker to have lunch, Cavalli thought.

Cavalli was dropped outside his father's 75th Street brownstone just before one, leaving Angelo to go on to the Wall Street office and monitor the checking-in calls as each member of the team filed his report.

The butler held open the front door of No. 23 as Tony stepped out of the car.

'Can I take that for you, sir?' he asked, eyeing the plastic tube.

'No, thank you, Martin,' said Tony. 'I'll hold onto it for the moment. Where's my father?'

'He's in the boardroom with Mr Vicente, who arrived a few minutes ago.'

Tony jogged down the staircase that led to the basement and continued across the corridor. He strode into the boardroom to find his father sitting at the head of the table, deep in conversation with Nick Vicente. The chairman stood up to greet his son, and Tony passed him the plastic tube.

'Hail, conquering hero,' were his father's first words. 'If you'd pulled off the same trick for George III, he would have made you a knight. "Arise, Sir Antonio." But as it is, you'll have to be satisfied with a hundred million dollars' compensation. Is it permissible for an old man to see the original before Nick whisks it away?'

Cavalli laughed and removed the cap from the top of the cylinder before slowly extracting the parchment and placing it gently on the boardroom table. He then unrolled two hundred years of history. The three men stared down at the Declaration of Independence and quickly checked the spelling of 'Brittish'.

'Magnificent,' was all Tony's father said as he began licking his lips.

'Interesting how the names on the bottom were left with so little space for their signatures,' observed Nick Vicente after he had studied the document for several minutes.

'If they'd all signed their names the same size as John Hancock, we would have needed a Declaration of twice the length,' added the chairman as the phone on the boardroom table started to ring.

The chairman flicked a button on his intercom. 'Yes, Martin?'

'There's a Mr Al Obaydi on the private line, says he would like to have a word with Mr Tony.'

'Thank you, Martin,' said the chairman, as Tony leaned over to pick up the call. 'Why don't you take it in my office, then I can listen in on the extension.'

Tony nodded and left the room to go next door, where he picked up the receiver on his father's desk. 'Antonio Cavalli,' he said.

'Hamid Al Obaydi here. Your father suggested I call back around this time.'

'We are in possession of the document you require,' was all Cavalli said.

'I congratulate you, Mr Cavalli.'

'Are you ready to complete the payment as agreed?'

'All in good time, but not until you have delivered the document to the place of our choosing, Mr Cavalli, as I'm sure you will recall was also part of the bargain.'

'And where might that be?' asked Cavalli.

'I shall come to your office at twelve o'clock tomorrow, when you will receive your instructions.' He paused. 'Among other things.' The line went dead.

Cavalli put the phone down and tried to think what Al Obaydi could possibly mean by 'Among other things.' He walked slowly back to the boardroom to find his father and Nick poring over the Declaration. Tony noticed that the parchment had been turned round.

174

'What do you think he meant by "Among other things"?' Tony asked.

'I've no idea,' replied his father as he gave the parchment one last look and then began slowly to roll it up.

'No doubt I'll find out tomorrow,' said Tony as the chairman handed the document to his son, who carefully slipped it back into its plastic container.

'So where's its final destination to be?' asked Nick.

'I'll be given the details at twelve o'clock tomorrow,' said Tony, a little surprised that his father hadn't reported his phone conversation with Al Obaydi to his oldest friend.

16

HE LAY WATCHING HER, his head propped up in the palm of his hand, as the first sunlight of the morning crept into the room. She stirred but didn't wake as Scott began to run a solitary finger down her spine. He couldn't wait for her to open her eyes and revive his memories of the previous night.

When Scott had, in those early days, watched Hannah walking from the Jordanian Embassy, dressed in those drab clothes so obviously selected with Karima Saib's tastes in mind, he thought she still looked stunning. Some packages, when you remove the brightly-coloured wrapping, fail to live up to expectation. When Hannah had first taken off the dowdy little two-piece suit she had been wearing that day, he had stood there in disbelief that anyone could be so beautiful.

He pulled back the single sheet that covered her and admired the sight that had taken his breath away the night before. Her short-cropped hair; he wondered how the long flowing strands would look when they fell on her shoulders as she wanted them to. The nape of her neck, the smooth olive skin of her back, and the long, shapely legs.

His hands were like a child's that had opened a stocking full of presents and wanted to touch everything at once. He ran his fingers down her shoulders to the arch of her back, hoping she would turn over. He moved a little closer, leaned across and began to circle her firm breasts with a single finger. The circles became smaller and smaller until he reached her soft nipple. He heard her sigh, and this time she did turn and fall into his arms, her fingers clinging to his shoulders as he pulled her closer.

'It's not fair, you're taking advantage of me,' she said drowsily as his hand moved up the inside of her thigh.

'I'm sorry,' he said, removing his hand and kissing her cheek.

'Don't be sorry. For heaven's sake, Simon, I want you to take advantage of me,' she said, pulling his body closer to her. He continued to stroke her skin, all the time discovering new treasures.

When he entered her, she sighed a different sigh, the sigh of morning love, calmer and more gentle than the demands of the night, but every bit as enjoyable.

For Scott it had been a new experience. Although he had made love many more times than he cared to remember, it had never been with the same excitement.

When they finished making love, she rested her head on his shoulder and he brushed a hair from her cheek, praying the next hour would go slowly. He hated the thought of her returning to the embassy that morning as he knew she eventually must. He didn't want to share her with anybody.

The room was now bathed in the morning sun, which only made him wonder when he would next be allowed to spend a whole night with her.

The Head of Interest Section had been called straight back to Geneva on urgent business, and had taken only one secretary with him, leaving Hannah in Paris on her own for the weekend. She only wished she could tell Simon what it was all about, so he could pass the information on to Kratz.

She had double-locked her room and left the embassy compound by the fire escape. Hannah told him that she had felt like a schoolgirl creeping out of her dormitory to join a midnight feast.

'Better than any feast I can remember,' were his last words before they fell asleep in each other's arms.

The day had begun when they had gone shopping together in the boulevard Saint-Michel and bought clothes she couldn't wear and a tie he would never have considered before he met her. They'd had lunch at a corner café and taken two hours to eat a salad and drink a bottle of wine. They had strolled down the Champs-Élysées, hand in hand as lovers should, before joining the queue to see the Clodion exhibition at the Louvre. A chance to teach her something he thought he knew about, only to find it was he who did the learning. He bought her a floppy tourist hat in the little shop at the base of the Eiffel Tower and was reminded that she always looked stunning whatever she wore.

They had dinner at Maxim's but only ate one course, as they both knew by then that all they really wanted to do was return to his little flat on the Left Bank.

He remembered how he had stood there mesmerised as Hannah removed each garment until she became so embarrassed that she began to take off his clothes. It was almost as if he didn't want to make love to her, because he hoped the anticipation might go on forever.

Of all the women, including the occasional promiscuous student, with whom he had had one-night stands, casual affairs, even sometimes what he had imagined was love, he had never known anything like this. And afterwards, he discovered something else he had never experienced before: the sheer joy of just lying in her arms was every bit as exhilarating as making love.

His finger ran down the nape of her neck. 'What time do you have to be back?' he asked, almost in a whisper.

'One minute before the Ambassador.'

'And when's he expected?'

'His flight's due in from Geneva at 11.20. So I'd better be at my desk before twelve.'

'Then we still have time to make love once more,' he said as he placed a finger on her lips.

She bit the finger gently.

'Ow,' he said mockingly.

'Only once?' she replied.

*　　*　　*

Debbie brought the Deputy Ambassador through to Cavalli's office at twenty past twelve. Neither man commented on the fact that Al Obaydi was late. Tony indicated the chair on the other side of his desk, and waited for his visitor to be seated. For the first time, he felt strangely uneasy about the Arab.

'As I mentioned yesterday,' Cavalli began, 'we are now in possession of the document you require. We are ready to exchange it for the sum agreed.'

'Ah, yes, ninety million dollars,' said the Iraqi, placing the tips of his fingers together just below his chin while he considered his next statement. 'Cash on delivery, if I remember correctly.'

'You do,' said Cavalli. 'So now all we need to know is where and when.'

'We require the document to be delivered to Geneva by twelve o'clock next Tuesday. The recipient will be a Monsieur Pierre Dummond of the bankers Dummond et cie.'

'But that only gives me six days to find a safe route out of the country and . . .'

'Your God created the world in that time, if I remember Genesis correctly. Such a fatuous story,' added Al Obaydi, 'that I didn't bother with Exodus.'

'The Declaration will be in Geneva by Tuesday midday,' said Cavalli.

'Good,' said Al Obaydi. 'And if Monsieur Dummond is satisfied that the document is authentic, he has been given instructions to release the sum of ninety million dollars by wire transfer to any bank of your choice in the world. If, on the other hand, you fail to deliver, or the document proves to be a fake, we will have lost ten million dollars, with nothing to show for it but a three-minute film made by a world-famous director. In that eventuality, a package similar to this one will be posted to the Director of the FBI and the Commissioner of the IRS.'

Al Obaydi removed a thick envelope from his inside pocket and tossed it across the table. Cavalli's expression did not change as the Deputy Ambassador rose, bowed and walked out of the room without another word.

Cavalli felt sure he was about to discover what 'Among other things' meant.

He ripped open the bulky yellow envelope and allowed the contents to spill out onto his desk. Photographs, dozens of them, and documents with banknote serial numbers attached to them. He glanced at the photographs of himself in deep conversation with Al Calabrese on the pavement in front of the National Café, another of himself with Gino Sartori in the centre of Freedom Plaza, and yet another with the director sitting on the dolly as they talked to the former Chief of the DC Police Department. Al Obaydi had even taken a photograph of Rex Butterworth entering the Willard Hotel and of the actor, bald-headed, sitting in the third car, and later getting into the limo outside the Archives' loading dock.

Cavalli began drumming his fingers on the table. It was then that he remembered the nagging doubt at the back of his mind. It was Al Obaydi he had seen in the crowd the previous day. He had underestimated the Iraqi. Perhaps the time had come to call their man in the Lebanon and inform him of the Swiss bank account he had opened in the Deputy Ambassador's name.

No. That would have to wait until the ninety million had been paid in full.

'What do I do, Simon, if he offers me the job?'

Scott hesitated. He had no idea what Mossad would expect her to do. He knew exactly what *he* wanted her to do. It was no use putting the question to Dexter Hutchins in Virginia, because they wouldn't have hesitated to tell him to continue using Hannah for their own purposes.

Hannah turned towards what Scott laughingly described as the kitchen. 'Perhaps you could ask Colonel Kratz what I should do,' she suggested when he didn't reply. 'Explain to him that the Ambassador wants me to take Muna's place, but that another problem has arisen.'

'What's that?' asked Scott anxiously.

'The Ambassador's term of office comes to an end early next month. He may well be asked to stay in Paris, but the Chief Administrator is telling everyone that he's going to be called back to Baghdad and promoted to Deputy Foreign Minister.'

Scott still didn't offer an opinion.

'What's the matter, Simon? Are you incapable of making a decision at this time in the morning?' Scott still said nothing. 'You're just as pathetic on your feet as you are in bed,' she teased.

Scott decided the time had come to tell her everything. He wasn't going to wait another minute. He walked out of the kitchen, took her in his arms and stroked her hair. 'Hannah, I need to –' he had begun, when the phone rang. He broke away to answer it.

He listened for a few moments before saying to Dexter Hutchins, 'Yes, sure. I'll call you back as soon as I've had time to think about it.' What was the man doing up in the middle of the night, wondered Scott as he replaced the receiver.

'Another lover, lover?' Hannah asked with a smile.

'My publishers wanting to know when my manuscript will be finished. It's already overdue.'

'And what will your answer be?'

'I'm currently distracted.'

'Only currently?' she said, pressing her finger on his nose.

'Well, perhaps permanently,' he admitted.

She kissed him gently on the cheek and whispered, 'I must get back to the embassy, Simon. Don't come down with me, it's too risky.'

He held her in his arms and wanted to protest but settled for 'When will I see you again?'

'Whenever the Ambassador's wife feels in need of a swim,' Hannah said. She broke away. 'But I'll keep on reminding her how good it is for her figure, and that perhaps she ought to be taking even more exercise.' She laughed and left without another word.

Scott stood by the window, waiting for her to reappear. He hated the fact that he couldn't just phone, write or make contact with her whenever he felt like it. He longed to send her flowers, letters, cards and notes to let her know how much he loved her.

Hannah ran out onto the pavement, a smile on her face. She looked up and blew Scott a kiss before she vanished around the corner.

Another man, who was cold and tired from hours of waiting, also watched her, not from a window in a warm room but from a doorway on the opposite side of the road.

The moment Scott disappeared from sight, the man stepped out of the shadows and followed the Ambassador's second secretary back to the embassy compound.

17

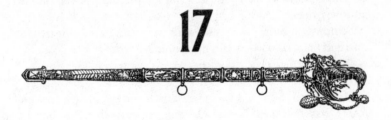

'I DON'T BELIEVE YOU,' she said.

'I fear that the truth of the matter is you don't want to believe me,' said Kratz, who had flown in from London that morning.

'But he can't be working for any enemy of Israel.'

'If that's the case, perhaps you can explain why he passed himself off as a Mossad agent?'

For the last two hours Hannah had tried to think of a logical reason why Simon would have deceived her, but had to admit that she had been unable to come up with a convincing answer.

'Have you told us everything you passed on to him?' Kratz demanded.

'Yes,' she said, suddenly feeling ashamed. 'But have you checked with all the friendly agencies?'

'Of course we have,' said Kratz. 'No one in Paris has ever heard of the man. Not the French, not the British, and certainly not the CIA. Their Head of Station told me personally that they have never had anyone on their books called Simon Rosenthal.'

'So what will happen to me now?' asked Hannah.

'Do you wish to continue working for your country?'

'You know I do,' she said, glaring back at him.

'And are you still hoping to be included in the team for Baghdad?'

'Yes, of course I am. Why would I have put myself through all this in the first place if I didn't want to be part of the final operation?'

'Then you will also want to abide by the oath you swore in the presence of your colleagues in Herzliyah.'

'Nothing would make me break that oath. You know that. Just tell me what you expect me to do.'

'I expect you to kill Rosenthal.'

Scott was delighted when Hannah confirmed on Thursday afternoon that she would be able to slip away for dinner on Friday evening, and might even find it possible to stay over-night. It seemed that the Ambassador had been called away to Geneva again. Something big was happening, but she still didn't know exactly what.

Scott had already decided that three things were going to take place when they next met. First, he would cook the meal himself, despite Hannah's comments about his inadequate kitchen. Second, he was going to tell her the truth about himself, whatever interruptions occurred. And third . . .

Scott felt more relaxed than he had in weeks once he had decided to 'come clean', as his mother had described it when-ever he'd tried to get away with something. He knew that he would be recalled to the States once he had informed Dexter of what had happened, and that a few weeks later he would be quietly discharged. But that was no longer of any significance, because third, and most important of all, he was going to ask Hannah to come back to America with him, as his wife.

Scott spent the afternoon shopping in the market for freshly baked bread, the finest wild mushrooms, succulent lamb chops and tiny ripe oranges. He returned home to prepare a feast he hoped she would never forget. He had also prepared a speech he believed she would, in time, find it possible to forgive.

During the evening, Scott found himself looking up at the kitchen clock every few moments. He felt robbed if she was ever more than a few minutes late. She had failed to turn up for their previous meeting, though he accepted that she had no way of letting him know when something unexpected came up. He was relieved to see her walk through the door soon after the clock had struck eight.

Scott smiled when Hannah removed her coat, and he saw she was wearing the dress he had chosen for her when they'd gone shopping together for the first time. A long blue dress that hung loosely off the shoulders, and made her appear both elegant and sexy.

He immediately took her in his arms, and was surprised by her response. She seemed distant, almost cold. Or was he being over-sensitive? Hannah broke away and stared at the table laid for two with its red-and-white check tablecloth and two sets of unmatching cutlery.

Scott poured her a glass of the white wine he had selected to go with the first course before he disappeared into the kitchen to put the final touches to his culinary efforts, aware that he and Hannah always had so little time together.

'What are you cooking?' she asked, in a dull, flat voice.

'Wait and see,' he replied. 'But I can tell you the starter is something I learned when –' He stopped himself. 'Many years ago,' he added rather lamely.

He didn't see her grimace at his failure to finish the original sentence.

Scott returned to join her a few moments later, carrying two plates of piping-hot wild mushrooms, with a small slice of garlic bread. 'But not too much garlic,' he promised her, 'for obvious reasons.' No witty or sharp response came flying back, and he wondered if she was unable to stay overnight. He might have questioned her more closely had he not been concentrating on the dinner as well as wanting to get his speech over with.

'I wish we could get out of Paris and see Versailles, like normal people,' said Scott as he dug his fork into a mushroom.

'That would be nice,' she said.

'And even better . . .' She looked up and stared at him.

'A weekend at the Colmendor. I promised myself long ago when I first read the life of Matisse at . . .' He hesitated once again, and she lowered her head. 'And that's only France,' he said, trying to recover. 'We could take a lifetime over Italy. They have a hundred Colmendors.'

He looked hopefully towards her but her eyes remained staring at the half-empty plate.

What had he done? Or was *she* fearful of telling *him* something? He dreaded the thought of learning that she was going to Baghdad when all he wanted to do was take her to Venice, Florence and Rome. If it was Baghdad that was making her anxious, he would do everything in his power to change her mind.

Scott cleared away the plates to return a few moments later with the succulent lamb Provençal. 'Madam's favourite, if I remember correctly.' But he was rewarded only with a weak smile.

'What is it, Hannah?' he asked as he took the seat opposite her. He leaned across to touch her hand, but she removed it quickly from the table.

'I'm just a little tired,' she replied unconvincingly. 'It's been a long week.'

Scott tried to discuss her work, the theatre, the Clodion exhibition at the Louvre and even Clinton's attempts to bring the three living Beatles together, but with each new effort he received the same bland response. They continued to eat in silence until his plate was empty.

'And now, we shall end on my *pièce de résistance*.' He expected to be playfully chastised about his efforts as a chef; instead he received only the flicker of a smile and a distant, sad look from those dark, beautiful eyes. He disappeared into the kitchen and returned immediately, carrying a bowl of freshly sliced oranges with a touch of Cointreau. He placed the delicate morsels in front of her, hoping they would change her mood. But while Scott continued with his monologue Hannah remained an unreceptive audience.

He removed the bowls, his empty, hers hardly touched, and returned moments later with coffee, hers made exactly as she liked it: black, with a touch of cream floating across the top, and no sugar. His black, steaming, with too much sugar.

Just as he sat down opposite her, determined this was the moment to tell her the truth, she asked for some sugar. Scott jumped up, somewhat surprised, returned to the kitchen, tipped some sugar into a bowl, grabbed a teaspoon and came back to see her snapping closed her tiny evening bag.

After he had sat down and placed the sugar on the table he smiled at her. He had never seen such sadness in those eyes before. He poured them both a brandy, whirled his round the balloon, took a sip of his coffee and then faced her. She had not touched her coffee or brandy, and the sugar she had asked for remained in the centre of the table, its little mound undented.

'Hannah,' Scott began softly, 'I have something important to tell you, and I wish I had told you a long time ago.' He looked up, to find her on the verge of tears. He would have asked her why, but feared that if he allowed her to change the subject he might never tell her the truth.

'My name is not Simon Rosenthal,' he said quietly. Hannah looked surprised, but not in the way he had expected – more anxious than curious. He took another sip of coffee and then continued. 'I have lied to you from the day we met, and the more deeply I fell in love with you, the more I lied.'

She didn't speak, for which he was grateful, because on this occasion, like his lectures, he needed to proceed without interruption. His throat began to feel a little dry, so he sipped his coffee again.

'My name is Scott Bradley. I am an American, but not from Chicago as I told you when we first met. I'm from Denver.' A puzzled look came into Hannah's eyes, but she still didn't interrupt him. Scott ploughed on.

'I am not Mossad's agent in Paris writing a travel book. Far from it, though I confess the truth is much stranger than the fiction.' He held her hand and this time she didn't try to remove it. 'Please, let me explain, and then perhaps you'll find it in your heart to forgive me.' His throat suddenly felt drier. He finished his coffee and quickly poured himself another cup, taking an extra teaspoonful of sugar. She still hadn't touched hers. 'I was born in Denver, where I went to school. My father was a local lawyer who ended up in jail for fraud. I was so ashamed that when my mother died, I took a post at Beirut University because I could no longer face anyone I knew.' Hannah looked up and her eyes began to show sympathy. It gave Scott the confidence to go on.

'I do not work for Mossad in any capacity, nor have I ever done so.' Her lips formed a straight line. 'My real job is nowhere near as romantic as that. After Beirut I returned to America to become a university professor.' She looked mystified, and then her expression suddenly changed to one of anxiety.

'Oh, yes,' he said, his words beginning to sound slightly slurred, 'this time I'm telling the truth. I teach Constitutional Law at Yale. Let's face it, no one would make up a story like that,' he added, trying to laugh.

He drank more coffee. It tasted less bitter than the first cup.

'But I am also what they call in the trade a part-time spy, and as it's turned out, not a very good one. Despite many years of training and lecturing other people on how it should be done.' He paused. 'But that was only in the classroom.'

She looked more anxious.

'You need have no fears,' he said, trying to reassure her. 'I work for the good side, though I suppose even that depends on where you're looking from. I'm currently a temporary Field Officer with the CIA.'

'The CIA?' she stammered in disbelief. 'But they told me . . .'

'What did they tell you?' he asked quickly.

'Nothing,' she said, and lowered her head again.

Had she already known about his background, or perhaps guessed his original story didn't add up? He didn't care. All he wanted to do was tell the woman he loved everything about himself. No more lies. No more deceit. No more secrets. 'Well, as I'm confessing, I mustn't exaggerate,' he continued. 'I go to

Virginia twelve times a year to discuss with agents the problems they've faced while working in the field. I was full of bright ideas to assist them in the peace and comfort of Langley, but I'll treat them with more respect now I've experienced some of the problems they come up against, especially having made such a mess of things myself.'

'It can't be true,' she said suddenly. 'Tell me you're making it up, Simon.'

'I'm afraid not, Hannah. This time it's all true,' he said. 'You must believe me. I only ended up in Paris after years of demanding to be tested in the field, because, with all my theoretical knowledge, I assumed I'd be a whizz if they just gave me the chance to prove myself. Scott Bradley, Professor of Constitutional Law. Infallible in the eyes of his adoring students at Yale and the senior CIA operatives at Langley. There'll be no standing ovation after this performance, of that we can both be sure.'

Hannah stood and stared down at him. 'Tell me it's not true, Simon,' she said. 'It mustn't be true. Why did you choose me? Why me?'

He stood and took her in his arms. 'I didn't choose you, I fell in love with you. They chose me. My people . . . my people needed to find out why Mossad had put you . . . put you in the Jordanian Embassy attached to the Iraqi Interest Section.' He was finding it difficult to remain coherent, and couldn't understand why he felt so sleepy.

'But why you?' she asked, clinging on to him for the first time that evening. 'Why not a regular CIA agent?'

'Because . . . because they wanted to put someone in . . . someone who wouldn't be recognised by any of the professionals.'

'Oh, my God, who am I meant to believe?' she said, breaking away. She stared helplessly at him.

'You can believe me, because I'll prove . . . prove all I've said is true.' Scott began to move away from the table. He felt unsteady as he walked slowly over to the sideboard, bent down to pull open the bottom drawer, and after some rummaging around removed a small leather case with the initials S.B. printed in gold on the top right-hand corner. He smiled a triumphant smile and turned back. He attempted to steady himself by resting one hand on the sideboard. He looked towards the blurred figure of the woman he loved, but could no longer see the desperate look on her face. He tried to remember how much he had already told her and how much she still needed to know.

'Oh, my darling, what have I done?' she said, her eyes now pleading.

'Nothing, it's all been my fault,' said Scott. 'But we'll have the rest of our lives to laugh about it. That, by the way, was a proposal. Feeble, I agree, but I couldn't love you any more than I do. You must surely realise that,' he added as he tried to take a pace towards her. She stood staring at him helplessly as he lurched forward before attempting to take a second step. Then he tried again, but this time he stumbled and collapsed across the table, finally landing with a thud on the floor at her feet.

'I can't blame you if you don't feel the same way as . . .' were his final words, as the leather case burst open, disgorging its contents all around a body that was suddenly still.

Hannah fell on her knees and took his head in her hands. She began to sob uncontrollably. 'I love you, of course I love you, Simon. But why didn't you trust me enough to tell me the truth?'

Her eyes rested on a small photo lodged between his fingers. She snatched it from his grasp. Written on the back were the words 'Katherine Bradley – Summer '66'. It must have been his mother. She grabbed the passport that lay by the side of his head and quickly turned the pages, trying to read through her tears. Male. Date of birth: 11.7.56. Profession: University Professor. She turned another page and a photo from *Paris Match* fell out. She stared at herself modelling an Ungaro suit from the spring collection of 1990.

'No, no. Don't let it be true,' Hannah said as she lifted him back into her arms. 'Let it be just more lies.'

And then her eyes settled on the envelope simply addressed 'Hannah'. She lowered his body gently to the ground, picked up the envelope and ripped it open.

My dearest Hannah,

I have tried to think of a hundred ways to begin this letter. There's one simple way. I love you. And, as important, I have never loved before, and now I know I can never love anyone like this again.

'No!' she screamed, 'No!' almost unable to read his words through her tears.

You are not only my lover but my closest friend. I'll never want or need anyone else ever again. I rejoice at the thought of spending the rest of my life with you, and wonder how I deserve to be so lucky.

'Please, God, no,' she wept as her head fell on his chest. 'I love you, too, Simon. I love you so much.'

I want three daughters and two sons and I must warn you that I won't settle for less. We'll discuss grandchildren later. I fear I'll be irascible and tiresome in old age, but I'll never stop loving you. Don't let's wait

191

'No, no, no . . .' Hannah cried as she bent down to kiss him. She suddenly leaped up and rushed over to the phone. She dialled 17 and screamed, 'Please God, let one pill not be enough. Answer, answer, answer!' she shrieked at the phone as the door of Scott's apartment flew open. Hannah turned to see Kratz and another man whom she didn't recognise come bursting in.

She dropped the phone on the floor and ran towards them, throwing herself at Kratz and knocking him to the ground.

'You bastard, you bastard!' she screamed. 'You made me kill the only person I ever really loved! I hope you rot in hell!' she said as her fists pumped down into his face.

The unknown man moved quickly across and threw Hannah to one side, before the two of them picked up Scott's limp body and carried him out of the room.

Hannah lay in the corner, weeping.

An hour passed, maybe two, before she crawled slowly back to the table, opened her bag and removed the second pill.

18

'WHITE HOUSE.'

'Mr Butterworth, please.'

There was a long silence. 'I don't show anyone by that name, sir. Just a moment and I'll put you through to Personnel.'

The Archivist waited patiently, made aware as each second passed that the new telephone system ordered by the Clinton administration was clearly overdue.

'Personnel office,' said a female voice. 'How can I help you?'

'I'm trying to locate Mr Rex Butterworth, Special Assistant to the President.'

'Who's calling?'

'Marshall, Calder Marshall, Archivist.'

'Of – ?'

'Of the United States of America.'

There was another long silence.

'The name Butterworth rings no bells with me, sir, but I'm sure you realise there are more than forty Special and Deputy Assistants to the President.'

'No, I didn't realise,' admitted Marshall. There followed another long silence.

'According to our records,' said the female voice, 'he seems to have returned to the Department of Commerce. He was a Schedule A – just here on temporary assignment.'

'Would you have a number where I might reach him?'

'No, I don't. But if you call the department locator at the

Commerce Department, I'm sure they will find him for you.'

'Thank you for your help.'

'Glad to have been of assistance, sir.'

Hannah could never recall how long she had lain huddled up in the corner of Simon's room. She couldn't think of him as Scott, she would always think of him as Simon. An hour, possibly two. Time no longer had any relevance for her. She could remember crawling back to the centre of the room, avoiding overturned chairs and tables that would have looked more appropriate in a nightclub that had just experienced a drunken brawl.

She removed the pill from her bag and flushed it down the lavatory, the automatic action of any well-drilled agent. She then began to search among the debris for any photographs she could find and, of course, the letter addressed simply to 'Hannah'. She stuffed these few mementoes into her bag and tried, with the help of a fallen chair, to get back on her feet.

Later that night she lay in her bed at the embassy, staring up at the blank white ceiling, unable to recall her journey back, the route she had taken or even if she had climbed the fire escape or entered by the front door. She wondered how many nights it would be before she managed to sleep for more than a few minutes at a time. How much time would have to pass before he wasn't her every other thought?

She knew Mossad would want to take her out, hide her, protect her – as they saw it – until the French police had completed their investigation. Governments would have their diplomatic arms twisted up their diplomatic backs. The Americans would expect a lot in return for killing one of their agents, but eventually a bargain would be struck. Hannah Kopec, Simon Rosenthal and Professor Scott Bradley would become closed files. For all three of them were numbers: interchangeable, dispensable and, of course, replaceable.

She wondered what they would do with his body, the body of the man she loved. An honourable but anonymous grave, she suspected. They would argue that it must be in the interest of the greater good. Wherever they buried him, she knew they would never allow her to find his grave.

She wouldn't have dropped the pill in the coffee in the first place if Kratz hadn't talked again and again of the thirty-nine Scuds that had landed on the people of Israel, and in particular of the one which had killed her mother, her brother and her sister.

She might even have drawn back at the last moment if they hadn't threatened to carry out the job themselves, should she refuse. They promised her that if that was the case, it would be a far more unpleasant death.

Just as Hannah was about to take the first pill out of her bag, she had asked Simon for some sugar, one last lifeline. Why hadn't he grabbed at it? Why didn't he question her, tease her about her weight, do anything that would have made her have second thoughts? But then why, why had he waited so long to tell her the truth?

If he had only realised that she had things to tell him, too. The Ambassador had been called back to Iraq – a promotion, he explained. He was, as Kanuk had been telling everyone, to become Deputy Foreign Minister, which meant that in the absence of Muhammad Saeed Al-Zahiaf, he would be working directly with Saddam Hussein.

His place at the embassy was to be taken by a Hamid Al Obaydi, the number two at the United Nations, who had recently rendered some great service for Iraq, of which she would eventually learn. The Ambassador had offered her the choice of remaining in Paris to serve under Al Obaydi, or returning to Iraq and continuing to work with him. Only days before, Mossad would have considered such an offer an irresistible opportunity.

Hannah so wanted to tell Simon that she no longer cared about Saddam, that he had made it possible for her to overcome her hatred of the Scuds, even made the death of her family a wound that might in time be healed. She knew that she was no longer capable of killing anyone, as long as she had someone to live for.

But now that Simon was dead, her desire for revenge was even stronger than before.

'Department of Commerce.'

'Rex Butterworth, please.'

'What agency?'

'I'm not sure I understand,' said the Archivist.

'What agency is Mr Butterworth with?' asked the operator, pronouncing each word slowly, as if she were addressing a four-year-old.

'I have no idea,' admitted the Archivist.

'We don't show anyone by that name.'

'But the White House told me –'

'I don't care what the White House told you. If you don't know which agency –'

'May I have the Personnel Office?'

'Just a minute.' It turned out to be far longer than a minute.

'Office of Personnel.'

'This is Calder Marshall, Archivist of the United States. May I speak to the director?'

'I'm sorry, but he's not available. Would you like to speak to his executive assistant, Alex Wagner?'

'Yes. That would be just fine,' said Marshall.

'She's not in today. Could you call again tomorrow?'

'Yes,' said Marshall with a sigh.

'Glad to have been of assistance, sir.'

When Kratz's car screeched to a halt outside the Centre Cardio-vasculaire on bois Gilbert there were three doctors, two orderlies and a nurse waiting for them on the hospital steps. The embassy must have pulled out every stop.

The two orderlies ran forward and lifted the body gently but firmly out of the back seat of the car, carrying Scott quickly up the steps before placing him on a waiting trolley.

Even as the trolley was being wheeled down the corridor the three doctors and the nurse surrounded the body and began their examination. The nurse quickly removed Scott's shirt and trousers while the first doctor opened his mouth to check his breathing. The second, a consultant, lowered his ear onto Scott's chest and tried to listen for a heartbeat, while the third checked his blood pressure; none of them looked hopeful.

The consultant turned to the Mossad leader and said firmly, 'Don't waste any time with lies. How did it happen?'

'We poisoned him, but he turned out not to be –'

'I'm not interested,' he said. 'What poison did you administer?'

'Ergot alkaloid,' said Kratz.

The consultant switched his attention to one of his assistants. 'Ring the Hospital Widal and get me details of its action and the correct antidote, fast,' he said as the orderlies crashed through the rubber doors and into a private operating theatre.

The first doctor had managed to keep Scott's mouth open during the short journey and create an airway. He had already pressed down the tongue to leave a clear passageway to the larynx. Once the trolley had come to a stop in the theatre he inserted a clear angled plastic tube of about five inches in length to ensure the tongue could not be swallowed.

The nurse then placed a mask over Scott's nose and mouth that was connected to an oxygen supply on the wall. Attached to the side of the mask was a rubber bag, which she began pumping regularly every three or four seconds with her left hand as she held his head steady with her right. Scott's lungs were immediately filled with oxygen.

The consultant placed an ear over Scott's heart again. He could still hear nothing. He raised his head and nodded to an orderly who began rubbing paste on different parts of Scott's chest. Another nurse followed him, placing small electronic

JEFFREY ARCHER

discs on the paste marks. The wires from the discs were
connected to a heart monitor machine that stood on a table by
the side of the trolley.

The fine line that ran across the machine and registered the
strength of the heartbeat produced a weak signal.

The consultant smiled below his mask, as the nurse continued to pump oxygen into the patient's mouth and nose.

Suddenly, without warning, the heart machine gave out a
piercing sound. Everyone in the operating theatre turned to
face the monitor, which was now showing a thin, flat line
running from one side of the screen to the other.

'Cardiac arrest!' shouted the consultant. He jumped forward
and placed the heel of his hand over Scott's sternum, and with
both arms firmly locked he began to rock backwards and forwards as he tried to push a volume of blood from the heart to
resuscitate his patient. Like a proficient weightlifter, he was able
to pump away with his arms at a rate of forty to fifty times a
minute.

A houseman wheeled forward the defibrillator. The consultant placed two large electric clamps onto the front and side of
Scott's chest.

'Two hundred joules,' said the consultant. 'Stand clear.'
They all took a pace back as a shock was transferred from the
electric discharge machine and ran through Scott's body.

They stared at the monitor as the consultant jumped forward
again and continued to pump Scott's chest with the palms of his
hands, but the thin green line did not respond. 'Two hundred
joules, stand clear,' he repeated firmly, and they all stood back
again to watch the effect of the electric shock. But the line
remained obstinately flat. The consultant quickly returned to
pumping Scott's chest with his hands.

'Three hundred and sixty joules, stand clear,' said the consultant in desperation, but the nurse who raised the number on the
dial knew the patient was already dead.

The consultant pressed a button, and they all watched the
highest shock allowed pass through Scott's body, assuming that

must be the end. They turned their attention to the monitor.

'We've lost him,' was on the consultant's lips, when to their astonishment they saw the line begin to show a faint flicker. He leaped forward and began pumping away with the palms of his hands as the flicker continued to show irregular fibrillation. 'Three hundred and sixty joules, stand clear,' he said once again. The button was pressed and their attention returned to the monitor. Fibrillation returned to a normal rhythm. The youngest doctor cheered.

The consultant quickly located a vein in Scott's left arm and jabbed a needle directly into it, leaving a cannula sticking out to which a saline drip was quickly attached.

Another doctor rushed into the theatre and, facing his superior, said, 'The antidote is GTN.'

A nurse went straight over to the poisons cabinet and extracted a phial of glyceryl trinitrate, which she passed to the consultant, who had a syringe ready. He extracted the blue liquid from the phial, shot a little into the air to be sure it was flowing freely, then pumped the antidote into a side valve of the intravenous drip. He turned to watch the monitor. The flicker maintained a constant rhythm.

The consultant turned to the senior nurse and said, 'Do you believe in miracles?'

'No,' she replied. 'I'm a Jew. Miracles are only for Christians.'

Hannah began to form a plan, a plan that would brook no interference from Kratz. She had made the decision to accept the job as senior secretary to the Ambassador, and to accompany him back to Iraq.

As the hours passed, her plan began to take shape. She was aware there would be problems. Not from the Iraqi side, but from her own people. Hannah knew that she would have to circumvent Mossad's attempts to take her out, which meant that she could never leave the embassy, even for one moment, until the time came for the Ambassador to return to Iraq. She would use all the techniques they had taught her over the past two years to defeat them.

When she was in Iraq, Hannah would make herself indispensable to the Ambassador, bide her time and, once she had achieved her objective, happily die a martyr's death.

She had been left with only one purpose in life now that Simon was dead. To assassinate Saddam Hussein.

'Department of Commerce.'

'Alex Wagner, please,' said the Archivist.

'Who?'

'Alex Wagner. Office of Personnel.'

'Just a minute.' Another stretched minute.

'Personnel.'

'This is Calder Marshall, Archivist of the United States. I called yesterday for Ms Wagner and you told me to try again today.'

'I wasn't here yesterday, sir.'

'Well, it must have been one of your colleagues. Is Ms Wagner available?'

'Just a minute.'

This time the Archivist waited several minutes.

'Alex Wagner,' said a brisk female voice.

'Ms Wagner, my name is Calder Marshall. I'm the Archivist of the United States, and it's extremely important that I contact Mr Rex Butterworth, who was recently detailed to the White House by the Commerce Department.'

'Are you a former employer of Mr Butterworth's?' asked the brisk voice.

'No, I am not,' replied Marshall.

'Are you a relative?'

'No.'

'Then I'm afraid I cannot help you, Mr Marshall.'

'Why's that?' asked the Archivist.

'Because the Privacy Act prohibits us from giving out any personal information about government employees.'

'Can you tell me the name of the Commerce Director, or is that covered by the Privacy Act too?' the Archivist asked.

'Dick Fielding,' said the voice abruptly.

'Thank you for your assistance,' said the Archivist.

The phone went dead.

When Scott woke, his first memory was of Hannah. And then he slept.

When he woke a second time, all he could make out were blurred figures who appeared to be bending over him. And then he slept.

When he woke again, the blurs began to take some shape. Most of them seemed to be dressed in white. And then he slept.

When he woke the next time it was dark and he was alone. He felt so weak, so limp, as he tried to remember what had happened. And then he slept.

When he woke, for the first time he could hear their voices, soothing, gentle, but he could not make out the words, however hard he tried. And then he slept.

When he woke again, they had propped him up in bed. They were trying to feed him a warm, tasteless liquid through a plastic straw. And then he slept.

When he woke, a man in a long white coat, with a stethoscope and a warm smile, was asking in a pronounced accent, 'Can you hear me?' He tried to nod, but fell asleep.

When he woke, another doctor – this time he could see him clearly – was listening attentively as Scott attempted his first words. 'Hannah. Hannah,' was all he said. And then he slept.

He woke again, and an attractive woman with short dark hair and a caring smile was leaning over him. He returned her smile and asked the time. It must have sounded strange to her, but he wanted to know.

'It's a few minutes after three in the morning,' the nurse told him.

'How long have I been here?' he managed.

'Just over a week, but you were so close to death. I think in English you have the expression "touch and go". If your friends had been a moment –' And then he slept.

When he woke, the doctor told Scott that when he'd first arrived they thought it was too late, and twice he'd been pronounced technically dead. 'Antidotes and electrostimulation of the heart, combined with a rare determination to live and one nurse's theory that you might be a Gentile, defied the technical pronouncement,' he declared with a smile.

Scott asked if someone called Hannah had been to see him. The doctor checked the board at the end of his bed. There had been only two visitors that he was aware of, both of them men. They came every day. And then Scott slept.

When he woke, the two men the doctor had mentioned were standing one on each side of his bed. Scott smiled at Dexter Hutchins, who was trying not to cry. Grown men don't cry, he wanted to say, especially when they work for the CIA. He turned to the other man. He had never seen a face so full of shame, so ridden with guilt, or eyes so red from not sleeping. Scott tried to ask what had caused him such unhappiness. And then he slept.

When he woke, both men were still there, now resting on uncomfortable chairs, half asleep.

'Dexter,' he whispered, and they both woke immediately. 'Where's Hannah?'

The other man, who Scott noticed was recovering from a black eye and a broken nose, took some time answering his question. And then Scott slept, never wanting to wake again.

19

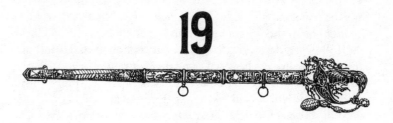

CAVALLI CHECKED INTO the Hôtel de la Paix around noon. He had booked a modest suite that overlooked the lake. Neither expensive nor conspicuous.

Once he had unpacked his small suitcase and hung up his suitbag, he strolled across to the window and admired the fountain in the centre of the lake whose water spouted like a gushing well high into the air.

On the previous evening he had taken a Yellow Cab to Kennedy and booked British Airways, Club Class, to London. The flight had landed at Heathrow, disgorging most of its passengers before changing its crew and adding new passengers for the journey on to Geneva.

The plane had touched down in Switzerland at 10.55 a.m., and another cab, this time blue, had deposited him outside the Hôtel de la Paix.

Cavalli felt confident that he had not been followed on any part of the journey, and that no one other than his father and Nick Vicente knew exactly where he was. After a light lunch he made two phone calls before placing the 'Do Not Disturb' sign on his door. Cavalli could never sleep on a plane.

At a few minutes past eight he dressed and went downstairs for dinner. Despite the recommendation of the maître d', he chose to be seated by a window in the corner, where only the most observant waiter would have been aware he was there.

As he toyed with a rare steak, he couldn't help wondering

where Nick was at that very moment and, more importantly, how he had smuggled the Declaration out of New York so that it would be in the offices of Dummond et cie by twelve o'clock the following day. Cavalli had already phoned and fixed an appointment to see his own banker, Monsieur Franchard, an hour before. A few minutes after ten the maître d' offered him a coffee, but he waved his hand dismissively and requested the bill. He paid in cash, and left a tip before retiring to his room.

When he opened the door, he was not surprised to find an envelope marked 'Private' lying on the carpet.

He assumed that it was one of those notes from the manager welcoming you to the hotel while at the same time apologising for missing you personally. The anonymous manager usually hoped that a complimentary bottle of champagne and a selection of fine chocolates would make up for his discourtesy. Cavalli tossed the envelope onto the bed, as he always considered the word complimentary meant 'Don't worry, we'll find another way of putting it onto your bill.'

After he had undressed, he climbed into bed and pressed several buttons on the remote control before he was able to tune into CNN. Why couldn't the channel have the same number in every country, he wondered.

He watched for a few moments, but found that the news of how Hillary Clinton had caused the first resignation from the senior White House staff ended up getting more coverage than the Americans shooting down a plane in the no-fly zone over Iraq. It seemed Clinton was determined to prove to Saddam that he was every bit as tough as Bush.

Still tired from his flight, Cavalli abandoned CNN in favour of sleep. As he began bashing the brick-hard pillow into shape with his fist, his attention was caught by the envelope that still lay on the other side of the bed. He tore it open to discover the enclosure was not a note from the manager, but a confirmation of his appointment to 'take tea' with his banker, Monsieur Franchard, at eleven o'clock the following morning.

He laughed and was about to see if he could flick the card into the waste-paper basket on the far side of the room without getting out of bed when he noticed some words scribbled on the bottom:

I do hope you find the brand appropriate.
Have a good party.
N.V.

'Department of Commerce.'

'The Director, please.'

'Who's calling?'

'Marshall, Calder Marshall.'

'Is he expecting your call?'

'No, he is not.'

'Mr Fielding only takes calls from people who have previously booked to speak to him.'

'What about his secretary?' asked Marshall.

'She never takes calls.'

'So how do I get a booking with Mr Fielding?'

'You have to speak to Miss Zelumski in reservations.'

'Can I be put through to Miss Zelumski, or do I have to make a reservation to speak to her as well?'

'There is no need to be sarcastic, sir. I'm only doing my job.'

'I'm sorry. Perhaps you'd put me through to Miss Zelumski.' Marshall waited patiently.

'Miss Zelumski speaking.'

'I'd like to reserve a call to speak to Mr Fielding.'

'Is it domestic, most-favoured status or foreign?' asked a bored-sounding voice.

'It's personal.'

'Does he know you?'

'No, he doesn't.'

'Then I can't help. I only deal with domestic, most-favoured status or foreign.'

The Archivist hung up before Miss Zelumski was given the chance to say 'Glad to have been of assistance, sir.'

After a light breakfast in his room, Cavalli packed his suitcase and hanging bag before going downstairs. The doorman answered his questions in perfect English, and confirmed the directions to Franchard et cie. In Switzerland hall porters know the location of banks, just as their London counterparts can direct you to theatres and football grounds.

As Cavalli left the hotel and started the short walk to the bank, he couldn't help feeling something wasn't quite right. And then he realised that the streets were clean, the people he passed were well-dressed, sober and silent. A contrast in every way to New York.

Once he reached the front door of the bank, Cavalli pressed the discreet bell under the equally discreet brass plate announcing 'Franchard et cie'.

A doorman responded to the call. Cavalli walked into a marble-pillared hall of perfect proportions.

'Perhaps you would like to go straight to the tenth floor, Mr Cavalli? I believe Monsieur Franchard is expecting you.'

Cavalli had only entered the building twice before in his life. How did they manage it? And the porter turned out to be as good as his word, because when Cavalli stepped out of the lift, the chairman of the bank was waiting there to greet him.

'Good morning, Mr Cavalli,' he said. 'Shall we go to my office?'

The chairman's office was a modest, tastefully decorated room, Swiss bankers not wishing to frighten away their customers with a show of conspicuous wealth.

Cavalli was surprised to see a large brown parcel placed in the centre of the boardroom table, giving no clue as to its contents.

'This arrived for you this morning,' the banker explained. 'I thought it might have something to do with our proposed meeting.'

Cavalli smiled, leaned over and pulled the parcel towards him. He quickly ripped off the brown-paper covering to find a packing case with the words 'TEA: BOSTON' stamped across it.

With the help of a heavy silver letter-opener which he picked up from a side table, Cavalli prised the wooden lid slowly open. He didn't notice the slight grimace that came over the chairman's face.

Cavalli stared inside. The top of the box was filled with styrofoam packing material, which he cupped out with his hands and scattered all over the boardroom table.

The chairman quickly placed a wastepaper basket by his side, which Cavalli ignored as he continued to dig into the box until he finally came to some objects wrapped in tissue-paper.

He removed a piece of the tissue-paper to reveal a teacup in the Confederate colours of the First Congress.

It took Cavalli several minutes to unwrap an entire tea set, which he laid out on the table in front of the puzzled banker. Once it was unpacked, Cavalli also appeared a little mystified. He dug into the box again, and retrieved an envelope. He tore it open and began reading the contents out loud.

This is a copy of the famous tea set made in 1777 by Pearson and Son to commemorate the Boston Tea Party. Each set is accompanied by an authentic copy of the Declaration of Independence. Your set is number 20917, and has been recorded in our books under the name of J. Hancock.

The letter had been signed and verified by the present chairman, H. William Pearson VI.

Cavalli burst out laughing as he dug deeper into the wooden box, removing yet more packing material until he came across a thin plastic cylinder. He had to admire the way Nick Vicente had fooled the US Customs into allowing him to export the original. The banker's expression remained one of bafflement. Cavalli placed the cylinder in the centre of the table, before going over in considerable detail how he wanted the meeting at twelve to be conducted.

The banker nodded from time to time, and made the occasional note on the pad in front of him.

'I would also like the plastic tube placed in a strongbox for the time being. The key to the box should be handed over to Mr Al Obaydi when, and only when, you have received the full payment by wire transfer. The money should then be deposited in my No. 3 account in your Zurich branch.'

'And are you able to tell me the exact sum you anticipate receiving from Mr Al Obaydi?' asked the banker.

'Ninety million dollars,' said Cavalli.

The banker didn't raise an eyebrow.

The Archivist looked up the name of the Commerce Secretary in his government directory, then picked up his phone and pressed one button. 482 2000 was now programmed into his speed dial.

'Department of Commerce.'

'Dick Fielding, please.'

'Just a moment.'

'Office of the Director.'

'This is Secretary Brown.'

The Archivist had to wait only a few seconds before the call was put through.

'Good morning, Mr Secretary,' said an alert voice.

'Good morning, Mr Fielding. This is Calder Marshall, Archivist of the United States of America.'

'I thought . . .'

'You thought . . .?'

'I guess I must have picked up the wrong phone. How may I help you, Mr Marshall?'

'I'm trying to trace a former employee of yours. Rex Butterworth.'

'I can't help you on that one.'

'Why? Are you bound by the Privacy Act as well?'

Fielding laughed. 'I only wish I was.'

'I don't understand,' said the Archivist.

'Last week we sent Butterworth a merit bonus, and it was returned, "No forwarding address".'

'But he has a wife.'

'She got the same response to her last letter.'

'And his mother in South Carolina?'

'She's been dead for years.'

'Thank you,' said Calder Marshall, and put the phone down. He knew exactly who he had to call next.

Dummond et cie is one of Geneva's more modern banking establishments, having been founded as late as 1781. Since then the bank has spent over two hundred years handling other people's money, without religious or racial prejudice. Dummond et cie had always been willing to deal with Arab sheik or Jewish businessman, Nazi Gauleiter or British aristocrat, in fact anyone who required their services. It was a policy that had reaped dividends in every trading currency throughout the world.

The bank occupied twelve floors of a building just off the place de la Fusterie. The meeting that had been arranged that Tuesday at noon was scheduled to take place in the boardroom on the eleventh floor, the floor below the chairman's office.

The chairman of the bank, Pierre Dummond, had held his present position for the past nineteen years, but even he had rarely experienced a more unlikely coupling than that between an educated Arab from Iraq and the son of a former Mafia lawyer from New York.

The boardroom table could seat sixteen, but on this occasion it was only occupied by four. Pierre Dummond sat in the centre of one of the long sides under a portrait of his uncle, the former chairman, François Dummond. The present chairman wore a dark suit of elegant cut and style that would not have looked out of place had it been worn by any of the chairmen of the forty-eight banks located within a square mile of the building. His shirt was of a shade of blue that was not influenced by Milan fashions, and his tie was so discreet that, moments after leaving the room, only a remarkably observant client would have been able to recall its colour or pattern.

On Monsieur Dummond's right sat his client, Mr Al Obaydi, whose dress, although slightly more fashionable, was nonetheless equally conservative.

Opposite Monsieur Dummond sat the chairman of Franchard et cie, who, any observer would have noticed, must have shared the same tailor as Monsieur Dummond. On Franchard's left sat Antonio Cavalli, wearing a double-breasted Armani suit, who looked as if he had dropped in on the wrong meeting.

The little carriage clock that sat on the Louis-Philippe mantelpiece behind Monsieur Dummond completed twelve strokes. The chairman cleared his throat and began the proceedings.

'Gentlemen, the purpose of this meeting, which was called at our instigation but with your agreement, is to exchange a rare document for an agreed sum of money.' Monsieur Dummond pushed his half-moon spectacles further up his nose. 'Naturally, I must begin, Mr Cavalli, by asking if you are in possession of that document?'

'No, he is not, sir,' interjected Monsieur Franchard, as prearranged with Cavalli, 'because he has entrusted the document's safekeeping to our bank. But I can confirm that, as soon as the sum has been transferred, I have been given power of attorney to release the document immediately.'

'But that is not what we agreed,' interrupted Dummond, who leaned forward, feigning shock, before adding, 'My client's government has no intention of paying another cent without full scrutiny of the document. You agreed to deliver it here by midday, and in any case we still have to be convinced of its authenticity.'

'That is understood by my client,' said Monsieur Franchard. 'Indeed, you are most welcome to attend my office at any time convenient to you in order to carry out such an inspection. Following that inspection, the moment you have transferred the agreed amount the document will be released.'

'This is all very well,' countered Monsieur Dummond, pushing his half-moon spectacles back up his nose, 'but your client has failed to keep to his original agreement, which in my view allows my client's government' – he emphasised the word 'government' – 'to reconsider its position.'

'My client felt it prudent, in the circumstances, to protect his interest by depositing the document in his own bank for safekeeping,' came back the immediate reply from Monsieur Franchard.

Anyone watching the two bankers sparring with each other might have been surprised to learn that they played chess together every Saturday night, which Monsieur Franchard invariably won, and tennis after lunch on Sunday, which he regularly lost.

'I cannot accept this new arrangement,' said Al Obaydi, speaking for the first time. 'My government has charged me to pay only a further forty million dollars if the original agreement is breached in any way.'

'But this is ridiculous!' said Cavalli, his voice rising with every word. 'We are quibbling over a matter of a few hours at the most and a building less than half a mile away. And as you well know, the figure agreed on was ninety million.'

'But you have since broken our agreement,' said Al Obaydi, 'so the original terms can no longer be considered valid by my government.'

'No ninety million, no document!' said Cavalli, banging his fist on the table.

'Let us be realistic, Mr Cavalli,' said Al Obaydi. 'The document is no longer of any use to you, and I have a feeling you would have settled for fifty million in the first place.'

'That is not the –'

Monsieur Franchard touched Cavalli's arm. 'I would like a few minutes alone with my client, and, if I may, the use of a telephone.'

'Of course,' said Monsieur Dummond, rising from his place. 'We will leave you. Please press the button under the table the moment you wish us to return.'

Monsieur Dummond and his client left the room without another word.

'He's bluffing,' said Cavalli. 'He'll pay. I know it.'

'I don't think so,' said Franchard.

'What makes you say that?'

'The use of the words "my government".'

'What does that tell us that we didn't already know?'

'The expression was repeated four times,' said Franchard, 'which suggests to me that the financial decision has been taken out of the hands of Mr Al Obaydi, and only forty million has been deposited by his government with Dummond et cie.'

Cavalli began pacing round the room, but stopped by the phone which rested on a small side table.

'I presume that's bugged,' said Cavalli, pointing at the phone.

'No, Mr Cavalli, it is not.'

'How can you be so sure?' asked his client.

'Monsieur Dummond and I are currently involved in several transactions, and he would never allow our relationship to suffer for the sake of one deal. And in any case, he sits on the opposite side of the table from you today but, like every Swiss banker, that won't stop him from thinking of you as a potential customer.'

Cavalli checked his watch. It was 6.20 a.m. in New York. His father would have been up for at least an hour. He jabbed out the fourteen numbers and waited.

His father answered the phone, sounding wide awake, and after preliminary exchanges listened carefully to his son's account of what had taken place in the bank's boardroom. Cavalli also repeated Monsieur Franchard's view of the situation. The chairman of Skills didn't take long considering what advice he should give his son, advice which took Cavalli by surprise.

He replaced the phone and informed Monsieur Franchard of his father's opinion.

Monsieur Franchard nodded as if to show he agreed with the older man's judgement.

'Then let's get on with it,' said Cavalli reluctantly. Monsieur Franchard pressed the button under the boardroom table.

Monsieur Dummond and his client entered the room a few moments later and returned to the seats they had previously occupied. The old banker pushed his half-moon spectacles up his nose once again and stared over the top of them as he waited for Monsieur Franchard to speak.

'If the transaction is completed within one hour, we will settle for forty million dollars. If not, the deal is off and the document will be returned to the United States.'

Dummond removed his spectacles and turned to glance at his client. He was pleased that Franchard had picked up the significance of 'my government', a phrase he had recommended Mr Al Obaydi should use as often as possible.

'White House?'

'Yes, sir.'

'May I speak to the President's scheduler, please?'

'Can I ask who's calling?'

'Marshall, Calder Marshall, Archivist of the United States. And before you ask, yes, I do know her, and yes, she is expecting my call.'

The line went dead. Marshall wondered if he had been cut off.

'Patty Watson speaking.'

'Patty, this is Calder Marshall. I'm the –'

'Archivist of the United States.'

'I don't believe it.'

'Oh, yes, I'm a great fan of yours, Mr Marshall. I've even read your book on the history of the Constitution, the Bill of Rights and the Declaration. How can I help you? – Are you still there, Mr Marshall?'

'Yes, Patty, I am. I only wanted to check on the President's schedule on the morning of May 25th this year.'

'Certainly, sir. I'll just be a moment.'

The Archivist did not have long to wait.

'Ah yes, May 25th. The President spent the morning in the Oval Office with his speech writers, David Kusnet and Carolyn Curiel. He was preparing the text for his address on the GATT at the Chicago Council on Foreign Relations which was held the following day. He took a break to have lunch with Senator Mitchell, the Majority Leader. At three, the President –'

'Did President Clinton remain in the White House the whole morning?'

'Yes, sir. He didn't leave the White House all day. He spent the afternoon with Mrs Clinton in discussions with her health-policy task unit.'

'Could he have slipped out of the building without even you knowing, Patty?'

The scheduling secretary laughed. 'That's not possible, sir. If he had done that, the Secret Service would have informed me immediately.'

'Thank you, Patty.'

'Glad to have been of assistance, sir.'

Once the meeting at Dummond et cie had broken up, Cavalli returned to his hotel room to wait for Franchard to call and confirm that the sum of forty million dollars had been deposited in his No. 3 account in Zurich.

As long as the transaction was closed within the hour, he would still have easily enough time to catch the 4.45 out of Geneva for Heathrow and make the early-evening connection to New York.

Cavalli began to get a little anxious after thirty minutes passed and there had been no call, and even more so after forty. After fifty, he found himself pacing around the room, staring out at the fountain, and checking his watch every few moments.

When the phone eventually rang, he grabbed it.

'Mr Cavalli?' enquired a voice.

'Speaking.'

'Franchard here. The document has been verified and taken away. It might interest you to know that Mr Al Obaydi studied one word on the parchment for some time before he agreed to transfer the money. The agreed sum has been credited to your No. 3 account in Zurich as you specified.'

'Thank you, Monsieur Franchard,' said Cavalli without further comment.

'My pleasure, as always, Mr Cavalli. And is there anything else we can do for you while you're here?'

'Yes,' replied Cavalli. 'I need to transfer a quarter of a million dollars to a bank in the Cayman Islands.'

'The same name and account as the last three transactions?' asked the banker.

'Yes,' replied Cavalli. 'And the Zurich account, presently registered in the name of Mr Al Obaydi: I want to withdraw one hundred thousand dollars from it and . . .'

Monsieur Franchard listened carefully to his client's further instructions.

'State Department.'

'Can I speak to the Secretary of State?'

'Just a moment.'

'Office of the Secretary.'

'This is Calder Marshall. I'm the Archivist of the United States. It's vitally important that I speak with Secretary Christopher.'

'I'll put you through to his executive assistant, sir.'

'Thank you,' said Marshall, and waited for a very short time.

'This is Jack Leigh. I'm executive assistant to the Secretary. How may I help you, sir?'

'To start with, Mr Leigh, how many executive assistants does the Secretary of State have?'

'Five, sir, but there is only one senior to me.'

'Then I need to speak to the Secretary of State urgently.'

'Right now he's out of the office. Perhaps the Deputy Secretary can help?'

'No, Mr Leigh, he cannot help.'

'Well, I'll certainly let Secretary Christopher know you called, sir.'

'Thank you, Mr Leigh. And perhaps you'd be kind enough to pass a message on to him?'

'Of course, sir.'

'Would you let him know that my resignation will be on his desk tomorrow morning by nine a.m. This call is simply to apologise for the harm it will undoubtedly do to the President, particularly given the short period of time he has been in office.'

'You haven't spoken to anyone from the media about this, have you, sir?' asked the executive assistant, sounding anxious for the first time.

'No, I have not, Mr Leigh, and I shall not do so until noon tomorrow, which should give the Secretary ample time in which to prepare answers to any questions that he and the President will undoubtedly be asked by the press when they learn my reason for resigning.'

'I'll have the Secretary get back to you as quickly as I can, sir.'

'Thank you, Mr Leigh.'

'Glad to have been of assistance, sir.'

She flew into the Cayman Islands that morning and took a taxi to Barclays Bank in Georgetown. She checked her account to find it had been credited with three payments of two hundred and fifty thousand dollars. One on March 9th, another on April 27th, and a further one on May 30th.

There was one still to come. But, to be fair, Cavalli might not learn of the death of T. Hamilton McKenzie until he had returned from Geneva.

'And we have another package for you, Miss Webster,' said the smiling West Indian behind the counter.

Far too familiar, she thought. Once again the time had come for her to move her account to another bank in another country, in another name. She dropped the package into her carrier bag, threw it over her shoulder and left without a word.

She didn't attempt to open the thick brown envelope until she had called for coffee at the end of an unhurried meal at a hotel she would never book into. She then carefully slit open the top of the bulky package with her bread knife, allowing the contents to spill out onto the table.

The usual photos, from every angle, plus addresses past and present, and the daily habits and haunts of the intended victim. Cavalli never left any room for mistakes.

She studied the photos of a little fat man sitting on a bar stool. He looked harmless enough. The contract was always the same. To be carried out within fourteen days. Payment two hundred and fifty thousand dollars to account specified.

It wasn't Columbus or Washington this time, but San Francisco. She hadn't been to the West Coast in years, and she tried to remember if they had a Laura Ashley store.

'National Archives.'

'Mr Marshall.'

'Who's calling?'

'Christopher. Warren Christopher.'

'And you're with which agency?'

'I have a feeling he'll know.'

'I'll put you through, sir.' The Secretary waited patiently.

'Calder Marshall speaking.'

'Calder, it's Warren Christopher.'

'Good morning, Mr Secretary.'

'Good morning, Calder. I've just received your letter of resignation.'

'Yes, sir. I thought it was the only course of action I could take in the circumstances.'

'Very commendable, I feel sure, but have you let anyone else into your confidence?'

'No, sir. I intended to brief my staff at eleven and hold a press conference at twelve, as stated in my letter. I hope that doesn't inconvenience you, sir.'

'Well, I wondered if before you did that, you might find the time to have a meeting with the President and myself?'

Marshall hesitated only because the request had taken him by surprise.

'Of course, sir. What time would suit you?'

'Shall we say ten o'clock?'

'Yes, sir. Where would you like me to come?'

'The North Entrance of the White House.'

'The North Entrance, of course.'

'Jack Leigh, my executive assistant, will meet you in the West Wing reception area and accompany you to the Oval Office.'

'The Oval Office.'

'And Calder . . .'

'Yes, Mr Secretary?'

'Please do not mention your resignation to anyone until you've seen the President.'

'Until I've seen the President. Of course.'

'Thank you, Calder.'

'Glad to have been of assistance, sir.'

20

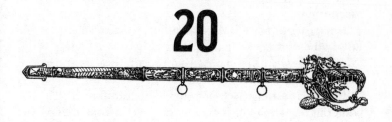

'I'D LIKE TO BEGIN by thanking you all for attending this meeting at such short notice,' said the Secretary of State. 'And, in particular, Scott Bradley, who has only recently recovered from . . .' Christopher hesitated for a moment, '. . . a near-tragic accident. I know we are all delighted by the speed of his recovery. I should also like to welcome Colonel Kratz, who is representing the Israeli Government, and Dexter Hutchins, the Deputy Director of the CIA.

'Only two of my staff are with me today: Jack Leigh, my executive assistant, and Susan Anderson, one of my senior Middle East advisers. The reason for numbers being limited on this occasion will become all too obvious to you. The issue we are about to discuss is so sensitive that the fewer people who are aware of it, the better. To suggest in this instance that silence is golden would be to underestimate the value of gold.

'Perhaps, at this juncture, I could ask the Deputy Director of the CIA to bring us up to date on the latest situation. Dexter.'

Dexter Hutchins unlocked his briefcase and removed a file marked 'For the Director's Eyes Only'. He placed the file on the table in front of him and turned its cover.

'Two days ago, Mr Marshall, the Archivist of the United States, reported to the Secretary of State that the Declaration of Independence had been stolen from the National Archives; or, to be more accurate, had been switched for a quite brilliant copy that had not only passed the scrutiny of Mr

Marshall, but also that of the Senior Conservator, Mr Mendelssohn.

'It was only when Mr Marshall attempted to re-contact a Mr Rex Butterworth, who had been temporarily assigned to the White House as a Special Assistant to the President, that he became worried.'

'If I could just interject, Mr Hutchins,' said Jack Leigh, 'and point out that though Mr Butterworth was a former employee of the Commerce Department, should the press ever get hold of this you can be certain they would only refer to him as a "Special Assistant to the President".' Warren Christopher nodded his agreement.

'When Calder Marshall discovered that Butterworth hadn't returned after his vacation,' continued Dexter Hutchins, 'and that he had also left without giving a forwarding address, he naturally became suspicious. Under the circumstances, he considered it prudent to ask Mr Mendelssohn to check and see if the Declaration had in any way been tampered with. After putting the parchment through several preliminary tests – a separate memorandum has been sent to all of you on this – he came to the conclusion that they were still in possession of the original document.

'But Mr Marshall, a cautious man, remained sceptical, and contacted the President's scheduler, Miss Patty Watson – details also enclosed. Following that conversation, he asked the Conservator to carry out a more rigorous scrutiny.

'Mr Mendelssohn spent several hours alone that evening going over the parchment word by word with a magnifying glass. It was when he came to the sentence, "Nor have We been wanting in attentions to our British brethren", that the Conservator realised that the word "British" had been spelt correctly, and not with two *t*s as in the original Declaration executed by Timothy Matlock. When this piece of news was imparted to Mr Marshall, he immediately offered his resignation to the Secretary of State, a copy of which you all have.'

'If I could come in here, Dexter,' said Secretary Christopher. 'Just for the record, the President and I saw Mr Marshall in the Oval Office yesterday. He could not have been more co-operative. He assured us that he and his colleague, Mr Mendelssohn, will say and do nothing in the immediate future. He did add, however, his feeling of disgust at continuing to display a counterfeit copy of the Declaration to the general public. He made us both, that is to say the President and myself, agree that should we fail to recover the original document before its disappearance becomes common knowledge, we would confirm that his resignation had been dated May 25th 1993 and accepted by myself as custodian of the Declaration. He wished it to be confirmed in writing that he had in no way connived to deceive his staff or the nation he served. "I am not in the habit of being deceitful," were his final words before leaving the Oval Office.

'If it is possible,' continued Christopher, 'for a public servant to make the President and the Secretary of State feel morally inferior, Mr Marshall achieved it with considerable dignity. However, that does not change the fact that if we don't get the original parchment back before its theft becomes public knowledge, the media are going to roast the President and myself slowly over a spit. One thing's also for sure: the Republicans, led by Dole, will happily wash their collective hands in public. Carry on, Dexter.'

'Under the Secretary of State's instructions, we immediately formed a small task force at Langley to profile every aspect of the problem we are facing. But we quickly discovered that we were working under some severe restrictions. To begin with, because of the sensitivity of the subject and the people involved, we could not do what we automatically would have done in normal circumstances, namely consult the FBI and liaise with the DC Police Department. That, we felt, would have guaranteed us the front page of the *Washington Post*, and probably the following morning. We mustn't forget that the FBI is still smarting over the Waco siege, and they'd like nothing better than for the CIA to replace them on the front pages.

'The next problem we faced was having to tiptoe round people we'd usually bring in for questioning, for fear that they too might discover our real purpose. However, we have been able to come up with several leads without talking to any members of the public. Following a routine check of permit records at the DCPD, we discovered that a movie was being made in Washington on the same day as the document was stolen. The director of that movie was Johnny Scasiatore, who is currently on bail facing an indecency charge. Three others involved in the enterprise turn out to have criminal records. And some of those people fit the descriptions Mr Marshall and Mr Mendelssohn have given us of the group who arrived at the National Archives posing as the Presidential party. They include a certain Bill O'Reilly, a well-known forger who has spent several years in more than one of our state penitentiaries, and an actor who played the President so convincingly that both Mr Marshall and Mr Mendelssohn accepted it was him without question.'

'Surely we can discover who that was,' said Christopher.

'We already have. His name is Lloyd Adams. But we daren't bring him in.'

'How did you find him?' asked Leigh. 'After all, there are quite a few actors who can manage a passable resemblance to Clinton.'

'Agreed,' said the Deputy Director, 'but only one who's been operated on by America's leading plastic surgeon within the past few months. We have reason to believe that the ring-leaders killed the surgeon and his daughter, which is why his wife reported everything she knew to the local Chief of Police.

'However, the whole operation would never have got off the ground without the inside help of Mr Rex Butterworth, who was last seen on the morning of May 25th and has since disappeared off the face of the earth. He booked a flight to Brazil, but he never showed. We have agents across the globe searching for him.'

'None of this is of any importance if we are no nearer to finding out where the original Declaration is at this moment, and who took it,' said Christopher.

'That's the bad news,' replied Dexter. 'Our agents spend hours on routine investigations that many American citizens consider a waste of taxpayers' money. But just now and then, it pays off.'

'We're all listening,' said Christopher.

'The CIA keeps under surveillance several foreign diplomats who work at the United Nations. Naturally, they would be outraged if any of them could prove what we were up to, and if we ever think they're onto us we back off immediately. In the case of Iraqis at the UN, we have people shadowing them round the clock. Our problem is that we can't operate within the UN complex itself, because if we were caught inside that building it would cause an international outcry. So, occasionally, their representatives are bound to slip our net.

'But we believe it was not a coincidence that Iraq's Deputy Ambassador to the United Nations, a Mr Hamid Al Obaydi, was in Washington on the day the Declaration was switched, and took several photographs of the bogus filming that was taking place. The agent who was tracking Al Obaydi at the time also reported that, at 10.37, after the Declaration had gone back on display in the National Archives, Al Obaydi joined the public queue, waiting over an hour to view the parchment. But here's the clincher. He studied the document once, and then he looked at it a second time, with glasses.'

'Perhaps he's near-sighted,' said Susan.

'Our agent reports that he's never before or since seen him wearing glasses of any kind,' replied Dexter Hutchins. 'Now for the *really* bad news,' he continued.

'That wasn't it?' said Christopher.

'No, sir. Al Obaydi flew on to Geneva a week later and was spotted by our local station officer leaving a bank.' Dexter referred to his notes. 'Franchard et cie. He was carrying a plastic cylinder, and I quote, "a little over two feet in length and about two inches in diameter".'

'Who's going to tell the President?' said Christopher, putting his hands over his eyes.

'He took this cylinder by car straight to the Palais des Nations, and it hasn't been seen since.'

'And Barazan Al-Tikriti, Saddam's half-brother, is the Iraqi Ambassador to the United Nations in Geneva,' said Susan.

'Don't remind me,' said Christopher. 'But what I want to know is, why the hell didn't your man jump Al Obaydi when it was obvious what he was carrying? I would have found a way of keeping the Swiss in line.'

'We would have done so if we'd known what he was carrying, but at that stage we weren't even aware the Declaration had been stolen, and our surveillance was just routine.'

'So what you're telling us is that the Declaration could well be in Baghdad by now,' said Leigh. 'Because if it was sent through the diplomatic pouch, the Swiss wouldn't have let us get anywhere near it.'

No one spoke for several moments.

'Let's work on the worst-case scenario,' said the Secretary of State finally. 'The Declaration is already in Saddam's possession. So what's his next move going to be? Scott, you're our man of logic. Can you second-guess what he might get up to?'

'No, sir, Saddam's not a man you can second-guess. But two things have worried me recently about his behaviour,' said Scott. 'First, we shoot down one of his fighters in the no-fly zone to protect the Shi'ites, and how does he react? Not with the usual bellicose shouting and screaming, followed by the massacre of innocent victims. No. The news is met by a reasoned, coherent statement from their Ambassador at the UN. Why? The press tells us it's because Saddam is hoping Clinton will be more reasonable in the long term than Bush. I don't believe it. I suspect Saddam realises that Clinton's position doesn't differ greatly from that of Bush. I don't think that's his reasoning at all. No, I suspect he believes that with the Declaration in his possession, he has a weapon so powerful that he can humiliate the United States, and in particular the new President, as and when he pleases.'

'When and how, Scott? If we knew that . . .'

'I have two theories on that, sir,' replied Scott.

'Let's hear them both.'

'Neither is going to make you feel any happier, Mr Secretary.'

'Nevertheless . . .'

'First he sets up a press conference, inviting the world's media to attend. He selects some public place in Baghdad where he is safely surrounded by his own people, and then he tears up, burns, destroys, does whatever he likes to the Declaration. I have a feeling it would make prime-time television.'

'But we'd bomb Baghdad to the ground if he tried that,' said Dexter Hutchins.

'I doubt it,' said Scott. 'How would our allies, the British, the French, not to mention the other friendly Arab nations, react to our bombing innocent civilians because Saddam had stolen the Declaration of Independence from right under our eyes?'

'You're right, Scott,' said Warren Christopher. 'The President would be vilified as a barbarian if he retaliated by bombing innocent Iraqis after what a lot of the world would consider nothing more than a public relations coup. So *when*'s he likely to move?'

'That's not so easy to answer, sir,' replied Scott, 'because you have to think the way he thinks. What makes that almost impossible is that he's capable of changing his mind from hour to hour. But if he thinks the problem through logically, my guess is he'll be considering two alternatives. Either on some symbolic date, maybe an anniversary associated with the Gulf War, or . . .'

'Or . . .?' said Christopher.

'Or he intends to hold on to it as a bargaining chip to allow him to retake the oilfields in Kuwait. After all, he's always claimed he had an agreement with us on that in the first place.'

'Either scenario is too horrific to contemplate,' said the Secretary of State. Turning to the Deputy Director, he asked, 'Have you begun to form any plan for getting the document back?'

'Not at the moment, sir,' replied Dexter Hutchins, 'as I suspect the parchment will be every bit as well protected as Saddam himself, and frankly we only learned of its likely destination last night.'

'Colonel Kratz,' said Christopher, turning his attention to the Mossad man, who had not uttered a word. 'Your Prime Minister informed us a few weeks ago that he was considering a plan to take out Saddam at some time in the near future.'

'Yes, sir, but he recognises your present dilemma, and all our activities have been shelved until the problem over the Declaration has been resolved, one way or the other.'

'I have already informed Mr Rabin how much I appreciate his support, especially as he can't even tell his own cabinet the true reason for his change of heart.'

'But we have our own problem, sir,' said the Israeli.

'Make my day, Colonel.'

The burst of laughter that followed helped to ease the tension for a moment – but only for a moment.

'We have been training an agent who was going to be part of the team for the final operation to eliminate Saddam, a Hannah Kopec.'

'The girl who . . .' said Christopher, half-glancing towards Scott.

'Yes, sir. She was totally blameless. But that is not the problem. After she returned to the Iraqi Embassy that evening, we were unable to get anywhere near Miss Kopec to let her know what had happened, because during the next few days she never once left the building, night or day. She and the

Iraqi Ambassador have since returned to Baghdad under heavy guard. However, Agent Kopec remains under the misapprehension that she has killed Scott Bradley, and we suspect her only interest now is to eliminate Saddam.'

'She'll never get anywhere near him,' said Leigh.

'I wish I believed that,' said Scott quietly.

'She is a bold, imaginative and resourceful young woman,' said Kratz. 'And, worse, she has the assassin's greatest weapon.'

'Namely?' said Christopher.

'She no longer cares about her own survival.'

'Can this get any worse?' asked Christopher.

'Yes, sir. She knows nothing about the disappearance of the Declaration, and we have no way of contacting her to let her know.'

The Secretary of State paused for a moment, as if he was coming to a decision. 'Colonel Kratz, I want to put something to you which is likely to stretch your personal loyalty.'

'Yes, Mr Secretary,' said Kratz.

'This plan to assassinate Saddam. How long have you been working on it?'

'Nine months to a year,' replied Kratz.

'And it obviously entailed you getting a person or persons into Saddam's palace or bunker?'

Kratz hesitated.

'Yes or no will suffice,' said Christopher.

'Yes, sir.'

'My question is extremely simple, Colonel. May we therefore take advantage of the year's preparation you've already carried out and – dare I suggest – steal your plan?'

'I would have to take advice from my government before I could consider . . .'

Christopher took an envelope from his pocket. 'I will be happy to let you see Mr Rabin's letter to me on this subject, but first allow me to read it to you.'

The Secretary opened the envelope and extracted the letter.

He placed his glasses on the end of his nose and unfolded the single sheet.

From the Prime Minister

Dear Mr Secretary,
You are correct in thinking that the Prime Minister of the State of Israel is Chief Minister and Minister of Defence while at the same time having overall responsibility for Mossad.

However, I confess that when it comes to any ideas we may be considering for future relations with Saddam, I have only been kept in touch with the outline plan. I have not yet been fully briefed on the finer details.

If you believe on balance that such information as we possess may make the difference between success or failure with your present difficulties, I will instruct Colonel Kratz to brief you fully and without reservation.

    Yours
    Yitzhak Rabin

Christopher turned the letter around and pushed it across the table.

'Colonel Kratz, let me assure you on behalf of the United States Government that I believe such information as you have in your possession may make the difference between success and failure.'

PART TWO

*'Nor have We been wanting
in attentions to
our Brittish brethren.'*

21

THE DECLARATION OF INDEPENDENCE was nailed to the wall behind him.

Saddam continued puffing at his cigar as he lounged back in his chair. All of them seated around the table waited for him to speak. He glanced to his right.

'My brother, we are proud of you. You have served our country and the Ba'ath Party with distinction, and when the moment comes for my people to be informed of your heroic deeds, your name will be written in the history of our nation as one of its great heroes.'

Al Obaydi sat at the other end of the table, listening to the words of his leader. His fists, hidden under the table, were clenched to stop himself shaking. Several times on the journey back to Baghdad he had been aware that he was being shadowed. They had searched his luggage at almost every stop, but they had found nothing, because there was nothing to find. Saddam's half-brother had seen to that. Once the Declaration had reached the safety of their mission in Geneva he hadn't even been allowed to pass it over to the Ambassador in person. Its guaranteed route in the diplomatic pouch made it impossible to intercept even with the combined efforts of the Americans and the Israelis.

Saddam's half-brother now sat on the President's right-hand side, basking in his leader's eulogy.

Saddam swung himself slowly back round and stared down at the other end of the table.

'And I also acknowledge,' he continued, 'the role played by Hamid Al Obaydi, whom I have appointed to be our Ambassador in Paris. His name must not, however, be associated with this enterprise, lest it harm his chances of representing us on foreign soil.'

And thus it had been decreed. Saddam's half-brother was to be acknowledged as the architect of this triumph, while Al Obaydi was to be a footnote on a page, quickly turned. Had Al Obaydi failed, Saddam's half-brother would have been ignorant of even the original idea, and Al Obaydi's bones would even now be rotting in an unmarked grave. Since Saddam had spoken no one round that table, except for the State Prosecutor, had given Al Obaydi a second look. All other eyes, and smiles, rested on Saddam's half-brother.

It was at that moment, in the midst of the meeting of the Revolutionary Command Council, that Al Obaydi came to his decision.

Dollar Bill sat slouched on a stool, leaning on the bar in unhappy hour, happily sipping his favourite liquid. He was the establishment's only customer, unless you counted the slip of a woman in a Laura Ashley dress who sat silently in the corner. The barman assumed she was drunk, as she hadn't moved a muscle for the past hour.

Dollar Bill wasn't at first aware of the man who stumbled through the swing doors, and wouldn't have given him a second look had he not sat himself on the stool next to his. The intruder ordered a gin and tonic. Dollar Bill had a natural aversion to any man who drank gin and tonic, especially if they occupied the seat next to his when the rest of the bar was empty. He considered moving but decided on balance that he didn't need the exercise.

'So how are you, old timer?' the voice next to him asked. Dollar Bill didn't care to think of himself as an 'old timer', and refused to grace the intruder with a reply.

'What's the matter, not got a tongue in your head?' the man

asked, slurring his words. The barman turned to face them when he heard the raised voice, and then returned to drying the glasses left over from the lunchtime rush.

'I have, sir, and it's a civil one,' replied Dollar Bill, still not so much as glancing at his interrogator.

'Irish. I should have known it all along. A nation of stupid, ignorant drunks.'

'Let me remind you, sir,' said Dollar Bill, 'that Ireland is the land of Yeats, Shaw, Wilde, O'Casey and Joyce.' He raised his glass in their memory.

'I've never heard of any of them. Drinking partners of yours, I suppose?' This time the young barman put his cloth down and began to pay closer attention.

'I never had that honour,' replied Dollar Bill, 'but, my friend, the fact that you have not heard of them, let alone read their works, is your loss, not mine.'

'Are you accusing me of being ignorant?' said the intruder, placing a rough hand on Dollar Bill's shoulder.

Dollar Bill turned to face him, but even at that close range he couldn't focus clearly through the haze of alcohol he had consumed during the past two weeks. He did, however, observe that, although he appeared to be part of the same alcoholic haze, the intruder was somewhat larger than himself. Such a consideration had never worried Dollar Bill in the past.

'No, sir, it was not necessary to accuse you of ignorance. For you have been condemned by your own utterances.'

'I won't take that from anyone, you Irish drunk,' said the intruder. Keeping his hand on Dollar Bill's shoulder, he swung at him and landed a blow on the side of his jaw. Dollar Bill staggered back off his high stool, falling to the floor in a heap.

The intruder waited some time for Bill to rise to his feet before he aimed a second blow to the stomach. Once again, Dollar Bill ended up on the floor.

The young man behind the bar had already begun dialling the number his boss had instructed he should call if ever such a situation arose. He only hoped they would come quickly as he watched the Irishman somehow get back on his feet. This time it was his turn to aim a punch at the intruder's nose, a punch which ended up flying through the air over his assailant's right shoulder. A further blow landed on the side of Dollar Bill's throat. Down he went a third time, which in his days as an amateur boxer would have been considered a technical knock-out; but as there seemed to be no referee present to officiate, he rose once again.

The young barman was relieved to hear a siren in the distance, and was praying they weren't on their way to another call when suddenly four policemen came bursting through the swing doors.

The first one caught Dollar Bill just before he hit the ground for a fourth time, while two of the others grabbed the intruder, thrust his arms behind his back and forced a pair of handcuffs on him. Both men were bundled out of the bar and thrown into the back of a waiting police van. The siren continued its piercing sound as the two drunks were driven away.

The barman was grateful for the speed with which the San Francisco Police Department had come to his aid. It was only later that night that he remembered he hadn't given them an address.

Both men remained silent until David Kratz had come to the end of his outline plan.

Dexter was the first to speak. 'I must admit, Colonel, I'm impressed. It just might work.'

Scott nodded his agreement, and then turned to the Mossad man who only a few weeks before had given Hannah the order that he should be killed. Some of the guilt had been lifted since they had been working so closely with each other, but the lines on the forehead and the prematurely grey hair of the Israeli leader remained a perpetual reminder of what he had been through. During their time together Scott had come to admire the sheer professional skill of the man who had been put in charge of the operation.

'I still need some queries answered,' said Scott, 'and a few other things explained.'

The Israeli Councillor for Cultural Affairs to the Court of St James nodded.

'Are you certain that they plan to put the safe in the Ba'ath Party headquarters?'

'Certain, no. Confident, yes,' said Kratz. 'A Dutch company completed some building work in the basement of the headquarters nearly three years ago, and among their final drawings was a brick construction, the dimensions of which would house the safe perfectly.'

'And is this safe still in Kalmar?'

'It was three weeks ago,' replied Kratz, 'when one of my agents carried out a routine check.'

'And does it belong to the Iraqi Government?' asked Dexter Hutchins.

'Yes, it has been fully paid for, and is now legally the property of the Iraqis.'

'Legally that may be the position, but since the Gulf War the UN has imposed a new category of sanctions,' Scott reminded him.

'How can a safe be considered a piece of military equipment?' asked Dexter.

'Exactly the Iraqis' argument,' replied Kratz. 'But, unfortunately for them, when they placed the original order with the Swedes, among the explicit specifications was the requirement that the safe "must be able to withstand a nuclear attack". The word "nuclear" was all that was needed to start the bells ringing at the UN.'

'So how do you plan to get round that problem?' asked Scott.

'Whenever the Iraqi Government submits a new list of items that they consider do not break UN Security Council Resolution 661, the safe is always included. If the Americans, the British and the French didn't raise any objection, it could slip through.'

'And the Israeli Government?'

'We would protest vociferously in front of the Iraqi delegation, but not behind closed doors to our friends.'

'So let us imagine for one moment that we're in possession of a giant safe that can withstand a nuclear attack. What good does that do us?' asked Scott.

'Someone has to be responsible for getting that safe from Sweden to Baghdad. Someone has to install it when they get there, and someone has to explain to Saddam's people how to operate it,' said Kratz.

'And you have someone who is six feet tall, a karate expert, and speaks fluent Arabic?'

'We did have, but she was only five feet ten.' The two men stared at each other. Scott remained silent.

'And how were you proposing to assassinate Saddam?' asked Dexter quickly. 'Lock him up in the safe and hope he would suffocate?'

Kratz realised the comment had been made to take Scott's mind off Hannah, so he responded in kind. 'No, we discovered that was the CIA's plan, and dismissed it. We had something more subtle in mind.'

'Namely?' asked Scott.

'A tiny nuclear device was to be planted inside the safe.'

'And the safe would be in the passage next to where the Revolutionary Command Council meet. Not bad,' said Dexter.

'And the device was to be set off by a five-foot-ten, Arabic-speaking Jewish girl?' asked Scott.

Kratz nodded.

It had been many years since Dollar Bill had seen the inside of a jail, but not so long that he had forgotten how much he detested having to associate with drug peddlers, pimps and muggers.

Still, the last time he had been foolish enough to get himself involved in a bar-room brawl, he had started it. But even then he only ended up with a fifty dollar fine. Dollar Bill felt confident that the jails were far too overcrowded for any judge to consider the thirty-day mandatory sentence for such cases.

In fact he had tried to give one of the policemen in the van fifty dollars. They normally happily accepted the money, opened the back door of the van and kicked you out. He couldn't imagine what the San Francisco police were coming to. Surely with all the muggers and drug addicts around they had more important things to deal with than mid-afternoon middle-aged bar-room drunks.

As Dollar Bill began to sober up, the stench got to him, and he hoped that he'd be among the first to be put up in front of the night court. But as the hours passed, and he became more sober and the stench became greater, he began to wonder if they might end up keeping him overnight.

'William O'Reilly,' shouted the police Sergeant as he looked down the list of names on his clipboard.

'That's me,' said Bill, raising his hand.

'Follow me, O'Reilly,' the policeman barked as the cell door clanked open and the Irishman was gripped firmly by the elbow.

He was marched along a corridor that led into the back of a courtroom. He watched the little line of derelicts and petty criminals who were waiting for their moment in front of the judge. He didn't notice a woman a few paces away from him, tightly gripping the rope handle of a holdall.

'Guilty. Fifty dollars.'

'Can't pay.'

'Three days in jail. Next.'

After three or four cases were dispensed with in this cursory manner within as many minutes, Dollar Bill watched the man who had shown no respect for the canon of Irish literature take his place in front of the judge.

'Drunk and disorderly, disturbing the peace. How do you plead?'

'Guilty, Your Honour.'

'Any previous known record?'

'None,' said the Sergeant.

'Fifty dollars,' said the judge.

It interested Dollar Bill that his adversary had no previous convictions, and was also able to pay his fine immediately.

When it came to Dollar Bill's own turn to plead, he couldn't help thinking, as he looked up at the judge, that he appeared to be awfully young for the job. Perhaps he really was now an 'old timer'.

'William O'Reilly, Your Honour,' said the Sergeant, looking down at the charge sheet. 'Drunk and disorderly, disturbing the peace.'

'How do you plead?'

'Guilty, Your Honour,' said Dollar Bill, fingering a small wad of bills in his pocket as he tried to remember the location of the nearest bar that served Guinness.

'Thirty days,' said the judge, without raising his head. 'Next.'

Two people in the courtroom were stunned by the judge's decision. One of them reluctantly loosened her grip on the rope handle of her holdall, while the other stammered out, 'Bail, Your Honour?'

'Denied.'

22

AS HANNAH SAT ALONE at the back of the plane bound for Amman, she began to consider the task she had set herself.

Once the Ambassador's party had left Paris, she had returned to the traditional role of an Arab woman. She was dressed from head to toe in a black yashmak, and apart from her eyes, her face was covered by a small mask. She spoke only when asked a question directly, and never posed a question herself. She felt her Jewish mother would not have survived such a regime for more than a few hours.

Hannah's one break had come when the Ambassador's wife had enquired where she intended to stay once they had returned to Baghdad. Hannah explained that she had made no immediate plans as her mother and sister were living in Karbala, and she could not stay with them if she hoped to hold on to her job with the Ambassador.

Hannah had hardly finished the second sentence before the Ambassador's wife insisted that she come and live with them. 'Our house is far too large,' she explained, 'even with a dozen servants.'

When the plane touched down at Queen Alia airport, Hannah looked out of the tiny window to watch a large black limousine that would have looked more in place in New York than Amman driving towards them. It drew up by the side of the aircraft and a driver in a smart blue suit and dark glasses jumped out.

Hannah joined the Ambassador and his wife in the back of

the car and they sped away from the airport in the direction of the border with Iraq.

When the car reached the customs post, they were waved straight through with bows and salutes, as if the border didn't exist. They travelled a further mile and passed a second customs post on the Iraqi side, where they were treated in much the same manner as the first, before joining the six-lane highway to Baghdad.

On the long journey to the capital, the speedometer rarely fell below sixty miles per hour. Hannah soon became bored with the beating sun and the sight of miles and miles of flat sand that stretched to the horizon and beyond, with only the occasional cluster of palm trees to break the monotony. Her thoughts returned to Simon and what might have been . . .

Hannah dozed off as the air-conditioned limousine sped quietly along the highway. Her mind drifted from Simon to her mother, to Saddam, and then back to Simon.

She woke with a start to find they were entering the outskirts of Baghdad.

'Thirty days? What did I do to deserve thirty days, that's what I want to know.' But no one was listening as Dollar Bill was hustled out of the courtroom, along the corridor and then out through a door at the rear of the building, before being pushed into the back seat of an unmarked car. Three men with military-style haircuts, Ray-Bans, and small earplugs connected to wires running down the backs of their collars, accompanied him.

'Why wasn't I given bail? And what about my appeal? I have the right to a lawyer, damn it. And by the way, where are we going?' However many questions he asked, Dollar Bill received no answers.

Although he was unable to see anything out of the smoked-glass side windows, Dollar Bill could tell by looking over the driver's shoulder when they reached the Golden Gate Bridge. As they proceeded along Route 101, the speedometer touched fifty-five for the first time, but the driver never once exceeded the speed limit.

When twenty minutes later the car swung off the highway at the Belvedere exit, Dollar Bill had no idea where he was. The driver continued up a small, winding road, until the car slowed down as a massive set of wrought-iron gates loomed up in front of them.

The driver flashed his lights twice and the gates swung open to allow the car to continue its journey down a long, straight gravel drive. It was another three or four minutes before they came to a halt in front of a large country house which reminded Dollar Bill of his youth in County Kerry, when his mother had been a scullery maid up at the manor house.

One of Dollar Bill's escorts leaped out of the car and opened the door for him. Another ran ahead of them up the steps and pressed a bell, as the car sped away across the gravel.

The massive oak door opened to reveal a butler in a long black coat and a white bow tie.

'Good evening, Mr O'Reilly,' he declared in a pronounced English accent even before Dollar Bill had reached the top step. 'My name is Charles. Your room is already prepared. Perhaps you'd be kind enough to accompany me, sir.' Dollar Bill followed him into the house and up the wide staircase without uttering a word. He would have tried some of his questions on Charles, but as he was English, Dollar Bill knew he couldn't expect an honest reply. The butler guided him into a small, well-furnished bedroom on the first floor.

'I do hope you will find that the clothes are the correct fitting, sir,' said Charles, 'and that everything else is to your liking. Dinner will be served in half an hour.'

Dollar Bill bowed and spent the next few minutes looking round the suite. He checked the bathroom. French soap, safety razors and fluffy white towels; even a toothbrush and his favourite toothpaste. He returned to the bedroom and tested the double bed. He couldn't remember when he had last slept on anything so comfortable. He then checked the wardrobe and found three pairs of trousers and three jackets, not unlike the ones he had purchased a few days after returning from Washington. How did they know?

He looked in the drawers: six shirts, six pairs of pants and six pairs of socks. They had thought of everything, even if he didn't care that much for their choice of ties.

Dollar Bill decided to join in the game. He took a bath, shaved and changed into the clothes provided. They were, as Charles had promised, the correct fitting.

He heard a gong sound downstairs, which he took as a clear signal that he had been summoned. He opened the door, stepped into the corridor and proceeded down the wide stair-case to find the butler standing in the hall.

'Mr Hutchins is expecting you. You'll find him in the drawing room, sir.'

'Yes, of course I will,' said Dollar Bill, and followed Charles into a large room where a tall, burly man was standing by the fireplace, the stub of a cigar in the corner of his mouth.

'Good evening, Mr O'Reilly,' he said. 'My name is Dexter Hutchins. We've never met before, but I've long been an admirer of your work.'

'That's kind of you, Mr Hutchins, but I don't have the same advantage of knowing what you do to pass the unrelenting hour.'

'I do apologise. I am the Deputy Director of the CIA.'

'After all these years, I get to have dinner in a large country house with the Deputy Director of the CIA simply because I was involved in a bar-room brawl. I'm tempted to ask, what do you lay on for mass murderers?'

'I must confess, Mr O'Reilly, that it was one of my men who threw the first punch. But before we go any further, what would you like to drink?'

'I don't think Charles will have my favourite brew,' said Dollar Bill, turning to face the butler.

'I fear the Guinness is canned and not on tap, sir. If I had been given more notice . . .' Dollar Bill bowed again and the butler disappeared.

'Don't you think I'm entitled to know what this is all about, Mr Hutchins? After all . . .'

'You are indeed, Mr O'Reilly. The truth is, the government is in need of your services, not to mention your expertise.'

'I didn't realise that Clintonomics had resorted to forgery to help balance the budget deficit,' said Dollar Bill as the butler returned with a large glass of Guinness.

'Not quite as drastic as that, but every bit as demanding,' said Hutchins. 'But perhaps we should have a little dinner before I go into any details. I fear it's been a long day for you.' Dollar Bill nodded and followed the Deputy Director through to a small dining room, where the table had been set for two. The butler held a chair back for Dollar Bill, and when he was comfortably seated asked, 'How do you like your steak done, sir?'

'Is it sirloin or entrecôte?' asked Dollar Bill.

'Sirloin.'

'If the meat is good enough, tell the chef to put a candle under it – but only for a few moments.'

'Excellent, sir. Yours, Mr Hutchins, will I presume be well done?'

Dexter Hutchins nodded, feeling the first round had definitely gone to Dollar Bill.

'I'm enjoying this charade enormously,' said Dollar Bill, taking a gulp of Guinness. 'But I'd like to know what the prize is, should I be fortunate enough to win.'

'You might equally well be interested to know what the forfeit will be if you are unfortunate enough to lose.'

'I should have realised this had to be too good to last.'

'First, allow me to fill you in with a little background,' said Dexter Hutchins as a lightly grilled steak was placed in front of his guest. 'On May 25th this year, a well-organised group of criminals descended on Washington and carried out one of the most ingenious crimes in the history of this country.'

'Excellent steak,' said Dollar Bill. 'You must give my compliments to the chef.'

'I certainly will, sir,' said Charles, who was hovering behind his chair.

'This crime consisted of stealing from the National Archives, in broad daylight, the Declaration of Independence, and replacing it with a brilliant copy.'

Dollar Bill looked suitably impressed, but felt it would be unwise to comment at this stage.

'We have the names of several people involved in that crime, but we cannot make any arrests for fear of making those who are now in possession of the Declaration aware that we might be after them.'

'And what's this got to do with me?' asked Dollar Bill, as he devoured another succulent piece of meat.

'We thought you might be interested to know who had financed the entire operation, and is now in possession of the Declaration of Independence.'

Until that moment, Dollar Bill had learned nothing new, but he had long wanted to know where the document had ended up. He had never believed Angelo's tale of 'in private hands, an eccentric collector'. He put his knife and fork down and stared across the table at the Deputy Director of the CIA, who had at last captured his attention.

'We have reason to believe that the Declaration of Independence is currently in Baghdad, in the personal possession of Saddam Hussein.'

Dollar Bill's mouth opened wide, although he remained silent for some considerable time. 'Is there no longer honour among thieves?' he finally said.

'There still could be,' said Hutchins, 'because our only hope of returning the parchment to its rightful home rests in the hands of a small group who are willing to risk their lives by switching the document, in much the same way as the criminals did originally.'

'If I had known . . .' Dollar Bill paused. 'How can I help?' he asked quietly.

'At this moment, we are in urgent need of a perfect copy of

the original. And we believe you are the only person who is capable of producing one.'

Dollar Bill knew exactly where there was a perfect copy, hanging on a wall in New York, but couldn't admit as much without bringing on himself even greater wrath than Mr Hutchins was capable of.

'You made mention of a prize,' said Dollar Bill.

'And a forfeit,' said Dexter Hutchins. 'The prize is that you remain here at our West Coast safe house, in what I think you will admit are agreeable surroundings. While you are with us, you will produce a counterfeit of the Declaration that would pass an expert's eye. If you achieve that, you will go free, with no charges preferred against you.'

'And the forfeit?'

'After coffee has been served you will be released and allowed to leave whenever you wish.'

'Released,' repeated Dollar Bill in disbelief, 'and allowed to leave whenever I wish?'

'Yes,' said the Deputy Director.

'Then why shouldn't I just enjoy the rest of this excellent meal, return to my humble establishment in Fairmont, and forget we ever met?'

The Deputy Director removed an envelope from an inside pocket. He extracted four photographs and pushed them across the table. Dollar Bill studied them. The first was of a girl aged about seventeen lying on a slab in a morgue. The second was of a middle-aged man huddled foetus-like in the boot of a car. The third was of a heavily-built man dumped by the side of a road. And the fourth was of an older, distinguished-looking man. A broken neck was all the four of them had in common. Dollar Bill pushed the photos back across the table.

'Four corpses. So what?'

'Sally McKenzie, Rex Butterworth, Bruno Morelli, and Dr T. Hamilton McKenzie. And we have every reason to believe someone out there is planning the same happy ending for you.'

Dollar Bill speared the last pea left on his plate and downed the final drop of Guinness. He paused for a moment as if searching for inspiration.

'I'll need paper from Bremen, pens from a museum in Richmond, Virginia, and nine shades of black ink that can be made up for me by a firm in Cannon Street, London EC4.'

'Anything else?' asked Dexter Hutchins once he had finished writing down Dollar Bill's shopping list on the back of the envelope.

'I wonder if Charles would be kind enough to bring me another large Guinness. I have a feeling it may be my last for some considerable time.'

23

BERTIL PEDERSSON, the chief engineer of Svenhalte AC, was at the factory gate in Kalmar to greet Mr Riffat and Mr Bernstrom when the two men arrived that morning. He had received a fax from the United Nations the previous day confirming their flight times to Stockholm, and had checked with the arrivals desk at the airport to be informed that their plane had touched down only a few minutes late.

As they stepped out of their car, Mr Pedersson came forward, shook hands with both men and introduced himself.

'We are pleased to meet you at last, Mr Pedersson,' said the shorter of the two men, 'and grateful to you for making the time to see us at such short notice.'

'Well, to be frank with you, Mr Riffat, it came as quite a surprise to us when the United Nations lifted the restrictions on Madame Bertha.'

' "Madame Bertha"?'

'Yes, that is how we at the factory refer to the safe. I promise you, gentlemen, that despite your neglect, she has been a good girl. Many people have come to admire her, but nobody touches,' Mr Pedersson laughed. 'But I feel sure that after such a long journey you will want to see her for yourself, Mr Riffat.'

The short, dark-haired man nodded, and they both accompanied Pedersson as he led them across the yard.

'You responded most quickly to the UN's sudden change of heart, Mr Riffat.'

'Yes, our leader had given orders that the safe should be delivered to Baghdad the moment the embargo was lifted.'

Pedersson laughed again. 'I fear that may not be so easy,' he said once they reached the other side of the yard. 'Madame Bertha was not built for speed, as you are about to discover.'

The three men continued to walk towards a large, apparently derelict building, and Pedersson strode through an opening where there must once have been a door. It was so dark inside that the two foreigners were unable to see more than a few feet in front of them. Pedersson switched on a single light, which was followed by what sounded like the sigh of an unrequited lover.

'Mr Riffat, Mr Bernstrom, allow me to introduce you to Madame Bertha.' The two men stared at the massive structure that stood majestically in the middle of the old warehouse floor.

'Before I make a formal introduction,' Pedersson continued, 'first let me tell you Madame Bertha's vital statistics. She is nine feet tall, seven feet wide and eight feet deep. She is also thicker skinned than any politician, about six inches of solid steel to be precise, and she weighs over five tons. She was built by a specialist designer, three craftsmen and eight engineers. Her gestation from conception to delivery was eighteen months. But then,' he whispered, 'to be fair, she is almost the size of an elephant. I lower my voice only because she can hear every word I say, and I have no wish to offend her.'

Mr Pedersson did not see the puzzled looks that came over the faces of his two visitors. 'But, gentlemen, you have only seen her exterior, and I can promise you that what she has to offer is more than skin deep.

'First, I must tell you that Madame Bertha will not allow anyone to enter her without a personal introduction. She is, gentlemen, not a promiscuous lady, despite what you may have been told about the Swedes. She requires to know three things about you before she will consider revealing her innermost parts.'

Although the two guests remained puzzled as to what he meant, they did not interrupt Mr Pedersson's steady flow.

'And so, gentlemen, to begin with you must study Bertha's chest. You will observe three red lights above three small dials. By knowing the code on all three dials, you will be able to turn one of the lights from red to green. Allow me to demonstrate. The three dials all have a six-number code. First number to the right, second to the left, third to the right, fourth to the left, fifth to the right, sixth to the left. The first number for the first dial is 2, the second is 8, the third zero, the fourth 4, the fifth 3 and the sixth 7. 2-8-0-4-3-7.'

'The date of Sayedi's birthday,' said the tall, fair-haired visitor.

'Yes, I worked that one out, Mr Bernstrom,' said Pedersson. 'The second,' he said, turning his attention to the middle dial, 'is 1-6-0-7-7-9.' He turned the final number to the left.

'The day Sayedi became President.'

'We also managed that one, Mr Riffat. But I confess the third sequence fooled me completely. No doubt you will know what our client has planned for that particular day.' Mr Pedersson began twirling the third dial: 0-4-0-7-9-3.

Pedersson looked hopefully towards Mr Bernstrom, who shrugged his shoulders. 'I've no idea,' he lied.

'You will now note, gentlemen, that after entering the correct figures on all three dials, only one of Madame Bertha's lights has turned green, while two still remain obstinately red. But now that you have discovered her three codes, she will consider a more personal relationship. You will observe that below the three dials there is painted a small white square about the size of your hand. Watch carefully.' Pedersson took a pace forward and placed his right hand firmly on the white square. He left it there for several seconds, until the second light turned green.

'Even when she knows your palm print, she still won't open her heart. Not until I have spoken to her. If you look even more closely, gentlemen, you will see that the white square conceals a thin wire mesh, which houses a voice activator.' Both men stepped forward to look.

'At the present time, Bertha is programmed to react only to

my vocal cords. It doesn't matter what I say, because as soon as she recognises the voice, the third light will turn green. But she will not even consider listening to me unless the first two lights are already green.'

Pedersson stepped forward and placed his lips opposite the wire mesh. 'Two gentlemen have come from America to see you, and desire to know what you look like inside.'

Even before he had finished the sentence, the third red light had flicked to green, and a noisy unclamping sound could be heard.

'Now, gentlemen, we come to the part of the demonstration of which my company is particularly proud. The door, which weighs over a ton, is nevertheless capable of being opened by a small child. Our company has developed a system of phosphor-bronze bearings that are a decade ahead of their time. Please, Mr Riffat, why don't you try for yourself?'

The shorter man stepped forward, gripped the handle of the safe firmly, and pulled. All three lights immediately turned red, and a noisy clamping sound began again.

Pedersson chuckled. 'You see, Mr Riffat, unless Madame Bertha knows you personally, she clams up and sends you back to the red-light district.' He laughed at a joke his guests suspected he had told many times before. 'The hand that opens the safe,' he continued, 'must be the same one that passed the palm-print test. A good safety device, I think you'll agree.' Both men nodded in admiration as Pedersson quickly fiddled with the three dials, placed his hand on the square and then spoke to Madame Bertha. One by one the three lights dutifully turned from red to green.

'She is now prepared to let me, and me alone, open her up. So watch carefully. Although, as I said, the door weighs a ton, it can be opened with the gentlest persuasion, thus.'

Pedersson pulled back the ton of massive steel with no more exertion than he would have used to open the front door of his home. He jumped inside the safe and began walking around, first with his arms outstretched to show that he could not touch the sides while standing in the centre, and then with his hands above his head, showing he was unable to reach the roof. 'Do please enter, gentlemen,' he cried from inside.

The two men stepped up gingerly to join him.

'In this case, three is not a crowd,' said Pedersson, laughing again. 'And you will be happy to discover that it is impossible for me to get myself locked in.' He gripped the handle on the inside of the safe and pulled the great door shut.

Two of the occupants did not find this part of the experiment quite so appealing.

'You see, gentlemen,' continued Pedersson, who could not hide the satisfaction in his voice, 'Bertha cannot lock herself again unless it is my hand on the outside handle.' With one small push, the door swung open and Pedersson stepped out, closely followed by his two customers.

'I once had to spend an evening inside her before the system was completely perfected – a sort of one-night stand, you might call it,' said Pedersson. He laughed even louder as he pushed the door back in place. The three lights immediately flashed to red and the clamps noisily closed in place.

He turned to face them. 'So, gentlemen, you have been introduced to Madame Bertha. Now, if you would be kind enough to accompany me back to my office, I will present you with a delivery note and, more important, Bertha's bible.'

As they returned across the yard, Pedersson explained to his two visitors that the book of instructions had been treated by the company as top secret. They had produced one in Swedish, which the company retained in its own safe, and another in Arabic, which Pedersson said he would be happy to hand over to them.

'The bible itself is 108 pages in length, but simple enough to understand if you are an engineer with a first-class honours degree.' He laughed again. 'We Swedish are a thorough race.'

Neither of the men felt able to disagree with him.

'Will you require anyone to accompany Madame Bertha on her journey?' Pedersson asked, his eyes expressing hope.

'No, thank you,' came back the immediate reply. 'I think we can handle the problem of transport.'

'Then I have only one more question for you,' Pedersson said, as he entered his office. 'When do you plan to take her away?'

'We hoped to collect the safe this afternoon. We understood from the fax you sent to the United Nations that your company has a crane that can lift the safe, and a trolley on which it can be moved from place to place.'

'You are right in thinking we have a suitable crane, and a trolley that has been specially designed to carry Madame Bertha on short journeys. I am also confident I can have everything ready for you by this afternoon. But that doesn't cover the problem of transport.'

'We already have our own vehicle standing by in Stockholm.'

'Excellent, then it is settled,' said Mr Pedersson. 'All I need to do in your absence is to programme out my hand and voice so that she can accept whoever you select to take my place.' Pedersson looked forlorn for a second time. 'I look forward to seeing you again this afternoon, gentlemen.'

'I'll be coming back on my own,' said Riffat. 'Mr Bernstrom will be returning to America.'

Pedersson nodded and watched the two men climb into their car before he walked slowly back to his office. The phone on his desk was ringing.

He picked it up, said, 'Bertil Pedersson speaking,' and listened to the caller's request. He placed the receiver on his desk and ran to the window, but the car was already out of sight. He returned to the phone. 'I am so sorry, Mr Al Obaydi,' said Pedersson, 'the two gentlemen who came to see the safe have just this moment left, but Mr Riffat will be returning this afternoon to take her away. Shall I let him know you called?'

Al Obaydi put the phone down in Baghdad, and began to consider the implications of what had started out as a routine call.

As Deputy Ambassador to the UN, it was his responsibility to keep the sanctions list up to date. He had hoped to pass on the file within a week to his as-yet-unappointed successor.

In the past two days, despite phones that didn't connect and civil servants who were never at their desks – and even when they were, were too terrified to answer the most basic questions – he was almost in a position to complete the first draft of his report.

The problem areas had been: agricultural machinery, half of which the UN Sanctions Committee took for granted was military equipment under another name; hospital supplies, including pharmaceuticals, on which the UN accepted most of their requests; and food, which they were allowed to purchase – although most of the produce that came across the border seemed to disappear on the black market long before it reached the Baghdad housewife.

A fourth list was headed 'miscellaneous items', and included among these was a massive safe which, when Al Obaydi checked its measurements, turned out to be almost the size of the room he was presently working in. The safe, an internal report confirmed, had been built in Sweden before the planned liberation of the Nineteenth Province, and was now sitting in a warehouse in Kalmar, waiting to be collected. Al Obaydi's boss at the UN had confessed privately that he was surprised that the Sanctions Committee had lifted the embargo on the safe, but this did not deter him from assuring the Foreign Minister that they had only done so as a result of his painstaking negotiating skills.

Al Obaydi sat at his laden desk for several minutes, considering what his next move should be. He wrote a short list of headings on the notepad in front of him:

1   M.o.I.
2   State Security
3   Deputy Foreign Minister
4   Kalmar

Al Obaydi glanced at the first heading, M.o.I. He had re-mained in contact with a fellow student from London Univer-sity days who had risen to Permanent Secretary status at the Ministry of Industry. Al Obaydi felt his old friend would be able to supply the information he required without suspecting his real motive.

He dialled the Permanent Secretary's private number, and was delighted to find that someone was at his desk.

'Nadhim, it's Hamid Al Obaydi.'

'Hamid, I heard you were back from New York. The rumour is that you've got what remains of our embassy in Paris. But one can never be sure about rumours in this city.'

'For once, they're accurate,' Al Obaydi told his friend.

'Congratulations. So, what can I do for you, Your Excel-lency?'

Al Obaydi was amused that Nadhim was the first person to address him by his new title, even if he was being sarcastic.

'UN sanctions.'

'And you claim you're my friend?'

'No, it's just a routine check. I've got to tie up any loose ends for my successor. Everything's in order as far as I can tell, except I'm unable to find out much about a gigantic safe that was made for us in Sweden. I know we've paid for it, but I can't discover what is happening about its delivery.'

'Not this department, Hamid. The responsibility was taken out of our hands about a year ago after the file was marked "High Command", which usually means for the President's personal use.'

'But someone must be responsible for a movement order from Kalmar to Baghdad,' said Al Obaydi.

'All I know is that I was instructed to pass the file on to our UN office in Geneva. I'm surprised you didn't know that, Hamid. More your department than mine, I would have thought.'

'Then I'll have to get in touch with Geneva and find out what they're doing about it,' said Al Obaydi, not adding that New

York and Geneva rarely informed each other of anything they were up to. 'Thanks for your help, Nadhim.'

'Any time. Good luck in Paris, Hamid. I'm told the women are fabulous, and despite what you hear, they like Arabs.'

Al Obaydi put the phone down and stared at the list on his pad. He took even longer deciding if he should make the second call.

The correct course of action with the information he now possessed would be to contact Geneva, alert the Ambassador of his suspicions and let Saddam's half-brother once again take the praise for something he himself had done the work on. He checked his watch. It was midday in Switzerland. He asked his secretary to get Barazan Al-Tikriti on the phone, knowing she would log every call. He waited for several minutes before a voice came on the line.

'Can I speak to the Ambassador?' he asked politely.

'He's in a meeting, sir,' came back the inevitable reply. 'Shall I disturb him?'

'No, no, don't bother. But would you let him know that Hamid Al Obaydi called from Baghdad, and ask him if he would be kind enough to return my call.'

'Yes, sir,' said the voice, and Al Obaydi replaced the phone. He had carried out the correct procedure.

He opened the sanctions file on his desk and scribbled on the bottom of his report: 'The Ministry of Industry have sent the file concerning this item direct to Geneva. I phoned our Ambassador there, but was unable to make contact with him. Therefore, I cannot make any progress from this end until he returns my call. Hamid Al Obaydi.'

Al Obaydi considered his next move extremely carefully. If he decided to do anything, his actions must once again appear on the surface to be routine, and well within his accepted brief. Any slight deviation from the norm in a city that fed on rumour and paranoia, and it would be him who would end up dangling from a rope, not Saddam's half-brother.

Al Obaydi looked down at the second heading on his notepad.

He buzzed his secretary and asked her to get General Saba'awi Al-Hassan, Head of State Security, on the line. The post was one that had been held by three different people in the last seven months. The General was available immediately, there being more Generals than Ambassadors in the Iraqi regime.

'Ambassador, good morning. I've been meaning to call you. We ought to have a talk before you take up your new appointment in Paris.'

'My thoughts exactly,' said Al Obaydi. 'I have no idea who we still have representing us in Europe. It's been a long time since I served in that part of the world.'

'We're a bit thin on the ground, to be honest. Most of our best people have been expelled, including the so-called students whom we've always been able to rely on in the past. Still, not a subject to be discussed over the phone. When would you like me to come and see you?'

'Are you free between four and five this afternoon?'

There was a pause before the General said, 'I could be with you around four, but would have to be back in my office by five. Do you think that will give us enough time?'

'I feel sure you'll be able to brief me fully in that period, General.' Al Obaydi put the phone down on another routine call.

He stared at the third name on the list, who he feared might prove a little harder to bluff.

He spent the next few minutes rehearsing his questions before dialling an internal number. A Miss Saib answered the phone.

'Is there a particular subject you wish to raise with the Deputy Foreign Minister?' she asked.

'No,' replied Al Obaydi, 'I'm phoning at his specific request. I'm due for a little leave at the end of the week, and the Deputy Foreign Minister made it clear he wished to brief me before I take up my new post in Paris.'

'I'll come back to you with a time as soon as I've had a chance to discuss your request with the Minister,' Miss Saib promised.

Al Obaydi replaced the phone. Nothing to raise any suspicions there. He looked back at his pad and added a question mark and another word to his list.

$$Kalmar \leftarrow ? \rightarrow Geneva$$

Some time in the next forty-eight hours, he was going to have to decide which direction he should take.

The first question Kratz put to Scott on the journey from Kalmar to Stockholm was the significance of the numbers 0-4-0-7-9-3. Scott snapped out of a daydream where he was rescuing Hannah on a white charger, and returned to the real world, which looked a lot less promising.

'The fourth of July,' he responded. 'What better day could Saddam select to humiliate the American people, not to mention a new President.'

'So now at least we know when our deadline is,' said Kratz.

'Yes, and it leaves us with just eleven days,' replied Scott. 'One way or the other.'

'Still, we've got Madame Bertha,' said Kratz, trying to lighten the mood.

'True,' said Scott. 'And where do you intend to take her on her first date?'

'All the way,' said Kratz. 'That is to say, Jordan, which is where I'm expecting you to join up with us again. In fact, my full team is already in Stockholm waiting to pick her up before they begin the journey to Baghdad. All the paperwork has been sorted out for us by Langley, so there should be no hold-ups on the way. Our first problem will be crossing the Jordanian border, but as we have all the requisite documents demanded by the UN, a few extra dollars supplied to the right customs official should ensure that his stamping hand lands firmly on the correct page of all our passports.'

'How much time have you allocated for the journey to

Jordan?' Scott asked, remembering his own tight schedule.

'Six or seven days, eight at the outside. I've got a six-man team, all with considerable field experience. None of them will have to drive for more than four hours at a time without then getting sixteen hours' rest. That way there will be no need to stop at any point, other than to fill up with petrol.' They passed a sign indicating ten kilometres to Stockholm.

'So I've got a week,' said Scott.

'Yes, and we must hope that that's enough time for Bill O'Reilly to complete a perfect new copy of the Declaration,' said Kratz.

'It ought to be a lot easier for him a second time,' said Scott. 'Especially as every one of his requests was dealt with within hours of his asking. They even flew over nine shades of black ink from London on Concorde the next morning.'

'I wish we could put Madame Bertha on Concorde.'

Scott laughed. 'Tell me more about your back-up team.'

'The best I've ever had,' said Kratz. 'All of them have had front-line experience in several official and unofficial wars. Five Israelis and one Kurd.'

Scott raised an eyebrow.

'Few people realise,' continued Kratz, 'that Mossad has an Arab section, not large in numbers, but once we've trained them, only the Gurkhas make better killers. The test will be if you can spot which one he is.'

'How many are coming over the border with us?'

'Only two. We can't afford to make it look like an army. One engineer and a driver. At least, that's how they'll be described on the manifest, but they only have one job description as far as I'm concerned, and that's to get you into Baghdad and back out with the Declaration in the shortest possible time.'

Scott looked straight ahead of him. 'And Hannah?' he said simply.

'That would be a bonus if we got lucky, but it's not part of my brief. I consider the chances of your even seeing her are remote,' he said as they passed a 'Welcome to Stockholm' sign.

Scott began thumping Bertha's bible up and down on his knees. 'Careful with that,' said Kratz. 'It still needs to be translated, otherwise you won't know how to go about a proper introduction to the lady. After all, it will only be your palm and your voice she'll be opening her heart to.'

Scott glanced down at the 108-page book and wondered how long it would take him to master its secrets, even after it had been translated into English.

Kratz suddenly swung right without warning and drove down a deserted street that ran parallel to a disused railway line. All Scott could see ahead of him was a tunnel that looked as if it led nowhere.

When he was a hundred yards from the entrance, Kratz checked in his rear-view mirror to see if anyone was following them. Satisfied they were alone, he flashed his headlights three times. A second later, from what appeared to be the other end of a black hole, he received the same response. He slowed down and drove into the tunnel without his lights on. All Scott could now see was a torch indicating where they should pull up.

Kratz followed the light and came to a halt in front of what appeared to be an old army truck. It was stationed just inside the far end of the tunnel.

He jumped out of the car and Scott quickly followed, trying to accustom himself to the half-light. Then he saw three men standing on each side of the vehicle. The man nearest them came to attention and saluted. 'Good morning, Colonel,' he said.

'Put your men at ease, Feldman, and come and meet Professor Bradley,' said Kratz. Scott almost laughed at the use of his academic title among these men, but there were no smiles on the faces of the six soldiers who came forward to meet him.

After Scott had shaken hands with each of them he took a walk round the truck. 'Do you really believe this old heap is capable of carrying Madame Bertha to Baghdad?' he asked Kratz in disbelief.

'Sergeant Cohen.'

'Sir,' said a voice in the dark.

'You're the trained mechanic. Why don't you brief Professor Bradley?'

'Yes, sir.' Another figure appeared out of the gloom. Scott couldn't see his features clearly, as he was covered in grease, but from his accent he would have guessed he had spent most of his life in London. 'The Heavy Expanded Mobile Tactical Truck, or HEMTT, was built in Wisconsin. She has five gears, four forward, one reverse. She can be used on all terrains in most weather conditions in virtually any country. She weighs twenty tons and can carry up to ten tons, but with that weight on board you cannot risk driving over thirty miles per hour. Any higher than that and she would be impossible to stop, even though if pushed she can top 120 miles per hour.'

'Thank you, Cohen. A useful piece of kit, I think you'll agree,' said Kratz, looking back at Scott. 'We've wanted one of these for years, and then suddenly you arrive on the scene and Uncle Sam offers us the prototype model overnight. But then, at a cost of nearly a million dollars of taxpayers' money, you'd expect the Americans to be choosy about who they loan one out to.'

'Would you care to join us for lunch, Professor?' asked the man who had been introduced as Feldman.

'Don't tell me the HEMTT cooks as well,' said Scott.

'No, sir, we have to rely on the Kurd for that. Aziz's speciality is hamburger and French fries. If you've never had the experience before, it can be quite tasty.'

The eight of them sat cross-legged on the ground, using the reverse side of a backgammon board as a table. Scott couldn't remember enjoying a burnt hamburger more. He was also glad of the chance to chat to the men he would be working with on the operation. Kratz began to talk through the different contingency plans they would have to consider once they had reached the Jordan–Iraq border. It didn't take more than a few minutes for him to realise how professional these men were, or to see their desire to be part of the final team. Scott grew confident that the operation was in good hands, and that Kratz's team had not been chosen at random.

After a third hamburger he was sorry when the Mossad Colonel reminded him he had a flight to catch. He rose and thanked the cook for a memorable meal.

'See you in Jordan, sir,' said Sergeant Cohen.

'See you in Jordan,' said Scott.

As Scott was being driven to the airport, he asked Kratz, 'How are you going to select the final two?'

'They'll decide for themselves. Nothing to do with me, I'm only their commanding officer.'

'What do you mean?'

'They're going to play round-robin backgammon on the way to Jordan. The two winners get a day trip to Baghdad, all expenses paid.'

'And the losers?'

'Get a postcard saying "Wish you were here".'

24

HANNAH GATHERED UP all the files that the Deputy Foreign Minister would require for his meeting with the Revolutionary Command Council.

By working hours that no one else knew existed, and completing tasks the Minister had never thought would get done, Hannah had quickly made herself indispensable. Whenever the Minister needed something, it was there on his desk: she could anticipate his every need, and never sought praise for doing so. But, despite all this, she rarely left the office during the day or the house at night, and certainly seemed to be no nearer to coming into contact with Saddam. The Ambassador's wife tried valiantly to help on the social side, and on one occasion she even invited a young soldier round to dinner. He was good looking, Hannah thought, and seemed to be pleasant enough, although he hardly opened his mouth all evening and left suddenly without a word. Perhaps she was unable to hide the fact that she no longer had any interest in men.

Hannah had sat in on several meetings with individual Ministers, even members of the Command Council, including Saddam's half-brother, the Iraqi Ambassador to the UN in Geneva, but she felt no nearer to Saddam himself than she had been when she lived in a cul-de-sac in Chalk Farm. She was becoming despondent, and began to fear that her frustration might become obvious for all to see. As an antidote she channelled her energies into generating reports on interdepartmental spending, and set up a filing system that would have been the envy of the mandarins in Whitehall. But one of the many things Mossad had taught her during her arduous days of training was always to be patient, and ready, because in time an opening would appear.

It was early on a Thursday morning, when most of the Minister's staff had begun their weekends, that the first opening presented itself. Hannah was typing up her notes from a meeting the Deputy Minister had had the previous day with the newly-appointed Head of Interest Section in Paris, a Mr Al Obaydi, when the call came through. Muhammad Saeed Al-Zahiaf, the Foreign Minister, wished to speak to his deputy.

A few moments later, the Deputy Minister came rushing out of his office, barking at Hannah to follow him. Hannah grabbed a notepad and chased after the Minister down the long passageway.

Although the Foreign Minister's office was only at the other end of the corridor, Hannah had never been inside it before. When she followed her Minister into the room, she was surprised to find how modern and dull it was, with only the panoramic view over the Tigris as compensation.

The Foreign Minister did not bother to rise, but hastily ushered his subordinate into a chair on the opposite side of the desk, explaining that the President had requested a full report on the subject they had discussed at the Revolutionary Council the previous evening. He went on to explain that his own secretary had gone home for the weekend, so Miss Saib should take down a record of their meeting.

Hannah could not believe the discussion that followed. Had she not been aware that she was listening to two Ministers who were loyal members of the Revolutionary Command Council, she would have dismissed their conversation as an outrageous piece of propaganda. The President's half-brother had apparently succeeded in stealing the Declaration of Independence from the National Archives in Washington, and the document was now nailed to a wall of the room in which the Council met.

The discussion concentrated on how the news of this triumph should be released to an astonished world, and the date that had been selected to guarantee the greatest media coverage. Details were also discussed as to which square in the capital the President should deliver his speech from before he publicly burned the document, and whether Peter Arnett or Bernard Shaw of CNN should be granted special access to film the President standing next to the parchment the night before the burning ceremony took place.

After two hours the meeting broke up and Hannah returned with the Deputy Minister to his office. Without so much as a glance in her direction, he ordered her to make a fair copy of the decisions that had been taken that morning.

It took Hannah the rest of the morning to produce a first draft, which the Minister read through immediately. After making a few changes and emendations, he told her to produce a final copy to be delivered to the Foreign Minister with a recommendation that it should, if it met with his approval, be sent on to the President.

As she walked home through the streets of Baghdad that evening, Hannah felt helpless. She wondered what she could possibly do to warn the Americans. Surely they were planning some counter-measures in order to try to recapture the Declaration, or would at least be preparing some form of retaliation once they knew the day that had been selected for the public burning.

Did they even know where it was at that moment? Had Kratz been informed? Had Mossad been called in to advise the Americans on the operation they had themselves been planning for the past year? Were they now trying to get in touch with her? What would Simon have expected her to do?

She stopped at a cigarette kiosk and purchased three postcards of Saddam Hussein addressing the Revolutionary Command Council.

Later, in the safety of her bedroom, she wrote the same

message to Ethel Rubin, David Kratz and the Professor of Arabic Studies at London University. She hoped one of them would work out the significance of the date in the top right-hand corner and the little biro'd square full of stars she had drawn on the wall by the side of Saddam's head.

'What time is the flight for Stockholm expected to depart?' he asked.

'It shouldn't be long now,' said the girl behind the SAS desk at Charles de Gaulle. 'I'm afraid it's only just landed on its inward journey, so it's difficult for me to be more precise.'

Another opportunity to turn back, thought Al Obaydi. But following his meeting with the Head of State Security and, the next morning, with the Deputy Foreign Minister, he felt confident that they had both considered what he had told them no more than routine. Al Obaydi had dropped into the conversation the fact that he was due for some leave before taking up his new appointment in Paris.

After Al Obaydi had collected his luggage from the carousel, he deposited all the large cases in storage, retaining only one bulky briefcase. He then took a seat in the corner of the departure lounge and thought about his actions during the past few days.

The Head of State Security hadn't had a lot to offer. The truth – not that he was going to admit it – was that he had enough problems at home without worrying about what was going on abroad. He had supplied Al Obaydi with an out-of-date instruction book on what precautions any Iraqi citizen should take when in Europe, including not to shop at Marks and Spencers or to mix socially with foreigners, and an out-of-date collection of photographs of known Mossad and CIA agents active on the Continent. After looking through the photographs, Al Obaydi wouldn't have been surprised to find that most of them had long retired, and that some had even died peacefully in their beds.

The following day, the Deputy Foreign Minister had been

courteous without being friendly. He had given him some useful tips about how to conduct himself in Paris, including which embassies would be happy to deal with him despite their official position, and which would not. When it came to the Jordanian Embassy itself and the Iraqi annexe, he gave Al Obaydi a quick briefing on the resident staff. He had left Miss Ahmed there to guarantee some sort of continuity. He described her as willing and conscientious, the cook as awful but friendly, and the driver as stupid but brave. His only guarded warning was to be wary of Abdul Kanuk, the Chief Administrator, a wonderful title which did not describe his true position, his only qualification being that he was a distant cousin of the President. The Deputy Foreign Minister was careful not to voice a personal opinion, but his eyes told Al Obaydi everything he needed to know. As he left, the Minister's secretary, Miss Saib, had presented him with another file. This one turned out to be full of useful information about how to get by in Paris without many friends. Places where he would be made welcome and others he should avoid.

Perhaps Miss Saib should have listed Sweden as somewhere to avoid.

Al Obaydi felt little apprehension about the trip, as he had no intention of remaining in Sweden for more than a few hours. He had already contacted the chief engineer of Svenhalte AC, who assured him he had made no mention of his earlier call to Mr Riffat when he returned that afternoon. He was also able to confirm that Madame Bertha, as he kept calling the safe, was definitely on her way to Baghdad.

'Would passengers travelling to Stockholm...' Al Obaydi made his way through the departure lounge to the exit gate and, after his boarding card had been checked, was shown to a window seat in economy. This section of the journey would not be presented as a claim against expenses.

On the flight across northern Europe, Al Obaydi's mind drifted from his work in Baghdad back to the weekend, which he had spent with his mother and sister. It was they who had helped him make the final decision. His mother had no interest in leaving their comfortable little home on the outskirts of Baghdad, and even less in moving to Paris. So now Al Obaydi accepted that he could never hope to escape: his only future rested in trying to secure a position of power within the Foreign Ministry. He was in no doubt that he could now perform a service for the President that would make him indispensable in Saddam's eyes; it might even present him with the chance of becoming the next Foreign Minister. After all, the Deputy was due for retirement in a couple of years, and sudden promotion never surprised anyone in Baghdad.

When the plane landed at Stockholm, Al Obaydi disembarked, using the diplomatic channel to escape quickly.

The journey to Kalmar by taxi took just over three hours, and the newly-appointed Ambassador spent most of the time gazing aimlessly out of the grubby window, pondering the unfamiliar sight of green hills and grey skies. When the taxi finally came to a halt outside the works entrance of Svenhalte AC, Al Obaydi was greeted by the sight of a man in a long brown coat who looked as if he had been standing there for some time.

Al Obaydi noticed that the man had a worried expression on his face. But it turned to a smile the moment the Ambassador stepped out of the car.

'How agreeable to meet you, Mr Al Obaydi,' said the chief engineer in English, the tongue he felt they would both feel most comfortable in. 'My name is Pedersson. Won't you please come to my office?'

After Pedersson had ordered coffee – how nice to taste cappuccino again, Al Obaydi thought – his first question proved just how anxious he was.

'I hope we did not do wrong?'

'No, no,' said Al Obaydi, who had himself been put at ease by the chief engineer's gushing words and obvious anxiety. 'I assure you this is only a routine check.'

'Mr Riffat was in possession of all the correct documents, both from the UN and from your government.'

Al Obaydi was becoming painfully aware that he was dealing with a group of highly-trained professionals.

'You say they left here on Wednesday afternoon?' Al Obaydi asked, trying to sound casual.

'Yes, that is correct.'

'How long do you imagine it will take them to reach Baghdad?'

'At least a week, perhaps ten days in that old truck, if they make it at all.'

Al Obaydi looked puzzled. 'An old truck?'

'Yes, they came to pick up Madame Bertha in an old army truck. Though, I must confess, the engine had a good sound to it. I took some pictures for my album. Would you like to see them?'

'Pictures of the truck?' said Al Obaydi.

'Yes, from my window, with Mr Riffat standing by the safe. They didn't notice.'

Pedersson opened the drawer of his desk and took out several pictures. He pushed them across his desk with the same pride that another man might have displayed when showing a stranger snapshots of his family.

Al Obaydi studied the photographs carefully. Several of them showed Madame Bertha being lowered onto the truck.

'There is a problem?' asked Pedersson.

'No, no,' said Al Obaydi, and added, 'Would it be possible to have copies of these photographs?'

'Oh yes, please keep them, I have many,' said the chief engineer, pointing to the open drawer.

Al Obaydi picked up his briefcase, opened it and placed the pictures in a flap at the front before removing some photographs of his own.

'While I'm here, perhaps you could help me with one more small matter.'

'Anything,' said Pedersson.

'I have some photographs of former employees of the state, and it would be helpful if you were able to remember if any of them were among those who came to collect Madame Bertha.'

Once again, Pedersson looked unsure, but he took the photographs and studied each one at length. He repeated, 'No, no, no,' several times, until he came to one which he took longer over. Al Obaydi leaned forward.

'Yes,' said Pedersson eventually. 'Although it must have been taken some years ago. This is Mr Riffat. He has not put on any weight, but he has aged and his hair has turned grey. A very thorough man,' Pedersson added.

'Yes,' said Al Obaydi, 'Mr Riffat is a very thorough man,' he repeated as he glanced at the details in Arabic printed on the back of the photograph. 'It will be a great relief for my government to know that Mr Riffat is in charge of this particular operation.'

Pedersson smiled for the first time as Al Obaydi downed the last drop of his coffee. 'You have been most helpful,' the Ambassador said. He rose before adding, 'I feel sure my government will be in need of your services again in the future, but I would be obliged if you made no mention of this meeting to anyone.'

'Just as you wish,' said Pedersson as they walked back down to the yard. The smile remained on his face as he watched the taxi drive out of the factory gate, carrying off his distinguished customer.

But Pedersson's thoughts did not match his expression. 'All is not well,' he muttered to himself. 'I do not believe that gentleman feels Madame Bertha is in safe hands, and I am certain he is no friend of Mr Riffat.'

It surprised Scott to find that he liked Dollar Bill the moment he met him. It didn't surprise him that once he had seen an example of his work, he also respected him.

Scott landed in San Francisco seventeen hours after he had taken off from Stockholm. The CIA had a car waiting for him at the airport. He was driven quickly up into Marin County and deposited outside the safe house within the hour.

After snatching some sleep, Scott rose for lunch, hoping to meet Dollar Bill straight away, but to his disappointment the forger was nowhere to be seen.

'Mr O'Reilly takes breakfast at seven and doesn't appear again before dinner, sir,' explained the butler.

'And what does he do for sustenance in between?' asked Scott.

'At twelve, I take him a bar of chocolate and half a pint of water, and at six, half a pint of Guinness.'

After lunch, Scott read an update on what had been going on at the State Department during his absence, and then spent the rest of the afternoon in the basement gym. He staggered out of the session around five, nursing several aches and pains from excessive exercise and one or two bruises administered by the judo instructor.

'Not bad for thirty-six,' he was told condescendingly by the instructor, who looked as if he might have been only a shade younger himself.

Scott sat in a warm bath trying to ease the pain as he turned the pages of Madame Bertha's bible. The document had already been translated by six Arabic scholars from six universities within fifty miles of where he was soaking. They had been given two non-consecutive chapters each. Dexter Hutchins had not been idle since his return.

When Scott came down for dinner, still feeling a little stiff, he found Dollar Bill standing with his back to the fire in the drawing room, sipping a glass of water.

'What would you like to drink, Professor?' asked the butler.

'A very weak shandy,' Scott replied before introducing himself to Dollar Bill.

'Are you here, Professor, out of choice, or were you simply arrested for drunk driving?' was Dollar Bill's first question. He had obviously decided to give Scott just as hard a time as the judo instructor.

'Choice, I fear,' replied Scott with a smile.

'From such a reply,' said Dollar Bill, 'I can only deduce you teach a dead subject or one that is no use to living mortals.'

'I teach Constitutional Law,' Scott replied, 'but I specialise in Logic.'

'Then you manage to achieve both at once,' said Dollar Bill as Dexter Hutchins entered the room.

'I'd like a gin and tonic, Charles,' said Dexter as he shook Scott's hand warmly. 'I'm sorry I didn't catch up with you earlier, but those guys in Foggy Bottom haven't been off the phone all afternoon.'

'There are many reasons to be wary of your fellow creatures,' Dollar Bill observed, 'and by asking for a gin and tonic, Mr Hutchins has just demonstrated two of them.'

Charles returned a moment later carrying a shandy and a gin and tonic on a silver tray, which he offered to Scott and the Deputy Director.

'In my university days, logic didn't exist,' said Dollar Bill after Dexter Hutchins had suggested they go through to dinner. 'Trinity College, Dublin would have no truck with the subject. I can't think of a single occasion in Irish history when any of my countrymen have ever relied on logic.'

'So what did you study?' asked Scott.

'A lot of Fleming, a little of Joyce, with a few rare moments devoted to Plato and Aristotle, but I fear not enough to engage the attention of any member of the board of examiners.'

'And how is the Declaration coming on?' asked Dexter, as if he hadn't been following the conversation.

'A stickler for the work ethic is our Mr Hutchins, Professor,' said Dollar Bill as a bowl of soup was placed in front of him. 'Mind you, he *is* a man who would rely on logic to see him through. However, as there is no such thing in life as a free meal, I will attempt to answer my jailer's question. Today, I completed the text as originally written by Timothy Matlock, Assistant to the Secretary of Congress. It took him seventeen hours you know. I fear it has taken me rather longer.'

'And how long do you think it will take you to finish the names?' pressed Dexter.

'You are worse than Pope Julius II, forever demanding of Michelangelo how long it would take him to finish the ceiling of the Sistine Chapel,' said Dollar Bill as the butler removed the soup bowls.

'The names,' demanded Dexter. 'The names.'

'Oh, impatient and unsubtle man.'

'Shaw,' said Scott.

'I grow to like you more by the minute,' said Dollar Bill.

'The names,' repeated Dexter as Charles placed an Irish stew on the table. Dollar Bill immediately helped himself.

'Now I see why you are the *Deputy* Director,' said Dollar Bill. 'Do you not realise, man, that there are fifty-six names on the original document, each one of them a work of art in itself? Let me demonstrate to you, if I may. Paper, please, Charles. I require paper.'

The butler took a pad that lay next to the telephone and placed it by O'Reilly's side. Dollar Bill removed a pen from his inside pocket and began to scribble.

He showed his two dinner companions what he had written: 'Mr O'Reilly may have the unrestricted use of the company helicopter whenever he wishes.'

'What does that prove?' asked Dexter.

'Patience, Mr Hutchins, patience,' said Dollar Bill, as he retrieved the piece of paper and signed it first with the signature of Dexter Hutchins, and then, changing his pen, wrote 'Scott Bradley'.

Once again he allowed them to study his efforts.

'But how . . .?' said Scott.

'In your case, Professor, it was easy. All I needed was the visitors' book.'

'But *I* didn't sign the visitors' book,' said Dexter.

'I confess it would be a strange thing for you to do when you are the Deputy Director,' said Dollar Bill, 'but, in your case nothing would surprise me. However, Mr Hutchins, you do have the infuriating habit of signing and dating the inside cover of any book you have purchased recently. I suspect in the case of first editions it will be the nearest you get to posterity.' He paused. 'But enough of this idle banter. You can both see for yourself the task I face.' Without warning, Dollar Bill folded his napkin, rose from the table leaving his half-finished stew, and walked out of the room. His companions jumped up and quickly followed him across to the west wing without another word being spoken. After they had climbed a small flight of stone steps they entered Dollar Bill's makeshift study.

On an architect's drafting board below a bright light rested the parchment. Both men walked across the room, stood over the board and studied the completed script. It had been inscribed above a large empty space covered in tiny pencil crosses that awaited the fifty-six signatures.

Scott stared in admiration at the work.

'But why didn't you . . .'

'Take up a proper occupation?' asked Dollar Bill, anticipating the question. 'And have ended up as a schoolmaster in Wexford, or perhaps have climbed to the dizzy heights of being a councillor in Dublin? No, sir, I would prefer the odd stint in jail rather than be considered by my fellow men as mediocre.'

'How many days before you have to leave us, young man?' Dexter Hutchins asked Scott.

'Kratz phoned this afternoon,' Scott replied, turning to face the Deputy Director. 'He says they caught the Trelleborg–Sassnitz ferry last night. They're now heading south, hoping to cross the Bosphorus by Monday morning.'

'Which means they should be at the border with Iraq by next Wednesday.'

'The perfect time of year to be sailing the Bosphorus,' said Dollar Bill. 'Especially if you hope to meet a rather remarkable girl when you reach the other side,' he added, looking up at Scott. 'So, I'd better have the Declaration finished by Monday, hadn't I, Professor?'

'At the latest,' said Hutchins as Scott stared down at the little Irishman.

25

WHEN AL OBAYDI ARRIVED back in Paris he collected his bags from the twenty-four-hour storage depot, then joined the queue for a taxi.

He gave the driver an address, without saying it was the Iraqi annexe to the Jordanian Embassy – one of the tips in Miss Saib's 'do's and don'ts' in Paris. He hadn't warned the staff at the embassy that he would be arriving that day. He wasn't officially due to take up his appointment for another fortnight, and he would have gone straight on to Jordan that evening if there had been a connecting flight. Once he had realised who Mr Riffat was, he knew he would have to get back to Baghdad as quickly as possible. By reporting direct to the Foreign Minister, he would have gone through the correct channels. This would protect his position, while at the same time guaranteeing that the President knew exactly who was responsible for alerting him to a possible attempt on his life, and which Ambassador, however closely related, had left several stones unturned.

The taxi dropped Al Obaydi outside the annexe to the embassy in Neuilly. He pulled his cases out of the back without any help from the driver, who remained seated obstinately behind the wheel of his car.

The embassy front door opened just an inch, and was then flung wide, and a man of about forty came running down the steps towards him, followed by two girls and a younger man.

'Excellency, Excellency,' the first man exclaimed. 'I am sorry, you must forgive me, we had no idea you were coming.' The younger man grabbed the two large cases and the girls took the remaining three between them.

Al Obaydi was not surprised to learn that the first man down the steps was Abdul Kanuk.

'We were told you would be arriving in two weeks' time, Excellency. We thought you were still in Baghdad. I hope you will not feel we have been discourteous.'

Al Obaydi made no attempt to interrupt the non-stop flow of sycophancy that came pouring out, feeling the man must eventually run out of steam. In any case, Kanuk was not a man to get on the wrong side of on his first day.

'Would Your Excellency like a quick tour of our quarters while the maid unpacks your bags?'

As there were questions Al Obaydi felt only this man could answer, he took advantage of the offer. Not only did he get the guided tour from the Chief Administrator, but he was also subjected to a stream of uninterrupted gossip. He stopped listening after only a few minutes; he had far more important things on his mind. He soon longed to be shown to his own room and left alone to be given a chance to think. The first flight to Jordan was not until the next morning, and he needed to prepare in his mind how he would present his findings to the Foreign Minister.

It was while he was being shown round what would shortly be his office looking out over a Paris that was turning from the half-light of dusk to the artificial light of night, that the Administrator said something Al Obaydi didn't quite catch. He felt he should have been paying closer attention.

'I'm sorry to say that your secretary is on holiday, Excellency. Like the rest of us, Miss Ahmed wasn't expecting you for another fortnight. I know she had planned to be back in Paris a week ahead of you, so that she would have everything ready by the time you arrived.'

'It's not a problem,' said Al Obaydi.

'Of course, you'll know Miss Saib, the Deputy Foreign Minister's secretary?'

'I came across Miss Saib when I was in Baghdad,' replied Al Obaydi.

The Chief Administrator nodded, and seemed to hesitate for a moment.

'I think I'll have a rest before dinner,' the Ambassador said, taking advantage of the temporary halt in an otherwise unending flow.

'I'll have something sent up to your room, Excellency. Would eight suit you?'

'Thank you,' said Al Obaydi, in an attempt to put an end to the conversation.

'Shall I place your passport and tickets in the safe, as I always did for the previous Ambassador?'

'A good idea,' said Al Obaydi, delighted to have at last found a way of getting rid of the Chief Administrator.

Scott put the phone down and turned to face Dexter Hutchins, who was leaning back in the large leather chair at his desk, his hands clasped behind his head and a questioning look on his face.

'So where are they?' asked Dexter.

'Kratz wouldn't give me the exact location, for obvious reasons, but at his current rate of progress he feels confident they'll reach the Jordanian border within the next three days.'

'Then let's pray that the Iraqi Ministry of Industry is as inefficient as our experts keep telling us it is. If so, the advantage should be with us for at least a few more days. After all, we did move the moment sanctions were lifted, and until you showed up in Kalmar, Pedersson hadn't heard a peep out of anyone for the past two years.'

'I agree. But I worry that Pedersson might be the one weak link in Kratz's chain.'

'If you're going to take those sorts of risks, no plan can ever be absolutely watertight,' said Dexter.

Scott nodded.

'And if Kratz is less than three days from the border, you'll have to catch a flight for Amman on Monday night, assuming Mr O'Reilly has finished his signatures by then.'

'I don't think that's a problem any longer,' said Scott.

'Why? He still had a lot of names to copy when I last looked at the parchment.'

'It can't be that many,' said Scott, 'because Mr Mendels-sohn flew in from Washington this morning in order to pass his judgement, and that seems to be the only opinion Bill is interested in.'

'Then let's go and see for ourselves,' said Dexter as he swung himself up out of his chair.

As they left the office and made their way down the corridor, Dexter asked, 'And how's Bertha's bible coming along? I turned a few pages of the introduction this morning and couldn't begin to get a grasp of why the bulbs turn from red to green.'

'Only one man knows Madame Bertha more intimately than I do, and at this moment he's pining away in Scandinavia,' said Scott as they climbed the stone steps to Dollar Bill's private room.

'I also hear that Charles has designed a special pair of trousers for you,' Dexter said.

'And they're a perfect fit,' replied Scott with a smile.

As they reached the top of the steps, Dexter was about to barge in when Scott put an arm on his shoulder.

'Perhaps we should knock? He might be . . .'

'Next you'll be wanting me to call him "sir".'

Scott grinned as Dexter knocked quietly, and when there was no reply, eased the door open. He crept in to see Mendelssohn stooping over the parchment, magnifying glass in hand.

'Benjamin Franklin, John Morton and George Clymer,' muttered the Conservator.

'I had a lot of trouble with Clymer,' said Dollar Bill, who was looking out of the window over the bay. 'It was the damn man's squiggles, which I had to complete in one flow. You'll find a couple of hundred of them in the waste-paper basket.'

'May we approach the bench?' asked Dexter. Dollar Bill turned and waved them in.

'Good afternoon, Mr Mendelssohn. I'm Dexter Hutchins, Deputy Director of the CIA.'

'Could you possibly be anything else?' asked Dollar Bill.

Dexter ignored the comment and asked Mendelssohn, 'What's your judgement, sir?'

Dollar Bill continued to stare out of the window.

'It's every bit as good as the copy we currently have on display at the National Archives.'

'You are most generous, sir,' said Dollar Bill, who turned round to face them.

'But I don't understand why you have spelt the word "British" correctly, and not with two *t*s as it was on the original,' said Mendelssohn, returning his attention to the document.

'There are two reasons for that,' said Dollar Bill as six suspicious eyes stared back at him. 'First, if the exchange is carried out successfully, Saddam will not be able to claim he still has his hands on the original.'

'Clever,' said Scott.

'And second?' asked Dexter, who remained suspicious of the little Irishman's motives.

'It will stop the Professor from bringing back this copy and trying to pass it off as the original.'

Scott laughed. 'You always think like a criminal,' he said.

'And you'd better be thinking like one yourself over the next few days, if you're going to get the better of Saddam Hussein,' said Dollar Bill as Charles entered the room, carrying a pint of Guinness on a silver tray.

Dollar Bill thanked Charles, removed his reward from the tray and walked to the far side of the room before taking the first sip.

'May I ask . . .?' began Scott.

'I once spilt the blessed nectar all over a hundred-dollar etching that I had spent some three months preparing.'

'So what did you do then?' asked Scott.

'I fear that I settled for second best, which caused me to end up in the slammer for another five years.' Even Dexter joined in the laughter. 'However, on this occasion I raise my glass to Matthew Thornton, the final signatory on the document. I wish him good health wherever he is, despite the damn man's *t*s.'

'So, am I able to take the masterpiece away now?' asked Scott.

'Not yet, young man,' said Dollar Bill. 'I fear you must suffer another evening of my company,' he added before placing his drink on the window ledge and returning to the document. 'You see, the one problem I have been fighting is time. In Mr Mendelssohn's judgement, the parchment has an 1830s feel about it. Am I right, sir?'

The Conservator nodded, and raised his arms as if apologising for daring to mention such a slight blemish.

'So what can be done about that?' asked Dexter Hutchins.

Dollar Bill flicked on a switch and the Xenon lamps above his desk shone down on the parchment and filled the room with light, making it appear like a film set.

'By nine o'clock tomorrow morning the parchment will be nearer 1776. Even if, because you have failed to give me enough time, I miss perfection by a few years, I remain confident that there'll be no one in Iraq who'll be able to tell the difference, unless they are in possession of a Carbon 14 dating machine, and know how to use it.'

'Then we can only hope that the original hasn't already been destroyed,' said Dexter Hutchins.

'Not a chance,' said Scott.

'What makes you feel so confident?' asked Dexter.

'The day Saddam destroys that parchment, he will want the whole world to witness it. Of that I'm confident.'

'Then, I'm thinking a toast might be in order,' said the Irishman. 'That is, with my gracious host's permission.'

'A toast, Bill?' said the Deputy Director, sounding surprised. 'Who do you have in mind?' he asked suspiciously.

'To Hannah,' said the little Irishman, 'wherever she may be.'

'How did you know?' asked Scott. 'I've never mentioned her name.'

'No need to, when you write it on everything from the backs of envelopes to steaming windows. She must be a very special lady, Professor.' He raised his glass and repeated the words, 'To Hannah.'

The Chief Administrator sat and waited patiently until the maid had removed the Ambassador's dinner tray. He then closed his door at the other end of the corridor.

He waited for another two hours, until he felt certain all the embassy staff had gone to bed. Confident he would be the only one left awake, he crept back down to his office and looked up a telephone number in Geneva. He dialled the code slowly and deliberately. It rang for a long time before it was eventually answered.

'I need to speak to the Ambassador,' he whispered.

'His Excellency retired to bed some time ago,' said a voice. 'You'll have to call back in the morning.'

'Wake him. Tell him it's Abdul Kanuk in Paris.'

'If you insist.'

'I do insist.'

The Chief Administrator waited for some time before a sleepy voice eventually came on the line.

'This had better be good, Abdul.'

'Al Obaydi has arrived in Paris unannounced, and two weeks before he was expected.'

'You woke me in the middle of the night to tell me this?'

'But he didn't come direct from Baghdad, Excellency. He made a slight detour.'

'How can you be so sure?' said the voice, sounding a little more awake.

'Because I am in possession of his passport.'

'But he's on holiday, you fool.'

'I know. But why spend the day in a city not known for attracting tourists?'

'You're talking in riddles. If you've got something to tell me, tell me.'

'Earlier today, Ambassador Al Obaydi paid a visit to Stockholm, according to the stamp on his passport, but he returned to Paris the same evening. Not my idea of a holiday.'

'Stockholm . . . Stockholm . . . Stockholm . . .' repeated the voice on the other end of the line, as if trying to register its significance. A pause, and then, 'The safe. Of course. He must have gone on to Kalmar to check on Sayedi's safe. What has he found out that he thought worth hiding from me, and does Baghdad know what he's up to?'

'I have no idea, Excellency,' said the Administrator. 'But I do know he's flying back to Baghdad tomorrow.'

'But if he's on holiday, why would he return to Baghdad so quickly?'

'Perhaps being the Head of Interest Section in Paris is not reward enough for him, Excellency. Could he have his eyes on some greater prize?'

There was a long pause before the voice in Geneva said, 'You did well, Abdul. You were right to wake me. I shall have to phone Kalmar first thing in the morning. First thing,' he repeated.

'You did promise, Excellency, should I once again manage to bring to your attention . . .'

Tony Cavalli briefed his father once Martin had poured them both a drink.

'Arrested in a bar-room brawl,' said his father after he had listened to his son's report.

'Yes,' said Cavalli, placing a file on the table by his side, 'and what's more, he was sentenced to thirty days.'

'Thirty days?' said his father in disbelief. The old man paused before he added, 'What instructions have you given Laura?'

281

'I've put her on hold until July 15th, when Dollar Bill will be released,' Tony replied.

'So where have they locked him up this time? The county jail?'

'No. According to the records at the district court in Fairmont, they've thrown him back into the state pen.'

'For being involved in a bar-room brawl,' said the older man. 'It doesn't make sense.' He stared up at the Declaration of Independence on the wall behind his desk and didn't speak again for some moments.

'Who have we got on the inside?'

Cavalli opened the file on the table by his side and extracted a single sheet of paper. 'One senior officer and six inmates,' he said, passing his research across, pleased to have anticipated his father's question.

The old man studied the list of names for some time before he began licking his lips. 'Eduardo Bellatti must be our best bet,' he said, looking up at his son. 'If I remember correctly, he was sentenced to ninety-nine years for blowing away a judge who once got in our way.'

'Correct, and what's more, he's always been happy to kill anyone for a packet of cigarettes,' said Tony. 'So, if he takes care of Dollar Bill before July 15th, it would also save us a quarter of a million dollars.'

'Something isn't quite right,' said his father as he toyed with a whisky, which he hadn't touched. 'Perhaps it's time to dig a little deeper,' he added, almost as if he was talking to himself. He checked down the list of names once again.

Al Obaydi woke early the following morning, restless to be on his way to Baghdad so that he could brief the Foreign Minister on everything he'd learned. Once he was back on Iraqi soil he would prepare a full, written report. He went over the outline again and again in his mind.

He would first explain to the Foreign Minister that, while he was carrying out a routine sanctions check, he had learned that the safe that had been ordered by the President was already on its way to Baghdad. On discovering this, he had become suspicious that an enemy of the state might be involved in an assassination attempt on the life of the President. Not being certain who could be trusted, he had used his initiative, and even his own time and money, to discover who was behind the plot. Within moments of his reporting the details to the Foreign Minister, Saddam was certain to find out whose responsibility the safe was and, more important, who had failed to take care of the President's well-being.

A tap on the door interrupted his thoughts. 'Come in,' he called, and a maid entered carrying a breakfast tray of two pieces of burnt toast and a cup of thick Turkish coffee. Once she had closed the door behind her, Al Obaydi rose, had a cold shower – not by choice – and dressed quickly. He then poured the coffee down the washbasin and ignored the toast.

The Ambassador left his room and walked down one flight of stairs to his office, where he found the Chief Administrator standing behind his desk. Had he been sitting in his chair a moment before?

'Good morning, Excellency,' he said. 'I hope you had a comfortable night. I was just confirming your flight reservation.'

'How thoughtful of you,' said Al Obaydi, barely concealing his irritation.

Kanuk bowed low. 'I will see that you are met at the airport when you return, Excellency, and that this time everything is fully prepared for your arrival. Meanwhile, I'll go and fetch your passport. If you'll excuse me.'

Al Obaydi sat down behind his desk. He wondered how long he would be merely Head of Interest Section in Paris once Saddam learned who had saved his life.

Tony dialled the number on his private line.

The phone was picked up by the Deputy Warden, who

confirmed in answer to Cavalli's first question that he *was* alone. He listened to Cavalli's second question carefully before he replied.

'If Dollar Bill's anywhere to be found in this jailhouse, then he's better hidden than Leona Helmsley's tax returns.'

'But the county court files show him as being registered with you on the night of June 16th.'

'He may have been registered with us, but he sure never showed up,' said the voice on the other end of the line. 'And it doesn't take eight days to get from San Francisco County Court to here, unless they've gone back to chaining cons up and making them walk the whole way. Perhaps that wouldn't be such a bad idea,' he added with a nervous laugh.

Cavalli didn't laugh. 'Just be sure you keep your mouth shut and your ears open, and let me know the moment you hear anything,' was all he said before putting the phone back down.

Cavalli remained at his desk for an hour after his secretary had left, working out what needed to be done next.

26

THE SECOND EMERGENCY meeting between the Foreign Minister and his deputy took place on the Tuesday morning, again at short notice. This time it was an unexpected direct call from the President that had both Ministers rushing off to the palace.

All Hannah had been able to piece together from the several phone calls that had gone back and forth that morning was that at some point Saddam's half-brother had called from Geneva, and from that moment the Deputy Foreign Minister appeared to be in a state of panic.

Hannah remained at her desk in the hope that she might pick up some more information as the day progressed. While both Ministers were at the palace, she continued to check through old files, aware that she now had enough material to fill several cabinets at Mossad headquarters, but no one to pass her findings on to.

The two Ministers returned from the palace in the late afternoon, and the Deputy Foreign Minister seemed relieved to find Miss Saib was still at her desk.

'I need to make a written report on what was agreed at the meeting this morning with the President,' he said, 'and I cannot overstress the importance of confidentiality in this matter. It would not be an exaggeration to suggest that if anything I am about to tell you became public knowledge, we could both end up in jail, or worse.'

'I hope, Minister,' said Hannah as she put her glasses back on, 'that I have never given you cause for concern in the past.'

The Minister stared across at her, and then began dictating at a rapid pace.

'The President invited the Foreign Minister and myself to a confidential meeting at the palace this morning – date this memo today. Barazan Al-Tikriti, our trusted Ambassador in Geneva, contacted the President during the night to warn him that, after weeks of diligent surveillance, he has uncovered a plot by a group of Zionists to steal a safe from Sweden and use it as a means of illegally entering Iraq. The safe was due for delivery to Baghdad following the lifting of an embargo under UN Security Council Resolution 661. The President has ordered that General Hamil be given the responsibility for dealing with the terrorists' – Hannah thought she saw the Deputy Foreign Minister shudder – 'while the Foreign Ministry has been asked to look into the role played in this particular conspiracy by one of its own staff, Hamid Al Obaydi.

'Our Ambassador in Geneva has also discovered that Al Obaydi visited the engineering firm of Svenhalte AC in Kalmar, Sweden, on Monday June 28th, without being directed to do so by any of his superiors. During that visit he was informed of the theft of the safe and the fact that it was being transported to Baghdad. Following his trip to Kalmar, Al Obaydi stayed overnight at our Interest Section in Paris, when he would have had every opportunity to inform Geneva or Baghdad of the Zionist plot, but he made no attempt to do so.

'Al Obaydi left Paris the following morning and, although we know he boarded a flight to Jordan, he has not yet shown up at the border. The President has ordered that if Al Obaydi crosses any of our national frontiers, he should be arrested and taken directly to General Hamil at the headquarters of the Revolutionary Command Council.'

Hannah's pencil flew across the pages of her shorthand notebook as she tried to keep up with the Minister.

'The safe,' continued the Deputy Foreign Minister, 'is

currently being transported aboard an old army truck, and is expected to arrive at the border with Jordan some time during the next forty-eight hours.

'All customs officers have received a directive to the effect that the safe is the personal property of the President, and therefore when it reaches the border it must be given priority to continue its journey on to Baghdad.

'Our Ambassador in Geneva, having had a long conversation with a Mr –' the Minister checked his notes '– Pedersson, is convinced that the group accompanying the safe are agents of the CIA, Mossad, or possibly even the British SAS. Like the President, the Ambassador feels the infiltrators' sole interest is in recovering the Declaration of Independence. The President has given orders that the document should not be moved from its place on the wall of the Council Chamber, as this could alert any internal agent to warn the terrorist group not to enter the country.

'Twenty of the President's special guards are already on their way to the border with Jordan,' continued the Minister. 'They will be responsible for monitoring the progress of the safe, and will report directly to General Hamil.

'Once the agents of the West have been apprehended and thrown in jail, the world's press will be informed that their purpose was to assassinate the President. The President will immediately appear in public and on television, and will make a speech denouncing the American and Zionist warmongers. Sayedi believes that neither the Americans nor the Israelis will ever admit to the real purpose of their raid, but that they will be unable to deny the President's claim. Sayedi feels this whole episode can be turned into a public relations triumph, because if the assassination attempt is announced on the same day that the President publicly burns the Declaration of Independence, it will make it even harder for the Americans to retaliate.

'Starting tomorrow, the President requires a situation update every morning at nine and every evening at six. Both the Foreign Minister and myself are to report to him direct. If Al

Obaydi is picked up, the President is to be informed, whatever the time, night or day.'

Hannah's pencil hadn't stopped scribbling across her note pad for nearly twenty minutes. When the Deputy Minister finally came to an end, she tried to take in the full significance of the information she now possessed.

'I need one copy of this report drafted as quickly as possible, no further copies to be made, nothing put on tape, and all your shorthand notes must be shredded once the memo has been handed to me.' Hannah nodded as the Deputy Foreign Minister picked up the phone and dialled the internal number of his superior.

Hannah returned to her room and began typing up the dictation slowly, at the same time trying to commit the salient points to memory. Forty-five minutes later she placed a single copy of the report on the Minister's desk.

He read the script carefully, adding the occasional note in his own hand. When he was satisfied that the memo fully covered the meeting that had taken place that morning, he set off down the corridor to rejoin the Foreign Minister.

Hannah returned to her desk, aware that the team bringing the safe from Sweden were moving inexorably towards Saddam's trap. And if they had received her postcard . . .

When Al Obaydi landed in Jordan, he could not help feeling a sense of triumph.

Once he had passed through customs at Queen Alia airport and was out on the road, he selected the most modern taxi he could find. The old seventies Chevy had no air conditioning and showed 187,000 miles on the clock. He asked the driver to take him to the Iraqi border as quickly as possible.

The car never left the slow lane on its six-hour journey to the border, and because of the state of the roads Al Obaydi was unable to sleep for more than a few minutes at a time. When the driver eventually reached the highway, he still couldn't go much faster because of the oil that had been spilt from lorries carrying loads they had illegally picked up in Basra, to sell at four times the price in Amman. Loads that Al Obaydi had assured the United Nations Assembly time and again were a figment of the Western world's imagination. He also became aware of trucks travelling in the opposite direction that were full of food that he knew would be sold to black-marketeers, long before any of it reached Baghdad.

Al Obaydi checked his watch. If the driver kept going at this speed he wouldn't reach the border before the customs post closed at midnight.

When Scott landed at Queen Alia airport later that day and stepped on to the tarmac, the first thing that hit him was a temperature of ninety-five degrees. Even dressed in an open-neck shirt, jeans and sneakers, he felt roasted before he had reached the airport terminal. Once he'd stepped into the build-ing, he was relieved to find it was air conditioned, and his one bag came up on the carousel just as quickly as it would have done in the States. He checked his watch and changed it to Central Eastern time.

The immigration officer hadn't seen many Swedish passports before, but as his father had been an engineer, he wished Mr Bernstrom a successful trip.

As Scott strolled through the green channel, he was stopped by a customs official who was chewing something. He in-structed the foreigner to open his bulky canvas bag. After rummaging around inside, the only thing the officer showed any interest in was a long, thin cardboard tube that had been wedged along the bottom of the bag. Scott removed the cap on the end of the tube, pulled out the contents and unrolled a large poster, which was greeted by the official with such puzzled amazement that he even stopped chewing for a moment. He waved Scott through.

Once Scott had reached the main concourse, he walked

out onto the road in search of a taxi. He studied the motley selection of cars that were parked bumper to bumper by the side of the pavement. They made New York Yellow Cabs look like luxury limousines.

He instructed the driver parked at the front of the queue to take him to the Roman theatre in the centre of the city. The eleven-mile journey into Amman took forty minutes, and when Scott was dropped outside the third-century theatre he handed the driver two ten-dinar notes – enough, the experts at Langley had told him, to cover the cost of the trip. The driver pocketed the notes but did not smile.

Scott checked his watch. He was still well in time for the planned reunion. He walked straight past the ancient monument that was, according to his guidebook, well worth a visit. As instructed by Kratz, he then proceeded west for three blocks, occasionally having to step off the pavement into the road to avoid the bustling crowds. When he reached a Shell petrol station he turned right, leaving the noisy shoppers behind. He then took the second turning on the left, and after that another to the right. The roads became less crowded with locals and more full of potholes with each stride he took. Another left, followed by another right, and he found himself entering the promised cul-de-sac. At the end of the road, when he could go no further, he came to a halt outside a scrapyard. He smiled at the sight that greeted him.

By the time Al Obaydi reached the border, it was already pitch dark. All three lanes leading to the customs post were bumper to bumper with waiting lorries, covered with tarpaulins for the night. The taxi driver came to a halt at the barrier and explained to his passenger that he would have to hire an Iraqi cab once he was on the other side. Al Obaydi thanked the driver and gave him a handsome tip before going to the front of the queue outside the customs shed. A tired official gave him a languid look and told him the border was closed for the night. Al

Obaydi presented his diplomatic passport and the official quickly stamped his visa and ushered him through, aware that there would be no little red notes accompanying such a document. Al Obaydi felt exhilarated as he strolled the mile between the two customs posts. He walked to the front of another queue, produced his passport once again, and received another smile from the customs officer.

'There is a car waiting for you, Ambassador,' was all the official said, pointing to a large limousine that was parked near the highway. A smiling chauffeur stood waiting. He opened the back door and touched the peak of his cap.

Al Obaydi smiled. The Chief Administrator must have warned them that he would be coming over the border late that night. He thanked the customs official, walked over to the highway and slipped into the back of the limousine. Someone else was already there, who also appeared to be waiting for him. Al Obaydi began to smile again, when suddenly an arm shot across his throat and threw him to the floor. His hands were pinned behind his back, and a pair of handcuffs clicked into place.

'How dare you?' shouted Al Obaydi. 'I am an Ambassador!' he screamed as he was hurled back up onto the seat. 'Don't you realise who I am?'

'Yes, I do,' came back the reply. 'And you're under arrest for treason.'

Scott had to admit that the HEMTT carrying Madame Bertha looked quite at home among the colourful collection of old American cars and lorries piled high on three sides of the scrapyard. He ran across to the truck and jumped up into the cab on the passenger side. He shook hands with Kratz, who seemed relieved to see him. When Scott saw who was seated behind the wheel, he said, 'Good to see you again, Sergeant Cohen. Am I to assume you play a mean game of backgammon?'

'Two doubles inside the board clinched it for me in the final game, Professor, though God knows how the Kurd even reached the semi-final,' Cohen said as he switched on the engine. 'And because he's a mate of mine, the others are all claiming I fixed the dice.'

'So where's Aziz now?' asked Scott.

'On the back with Madame Bertha,' said the Sergeant. 'Best place for him. Mind you, he knows the back streets of Baghdad like I know the pubs in Brixton, so he may turn out to be useful.'

'And the rest of the team?' asked Scott.

'Feldman and the others slipped over the border during the night,' said Kratz. 'They're probably in Baghdad waiting for us by now.'

Sergeant Cohen eased the massive vehicle slowly out of the yard and onto the street; this time the roads became wider with each turning he took.

'Are we keeping to the plan that was agreed in Stockholm?' asked Scott.

'With two refinements,' said Kratz. 'I spent yesterday morning phoning Baghdad. After seven attempts, I got through to someone at the Ministry of Industry who knew about the safe, but it's the age-old problem with the Arabs: if they don't see the damn thing in front of their eyes, they don't believe it exists.'

'So our first stop will have to be the Ministry?' said Scott.

'Looks like it,' replied Kratz. 'But at least we know we've got something they want. Which reminds me, have you brought the one thing they don't want?'

Scott unzipped his bag and pulled out the cardboard tube.

'Doesn't look a lot to be risking your life for,' said Kratz as Scott slipped it back into his bag.

'And the second refinement?' asked Scott.

Kratz removed a postcard from his inside pocket and passed it over to Scott. A picture of Saddam Hussein addressing the Revolutionary Command Council stared back at him. A little biro'd square full of stars had been drawn in by the side of his head. Scott turned the card over and studied her unmistakable handwriting: 'Wish you were here.'

292

Scott didn't speak for several moments.

'Notice the date, did you?'

Scott looked at the top right-hand corner: 4.7.93.

'So, now we know where it is, and she's also confirmed exactly when Saddam intends to let the rest of the world into his secret.'

'Who's Ethel Rubin?' asked Scott. 'And how did you get your hands on the card?'

'The lady Hannah was billeted with in London. Her husband is Mossad's legal representative in England. He took the card straight to the embassy the moment it arrived and they sent it overnight in the diplomatic pouch. It reached our embassy in Amman this morning.'

Once they had reached the outskirts of the town, Scott began to study the barren terrain as the lorry continued its progress along the oil-covered, potholed roads.

'Sorry to be going so slowly, Professor,' said Cohen, 'but if I throw my brakes on with the road in this condition, Madame Bertha might travel another hundred yards before the wheels even have a chance to lock.'

Kratz went over every contingency he could think of as Cohen drove silently towards the border. The Mossad leader ended up by describing the layout of the Ba'ath headquarters once again.

'And the alarm system?' asked Scott when he had come to an end.

'All you have to remember is that the red buttons by the light switches activate the alarm, but at the same time close all the exits.'

Scott nodded, but it was some time before he asked his next question. 'And Hannah?'

'Nothing's changed. My first task is to get you in and then back out with the original document. She still remains an unlikely bonus, although she obviously knows what's going on.'

Neither of them spoke again until Sergeant Cohen pulled off the highway into a large gravel layby packed with lorries. He parked the vehicle at an angle so that only the most inquisitive could observe what they were up to, then jumped out of the cab, pulled himself over the tailboard and grinned at the Kurd who was lounging against the safe. Between them they removed the tarpaulin that covered the massive structure as Scott and Kratz climbed up to join them in the back of the truck.

'What do you think, Professor?' asked Aziz.

'She hasn't lost any weight, that's for sure,' said Scott, as he tried to remember the nightly homework he had done in preparation for this single exam.

He stretched his fingers and smiled. All three bulbs above the white square were red. He first turned all three dials to a code that only he and a man in Sweden were aware of. He then placed his right hand on the white square, and left it there for several seconds. He leaned forward, put his lips up against the square and spoke softly. 'My name is Andreas Bernstrom. When you hear this voice, and only this voice, you will unlock the door.' Scott waited as the other three looked on in bemused silence. He then swivelled the dials. All three bulbs remained red.

'Now we discover if I understood the instructions,' said Scott. He bit his lip and advanced again. Once more he twiddled the dials, but this time to the numbers selected by Saddam, ending with 0-4-0-7-9-3. The first light went from red to green. Aziz smiled. Scott placed the palm of his hand in the white square and left it there for several seconds. The second light switched to green.

Scott heard Kratz sigh audibly as he stepped forward again. He put his lips to the white square so they just touched the thin wire mesh. 'My name is Andreas Bernstrom. It's now time for the safe to –' The third light turned green even before he had completed the sentence. Cohen offered up a suppressed cheer.

Scott grasped the handle and pulled. The ton of steel eased open.

'Not bad,' said Cohen. 'What do you do for an encore?'

'Use you as a guinea-pig,' said Scott. 'Why don't you try and close the safe, Sergeant?'

Cohen took a step forward and with both hands shoved the door closed. The three bulbs immediately began flashing red.

'Easy, once you get the hang of it,' he said.

Scott smiled and pulled the door back open with his little finger. Cohen stared open-mouthed as the lights returned to green.

'The lights might flash red,' said Scott, 'but Bertha can only handle one man at a time. No one else can open or close the safe now except me.'

'And I was hoping it was because he was a Jew,' said Aziz.

Scott smiled as he pushed the door of the safe closed, swivelled the dials and waited until all three bulbs turned red.

'Let's go,' said Kratz, who Scott felt sounded a little irritated – or was it just the first sign of tension? Aziz threw the tarpaulin back over Madame Bertha while his colleagues jumped over the side and returned to the cab.

No one spoke as they continued their journey to the border until Cohen let out a string of expletives when he spotted the queue of lorries ahead of them. 'We're going to be here all night,' he said.

'And most of tomorrow morning, I expect,' said Kratz. 'So we'd better get used to it.' They came to a halt behind the last lorry in the queue.

'Why don't I just drive on up front and try to bluff my way through?' said Cohen. 'A few extra dollars ought to . . .'

'No,' said Kratz. 'We don't want to attract undue attention at any time between now and when we cross back over that border.'

During the next hour, while the truck moved forward only a couple of hundred yards, Kratz went over his plans yet again, covering any situation he thought might arise once they reached Baghdad.

Another hour passed, and Scott was thankful for the evening breeze that helped him doze off, although he realised that he would soon have to wind the window up if he wished to avoid freezing. He began to drift into a light sleep, his mind switching between Hannah and the Declaration, and which, given the choice, he would rather bring home. He realised that Kratz was in no doubt why he had volunteered to join the team when the chances of survival were so slim.

'What's this joker up to then?' said Cohen in a stage whisper. Scott snapped awake and quickly focused on a uniformed official talking to the driver of the lorry in front of them.

'It's a customs official,' said Kratz. 'He's only checking to see that drivers have the right papers to cross the border.'

'Most of this lot will only have two little bits of red paper about five inches by three,' said Cohen.

'Here he comes,' said Kratz. 'Try and look as bored as he does.'

The officer strolled up to the cab and didn't even give Cohen a first look as he thrust a hand through the open window.

Cohen passed over the papers that the experts at Langley had provided. The official studied them and then walked slowly round the lorry. When he returned to the driver's side, he barked an order at Cohen that none of them understood.

Cohen looked towards Kratz, but a voice from behind rescued them.

'He says we're to go to the front of the queue.'

'Why?' asked Kratz suspiciously. Aziz repeated the question to the official.

'We're being given priority because of the letter signed by Saddam.'

'And who do we thank for that?' asked Kratz, still not fully convinced.

'Bill O'Reilly,' said Scott, 'who was only too sorry he couldn't join us on the trip. But he's been given to understand that it's quite impossible to get draught Guinness anywhere in Iraq.'

Kratz nodded, and Sergeant Cohen obeyed the official's instructions, allowing himself to be directed into the lane of oncoming traffic as he began an unsteady two-mile journey to the front of the queue. Vehicles legally progressing towards

Amman on the other side of the road found they had to swerve onto the loose rubble of the hard shoulder if they didn't want a head-on collision with Madame Bertha.

As Cohen completed the last few yards to the border post, an angry official came running out of the customs shed waving a fist. Once again it was Aziz who came to their rescue, by recommending that Kratz show him the letter.

After one look at the signature, the fist was quickly exchanged for a salute.

'Passport,' was the only other word he uttered.

Kratz passed over three Swedish and one Iraqi passport with two red notes attached to the first page of each document. 'Never pay above the expected tariff,' he had warned his team. 'It only makes them suspicious.'

The four passports were taken to a little cubicle, studied, stamped and returned by the official, who even offered them the suggestion of a smile. The barrier on the Jordanian side was raised, and the lorry began its mile-long journey towards the Iraqi checkpoint.

27

HAMID AL OBAYDI was dragged into the Council Chamber by two of the Presidential Guards and then dumped in a chair several yards away from the long table.

He raised his head and looked around at the twelve men who made up the Revolutionary Command Council. None of their eyes came into contact with his, with the exception of the State Prosecutor.

What had he done that these people had decided to arrest him at the border, handcuff him, throw him in jail, leave him to sleep on the stone floor and not even offer him the chance to use a lavatory?

Still dressed in the suit he had crossed the border in, he was now sitting in his own excrement.

Saddam raised a hand, and the State Prosecutor smiled.

But Al Obaydi did not fear Nakir Farrar. Not only was he innocent of any trumped-up charge, but he also had information they needed. The State Prosecutor rose slowly from his place.

'Your name is Hamid Al Obaydi?'

'Yes,' replied Al Obaydi, looking directly at the State Prosecutor.

'You are charged with treason and the theft of state property. How do you plead?'

'I am innocent, and Allah will be my witness.'

'If Allah is to be your witness, I'm sure he won't mind me asking you some simple questions.'

'I will be most happy to answer anything.'

'When you returned from New York earlier this month, you carried on with your work in the Foreign Ministry. Is that correct?'

'It is.'

'And was one of your responsibilities checking the government's latest position with reference to UN sanctions?'

'Yes. That was part of my job as Deputy Ambassador to the UN.'

'Quite so. And when you carried out these checks, you came across certain items on which embargoes had been lifted. Am I right?'

'Yes, you are,' said Al Obaydi confidently.

'Was one of those items a safe?'

'It was,' said Al Obaydi.

'When you realised this, what did you do about it?'

'I telephoned the Swedish company who had built the safe to ascertain what the latest position was, so that I could enter the facts in my report.'

'And what did you discover?'

Al Obaydi hesitated, not sure how much the Prosecutor knew.

'What did you discover?' insisted Farrar.

'That the safe had been collected that day by a Mr Riffat.'

'Did you know this Mr Riffat?'

'No, I did not.'

'So what did you do next?'

'I rang the Ministry of Industry, as I was under the impression that they were responsible for the safe.'

'And what did they tell you?'

'That the responsibility had been taken out of their hands.'

'Did they also tell you into whose hands the responsibility had been entrusted?' asked the Prosecutor.

'I don't remember exactly.'

'Well, let me try and refresh your memory – or shall I call the Permanent Secretary to whom you spoke on the phone that morning?'

'I think he may have said that it was no longer in their hands,' said Al Obaydi.

'Did he tell you whose hands it was in?' repeated the Prosecutor.

'I think he said something about the file being sent to Geneva.'

'It may interest you to know that the official has submitted written evidence to confirm just that.'

Al Obaydi lowered his head.

'So, once you knew that the file had been passed on to Geneva, what did you do next?'

'I phoned Geneva and was told the Ambassador was not available. I left a message to say that I had called,' said Al Obaydi confidently, 'and asked if he would call back.'

'Did you really expect him to call back?'

'I assumed he would.'

'You assumed he would. So what did you write in your report, in the sanctions file?'

'The file?' asked Al Obaydi.

'Yes. You were making a report for your successor. What information did you pass on to him?'

'I don't remember,' said Al Obaydi.

'Then allow me to remind you once again,' said the Prosecutor, lifting a slim brown file from the table. ' "The Ministry of Industry have sent the file concerning this item direct to Geneva. I phoned our Ambassador there, but was unable to make contact with him. Therefore, I cannot make any progress from this end until he returns my call. Hamid Al Obaydi." ' Did you write that?'

'I can't remember.'

'You can't remember what the Permanent Secretary said to you; you can't remember what you wrote in your own report when property of the state might have been stolen, or worse . . . But I shall come to that later. Perhaps you would like to check your own handwriting?' said the Prosecutor as he walked from the table and thrust the relevant sheet in front of Al Obaydi's face. 'Is that your writing?'

'Yes, it is. But I can explain.'

'And is that your signature at the bottom of the page?'

Al Obaydi leaned forward, studied the signature and nodded.

'Yes or no?' barked the Prosecutor.

'Yes,' said Al Obaydi quietly.

'Did you, that same afternoon, visit General Al-Hassan, the Head of State Security?'

'No. He visited me.'

'Ah, I have made a mistake. It was he who visited you.'

'Yes,' said Al Obaydi.

'Did you alert him to the fact that an enemy agent might be heading towards Iraq, having found a way of crossing the border with the intention of perhaps assassinating our leader?'

'I couldn't have known that.'

'But you must have suspected something unusual was going on?'

'I wasn't certain at that time.'

'Did you let General Al-Hassan know of your uncertainty?'

'No. I did not.'

'Was it because you didn't trust him?'

'I didn't know him. It was the first time we had met. The previous . . .' Al Obaydi regretted the words the moment he had said them.

'You were about to say?' said the Prosecutor.

'Nothing.'

'I see. So, let us move on to the following day, when you paid a visit – because I feel confident that he didn't visit you – to the Deputy Foreign Minister.' This induced some smiles around the table, but Al Obaydi did not see them.

'Yes, a routine call to discuss my appointment to Paris. He was, after all, the former Ambassador.'

'Quite. But is he not also your immediate superior?'

'Yes, he is,' said Al Obaydi.

'So, did you tell *him* of your suspicions?'

'I wasn't sure there was anything to tell him.'

'Did you tell him of your suspicions?' asked the Prosecutor, raising his voice.

'No, I did not.'

'Was he not to be trusted either? Or didn't you know him well enough?'

'I wasn't sure. I wanted more proof.'

'I see. You wanted more proof. So what did you do next?'

'I travelled to Paris,' said Al Obaydi.

'On the next day?' asked the State Prosecutor.

'No,' said Al Obaydi, hesitating.

'On the day after, perhaps? Or the day after that?'

'Perhaps.'

'Meanwhile, the safe was on its way to Baghdad. Is that right?'

'Yes, but –'

'And you *still* hadn't informed anyone? Is that also correct?'

Al Obaydi didn't reply.

'Is that also correct?' shouted Farrar.

'Yes, but there was still enough time –'

'Enough time for what?' asked the State Prosecutor.

Al Obaydi's head sank again.

'For you to reach the safety of our embassy in Paris?'

'No,' said Al Obaydi. 'I travelled on to –'

'Yes?' said Farrar. 'You travelled on to where?'

Al Obaydi realised he had fallen into the trap.

'To Sweden, perhaps?'

'Yes,' said Al Obaydi. 'But only because –'

'You wanted to check the safe was well on its way? Or was it, as you told the Foreign Minister, that you were simply going on holiday?'

'No, but . . .'

' "Yes but, no but." Were you on holiday in Sweden? Or were you representing the state?'

'I was representing the state.'

'Then why did you travel economy, and not charge the state for the expense that was incurred?'

Al Obaydi made no reply.

The Prosecutor leaned forward. 'Was it because you didn't want anyone to know you were in Sweden, when your superiors thought you were in Paris?'

'Yes, but in time . . .'

'After it was too late, perhaps. Is that what you're trying to tell us?'

'No. I did not say that.'

'Then why did you not pick up a phone and ring our Ambassador in Geneva? He could have saved you all the expense and the trouble. Was it because you didn't trust him either? Or perhaps he didn't trust you?'

'Neither!' shouted Al Obaydi, leaping to his feet, but the guards grabbed him by the shoulders and threw him back onto the chair.

'Now that you've got that little outburst out of the way,' said the Prosecutor calmly, 'perhaps we can continue. You travelled to Sweden, to Kalmar to be exact, to keep an appointment with a Mr Pedersson, whom you did seem willing to phone.' The Prosecutor checked his notes again. 'And what was the purpose of this visit, now that you have confirmed it was not a holiday?'

'To try and find out who it was who had stolen the safe.'

'Or was it to make sure the safe was on the route you had already planned for it?'

'Certainly not,' said Al Obaydi, his voice rising. 'It was I who discovered that Riffat was the Mossad agent Kratz.'

'You *knew* that Riffat was a Mossad agent?' queried the Prosecutor in mock disbelief.

'Yes, I found out when I was in Kalmar,' said Al Obaydi.

'But you told Mr Pedersson that Mr Riffat was a thorough man, a man who could be trusted. Am I right? So now at last we've found someone you can trust.'

'It was quite simply that I didn't want Pedersson to know what I'd discovered.'

'I don't think you wanted *anyone* to know what you had discovered, as I shall go on to show. What did you do next?'

'I flew back to Paris.'

'And did you spend the night at the embassy?'

'Yes, I did, but I was only stopping overnight on my way to Jordan.'

'I'll come to your trip to Jordan in a moment, if I may. But what I should like to know now is why, when you were back at our embassy in Paris, you didn't immediately call our Ambassador in Geneva to inform him of what you had discovered? Not only was the Ambassador in residence, but he took a call from another member of the embassy staff after you had gone to bed.'

Al Obaydi suddenly realised how Farrar knew everything. He tried to collect his thoughts.

'My only interest was getting back to Baghdad to let the Foreign Minister know the danger our leader might be facing.'

'So, you rushed home to warn the Foreign Minister. Stopping off in Paris for the night, but not bothering to phone anyone in either Baghdad or Geneva.'

'No, I wanted to present a complete report.'

'And where is that complete report?'

'I intended to write it on the journey from Jordan to Baghdad.'

'How convenient. And did you advise your trustworthy friend Mr Riffat to ring the Minister of Industry to find out if he was expected?'

'No, I did not,' said Al Obaydi. 'If any of this were true,' he added, 'why would I have worked so hard to see that our great leader secured the Declaration?'

'I'm glad you mentioned the Declaration,' said the State Prosecutor softly, 'because I'm also puzzled by the role you played in that particular exercise. But first, let me ask you, did you trust our Ambassador in Geneva to see that the Declaration was delivered to Baghdad?'

'Yes, I did.'

'And did it reach Baghdad safely?' asked the Prosecutor, glancing at the battered parchment, still nailed to the wall behind Saddam.

'Yes, it did.'

'Then why not entrust the knowledge you had acquired about the safe to the same man, remembering that it was his responsibility?'

'This was different.'

'It certainly was, and I shall show the Council just how different. How was the Declaration paid for?'

'I don't understand,' said Al Obaydi.

'Then let me make it easier for you. How was each payment dealt with?'

'Ten million dollars was to be paid once the contract had been agreed, and a further forty million when the Declaration was handed over.'

'And how much of that money – the state's money – did you keep for yourself?'

'Not one cent.'

'Well, let us see if that is totally accurate, shall we? Where did the meetings take place for the exchange of these vast sums of money?'

'The first payment was made to a bank in New Jersey, and the second to Dummond et cie, one of our banks in Switzerland.'

'And the first payment of ten million dollars, if I understand you correctly, you insisted should be in cash?'

'That is not correct,' said Al Obaydi. 'The other side insisted that it should be in cash.'

'How convenient. But then, once again, we only have your word for that, because our Ambassador in New York has stated it was you who insisted the first payment had to be in cash. Perhaps he misunderstood you as well. But let us move on to the second payment, and do correct me if I have misunderstood you.' He paused. 'That was paid direct into Franchard et cie?'

'That is correct,' said Al Obaydi.

'And did you receive, I think the word is a "kickback", after either of these payments?'

'Certainly not.'

'Well, what *is* certain is that, as the first payment was made in cash, it would be hard for anyone to prove otherwise. But as for the second payment...' The Prosecutor paused to let the significance of his words sink in.

'I don't know what you're talking about,' snapped Al Obaydi.

'Then you must be having another lapse of memory, because during your absence, when you were rushing back from Paris to warn the President of the imminent danger to his life, you received a communication from Franchard et cie which, because the letter was addressed to our Ambassador in Paris, ended up on the desk of the Deputy Foreign Minister.'

'I've had no communication with Franchard et cie.'

'I'm not suggesting you did,' said the Prosecutor, as he strode forward to within a foot of Al Obaydi. 'I'm suggesting *they* communicated with *you*. Because they sent you your latest bank statement in the name of Hamid Al Obaydi, dated June 25th 1993, showing that your account was credited with one million dollars on February 18th 1993.'

'It's not possible,' said Al Obaydi defiantly.

'It's not possible?' said the Prosecutor, thrusting a copy of the statement in front of Al Obaydi.

'This is easy to explain. The Cavalli family is trying to get revenge because we didn't pay the full amount of one hundred million as originally promised.'

'Revenge, you claim. The money isn't real? It doesn't exist? This is just a piece of paper? A figment of our imagination?'

'Yes,' said Al Obaydi. 'That is the truth.'

'So perhaps you can explain why one hundred thousand dollars was withdrawn from this account on the day after you had visited Franchard et cie?'

'That's not possible.'

'Another impossibility? Another figment of the imagination? Then you have not seen this withdrawal order for one hundred thousand dollars, sent to you by the bank a few days later? The signature on which bears a remarkable resemblance to the one on the sanctions report which you accepted earlier was authentic.'

The Prosecutor held both documents in front of Al Obaydi so they touched the tip of his nose. He looked at the two signatures and realised what Cavalli must have done. The Prosecutor proceeded to sign his death warrant, even before Al Obaydi had been given the chance to explain.

'And now, you are no doubt going to ask the Council to believe that it was Cavalli who also forged your signature?'

A little laughter trickled round the table, and Al Obaydi suspected that the Prosecutor knew that he had only spoken the truth.

'I have had enough of this,' said the one person in the room who would have dared to interrupt the State Prosecutor.

Al Obaydi looked up in a last attempt to catch the attention of the President, but with the exception of the State Prosecutor the Council were looking towards the top of the table and nodding their agreement.

'There are more pressing matters for the Council to consider.' He waved a hand as if he were swatting an irritating fly.

Two soldiers stepped forward and removed Al Obaydi from his sight.

'That was a whole lot easier than I expected,' said Cohen, once they had passed through the Iraqi checkpoint.

'A little too easy,' said Kratz.

'It's good to know that we've got one optimist and one pessimist on this trip,' said Scott.

Once Cohen was on the highway he remained cautious of pushing the vehicle beyond fifty miles per hour. The lorries that passed in the opposite direction on their way to Jordan rarely had more than two of their four headlights working, which sometimes made them appear like motorcycles in the distance, so overtaking became hazardous. But his eyes needed to be at their most alert for those lorries in front of him: for them, one red tail-light was a luxury.

Kratz had always thought the three-hundred-mile journey

from the border to Baghdad would be too long to consider covering in one stretch, so he had decided they should have a rest about forty miles outside the Iraqi capital. Scott asked Cohen what time he thought they might reach their rest point.

'Assuming I don't drive straight into a parked lorry that's been abandoned in the middle of the road or disappear down a pothole, I'd imagine we'll get there around four, five at the latest.'

'I don't like the sight of all these army vehicles on the road. What do you think they're up to?' asked Kratz, who hadn't slept a wink since they crossed the border.

'A battalion on the move, I'd say, sir. Doesn't look that unusual to me, and I don't think we'd need to worry about them unless they were going in the same direction as us.'

'Perhaps you're right,' said Kratz.

'You wouldn't give them a second thought if you'd crossed the border legally,' said Scott.

'Possibly. But Sergeant,' Kratz said, turning his attention back to Cohen, 'let me know the moment you spot anything you consider unusual.'

'You mean, like a woman worth a second glance?'

Kratz made no comment. He turned to ask Scott a question, only to find he had dozed off again. He envied Scott's facility to sleep anywhere at any time, especially under such pressure.

Sergeant Cohen drove on through the night, not always in a straight line, as he circumvented the occasional burned-out tank or large crater left over from the war. On and on they travelled, through small towns and seemingly uninhabited sleeping villages, until a few minutes past four, when Cohen swung off the highway and up a track that could have only considered one-way traffic. He drove for another twenty minutes, finally coming to a halt when the road ended at an overhanging ledge.

'Even a vulture wouldn't find us here,' said Cohen as he turned off the engine. 'Permission to have a smoke and a bit of shut-eye, Colonel?'

Kratz nodded and watched Cohen jump out of the cab and offer Aziz a cigarette before disappearing behind a palm tree. He checked the surrounding countryside carefully, and decided Cohen was right. When he returned to the truck, he found Aziz and the Sergeant were already asleep, while Scott was sitting on the ledge watching the sun come up over Baghdad.

'What a peaceful sight,' he said as Kratz sat down beside him, almost as though he had been talking to someone else. 'Only God could make a sunrise as beautiful as that.'

'Something isn't right,' muttered Kratz under his breath.

28

SADDAM NODDED TO THE PROSECUTOR. 'Now we have dealt with the traitor, let us move on to the terrorists. What is the latest position, General?'

General Hamil, known as the Barber of Baghdad, opened the file in front of him – he kept a file on everybody, including those sitting around the table. Hamil had been educated at Sandhurst and returned to Iraq to receive the King's Commission, only to find there was no King to serve. So he switched his loyalty to the new President, Abdul Karim Qasim. Then a young Captain changed sides in the 1963 coup and the Ba'ath Party took power. Once again Hamil switched his loyalty, and was rewarded with an appointment to the personal staff of the new Vice-President, Saddam Hussein. Since that day he had risen rapidly through the ranks. He was now Saddam's favourite General, and Commander of the Presidential Guard. He had the distinction of being the only man, with the exception of the President's bodyguards, allowed to wear a side-arm in Saddam's presence. His favourite hobby was to shave his victims' heads before they were hanged, with a blunt cut-throat razor that he never bothered to sharpen. Some of them disappointed him by dying before he could get the rope around their necks.

Hamil studied his file for a few moments before offering an opinion. 'The terrorists,' he began, 'crossed the border at 21.26 last night. Four passports were presented to the immigration officer for stamping. Three were of Swedish origin, and one was from Iraq.'

'I'll skin that one personally,' said Saddam.

'The four men are travelling in a truck that appears to be quite old, but as we are unable to risk taking too close a look, I cannot be sure if we are dealing with a Trojan horse or not. The safe that you ordered, Mr President, is undoubtedly on the back of the truck.

'The truck has driven non-stop through the night at a steady pace of around forty miles per hour in the direction of Baghdad, but at 4.09 this morning it turned off into the desert, and we ceased to monitor its movements, as that particular path leads nowhere. We believe they have simply come off the road to rest before travelling on to the capital later this morning.'

'How many miles are they from Baghdad at this moment?' asked the Minister of the Interior.

'Forty, perhaps fifty – an hour to an hour and a half at the most.'

'So, if we now have them trapped in the desert, General, why don't we just send troops in and cut them off?'

'While they are still bringing the safe to Baghdad?' said Saddam. 'No. That way lies our only danger.'

'I'm not sure I understand, Sayedi,' said the Minister of the Interior, turning to face his leader.

'Then I will explain, *Minister*,' Saddam said, exaggerating the final word cruelly. 'If we arrest them in the desert, who will believe us when we tell the world they are terrorists? The Western press will even claim that we planted their passports on them. No, I want them arrested right here in the Council Chamber, when it will be impossible for Mossad to deny their involvement and, more important, we will have exposed their plot and made fools of them in the eyes of the Zionist people.'

'Now I understand your profound wisdom, Sayedi.'

Saddam waved a hand and turned his attention to the Minister of Industry.

'Have my orders been carried out?'

'To the letter, Excellency. When the terrorists arrive at the Ministry, they will be made to wait, and will be treated curtly, until they produce the documentation that claims to come from your office.'

'They presented such a letter at the border,' interrupted General Hamil, still looking down at his file.

'The moment such a letter is presented to my office,' continued the Minister for Industry, 'a crane will be supplied so that the safe can be transferred into this building. I fear that we will have to remove the doors on the front of the building, but only –'

'I am not interested in the doors,' said Saddam. 'When do you anticipate that the safe will arrive outside the building?'

'Around midday,' said General Hamil. 'I shall personally take over the entire operation once the safe is inside the building, Mr President.'

'Good. And make sure the terrorists see the Declaration before they are arrested.'

'What if they were to try to destroy the document, Excellency?' asked the Interior Minister, attempting to recover some lost ground.

'Never,' said Saddam. 'They have come to Baghdad to steal the document, not to destroy their pathetic piece of history.' Two or three people round the table nodded their agreement. 'None of you except General Hamil and his immediate staff will come anywhere near this building for the next twenty-four hours. The fewer people who know what's really happening, the better. Don't even brief the officer of the day. I want the security to appear lax. That way they will fall right into our trap.'

General Hamil nodded.

'Prosecutor,' said Saddam, turning his attention to the other end of the table, 'what will the international community say when they learn I have arrested the Zionist pigs?'

'They are terrorists, Excellency, and for terrorists, there can be only one sentence.'

'Any other questions?' asked Saddam.

'Just one, Your Excellency,' said the Deputy Foreign Minister. 'What do you want to do about the girl?'

Saddam smiled for the first time. 'Ah, yes. Now that she has served her purpose, I must think of a suitable way to end her life. Where is she at the moment?'

As the truck began its slow journey back along the tiny desert path, with Aziz taking his turn behind the wheel and Cohen in the back with Madame Bertha, Scott felt the atmosphere inside the cab had changed. When they pulled off the highway to rest, he still believed they were in no real danger. But the grim silence of morning made him suddenly aware of the task they had set themselves.

They had Kratz to thank for the original idea, and mixed with his particular cocktail of imagination, discipline, courage, and the assumption that no one knew what they were up to, Scott felt they had a better than even chance of getting away with it, especially now they knew exactly where the Declaration was situated.

When they reached the main road, Aziz jokingly asked, 'Right or left?'

Scott said 'Left,' but Aziz turned dutifully right.

As they travelled along the highway towards Baghdad the sun shone from a cloudless sky that would have delighted any tourist board, although the burned-out tanks and the craters in the road might not have been considered obvious attractions. No one spoke as the miles sped by: there was no need for them to go over the plans another time. That would be like an Olympian training on the morning of a race – either too late, or no longer of any value.

For the last ten miles, they joined an expressway that was equal to anything they might have found in Germany. As they crossed a newly reconstructed bridge over the Euphrates, Scott began to wonder how close he was to Hannah, and whether he

313

could get himself into the Foreign Ministry without alerting Kratz, let alone the Iraqis.

When they reached the outskirts of Baghdad, with its glistening skyscrapers and modern buildings, they could have been entering any major city in the world – until they saw the people. There were lines of cars at petrol pumps in a land where the main asset was oil, but their length was dwarfed only by the queues for food. All four of them could see that sanctions were biting, however much Saddam denied it.

As they drove nearer to the city centre, along the road that passed under the Al-Naser, the massive archway of two crossed swords gripped by casts of Saddam's hand, there was no need to direct Aziz to the Ministry of Industry. He wished he still lived in Baghdad, but he hadn't entered the city since his father had been executed for his part in the failed coup of 1987. Looking out of the window at his countrymen, he could still smell their fear in his nostrils.

When Aziz saw the Ministry of Industry building looming up ahead of him, he pointed it out to Scott, who remembered the façade from the mass of photographs supplied by Kratz. But Scott's eyes had moved up to the gun turrets on top of the Foreign Ministry, a mere stone's throw away.

Aziz brought the lorry to a halt a hundred yards beyond the entrance to the Ministry. Scott said, 'I'll be as quick as I can,' as he jumped out of the cab and headed back towards the building.

As he climbed the steps to the Ministry, he did not see a man in a window of the building opposite who was speaking on the telephone to General Hamil.

'The truck has stopped about a hundred metres beyond the Ministry. A tall, fair-haired man who was in the front of the vehicle is now entering the building, but the other three, including Kratz, have remained with the safe.'

Scott pushed through the swing doors and strolled past two guards who looked as if they didn't move more than a few feet every day. He walked over to the information desk and joined the shortest of three queues. The one-handed clock above the desk indicated that it was approximately 9.30.

It took another fifteen minutes before Scott reached the counter. He explained to the girl that his name was Bernstrom and that he needed to see Mr Kajami.

'Do you have an appointment?' she asked.

'No,' said Scott. 'We called from Jordan to warn him that a safe the government had ordered was on its way to Baghdad. He asked us to inform him the moment it arrived.'

'I will see if he's in,' said the receptionist. Scott waited, staring up at a massive portrait of Saddam Hussein in uniform holding a Kalashnikov. It dominated the otherwise blank grey walls of the reception area.

The girl listened carefully to whoever it was on the other end of the line before saying, 'Someone will be down to see you in a few minutes.' She turned her attention to the next person in the queue.

Scott hung around for another thirty minutes before a tall, thin man wearing a smart Western suit stepped out of the lift and walked over to him.

'Mr Bernstrom?'

'Yes?' said Scott, as he swung round to face the man.

'Good morning,' he said confidently in English. 'I am Mr Ibrahim, Mr Kajami's personal assistant. How can I help you?'

'I have brought a safe from Sweden,' said Scott. 'It was ordered by the Ministry some years ago, but, due to the UN sanctions, could not be delivered any earlier. We were told that when we reached Baghdad we should report to Mr Kajami.'

'Do you have any papers to verify your claim?'

Scott removed a file from his bag and showed Mr Ibrahim its contents.

The man read through each document slowly until he came to the letter signed by the President. He read no further. Looking up, he asked, 'May I see this safe, Mr Bernstrom?'

'Certainly,' said Scott. 'Please follow me.' He led the official out onto the street and took him over to the truck.

Cohen stared down at them. When Kratz gave the order, he whipped the tarpaulin off the safe so that the civil servant could inspect Madame Bertha for himself.

Scott was fascinated by the fact that those passing in the street didn't give the safe a second look. If anything, they quickened their pace. Fear manifested itself among these people by their lack of curiosity.

'Please return with me, Mr Bernstrom,' said Ibrahim. Scott accompanied him back to the reception area, where he left without another word.

Scott was left waiting for another thirty minutes before Ibraham returned.

'You are to take the safe to Victory Square, where you will see a barrier with a tank in front of a large white building. They are expecting you.'

Scott was about to ask where Victory Square was when Ibrahim turned and walked away. He returned to the truck, and joined Kratz and Aziz in the front before passing on the news. Aziz didn't need to be told the way.

'No special treatment there, I'm glad to see,' said Kratz.

Scott nodded his agreement as Aziz eased the truck back into the road. The traffic was much heavier now. Lorries and cars were honking their horns, managing to move only a few inches at a time.

'It must be an accident,' said Scott, until they turned the corner and saw the three bodies hanging from a makeshift gallows: a man wearing an expensive designer suit, a woman perhaps a little younger, and another much older woman. It was hard to be certain, with their heads shaven.

Mr Kajami sat at his desk, dialled the number that had been passed to him, and waited.

'Deputy Foreign Minister's Office, Miss Saib speaking.'

'This is the Minister of Industry calling. Could you put me through to the Deputy Foreign Minister.'

'I'm afraid he's out of the office at the moment, Mr Kajami. Shall I ask him to return your call, or would you like to leave a message?'

'I will leave a message, but perhaps he could also call me when he gets back.'

'Certainly, Minister.'

'Could you let him know that the safe has arrived from Sweden and can therefore be crossed off the sanctions list.' There was a long pause. 'Are you still there, Miss Saib?'

'Yes. I was just writing down what you said, sir.'

'If he needs to see the relevant forms we still have them at the Ministry, but if it's the safe he wants to check on, it's already on its way to the Ba'ath headquarters.'

'I understand, sir. I'll see he gets the message just as soon as he comes in.'

'Thank you, Miss Saib.'

Kajami replaced the phone on the hook, glanced across his desk at the Deputy Foreign Minister and smiled.

29

AZIZ BROUGHT THE TRUCK to a halt in front of a tank. A few soldiers were moving around, but there didn't appear to be a great deal of activity.

'I was expecting a bigger show of force than this,' said Kratz. 'It's the Ba'ath Party headquarters, after all.'

'Saddam's probably at the palace, or even out of Baghdad,' suggested Aziz as two soldiers advanced towards the truck. The first one shouted 'Out!' and they obeyed slowly. Once all four of them were on the ground, the soldier ordered them to stand a few yards away from the truck while a couple of other soldiers jumped up on the back and removed the tarpaulin.

'This one's a Major,' whispered Aziz as a portly man covered in battle ribbons and carrying a mobile phone advanced towards them. He stopped and looked up at the safe suspiciously before turning to Kratz and introducing himself as Major Saeed.

'Open,' was all he added.

Kratz pointed to Scott, who climbed up onto the back of the lorry while several more soldiers surrounded the truck to watch him perform the opening ceremony. Once Scott had pulled the great door open, the Major joined him on the back of the truck, but not until one of the soldiers had given him a hand-up. He stood a pace back and ordered two of his men to go inside. They appeared apprehensive at first, but once they had entered the safe they began touching the sides and even jumping up to try to reach the roof. A few moments later, Saeed joined them, and banged the walls with his swagger stick. He then stepped back out, jumped heavily off the truck and turned towards Scott.

'Now we wait for a crane,' he said, sounding a little more friendly. He dialled a number on the phone.

Cohen climbed into the cab and sat behind the wheel, the keys still in the ignition, while Aziz remained on the back with the safe. Scott and Kratz leaned against a wall, trying to appear bored, while having a conversation on the alternatives they now faced.

'We must find some way of getting into the building ahead of the safe,' said Kratz. Scott nodded his agreement.

The clock in Victory Square had struck 12.30 before Aziz spotted the tall, thin structure progressing slowly round the massive statue of Saddam. The four of them watched as soldiers ran out into the street to hold up the flow of traffic and allow the vast crane to continue its progress uninterrupted.

Scott explained to the Major that the truck now needed to be moved to a position opposite the front door. He agreed without a phone call. When the truck was parked exactly where Scott wanted it, Major Saeed finally conceded that the doors would have to come off their hinges if they were ever going to get the safe and its trolley inside the building.

This time he did make a phone call, and to Scott's question, 'How long?' he simply shrugged his shoulders and replied, 'Must wait.'

Scott was determined to use the 'must wait' period, and explained to Major Saeed that he needed to walk the route that the safe would travel once they had entered the building.

The Major hesitated, made a further phone call, held on for some time before he received an answer, and then, pointing to Scott, said, 'You, only.'

Scott left Kratz to organise the crane as it prepared to lift the safe off the lorry, and followed the Major into the building.

The first thing that Scott noticed as he walked down the carpeted corridor was its width and solid feel. Every few paces there were soldiers lounging against the wall who sprang to attention the moment they saw Major Saeed.

At the end of the corridor was an elevator. The Major produced a key and turned it in a lock on the wall. The doors of the elevator opened slowly. It struck Scott that the size of the safe must have been determined by the width of the lift. He doubted if there would be much more than an inch to spare all round once they had succeeded in getting Madame Bertha on board.

The Major pressed a button marked '– 6', which, Scott noted, was as far down as they could go. The lift dropped slowly. When the doors opened Scott followed Major Saeed into a long corridor. This time he had the feeling that the passageway had been built to survive an earthquake. They came to a halt outside a pair of heavy, reinforced doors, guarded by two soldiers carrying rifles.

Saeed asked a question, and both guards shook their heads. 'The Chamber is empty, so we can go straight through,' he explained, then proceeded to unlock the door. Scott followed him into the Council Chamber.

His eyes searched quickly round the room. The first thing he saw on the far wall was another massive portrait of Saddam, this time in a dark double-breasted suit. Then he spotted one of the red alarm buttons next to a light switch that Kratz had warned him about. The Major hurried on through the Chamber, giving the impression of a man who hadn't the right to be there, while Scott went as slowly as he felt he could get away with. And then he saw it, just for a moment, and his heart sank: the Declaration of Independence was nailed to the wall, a corner torn and some of the signatures looking distinctly blurred.

The Major unlocked the far door and Scott reluctantly followed him through into the adjoining corridor. They continued for only a few more paces before coming to a halt in front of a massive recess of inlaid brick that Scott didn't need to measure to realise had been purpose-built in anticipation of the arrival of the safe.

Scott took some time measuring the space, as he tried to think of how he could get a longer look at the Declaration. After a few minutes, Major Saeed tapped him on the shoulder with his swagger stick and indicated that it was time for them to return to the courtyard. Scott reluctantly followed him back down the short corridor and into the Council Chamber, which the Major scurried through while Scott lingered to measure the doors. He was pleased to discover that they would have to be taken off their hinges. He stood a pace back as if considering the problem. The Major returned and slapped the side of his leg with his swagger stick, muttering something under his breath that Scott suspected wasn't altogether flattering.

Scott stole a glance to the right, and confirmed his worst fears: even if he were able to exchange the two documents, it would take an even greater genius than Dollar Bill to repair the damage that Saddam had already inflicted.

'Come. Come. We must go,' said the Major.

'And so must these doors,' said Scott, and turning, added, 'and those two as well,' pointing to the pair at the other end of the Chamber. But Major Saeed was already striding off down the long corridor towards the open lift.

Hannah put the phone down and tried to stop herself trembling. They had warned her many times at Herzliyah that however tough you think you are, and however well trained you've been, you will still tremble.

She checked her watch. Her lunch break was due in twenty minutes, and although she rarely left the building during the day except on official business, she knew she could no longer sit in that office and just wait for events to happen all around her.

The Deputy Foreign Minister had left for the palace at eight that morning, and had told her not to expect him back until five at the earliest. A muscle in her cheek twitched as she began to type out the Minister of Industry's message.

For fifteen minutes, she sat at her desk and planned how the hour could be best spent. As soon as she was clear in her mind what needed to be done, she picked up her phone and asked a girl on the switchboard to cover her calls during the lunch break.

Hannah put on her glasses, left the room and walked quickly down the corridor, remaining close to the wall with her head bowed, so that those passing didn't give her a second look.

She took the stairs rather than the lift, slipped across the hall past reception, through the swing doors and out onto the steps of the Foreign Ministry.

'Saib's just left the building,' said a voice from the other side of the road into a mobile phone. 'She's going in the direction of Victory Square.'

Hannah continued walking towards the square. The crowds were so large and noisy that she feared another public hanging must have taken place. When she reached the end of the road and turned the corner, she averted her eyes as she made a path between those who were standing, staring, some even laughing at the spectacle.

'Quite a high-up official,' someone joked. Another more serious voice said that he had heard he was a diplomat recently back from America who had been caught with his fingers in the till. A third, an elderly woman, wept when someone suggested that the other two were the man's innocent mother and sister.

Once Hannah could see the barrier she slowed her pace. She stopped and stared across the road at the Ba'ath Party headquarters. She was pleased to be hidden in such a large crowd, even if it did occasionally obscure her view.

'She's facing the Ba'ath Party headquarters. Everyone else is looking in the opposite direction.'

Hannah's eyes settled on the truck that was surrounded by soldiers, and then she saw the massive safe that was perched on the back of the vehicle and the two young men who were attaching large coils of steel to its base. One was Middle Eastern in appearance, the other vaguely European. And then she saw

Kratz – or was it Kratz? Whoever it was disappeared behind the far side of the truck. She waited for the man to reappear. When he did, a few moments later, she was left in no doubt that it was the Mossad leader.

She realised that she could not wait around in such a public place for much longer, and decided to return to her office and consider what needed to be done next. She gave Kratz one last look as a group of cleaners came out of the building, walked across the tarmac and passed by the barrier without any of the soldiers paying them the slightest attention.

Hannah began to walk away from Victory Square, just as Major Saeed and Scott emerged from the building into the courtyard.

'She's on the move again, but she doesn't seem to be returning to the Ministry.' The man on the mobile phone listened for a moment and then replied, 'I don't know, but I'll follow her and report back.'

When Scott stepped back into the courtyard he was pleased to see that Kratz had already got the crane into position to lift the safe off the truck. Aziz and Cohen were fastening long steel coils around the body of Madame Bertha while the specially constructed trolley, of which Mr Pedersson was so proud, had been placed on the ground between the front door and the side of the truck.

Scott looked up at the crane that was taller than the building itself and back down at the operator, sitting in his wide cab near the base. Once Cohen and Aziz had jumped off the truck Kratz gave the operator the thumbs-up.

After a few moments he heard the crunch of a gear shifting into place. He watched as the steel cords tightened, followed by a raucous revving of the engine. But Madame Bertha refused to budge an inch. The revving noise became even louder a second time, but Madame Bertha remained unmoved by their solicitations.

The operator pushed the long gear lever forward another notch, and tried a third time. Finally Bertha rose an inch off the back of the lorry, swaying gently from side to side. Some of the soldiers started to cheer, but they stopped immediately when the Major turned to stare in their direction.

Kratz nodded and Cohen ran across the tarmac and lowered the tailboard, before getting into the cab and jumping behind the wheel of the truck. He switched on the engine, pushed the gear lever into first and moved the vehicle slowly forward until the safe was left dangling in mid-air. Aziz and Kratz then pushed the trolley a few yards across the tarmac so that it was directly below the dangling safe, Kratz gave the thumbs-up a second time, and the crane operator slowly began lowering the five tons of steel, inch by inch, until it came to rest on the trolley, causing the large rubber wheels to compress abruptly.

The safe now rested in front of the double doors, waiting for the carpenter to arrive before it could progress on its inward journey. The Major shrugged his shoulders even before Kratz had mouthed the question.

As Cohen backed the lorry into a parking space designated by the Major, Scott pointed at the safe and beckoned to Kratz, who walked over, looking puzzled. He thought the operation was going rather well.

'What's the problem?' he asked. Scott continued pointing at the safe, and with exaggerated movements indicated how he thought it would have to be moved, while whispering to Kratz: 'I've seen the Declaration.' He moved to the other side of the safe. Kratz followed, now also pretending to take a close interest in the safe.

'Great news,' said Kratz. 'So where is it?'

'The news is not so great,' said Scott.

'What do you mean?' asked Kratz anxiously.

'It's in the Council Chamber, exactly where Hannah said it would be. But it's nailed to the wall,' replied Scott.

'Nailed to the wall?' said Kratz under his breath.

'Yes, and it looks as if it's beyond repair,' said Scott, as an Iraqi, dressed in a dishdash and a red-and-white keffiyeh and carrying a tool bag appeared at the barrier.

Once the guards had thoroughly checked the tool bag, tipping all its contents out onto the ground, they allowed him through. The carpenter gathered up his tools, took one look at the safe, another at the double doors, and understood immediately why his boss had described the problem as urgent. Scott stood back and watched the craftsman as he began to unscrew the hinges on one of the doors.

'So where's Dollar Bill's counterfeit at the moment?' asked Kratz.

'Still in my bag,' said Scott. 'I'm going to have to do some work on it, or they'll spot the difference the moment I've exchanged it for the original.'

'Agreed,' said Kratz. 'You'd better get on with it while the carpenter's working on the door. I'll try and keep the Major occupied.'

Kratz sauntered over to the carpenter and started chatting to him while Scott disappeared into the front of the truck carrying his bag. Once the Major saw what Kratz was doing he ran across to join them.

Scott stared through the cab window as he extracted Dollar Bill's copy from the cylinder and tried to recall where the main damage was on the original. First he made a tear in the top right-hand corner, then he spat on the names of John Adams and Robert Treat Paine. After he had studied his handiwork he decided he hadn't gone far enough and, placing the copy on the floor, he rubbed the soles of his shoes gently over the surface. He glanced up to see the Major ordering Kratz to let the carpenter get on with his job. Kratz shrugged his shoulders as Scott rolled up the copy of the Declaration and returned it to the cylinder, before sliding it down the specially-sewn long thin pocket on the inside of his trouser leg. A perfect fit.

A few moments later the carpenter got off his knees and smiled to show he had completed his task. At the Major's command four soldiers stepped forward and removed the doors. They carried them a few paces away and leaned them up against an outside wall.

The Major ordered several more soldiers to push the trolley as Scott guided Madame Bertha through the doorway. Kratz and Aziz tried to follow, but the Major waved an arm firmly to indicate that only Scott could enter the building. It was Scott's turn to shrug his shoulders.

Inch by inch, they eased the trolley down the long corridor. The lift doors had been left open, but it still took forty hands to lever the five tons of metal safely inside. Scott knew from his research that this part of the building had been built to survive a nuclear attack, but he wondered if the lift would ever recover from having to carry the five-ton safe down six floors. He was only thankful that Madame Bertha was going down, not up.

The lift doors slowly closed and the Major quickly led Scott through a side door and down the back stairs, followed by a dozen soldiers. When they reached the basement, the doors of the lift were already open and Madame Bertha stood there, majestically waiting. The Major pointed to the floor with his swagger stick: ten of the soldiers fell to their knees and began pulling the trolley inch by inch until they finally managed to coax it into the corridor. The lift was then sent up to – 5, and six of the soldiers ran back up the stairs, jumped into the empty lift and returned to the basement so they could push the safe from the other side.

The carpenter had already removed the first set of doors they would encounter when the safe entered the Council Chamber, but was still working on the second set when the trolley reached the entrance. The delay gave Scott an opportunity to supervise the moving of the large table up against the side wall and the placing of the chairs on the table so that the safe would have a clear passage into the far corridor.

As he went back and forth Scott had several opportunities to stare at the Declaration, even study the spelling of the word

'Brittish'. He quickly realised that the parchment was in an even worse condition than he had thought.

Once the doors were finally removed, the soldiers began pushing the safe across the Chamber and out into the short corridor on the last few yards of its journey. When they had reached the end of the corridor opposite the specially prepared recess, Scott supervised the last few inches of its move until they could push the five tons of steel no further. Madame Bertha had finally come to her resting place against the far wall.

Scott smiled, and Major Saeed made another phone call.

The old woman explained to Hannah that the next shift was to be at three o'clock that afternoon, and they would be expected to have the Council Chamber ready for the meeting that was to take place at six the following day. They hadn't been able to do a proper job on the first shift that morning because of that safe.

Hannah had followed the cleaners, watching as they peeled off one by one and went their separate ways. She selected an old woman carrying the heaviest bags, and offered to help her across the road. They quickly got into conversation, and Hannah continued to carry the bags all the way to her front door, explaining that she only lived a few streets away.

'Come inside, my dear,' the old lady said.

'Thank you,' replied Hannah, feeling more like the wolf than Little Red Riding Hood.

Slipping a small whisky into the old woman's coffee had proved harmless enough, and it certainly loosened her tongue. Two Valium dropped in the cleaner's second coffee ensured that it would be several hours before she woke. Mossad had taught Hannah five different ways of breaking into a car, a hotel room, a briefcase, even a small safe, so a drugged old woman's handbag was no great challenge. She removed the special pass and slipped out of the house.

'She's now heading back in the direction of the Ministry,' said the voice into the mobile phone. 'We've checked the old woman. She passed out and probably won't come round until this time tomorrow. The only thing that's been taken is her security pass.'

When Hannah arrived back at her desk there was no sign that the Deputy Foreign Minister had returned, so she checked with the switchboard. There had only been three calls: two said they would call back tomorrow, and the third didn't leave a message.

Hannah replaced the handset and typed out a note explaining that she had gone home as she wasn't certain whether the Deputy Foreign Minister would be returning that day. As long as he didn't check his messages until after five o'clock, there would be no reason for him to become suspicious.

In the privacy of her little room, Hannah exchanged her office clothes for the traditional black abaya with a pushi covering her face. She checked herself in the mirror before once again leaving the building, silently and anonymously.

'Now you open the safe,' said Major Saeed.

Scott swivelled the dials to their coded numbers, and the first bulb turned green. The Major was impressed. Scott then placed the palm of his hand on the white square, and a few seconds later the middle bulb turned green. The Major was mesmerised. Scott leaned forward and spoke into the voice box, and the third light turned green. The Major was speechless.

Scott pulled the handle and the door swung open. He jumped inside and immediately extracted the cardboard tube from the inside of his trouser leg.

The Major spotted it at once, and flew into a rage. Scott quickly flicked off the cap, took out the poster of Saddam Hussein and unpeeled it, letting the backing paper fall to the ground before he strolled to the far side of the safe and fixed the portrait of Saddam to the wall. A smile returned to the Major's face as Scott bent down, rolled up the backing paper and slid it into the tube.

'Now I teach you,' said Scott.

'No, no, not me,' said Major Saeed. He held his phone up in the air and said, 'We must go back upstairs.'

Scott felt like swearing as he stepped out of the safe, dropping the tube and allowing it to roll across the floor to the darkest corner. The plan he had so carefully prepared with Kratz would no longer be possible. He reluctantly left the open safe and joined the Major as he marched quickly towards the Council Chamber, this time not allowing Scott any opportunity to hold him up.

'I'm almost sure it's her coming out of the Ministry,' said the voice into the mobile phone, 'but she's changed into traditional dress and is no longer wearing glasses. She's heading towards Victory Square again. I'll keep you briefed.'

Hannah was back in Victory Square twenty minutes before the first cleaner was expected to arrive for work. Although the crowd was now smaller, she was still able to remain inconspicuous. She looked across the road towards the courtyard. The safe was no longer to be seen, and the crane too had disappeared. The truck was now backed up against the wall. Hannah strained to see if Kratz was one of the figures sitting in the front of the truck, but she couldn't penetrate the haze of smoke.

Hannah turned her attention to a building she had never entered but felt she knew so well. A full-scale plan of each floor was attached to a board in the operations room of Mossad's headquarters in Herzliyah, and you couldn't take the second paper of any exam on Iraq without being able to draw every floor of the building in detail. Information was added all the time, from the strangest sources: escaped refugees, former diplomats, ex-Cabinet Ministers who were Kurds or Shi'ites, even the former British Prime Minister Edward Heath.

The first cleaner arrived a few minutes before three, presented her pass and then hurried across the tarmac before disappearing into a side door of the building. The second appeared a few moments later, and followed the same procedure. When Hannah spotted the third making her way along the far side of the pavement, she slipped across the road and filed in behind her as she walked towards the barrier.

'She's crossed the road, reached the barrier, and the guard is now checking her pass,' said the voice into the mobile phone. 'As instructed, they've let her through. She's now walking across the tarmac and following another woman through the side door. She's in, the door's closed. We've got her.'

Hannah joined the other cleaners inside the building, and told them that her mother had been taken ill and that she had been sent to cover for her. She tried to assure them that it was not the first time she had done so, and was surprised when they asked no questions. She assumed that they were fearful of being involved with a stranger.

Hannah picked up a box of cleaning equipment and made her way down the back stairs. The plan displayed on the walls at Herzliyah was proving impressively accurate, even if nobody had managed the exact number of steps to the basement.

When she reached the door that led into the bottom corridor she could hear voices coming from the direction of the Council Chamber. Whoever it was must be heading for the lift. Hannah backed up against the wall so she could just see them through the thick pane of wire-mesh glass in the centre of the door.

The two men passed. Hannah didn't recognise the Major, but when she saw who was with him, her legs gave way and she almost collapsed onto the ground.

Once they were back in the courtyard, the Major dialled a number. Scott strolled over to Kratz, who was standing behind the truck.

'Did you manage to switch the Declaration?' were Kratz's first words.

'No, it's still on the wall of the Chamber.'

'Damn. And the copy?'

'I left it in the tube on the floor of the safe. I couldn't risk bringing it out.'

'So how are you going to get back into the building?' asked Kratz, looking towards the Major. 'You were meant to use the time –'

'I know. But it turns out he's not the one who'll be in charge of the safe. He's getting in touch with whoever it is I'll have to instruct.'

'Not what we needed. I suspect that with the Major our first plan would have been a lot easier,' said Kratz. 'I'd better brief the others so we can work on an alternative if things go wrong again.'

Scott nodded his agreement, and he and the Mossad leader strolled over to the truck where Aziz and Cohen were sitting in the cab smoking. As the Colonel climbed into the front, two cigarettes were quickly stubbed out. Kratz explained why they were still waiting, and warned them that this could be the Professor's last chance to get back into the Council Chamber. 'So when he comes out this time,' he explained, 'we must be ready to go. With a little luck, we might still make the border by midnight.'

How could he possibly be alive? Hannah thought. Hadn't she killed him? She had seen his dead body carried out of the room. She tried to organise her thoughts, which ranged from joy to fear. She recalled her senior instructor telling her, 'When you're in the front line, never be surprised by anything.' She felt she now had the right to contradict him, if she was ever given the chance.

Hannah pushed open the door and crept into the corridor, which was deserted except for a pair of soldiers chatting at the entrance to the Chamber. She realised she couldn't hope to get past them without being questioned.

With a pace to go, she was told to stop, and came to a halt between them. After they had checked the cleaning box thoroughly, the one with two stripes on his arm said, 'You know it's our duty to search you as well?' Hannah made no comment while he bent down, lifted her long black robe and placed his hands on her ankles. The second one let out a raucous laugh as he put his fingers round the front of her neck, and began moving his hands down over her shoulders and across her breasts, while his colleague moved his hands up her legs and onto her thighs. As the first soldier reached the top of her legs, his colleague pinched her nipples. Hannah pushed them both away and stepped into the Chamber. They made no attempt to follow, although their laughter increased in volume.

The table had been returned to the centre of the room and the chairs casually rearranged around it. She began by straightening the table before placing the chairs at an equal distance from each other. She was still trying to take in the fact that Simon was alive, and part of the team for Baghdad. But why would the CIA send him? Unless . . . she stared up at the massive portrait of Saddam Hussein as she straightened his chair at the head of the table. Then her eyes came to rest on the document that was nailed next to his picture.

The American Declaration of Independence was fixed to the wall in exactly the place the Deputy Foreign Minister had claimed it was.

30

TWO CARS SWEPT UP TO the barrier and were ushered quickly through without the suggestion of a check. Scott watched carefully as a large group of soldiers surrounded the vehicles.

When a tall, heavily-built man stepped out of the second car, Aziz said under his breath, 'General Hamil, the Barber of Baghdad. He carries a cut-throat razor on his keyring.'

Kratz nodded. 'I know his complete life history,' he said. 'Even the name of the young Lieutenant he's currently living with.'

Major Saeed was now standing to attention, saluting the General, and Scott didn't need to be told that this man was of a different rank and calibre to the one he had been dealing with until then. He studied the face of the man dressed in an immaculate tailored uniform with several more rows of battle ribbons than the Major, wearing black leather gloves and carrying a swagger stick. It was a cruel face. The troops who stood around him were unable to disguise their fear.

The Major pointed to Scott and said, 'You, come.'

'I've got a feeling he means you,' said Kratz.

Scott nodded and strolled across to join them.

'Mr Bernstrom,' the General said, removing the glove from his right hand, 'I am General Hamil.' Scott shook his hand. 'I am sorry to have kept you waiting. But don't let me hold you up any longer. Please show me your safe, which Major Saeed seems so impressed by.'

Without another word the General turned and began walking towards the building, leaving Scott with little choice but to follow. For the first time in his life, Scott was terrified.

Hannah picked up a duster and some polish and began to rub in small circles on the table while taking a more careful look at the Declaration of Independence. The parchment was in such terrible condition that she doubted if it could be repaired even if Simon were able to get it back to Washington.

She peered round the door into the short corridor, and spotted the safe she had seen on the truck earlier that day. It was open, but was guarded by two more thugs, chatting as much as the other two who were stationed at the door of the Council Chamber.

Hannah made her way slowly down the corridor, dusting and polishing the ledge of the wooden skirting until she was opposite the safe and had a clear view inside. She took a pace forward and peered in as if she had never seen anything like it in her life before. One of the soldiers kicked her and she fell into the safe. The inevitable raucous laughter followed. She was about to turn round and retaliate when she saw the long cardboard cylinder in one corner, almost hidden in the shadow. She leaned across and rolled it quickly towards her until it was safely under her long skirt. She wondered if she could use it to get a message to Simon. Hannah left her duster and polish on the floor of the safe, stepped out backwards and bolted down the corridor, as if to escape the guards.

Once she was back in the Chamber she removed another rag from the cleaning box and began polishing the table until she was in a position where no one could see her from either passageway. She then lowered herself slowly onto her knees until she was below the table, and let the cardboard tube fall to the floor in front of her. She quickly flicked off the cap, to find the cylinder wasn't empty. She pulled out the parchment, unrolled it and studied it in disbelief: a magnificent copy of the

Declaration of Independence, obviously made by a craftsman, even if someone had tried to deface it. She realised immediately that Simon must have been hoping to find some way of switching the copy for the original.

Kratz watched Scott follow General Hamil into the building, then walked slowly across to the truck and climbed into the cab. He stared through the front window. No one was taking any particular interest in what they were up to.

'This is too easy,' he said. 'Far too easy.' Cohen and Aziz looked straight ahead, but didn't offer an opinion. 'If Hamil is involved, they must suspect something. The time has come for us to find out who knows what.'

'What do you have in mind, sir?' asked Cohen.

'I have a feeling that our switchboard Major isn't fully aware of what's going on. Either they haven't briefed him, or they think he's not up to the job.'

'Or both,' suggested Aziz.

Kratz nodded. 'Or both. So let's find out. Aziz, I want you and Cohen to take a stroll down to the barrier. Tell the guards that you're going for something to eat, and that you'll be back in a few minutes. If they refuse to let you through, we've got a real problem, because that will mean they know what we're up to. In which case, come back to the cab and I'll start working on what we have to do next.'

'And if they let us through?' asked Cohen.

'Get out of sight,' said Kratz, 'but keep in visual contact with the truck. That shouldn't be too hard, with these gawking crowds. If Professor Bradley comes out with his cardboard tube and I rest my arm on the window ledge as I'm doing now, get back here fast, because we won't want to be hanging about. And by the way, Cohen: if I'm not around for any reason, and the Professor should suggest a detour to the Foreign Ministry, overrule him.' Cohen nodded, without a clue what the Colonel was talking about. 'But if you spot that we're in trouble, keep well out of the way for one hour, and then pray that the whopper works.'

'Understood, sir,' said Cohen.

'Take the keys with you,' said Kratz. 'Now get going.'

Kratz stepped back down onto the tarmac, strolled over to where Major Saeed was listening to one of his interminable phone calls, and placed himself a few feet to his left as if wanting to attract his attention. At the same time he looked over his shoulder to watch Aziz and Cohen walking towards the barrier.

Kratz continued to try and attract the Major's attention as Aziz came to a halt at the barrier and started joking with one of the guards.

A few moments later Kratz saw both of his men step under the barrier. Within seconds they were lost in the crowd.

Major Saeed came off the phone. 'What is the problem this time?' he asked. Kratz took out a cigarette and asked the Major for a light.

'Don't smoke,' he said, and waved him away.

Kratz walked slowly back to the cab and took his place behind the steering wheel, his eyes never leaving the open doorway of the Ba'ath Party headquarters.

Hannah stared at the Declaration hanging on the wall. It was only a few paces away from her. She waited until she heard another roar of laughter from the soldiers before walking over to the document and quickly trying to remove the nails. Three came out with the minimum of effort, but the one at the top right-hand corner refused to budge, and the Declaration continued to dangle from it. After a few more seconds, she felt she was left with no choice but to ease the document over the head of the nail. Once the parchment was in her hand she went back to the table, placed the original on the floor and returned quickly to attach the copy to the wall.

She hardly glanced at her handiwork before she turned back to the table, knelt on the ground, and rapidly rolled up the original, replacing it in the cylinder. Once again she tucked it under her skirt. It had been the longest two minutes of her life. She remained on her knees, trying to think. She knew she couldn't risk trying to get the tube out of the building, as the guards might decide to 'search' her again. There was no alternative. She walked quickly back down the short corridor and was in the safe even before the two soldiers had stopped talking. She let the cylinder fall to the floor, then pushed it back into the darkest corner, exactly where she had first seen it. Then she picked up the duster and polish she had left behind, stepped back out of the safe and showed them to the soldiers, and ran back down the corridor towards the Chamber.

Hannah knew she must get out of the building as quickly as possible, and somehow pass a message to Simon.

And then she heard the voices.

'And just how large is this safe?' the General asked Scott as they proceeded down the corridor.

'Nine feet in height, seven feet in width and eight feet in depth,' responded Scott immediately. 'You could hold a private meeting in there if you wished to, General.'

'Is that so?' said Hamil as he entered the lift. 'But I am informed the safe can only be operated by one person.' He pressed the bottom button with his gloved finger. 'Is that true?'

'That is correct, General. We followed the exact specifications your government requested.'

The lift doors slid apart at the basement floor. The General stepped out into the corridor and headed towards the Council Chamber.

'I am also told that the safe can withstand a nuclear attack. Is that the case?'

'Yes,' replied Scott. 'The safe has a six-inch skin and would be unaffected by any explosion other than a direct hit. In any other circumstances, everything in the safe would be preserved, even if the building it was standing in was completely demolished.'

'Impressive,' said the General as the guards sprang to attention and he touched the rim of his beret with his swagger stick. He marched into the Chamber and Scott followed, annoyed to find there was a woman polishing the table. He certainly didn't need her hanging around when he came back out. The General didn't even look at Hannah as he strode through the Chamber.

Scott glanced across at the parchment before he followed the General out of the room.

'Ah,' Hannah heard the General say when he was still several yards from the end of the corridor. 'Pure statistics don't do your safe justice, Mr Bernstrom.' The two soldiers remained rigidly at attention as the General studied the safe for some time, before stepping inside. When he saw the cardboard tube on the floor he bent down and picked it up.

'Just to protect the picture,' explained Scott, stepping in to join him. He pointed to the portrait of Saddam Hussein.

'You are a thorough man, Mr Bernstrom,' said Hamil. 'You would have made an excellent colonel in one of my regiments.' He laughed and passed the cardboard tube over to Scott.

Hannah listened intently to every word, and concluded that she must get out of the building as quickly as possible and alert Kratz to what she had done.

'Would you like me to show you how to programme the safe?' she heard Scott ask as she reached the entrance of the Chamber.

'No, no, not me,' said General Hamil. 'The President will be the only one who will be allowed to operate the safe.' Those were the last words Hannah heard as she walked out of the Chamber, past the guards, and continued purposefully down the long corridor.

When she reached the doors that led to the staircase she turned back to see the General striding into the Chamber and, some way behind him, Scott following. He was holding the tube.

Hannah wanted to scream with delight.

Scott realised he would never be given a chance to carry out the switch once Saddam was in the building. When he reached the Chamber he allowed the General to get a few paces ahead of him. His eyes swept the room, and he was relieved to find the cleaner was no longer anywhere to be seen. The guards sprang to attention as the General strode out of the Council Chamber into the far corridor.

Scott stared at the alarm button on the wall ahead of him. 'Don't look round,' he begged under his breath as he kept his eyes on the retreating back of the General. With a yard to go before he reached the door, Scott lunged forward and jabbed his thumb on the red button. The doors immediately slammed closed and clamped with a deafening noise.

Hannah was just about to push open the door that led to the back stairs when the alarm gave out a piercing sound and all the exits were immediately bolted. She turned to discover she was alone in the corridor with General Hamil and four of his republican guards.

The General smiled at her. 'Miss Kopec, I believe. I'm delighted to make your acquaintance. I fear it will be a couple of minutes before Professor Bradley is able to join us.'

The guards surrounded Hannah as the General looked up at a television screen above the door. He watched as Scott, inside the Chamber, pressed a button on the side of his watch. Scott then ran over to the wall, quickly extracted the copy of the document from the tube, and checked it against the original. He felt he had done a fair job back in the cab of the truck, but he spat on Lewis Morris and John Witherspoon for good measure, then spent a few seconds rubbing the parchment on the stone floor before comparing it once again to the one on the wall. He looked at his watch: forty-five seconds. He began to pull the nails out of the wall, but was unable to get the top right-hand one to budge, so he eased the Declaration over its head. Sixty seconds.

Hannah stared up at the television screen in horror, watching Simon undo all her work, while the General made a phone call.

Once Scott had removed the document from the wall he placed it on the table. He then fastened the original that he had taken out of the cardboard cylinder back on the wall, easing the parchment over the nail in the top right-hand corner, which still stubbornly refused to budge. Ninety seconds. He picked up Dollar Bill's copy from the table, rolled it up and dropped it into the cylinder. One hundred and ten seconds. He walked over to the door that led to the lifts and stood inhaling deeply for a moment before the alarm stopped and the doors swung open.

Scott knew that it would take them a few minutes before the source of the alarm could be checked, so when he saw the General, he shrugged his shoulders and smiled.

Kratz sat on the front seat of the truck, keeping a wary eye on Major Saeed. There was a ringing sound: Saeed pressed a button and placed his phone to his ear. Suddenly, without warning, he turned, whipped out his pistol and looked anxiously towards the cab. He barked out an order, and within seconds every soldier in sight surrounded the truck, their rifles pointing directly at Kratz.

The Major rushed up. 'Where are the other two?' he demanded. Kratz shrugged his shoulders. Saeed turned on his heels and ran into the building, shouting another order as he went.

Kratz placed his right hand over his left wrist and slowly began to unpeel the plaster, a second skin, secreted beneath his watch. He delicately removed the tiny green pill stuck to the plaster and transferred it to the palm of his hand. Sixty or seventy eyes were staring at him. He began coughing, and slowly put his hand up to his mouth, lowered his head and swallowed the pill.

Saeed came rushing back out of the building and began barking new orders. Within seconds, a car pulled up beside the truck.

'Out!' the Major screamed at Kratz, who stepped down onto the tarmac and allowed a dozen fixed bayonets to guide him towards the back door of the car. He was pushed onto the seat, and two men in dark suits took a place on each side of him. One quickly turned him and tied his hands behind his back, while the other blindfolded him.

Cohen and Aziz watched from the other side of the square as the car sped away from them.

31

THE GENERAL RETURNED Scott's smile.

'I won't introduce you to Miss Saib,' he said, 'as I believe you've already met.'

Scott looked blank as he stared at the woman dressed in a black abaya and a pushi that covered her face. She was surrounded by four soldiers, their bayonets drawn.

'We have a lot to thank Miss Saib for, because of course it was she who led us to you in the first place, not to mention her post-card to Mrs Rubin that helped you find the Declaration so quickly. We did try to make it as easy as possible for you.'

'I don't know Miss Saib,' said Scott.

'Oh, come, Professor – or should I call you Agent Bradley? I admire your gallantry, but while you may claim not to know Miss Saib, you certainly know Hannah Kopec,' the General said as he ripped off Hannah's pushi.

Scott stared at Hannah, but still said nothing.

'Ah, I see you do remember her. But then, it would be hard to forget someone who tried to kill you, wouldn't it?'

Hannah's eyes pleaded with Scott.

'How touching, my dear, he's forgiven you. But I fear I don't share his forgiving nature.' The General turned to see Major Saeed running towards him. He listened carefully to what the Major whispered to him, then began banging his swagger stick rapidly against his long leather boots.

'You're a fool!' he shouted at the top of his voice, and

suddenly struck the Major across the face with his swagger stick.

He turned back to face Scott. 'It seems,' he said, 'that the reunion I had planned for you and your friends will have to wait a little longer, because although we have Colonel Kratz safely locked up, the Jew and the Kurdish traitor have escaped. But it can only be a matter of time before we catch them.'

'How long have you known?' asked Hannah quietly.

'You made the mistake so many of our enemies make, Miss Kopec, of underestimating our great President,' replied the General. 'He dominates the affairs of the Middle East to a far greater extent than Gorbachev did the Russians, Thatcher the British, or Bush the American people. I ask myself, how many citizens in the West any longer believe the Allies won the Gulf War? But then, you were also stupid enough to underrate his cousin, Abdul Kanuk, our newly appointed Ambassador to Paris. Perhaps he wasn't quite that stupid when he followed you all the way to your lover's flat and stood in a doorway the rest of the night before following you back to the embassy. It was he who informed our Ambassador in Geneva what "Miss Saib" was up to.

'Of course, we needed to be sure, not least because our Deputy Foreign Minister found it so hard to accept such a tale about one of his most loyal members of staff. Such a naïve man. So, when you came to Baghdad, the Ambassador's wife invited Miss Saib's brother to dinner. But, sadly, he didn't recognise you. Your cover, as the more vulgar American papers would describe it, was blown. Those same papers keep asking pathetically, "Why doesn't Mossad assassinate President Saddam?" If only they knew how many times Mossad has tried and failed. What Colonel Kratz didn't tell you at your training school in Herzliyah, Miss Kopec, was that you are the seventeenth Mossad agent who has attempted to infiltrate our ranks during the past five years, and all of them have experienced the same tragic end as your Colonel is about to. And the real beauty of the whole exercise is that we don't have to admit we killed any of you in the first place. You see, the Jewish people are unwilling to accept, after Entebbe and Eichmann, that such a thing could possibly happen. I feel sure you will appreciate the logic of that, Professor.'

'I'll make a bargain with you,' said Scott.

'I'm touched, Professor, by your Western ethics, but I fear you have nothing to bargain with.'

'We'll trade Miss Saib if you release Hannah.'

The General burst out laughing. 'Professor, you have a keen sense of the ridiculous, but I won't insult you by suggesting that you don't understand the Arab mind. Do allow me to explain. You will be killed, and no one will comment because, as I have already explained, the West is too proud to admit that you even exist. Whereas we in the East will throw our hands in the air and ask why Mossad has kidnapped a gentle, blameless secretary on her way to Paris, and is now holding her in Tel Aviv against her will. We even know the house where she is captive. We have already arranged for sentimental pictures of her to be released to every paper in the Western world, and a distraught mother and son have been coached for weeks by one of your own public relations companies to face the Western press. We'll even have Amnesty International protesting outside Israeli embassies across the world on her behalf.'

Scott stared at the General.

'Poor Miss Saib will be released within days. Both of you, on the other hand, will die an unannounced, unheralded and unmourned death. To think that all you sacrificed your lives for was a scrap of paper. And while we are on that subject, Professor, I will relieve you of the Declaration.'

The four soldiers stepped forward and thrust their bayonets at Scott's throat as the General snatched the cardboard tube from his grasp.

'You did well to switch the documents in two minutes, Professor,' said the General, glancing up at the television screen above him. 'But you can be assured that it remains our intention to burn the original very publicly on the fourth of July, and I feel confident that we will destroy President Clinton's flimsy reputation along with it.' The General laughed. 'You know, Professor, I have for many years enjoyed killing people, but I shall gain a particular pleasure from your deaths, because of the appropriate way you will be departing this world.'

The soldiers surrounded Hannah and Scott and forced them back into the Chamber and on towards the short corridor. The General followed them down the passage. They all came to a halt in front of the open safe.

'Allow me,' said General Hamil, 'to inform you of one statistic you failed to mention, Professor, when you briefed me on this amazing feat of engineering. Perhaps you simply didn't know, although I am bound to admit that you have done your homework thoroughly. But did you realise that one person locked in a safe of this size, with a capacity of 504 cubic feet, can only hope to survive for six hours? I do not yet know the exact length of time two people can hope to survive while sharing the same amount of oxygen. But I will very shortly.' He removed a stopwatch from his pocket, waved his swagger stick, and the soldiers hurled first Hannah and then Scott into the safe. The smile remained on the General's face as two of the soldiers pushed the massive door closed. The lights all began flashing red.

The General clicked his stopwatch.

When the car came to a halt, Kratz reckoned that the distance they had travelled was under a mile. He heard the door open and felt a shove on his arm to indicate he should get out of the car. He was pushed up three stone steps before entering a building and walking into a long corridor. His footsteps echoed on the wooden floor. Then he was guided into a room on his left, where he was pushed down onto a chair, tied and gagged. His shoes and socks were removed. When he heard the door close, he sensed he was alone.

It was a long time – he couldn't be sure just how long – before the door opened again. The first voice he heard was General Hamil's. 'Remove the gag,' was all he said.

Kratz could hear him pacing round the chair, but at first the General said nothing. Kratz began to concentrate. He knew the pill was good for two hours, no more, and he suspected that it was already forty or fifty minutes since they had driven him away from Ba'ath headquarters.

'Colonel Kratz, I have waited some time for the privilege of making your acquaintance. I have long admired your work. You are a perfectionist.'

'Cut the crap,' said Kratz, 'because I don't admire you or your work.'

He waited for the first slap of gloves across his face or for a fist to come crashing into his jaw, but the General simply continued to circle the chair.

'You mustn't be too disappointed,' said the General. 'I feel sure, after all you've heard about us, that you must have expected at least some electric shocks by now, perhaps the Chinese water torture, even the rack, but I fear – unlike Mossad, Colonel – that when dealing with people of your seniority we long ago dispensed with such primitive methods. We have found them to be outmoded, a thing of the past. Worse, they just don't get results. You Zionists are tough and well trained. Few of you talk, very few. So we've had to resort to more scientific methods to gain the information we need.'

If it was still within the hour, thought Kratz, he had judged it well.

'A simple injection of PPX will ensure that we learn everything we want to know,' continued the General, 'and once we have the information we require, we'll simply kill you. So much more efficient than in the past, and with all the environmental complaints one gets nowadays, so much more tidy. Though, I must confess, I miss the old methods. So you'll appreciate why I couldn't resist locking Miss Kopec and Professor Bradley in their safe, especially as they hadn't seen each other for so long.'

Kratz's hand was pressed back and held against the arm of the chair. He felt fingers searching for a vein, and when the needle went in, he flinched. He began counting: one, two, three, four, five, six . . .

He was about to find out if one of Europe's leading chemists had, as she claimed, found the antidote for the Iraqis' latest truth drug. Mossad had tracked down the supplier in Austria. Strange how many people think there are no Jews left in Austria.

. . . thirty-seven, thirty-eight, thirty-nine . . .

The drug was still in its testing stage, and needed to be proved under non-laboratory conditions. If a person could remain fully in control of his senses while appearing to be under hypnosis, then they would know their antidote was a success.

. . . one minute, one minute one, one minute two, one minute three . . .

The test would come when they stuck the second needle in, and that might be anywhere. Then the trick was to show no reaction whatsoever, or the General would immediately realise that the original injection had failed to have the required effect. The training programme for this particular 'realistic experience' was not universally popular among agents, and although Kratz had experienced 'the prick', as it was affectionately known, once a month for the past nine months, you only had a single chance in 'non-laboratory conditions' to discover if you could pass the test.

. . . one minute thirty-seven, one minute thirty-eight, one minute thirty-nine . . .

The injection was meant to take effect after two minutes, and every agent had been taught to expect the second needle at some time between two and three minutes, thus the counting.

. . . one minute fifty-six, one minute fifty-seven . . .

Relax, it must come at any moment. Relax.

Suddenly the needle was jabbed in and out of the big toe on his left foot. Kratz stopped gritting his teeth; even his breathing remained regular. He had won the Israeli Pincushion Award, First Class. Mossad made jokes about everything.

32

'. . . AND ALL THAT TIME I really thought you were dead.'

'We had no way of letting you know,' said Scott.

'Still, it's not that important now, Simon.' said Hannah. 'Sorry. "Scott" will take a bit of getting used to. I may not be able to manage it in the time we've got left.'

Scott continued to cling onto her, until Hannah said, 'I know I ought to be hysterical, or at least crying, but I'm not. Perhaps all that will come later.'

'Or not at all,' said Scott, not letting her go.

'How can you say that?'

'One of the contingency plans that Kratz and I worked on was that if any of us were caught and tortured while someone else was still free, we'd hold out for one hour before telling them the whopper.'

Hannah knew exactly what Mossad meant by the whopper, even if on this occasion she didn't know the details.

'Although I have to admit this is one scenario we never considered,' said Scott. 'In fact, the exact opposite. We thought that if we were able to convince them we had another reason for bringing the safe to Baghdad, they'd immediately evacuate the building and clear the surrounding area.'

'And what would that have achieved?'

'We hoped that with the building empty, even if we'd been captured, the other agents who came over the border a day ahead of us might have a clear hour to get into the Council Chamber and remove the Declaration.'

'But the Iraqis would have taken the document with them.'

'Not necessarily. Our plan was that we would tell them exactly what would happen if the safe was closed by anyone other than me. We felt that would cause panic, and they'd probably leave everything behind.'

'So Kratz drew the short straw.'

'Yes,' said Scott quietly. 'Not that his original plan is relevant now, after I was stupid enough to hand over the Declaration to Hamil. So we'll have to use the time to get out, not in.'

'But you didn't hand it over,' said Hannah. 'The Declaration is still on the wall of the Chamber.'

'I'm afraid not,' said Scott. 'Hamil was right. I switched the copies after I set the alarm off. So I ended up giving Hamil back the original.'

'No, you didn't,' said Hannah. 'It's because you believed you switched the original that you fooled Hamil as well as yourself.'

'What are you talking about?' said Scott.

'I'm the one responsible,' said Hannah. 'I found the cardboard tube in the safe and switched the two documents, thinking I could get out of the building and then pass on a message to let Kratz know what I'd done. The trouble was, you and General Hamil arrived just as I was about to leave. So, when you locked yourself in the Chamber, you put the original back on the wall, and then you handed over the copy to Hamil.'

Scott took her in his arms again. 'You're a genius,' he said.

'No I'm not,' said Hannah. 'So you'd better let me in on the secret of what you've planned for this particular scenario. To start with, how do we get out of a locked safe?'

'That's the beauty of it,' said Scott. 'It isn't locked. It's programmed so that it can only be opened and closed by me.'

'Who dreamed that one up?'

'A Swede who would happily take our place, but he's stuck in Kalmar. The first thing I have to do is discover which wall is the door.'

'That's easy,' said Hannah. 'It has to be exactly opposite me because I'm sitting below the picture of Saddam, remember?'

Scott and Hannah began the short crawl on their hands and knees to the other side of the safe. 'Now we go to the right-hand corner,' he said, 'so that when we push, the leverage will be easier.'

Hannah nodded, and then remembered they couldn't see each other. 'Yes,' she said.

Scott checked the luminous dial of his watch. 'But not quite yet,' he added. 'We'll have to give Kratz a little more time.'

'Enough time to tell me what the whopper is?' asked Hannah.

'Good,' said the General, when Kratz didn't react to the needle being jabbed into his big toe. 'Now we can find out all we need to know. But to begin with, some simple questions. Your Mossad rank?'

'Colonel,' said Kratz. The secret was to tell them only facts you felt confident they already knew.

'Your initiation number?'

'78216,' he said. If in doubt, assume they know, otherwise you could be caught out.

'And your official position?'

'Councillor for Cultural Affairs to the Court of St James in London.' You are allowed three testing lies and one whopper, but no more.

'What are the names of your three colleagues who accompanied you on this mission?'

'Professor Scott Bradley, an expert on ancient manuscripts,' – the first testing lie – 'Ben Cohen, and Aziz Zeebari.' The truth.

'And the girl, Hannah Kopec, what is her rank in Mossad?'

'She is still a trainee.'

'How long has she been with Mossad?'

'Just over two years.'

'And her role?'

'To be placed in Baghdad to discover where the Declaration of Independence was located.' The second lie.

'You are doing well, Colonel,' said the General, looking at the long, thin cardboard tube he held in his right hand.

'And was this your overall responsibility as her commanding officer?'

'No. I was simply to accompany the safe from Kalmar.' The third lie.

'But surely that was nothing more than an excuse to locate the Declaration of Independence?'

Kratz hesitated. Experts had been able to show that even under the influence of a truth drug a highly trained agent would still hesitate when asked a secret he had never revealed in the past.

'What was the true purpose of your bringing the safe to Baghdad, Colonel?'

Kratz still remained silent.

'Colonel Kratz,' said the General, his voice rising with every word, 'what was the real reason you brought the safe to Baghdad?'

Kratz counted to three before he spoke.

'To blow up the Ba'ath Party headquarters with a tiny nuclear device secreted in the safe, in the hope of killing the President along with all the members of the Revolutionary Command Council.' The whopper.

How Kratz wished he could see the General's face. It was Hamil who was hesitating now.

'How was the bomb to be activated?'

Again Kratz did not reply.

'I will ask you once again, Colonel. How was the bomb to be activated?'

Still Kratz said nothing.

'When will it go off?' shouted the General.

'Two hours after the safe has been closed by anyone other than the Professor.'

The General checked his watch, rushed to the only phone in

the room and shouted to be put through to the President immediately. He waited until he heard Saddam's voice. He didn't notice that Kratz had fainted and fallen from his chair to the floor.

Scott eased himself into the corner before once again checking the little sulphur dots on his watch. It was 5.19. He and Hannah had been in the safe for an hour and seventeen minutes.

'I'm going to push now. If you hear anything, shove as hard as you can. If there's anyone still out there our only hope will be to take them by surprise.'

Scott began to exert the minimum amount of pressure on the corner of the door with the tips of his fingers, and it eased open an inch. He stopped and listened, but could hear nothing. He took a look through the tiny crack, and could see no one. He pushed another inch. Still no sound. Both of them now had a clear view of the corridor. Scott looked at Hannah and nodded, and together they shoved as hard as they could. The ton of steel shot open. They both leaped into the corridor, but there was no one to be seen. There was an eerie silence.

Scott and Hannah walked slowly down the short corridor, keeping to the sides until they reached the Chamber. Still no sound. Scott put a foot into the Chamber and glanced to his left. The Declaration of Independence was still hanging on the wall next to the portrait of Saddam.

Hannah moved silently to the far end of the Chamber and checked the long corridor. She then looked back at Scott and nodded. Scott checked the spelling of 'Brittish' before saying a silent hallelujah. He pulled out three of the nails, then eased the Declaration over the remaining nail in the top right-hand corner, trying to forget that he had spat on a national treasure and rubbed it in the dust. He gave Saddam one last look before rolling up the parchment and joining Hannah in the corridor.

Hannah slid along the wall, then pointed to the lift. She pulled a finger across her throat to show Scott she wanted to avoid using it in favour of the back stairs. He nodded his agreement and followed her out of the side door.

They moved quickly but silently up the six flights of stairs until they reached the ground floor. Hannah beckoned Scott into the side room where the cleaners had collected their boxes. She had reached the window on the far side of the room and was on her knees even before Scott had closed the door. He joined her and they stared out on a deserted Victory Square. There was no one to be seen in any direction.

'God bless Kratz,' said Scott.

Hannah nodded and beckoned him to follow her again. She led him back into the corridor and guided him quickly to the side door. Scott opened the door tentatively and slipped out ahead of her. A moment later she joined him on the tarmac.

He pointed to a group of palm trees halfway across the courtyard, and she nodded once again. They covered the twenty yards to its relative safety in under three seconds. Scott turned to look back at the building and saw the truck standing up against the wall. He assumed that, in the panic, it was just something else that had been left behind.

He tapped Hannah on the shoulder and indicated that he wanted to return to the building. They covered the ground at the same pace as before, ducking back inside the door. Scott led Hannah to the main corridor, where they found the front door was swinging on its hinges. He looked through the gap and pointed to the truck, mimed to which side he would go and touched her shoulder. Again they sprinted across the tarmac as if reacting to a starting pistol.

Scott jumped behind the wheel as Hannah leaped in the other side.

'Where the hell –' was Scott's first reaction when he discovered the ignition key wasn't in place. They began frantically to search the glove compartment, under the seats, on the dashboard. 'The bastards must have taken the key with them.'

'Simon, look out!' screamed Hannah. Scott turned to see a figure leaping up onto the footplate.

Hannah moved quickly into position to attack the intruder, but Scott blocked her.

'Good afternoon, miss,' said the stranger. 'Sorry we haven't been properly introduced,' he added before turning to Scott. 'Move over, Professor,' he said as he put the key back in the ignition. 'If you recall, it was agreed that I'd do the driving.'

'What in heaven's name are you doing here, Sergeant?' asked Scott.

'Now that's what I call a real American welcome,' replied Cohen. 'But, to answer your question, I was just obeying orders. I was told if you came out of that door carrying a cardboard tube, I was to get myself back here and move the hell out of it, but not under any circumstances to allow you to make a detour to the Foreign Ministry. By the way, where's the tube?'

'Look out!' shouted Hannah again, as she turned and saw an Arab charging towards them from the other side.

'That one won't do you any harm,' said Cohen, 'he's bloody useless. Doesn't even know the difference between a Diet Coke and a Pepsi.' Aziz leaped onto the running board and said to Scott, 'I think we've got about another twenty minutes, Professor, before they work out that there's no bomb in the safe.'

'Then let's get out of here,' said Scott.

'But where to?' asked Hannah.

'Aziz and I have already done a recce, sir. As soon as the sirens sounded we knew that Kratz must have sold them the whopper, because they couldn't move fast enough to get themselves below. Soldiers and police first seems to be the rule out here. Aziz and I have had the run of the city centre for the last hour. In fact the only person we bumped into was one of our own agents, Dave Feldman. He'd already sussed out the best route to give us a chance of avoiding any military.'

'Not bad, Cohen,' said Scott.

Cohen turned suddenly and stared at the Professor.

'I didn't do it for you, sir, I did it for Colonel Kratz. He got me out of jail once, and he's the only officer that's ever treated me like a human being. So whatever it is that you're holding in your hands, Professor, it had bloody well better be worth his life.'

'Thousands have given their lives for it over the years,' said Scott quietly. 'It's the American Declaration of Independence.'

'Good God,' said Cohen. 'How did the bastards get their hands on that?' He paused briefly. 'Am I meant to believe you?'

Scott nodded and unrolled the parchment. Cohen and Aziz stared in disbelief for several seconds.

'Right then, we'd better get you home, Professor, hadn't we?' said Cohen. 'Aziz will take over while we're in his neck of the woods.' He jumped out of the cab and the Kurd came running round to take his place behind the wheel. Once Cohen had clambered over the tailboard, he banged the roof of the truck and Aziz switched the engine on.

They accelerated round the courtyard, drove straight through the barrier and out onto Victory Square. The only other vehicles to be seen had long since been abandoned, and there was no sign of anyone on the streets.

'The area has been cleared for three miles in every direction, so it will be a little time before we come across anything,' Aziz said as he turned left into Kindi Street. He quickly moved the lorry up to sixty miles per hour, a speed only Saddam had ever experienced before on that particular road.

'I'm going to take the old Baquba Road out of the city, travelling through the areas where we're least likely to see any sign of the military,' explained Aziz as he passed the fountain made famous by Ali Baba. 'I'm still hoping to reach the highway out of Baghdad within the magic two hours.'

Aziz took a sudden right, switching gears but hardly losing any speed as he continued through what gave every impression of being a ghost town. Scott looked up at the sun as they crossed a bridge over the Tigris; in an hour or so it would have disappeared behind the highest buildings, and their chances of remaining undetected would greatly improve.

Aziz swung past Karmel Junblat University and into Jamila Street. There were still no people on the roads or pavements, and Scott felt that if anyone did see them now they would assume they were part of an army unit on patrol.

It was Hannah who spotted the first person: an old man, bent double, sitting on the edge of the pavement as if nothing in particular had taken place. They drove past him at sixty miles per hour, but he didn't even look up.

Aziz swung into the next road and found himself facing a group of young looters carrying off televisions and electronic equipment. They scattered when they saw the truck. Around the next corner there were more looters, but still no sign of police or soldiers.

When Aziz spotted the first dark-green uniforms he swerved quickly right, down a side street that on any other Wednesday would have been packed with shoppers and where a vehicle would have been lucky to average more than five miles per hour. But today Aziz managed to keep the speedometer above fifty. He turned right again, and they saw some of the first of the locals who had ventured back onto the streets. Once they had reached the end of the road, Aziz was able to join the main thoroughfare out of Baghdad. The traffic was still light.

Aziz eased the truck across into the outside lane, checking his rear-view mirror every few seconds and complying with the speed limit of fifty miles per hour. 'Never get stopped for the wrong reasons,' Kratz had warned him a thousand times.

When Aziz switched his sidelights on, Scott's hopes began to rise. Although the two hours had to be up, he doubted that anybody would be out searching for them yet, and it was well understood that with every mile out of Baghdad the citizens became less and less loyal to Saddam.

Once Aziz had left the Baghdad boundary sign behind him he pushed the speedometer up to sixty. 'Give me twenty minutes, Allah,' he said. 'Give me twenty minutes and I'll get them to Castle Post.'

'Castle Post?' said Scott. 'We're not on a Red Indian scouting mission.'

Aziz laughed. 'No, Professor, it's the site of a First World War British Army post, where we can hide for the night. If I can get there before –' All three of them spotted the first army lorry coming towards them. Aziz swung off to the left, skidded into a side road, and was immediately forced to drop his speed.

'So now where are we heading?' asked Scott.

'Khan Beni Saad,' said Aziz, 'the village where I was born. It will only be possible for us to stay for one night, but no one will think of looking for us there. Tomorrow, Professor, you will have to decide which of the six borders we're going to cross.'

General Hamil had been pacing around his office for the past hour. The two hours had long passed, and he was starting to wonder if Kratz might have got the better of him. But he couldn't work out how.

He was even beginning to regret that he had killed the man. If Kratz had still been alive, at least he could have fallen back on the tried and trusted method of torture. Now he would never know how he would have responded to his particular shaving technique.

Hamil had already ordered a reluctant lieutenant and his platoon back to the basement of the Ba'ath headquarters. The lieutenant had returned swiftly to report that the safe door was wide open and the truck had disappeared, as had the document that had been hanging on the wall. The General smiled. He remained confident that he was in possession of the original Declaration, but he extracted the parchment from the cylinder and laid it on his desk to double-check. When he came to the word 'British', he turned first white, and then, by several degrees, deeper and deeper shades of red.

He immediately gave an order to cancel all military leave, and then commanded five divisions of the elite guard to mount a search for the terrorists. But he had no way of knowing how much start they had on him, how far they might have already travelled, and in which direction.

However, he did know that they couldn't remain on the main roads in that truck for long, without being spotted. Once it was dark, they would probably retreat into the desert to rest overnight. But they would have to come out the following morning, when they must surely try to cross one of the six borders. The General had already given an order that if even one of the terrorists managed to cross any border, guards from every customs post would be arrested and jailed, whether they were on duty or not. The two soldiers who were supposed to have closed the safe door had already been shot for not carrying out his orders, and the Major detailed to supervise the moving of the safe had been immediately arrested. At least Major Saeed's decision to take his own life had saved Hamil the trouble of a court martial: within an hour the Major had been found hanging in his cell. Obviously leaving a coil of rope in the middle of the floor below a hook in the ceiling had proved to be a compelling enough hint. And as for the two young medical students who'd been responsible for the injections, and who had witnessed his conversation with Kratz, they were already on their way to the southern borders, to serve with a less than elite regiment. They were such nice-looking boys, the General thought; he gave them a week at the most.

Hamil picked up the phone and dialled a private number that would connect him to the palace. He needed to be certain that he was the first person to explain to the President what had taken place that afternoon.

33

SCOTT HAD ALWAYS CONSIDERED his own countrymen to be an hospitable race, but he had never experienced such a welcome as Aziz's family gave to the three strangers.

Khan Beni Saad, the village in which Aziz was born, had, he told them, just over 250 inhabitants at the last count, and barely survived on the income it derived from selling its small crop of oranges, tangerines and dates to the housewives of Kirkuk and Arbil.

The chief of the tribe, who turned out to be one of Aziz's uncles, immediately opened his little stone home to them so that they could make use of the one bath in the village. The women of the house – there seemed to be a lot of them – kept boiling water until all of the visitors were pronounced clean.

When Scott finally emerged from the chief's home, he found a table had been set up under a clump of citrus trees in the Huwaider fields. It was laden with strange fish, meat, fruit and vegetables. He feared they must have gathered something from every home in the village.

Under a clear starlit night, they devoured the fresh food and drank mountain water that, if bottled, a Californian would happily have paid a fortune for.

But Scott's thoughts kept returning to the fact that tomorrow they would have to leave these idyllic surroundings, and that he would somehow have to get them all across one of the six borders.

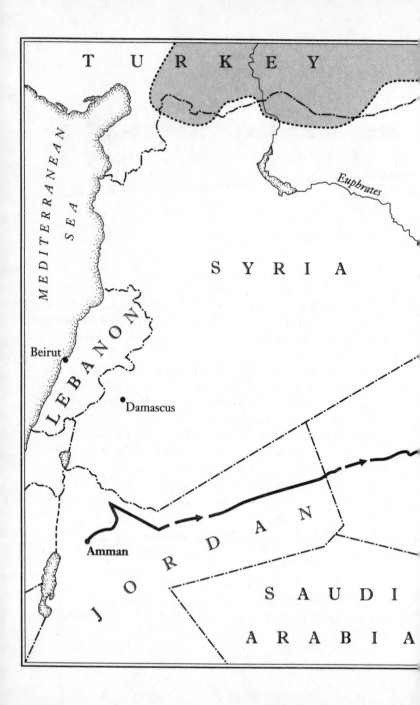

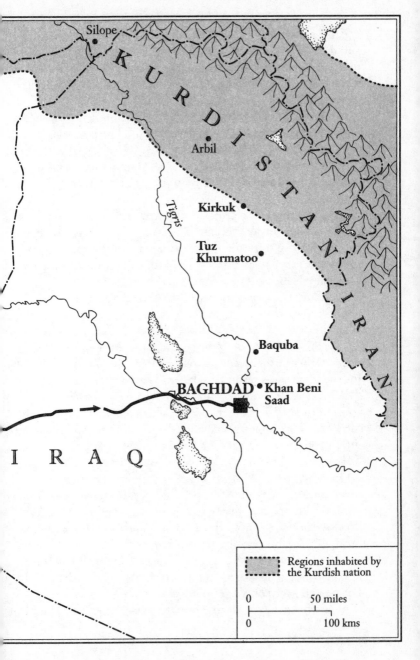

map 2   same size

After coffee had been served in various different-sized cups and mugs, the chief rose from his place at the head of the table to make a speech of welcome, which Aziz translated. Scott made a short reply which was applauded even before Aziz had been given the chance to interpret what he had said.

'That's one thing they have in common with us,' said Hannah, taking Scott's hand. 'They admire brevity.'

The chief ended the evening with an offer for which Scott thanked him, but felt unable to accept. He wanted to order all of his family out of the little house so that his guests could sleep indoors.

Scott continued to protest until Aziz explained, 'You must agree, or you insult his home by suggesting it is not good enough for you to rest in. And by the way, the greatest compliment you can pay an Arab is to make your woman pregnant while she sleeps under his roof.' Aziz shrugged.

Scott lay awake most of the night, staring through the glassless window, while Hannah hardly stirred in his arms. Having attempted to pay the chief the greatest possible compliment, Scott's mind went back to the problem of getting his team over one of the borders and ensuring that the Declaration of Independence was returned safely to Washington.

When the first ray of light crept across the woven rug that covered their bed, Scott released Hannah and kissed her on the forehead. He slipped from under the sheets to find that the little tin bath was already full of warm water, and the women had begun boiling more urns over an open fire.

Once Scott was dressed, he spent an hour studying maps of the country, searching for possible routes across Iraq's six borders. He quickly dismissed Syria and Iran as impossible, because the armies of both would be happy to slaughter them on sight. He also felt that to return over the Jordanian border would be far too great a risk. By the time Hannah had joined him he had also dismissed Saudi Arabia as too well guarded, and was now down to only five routes and two borders.

As his hosts began to prepare breakfast, Scott and Hannah

wandered down into the village hand in hand, as any lovers might on a summer morning. The locals smiled, and some bowed. Although none could hold a conversation with them, they all spoke so eloquently with their eyes that they both understood.

Once they had reached the end of the village, they turned and strolled back up the path towards the chief's house. Cohen was frying eggs on an open fire, and Hannah stopped to watch how the women baked the thin, circular pieces of bread which, covered in honey, were a feast in themselves. The chief, once again sitting at the head of the table, beckoned Scott to the place beside him. Cohen had already taken a seat on a stool and was about to begin his breakfast when a goat walked in and tugged the eggs straight off the plate. Hannah laughed and cracked Cohen another egg before he had a chance to voice his opinion.

Scott spread some honey on a piece of warm bread, and a woman placed a mug of goat's milk in front of him.

'Worked out what we have to do next, have you, Professor?' asked Cohen as Hannah dropped a second fried egg on to his plate. In one sentence, he had brought them all back to reality.

A villager came up to the table, knelt by the side of the chief and whispered in his ear. The message was passed on to Aziz.

'Bad news,' Aziz told them. 'There are soldiers blocking all the roads that lead back to the main highway.'

'Then we'll have to go across the desert,' said Scott. He unfolded his map and spread it across the table. Alternative routes were highlighted by a dozen blue felt-tip lines. He pointed to a path leading to a road which would take them to the city of Khalis.

'That is not a path,' said Aziz. 'It was once a river, but it dried up many years ago. We could walk along it, but we would have to leave the truck behind.'

'It won't be enough to leave the truck,' said Scott. 'We'll have to destroy it. If it were ever found by Saddam's soldiers, they would raze the village to the ground and massacre your people.'

The chief looked perplexed as Aziz translated all Scott had said. The old man stroked the rough morning stubble on his chin and smiled as Scott and Hannah listened to his judgement, unable to understand a word.

'My uncle says you must have his car,' Aziz translated. 'It is old, but he hopes that it still runs well.'

'He is kind,' said Scott. 'But if we cannot drive a truck across the desert, how can we possibly go by car?'

'He understands your problem,' said Aziz. 'He says you must take the car to pieces bit by bit, and his people will carry it the twelve miles across the desert until you reach the road that leads to Khalis. Then you can put it together again.'

'We cannot accept such a gesture,' said Scott. 'He is too generous. We will walk and find some form of transport when we reach Huwaider.' He pointed to the first village along the road.

Aziz translated once again: his uncle looked sad and murmured a few words. 'He says it is not really his car, it was his brother's car. It now belongs to me.'

For the first time, Scott realised that Aziz's father had been the village chief, and how much his uncle was willing to risk to save them from being captured by Saddam's troops.

'But even if we could disassemble and reassemble the car, what about army patrols once we reach that road?' he asked. 'By now thousands of Hamil's men are bound to be out there searching for us.'

'But not on those roads,' Aziz replied. 'The army will stick to the highway. They realise that's our only hope of getting across the border. No, our first problem will come when we reach the roadside check in Khalis.' He moved his finger a few inches across the map. 'There's bound to be at least a couple of soldiers on duty there.'

Scott studied the different routes again while Aziz listened to his uncle.

'And could we get as far as Tuz Khurmatoo without having to use the highway?' asked Scott, not looking up from the map.

'Yes, there's a longer route, through the hills, that the army would never consider, because they'd run the risk of being attacked by the Peshmerga guerrillas so near the border with Kurdistan. But once you've gone through Tuz Khurmatoo it's only a couple of miles to the main highway, though it's still another forty-five miles from there, with no other way of crossing the border.'

Scott held his head in his hands and didn't speak for some moments. 'So if we took that route we would be committed to crossing the border at Kirkuk,' he eventually said. 'Where both sides could prove to be unfriendly.'

The chief started tapping Kirkuk on the map with his finger while talking urgently to his nephew.

'My uncle says Kirkuk is our best chance. Most of the inhabitants are Kurdish and hate Saddam Hussein. Even the Iraqi soldiers have been known to defect and become Kurdish Peshmergas.'

'But how will they know which side we're on?' asked Scott.

'My uncle will get a message to the Peshmergas, so that when you reach the border they will do everything they can to help you to cross it. It's not an official border, but once you're in Kurdistan you'll be safe.'

'The Kurds sound our best bet,' said Hannah, who had been listening intently. 'Especially if they believe our original mission was to kill Saddam.'

'It might just work, sir,' said Cohen. 'That is, if the car's up to it.'

'You're the mechanic, Cohen, so only you can tell us if it's possible.'

Once Aziz had translated Scott's words the chief rose to his feet and led them to the back of his house. He came to a halt beside a large oblong object covered by a black sheet. He and Aziz lifted off the cover. Scott couldn't believe his eyes.

'A pink Caddy?' he said.

'A classic 1955 Sedan de Ville, to be exact, sir,' said Cohen, rubbing his hands with delight. He opened the long, heavy door and climbed behind the vast steering wheel. He pulled a lever under the dashboard and the bonnet flicked up. He got out, lifted the bonnet and studied the engine for some minutes.

'Not bad,' he said. 'If I can nick a few parts from the truck, I'll give you a racing car within a couple of hours.'

Scott checked his watch. 'I can only spare you an hour if we're hoping to cross the border tonight.'

Scott and Hannah returned to the house and once again pored over the map. The road Aziz had recommended was roughly twelve miles away, but across terrain that would be hard going even if they were carrying nothing.

'It could take hours,' Scott said.

'What's the alternative if we can't use the highway?' asked Hannah.

While she and Scott continued working on the route and Cohen on the car, Aziz rounded up thirty of the strongest men in the village. At a few minutes past the hour, Cohen re-appeared in the house, his hands, arms, face and hair covered in oil.

'It's ready to be taken apart, Professor.'

'Well done. But we'll have to get rid of the truck first,' said Scott as he rose from the table.

'That won't be possible, sir,' said Cohen. 'Not now that I've removed one or two of the best parts of its engine. That Cadillac should be able to do over a hundred miles per hour,' he said, with some pride. 'In third gear.'

Scott laughed, and accompanied by Aziz went in search of the chief. Once again he explained the problem.

This time the chief's face showed no anxiety. Aziz translated his thoughts. ' "Do not fear, my friend," he says. "While you are marching across the desert we will strip the truck and bury each piece in a place Saddam's soldiers could never hope to discover in a thousand years." '

Scott looked apprehensive, but Aziz nodded his agreement. Without waiting for Scott's opinion the chief led his nephew to the back of the house, where they found Cohen supervising the stripping of the Cadillac and the distribution of its pieces among the chosen thirty.

Four men would carry the engine on a makeshift stretcher, and another six would lift the chrome body onto their shoulders like pallbearers. Four more each carried a wheel with its white-rimmed tyre, while another four transported the chassis. Two held onto the red-and-white leather front seat, another two the back seat, and one the dashboard. Cohen continued to distribute the remaining pieces of the Cadillac until he came to the back of the line, where three children who looked no more than ten or eleven were given responsibility for two five-gallon cans of petrol and a tool bag. Only the roof was to be left behind.

Aziz's uncle led his people to the last house in the village so he could watch his guests begin their journey towards the horizon.

Scott shook hands with the chief, but could find no words adequate to thank him. 'Give me a call the next time you're passing through New Haven,' was what he would have said to a fellow American.

'I will return in better times,' he told the old man, and Aziz translated.

'My people wait for that day.'

Scott turned to watch Cohen, compass in hand, leading his improbable platoon on what appeared likely to be an endless journey. He took one of the five-gallon cans from the smallest of the children, and pointed back towards the village, but the little boy shook his head and quickly grabbed Scott's canvas bag.

Would history ever reveal this particular mode of transport for the Declaration of Independence, Scott wondered, as Cohen shouted 'Forward!'

General Hamil continued to pace round his office, as he waited for the phone to ring.

When Saddam had learned the news of Major Saeed's

incompetence in allowing the terrorists to escape with the Declaration, he was only furious that he had not been able personally to end the man's life.

The only order he had given the General was that a message should be put out on state radio and television stations hourly, stating that there had been an attempt on his life which had failed, but that the Zionist terrorists were still at large. Full descriptions of the would-be assassins were given, and he asked his beloved countrymen to help him in his quest to hunt down the infidels.

Had the matter been less urgent, the General would have counselled against releasing such information, on the grounds that most of those who came across the terrorists might want to help them, or at best turn a blind eye. The only advice he did give his leader was to suggest that a large reward should be offered for their capture. Enlightened self-interest, he had found, could so often overcome almost any scruples.

The General came to a halt in front of a map pinned to the wall behind his desk, temporarily covering a portrait of Saddam. His eye passed down the many thin red lines that wriggled between Baghdad and Iraq's borders. There were a hundred villages on both sides of every one of the roads, and the General was painfully aware that most of them would be only too happy to harbour the fugitives.

And then he remembered one of the names Kratz had given him. Aziz Zeebari – a common enough name, yet it had been nagging at him the whole morning.

'Aziz Zeebari . . . Aziz Zeebari . . . Aziz Zeebari . . .' he repeated. And then he remembered. He had executed a man of that name who had been involved in an attempted coup about seven years before. Could it possibly have been the traitor's father?

The load bearers halted every fifteen minutes to rest, change responsibilities and place the strain on yet-untested muscles.

'Pit stops', Cohen called them. They managed two miles in the first hour, and between them drank far more water than any car would have devoured.

When Scott checked his watch at midday, he estimated that they had only covered a little over two thirds of the distance to the road: it had been a long time since they had lost sight of the village but there was still no sign of life on the horizon. The sun beat down as they continued their journey, the pace slowing with each mile.

It was the eyes of a ten-year-old child that were the first to see movement. He ran to the front and pointed. Scott could see nothing as the little boy jogged ahead, and it was to be another forty minutes before they could all clearly see the dusty road. The sight made them quicken their pace.

Once they reached the side of the road, Aziz gave the order that the pieces of the car should be lowered gently to the ground, and a little girl, who Scott hadn't noticed before, handed out bread, goats' cheese and water while they rested.

Cohen was the first up and began walking around his platoon, checking on the various pieces. By the time he had returned to the chassis, they were all impatient to put the car together again.

Scott sat on the ground and watched as thirty untrained mechanics, under the direction of Sergeant Cohen, slowly bolted the old Cadillac together piece by piece. When the last wheel had been screwed on, Scott had to admit it *looked* like a car, but wondered if the old veteran would ever be able to start.

All the villagers surrounded the massive pink vehicle as Cohen sat in the driver's seat.

Aziz waited until the children had emptied their last drop of petrol into the tank. He then screwed on the big steel cap and shouted, 'Go for it!'

Cohen turned the key in the ignition.

The engine turned over slowly, but wouldn't catch. Cohen leaped out, lifted the bonnet and asked Aziz to take his place behind the wheel. He made a slight readjustment to the fan belt, checked the distributor and cleaned the spark plugs of the last few remaining grains of sand before screwing them in tightly. He stuck his head out from under the bonnet.

'Have a go, Kurd.'

Aziz turned the key and pressed the accelerator. The engine turned over a little more quickly but still didn't want to start. Sixty eyes stared beneath the bonnet, but offered no advice as Cohen spent several more minutes working on the distributor.

'Once again, and give it more throttle!' he shouted. Aziz switched on the ignition. The chug became a churn, and then suddenly a roar as Aziz pressed the accelerator – a noise only exceeded by the cheers of the villagers.

Cohen took Aziz's place in the front and lifted the gear lever on the steering column up into first. But the car refused to budge, as it bedded itself deeper and deeper into the sand. Cohen turned off the engine and jumped out. Sixty hands were flattened against the car as it was rocked backwards and forwards, and then, with one great shove, it was eased out of its deep trough. The villagers pushed it a further twenty yards and then waited for the Sergeant's next order.

Cohen pointed to the little girl who had distributed the food. She came shyly forward and he lifted her into the front of the car. With sign language, Cohen instructed her to kneel by the accelerator pedal and press down. Without getting into the car, Cohen leaned across, checked that the gears were in neutral, and switched on the engine. The little girl continued to push on the accelerator with both hands, and the engine revved into action. She immediately burst into tears, as the villagers cheered even louder. Cohen quickly lifted the little girl out onto the sand and then beckoned to Aziz.

'You're about half my weight, mate, so get in, put it into first gear and see if you can keep it going for about a hundred yards. If you can, we'll all jump in. If you can't, we'll have to push the bloody thing all the way to the border.'

Aziz stepped gingerly into the Cadillac. Sitting on the edge of the leather seat he gently lifted the lever into first gear and pressed down on the accelerator. The car inched forward and the villagers began to cheer again as Scott, Hannah and Cohen ran along beside it.

Hannah opened the passenger door, pushed the seat forward and jumped into the back as the car continued at its slow pace. Cohen leaped in after her and shouted, 'Second gear!'

Aziz pulled the lever down, across and up. The car lurched forward.

'That's third, you stupid Kurd!' shouted Cohen. He turned to see Scott running almost flat out. Cohen reached across to hold the door open as Scott threw his bag into the back. Scott leaped in and Cohen grabbed him round the shoulders. Scott's head landed in Aziz's lap, but although the Kurd swerved the car still kept going on the firmer sand.

'I can see why there aren't likely to be any army patrols on this road,' was Scott's only comment.

Aziz continued swinging the car from side to side to avoid the mounds of sand that had blown on to the road. Scott turned back to see the villagers waving frantically. Returning their wave seemed inadequate after all they had done. He hadn't thanked them properly or even said goodbye.

The villagers didn't move until the car was out of sight.

General Hamil swung round, angry that anyone had dared to enter his room without knocking. His ADC came to a halt in front of his desk. He was shaking, only too aware of the mistake he had made. The General raised his swagger stick and was about to strike the young officer across the face when he bleated out, 'We've discovered the village that the traitor Aziz Zeebari comes from, General.'

Hamil lowered his arm slowly until the swagger stick came to rest on the officer's right shoulder. The tip pushed forward until it was about an inch away from the ball of his right eye.

'Where?'

'Khan Beni Saad,' said the young man in terror.

'Show me.'

The Lieutenant ran over to the map, studied it for a few moments and then placed a finger on a village about ten miles north-east of Baghdad.

General Hamil stared at the spot and smiled for the first time that day. He returned to his desk, picked up the phone and barked out an order.

Within an hour, hundreds of troops would be swarming all over the little village.

Even if Khan Beni Saad did only have a population of 250, the General felt confident someone would talk, however young.

Aziz was able to keep up a steady thirty miles per hour while Scott tried to work out where they were on the map. He couldn't pinpoint their exact location until they had been driving for nearly an hour, when they came across a crude handpainted signpost lying in the road that read 'Khalis 25km'.

'Keep going for now,' said Scott. 'But we'll have to stop a couple of miles outside town so I can figure out how we get past the checkpoint.'

Scott's confidence in the old chief's judgement that there would be no army vehicles on that road was growing with every mile of flat desert road they covered. He continued to study the map carefully, now certain of the route that would have to be taken if they hoped to cross the border that day.

'So what *do* we do when we reach the checkpoint?' asked Cohen.

'Maybe it'll be easier than we think,' said Scott. 'Don't forget, they're looking for four people in a massive army truck.'

'But we *are* four people.'

'We won't be by the time we reach the checkpoint,' explained Scott, 'because by then you and I will be in the boot.'

Cohen scowled.

'Just be thankful it's a Caddy,' said Aziz, grinning as he maintained the steady speed.

'Perhaps I should take over the wheel now,' said Cohen.

'Not here,' said Scott. 'While we're on these roads, Aziz stays put.'

It was Hannah who saw her first. 'What the hell does she think she's up to?' she said, pointing to a woman who had jumped out into the middle of the road and was waving her arms excitedly.

Scott gripped the side of the window ledge as Cohen leaned forward to get a clearer view.

'Don't stop,' said Scott. 'Swerve round her if you have to.'
Suddenly Aziz began laughing.

'What's so funny, Kurd?' asked Cohen, keeping his eyes fixed on the woman, who remained determinedly in the middle of the road.

'It's only my cousin Jasmin.'

'Another cousin?' said Hannah.

'We are all cousins in my tribe,' Aziz explained as he brought the Cadillac to a halt in front of her. He leaped out of the car and threw his arms around the young woman, as the others joined them.

'Not bad,' said Cohen when he was finally introduced to cousin Jasmin, who hadn't stopped talking even when she shook hands with Scott and Hannah.

'So what's she jabbering on about, then?' demanded Cohen, before Aziz had been given the chance to translate his cousin's words.

'It seems the Professor was right. The soldiers have been warned to look out for an army truck being driven by four terrorists. But her uncle has already been in touch this morning to warn her we'd be in the Cadillac.'

'Then it must be a hell of a risk to try and get past them,' said Hannah.

'A risk,' agreed Aziz, 'but not a hell of a risk. Jasmin goes through this checkpoint twice a day, every day, to sell oranges, tangerines and dates from our village. So she's well known to them, and so is my uncle's car. My uncle says she must be in the

Cadillac when we go through the checkpoint. That way they won't be suspicious.'

'But if they decide to search the boot?'

'Then they won't get their daily ration of cigarettes, or fruit for their families, will they? You see, they all take it for granted we must be smuggling something.'

Jasmin started chattering again and Aziz listened dutifully. 'She says you must all climb into the boot before someone passing spots us.'

'It's still a hell of a risk, Professor,' said Cohen.

'It's just as big a risk for Jasmin,' said Scott, 'and I don't see any route back.' He folded up the map, walked round to the back of the car, opened the boot and climbed in. Hannah and Cohen followed without another word.

'Not as comfortable as the safe,' remarked Hannah as she put her arms round Scott. Aziz wedged the bag between her and Cohen. Hannah laughed.

'One bang on the side of the door,' said Aziz, 'and I'll be stopping at the checkpoint.'

He slammed down the boot. Jasmin grabbed her bags from the side of the road and jumped in next to her cousin.

The three of them in the boot heard the engine splutter into action and begin its more stately progress over the last few miles towards Khalis. Jasmin used the time to brief Aziz on her routine whenever she crossed the checkpoint.

34

THE CHIEF WAS HANGED FIRST. Then his brothers, one by one, in front of the rest of the village, but none of them uttered a word. Then they moved on to his cousins, until a twelve-year-old girl, who hoped to save her father's life, told them about the strangers who had stayed in the chief's house the previous night.

They promised the little girl that her father would be saved if she told them everything she knew. She pointed out into the desert to show them where they had buried the lorry. Twenty minutes of digging by the soldiers and they were able to confirm that she had been telling the truth.

They contacted General Hamil by field phone. He found it hard to believe that thirty of the Zeebari tribe had taken the chief's Cadillac to pieces and carried it bit by bit across the open desert.

'Oh, yes,' the little girl assured them. 'I know it's true because my brother carried one of the wheels all the way to the road on the other side of the desert,' she declared, pointing proudly towards the horizon.

General Hamil listened carefully to the information over the phone before ordering that the girl's father and brother should also be hanged.

He returned to the map on the wall and quickly pinpointed the only possible road they could have taken. His eye moved along the path across a stretch of desert until it joined another winding road, and then he realised which town they would have to pass through.

He looked at the clock on his desk: 4:39. 'Get me the check-point at Khalis,' he instructed the young Lieutenant.

Aziz saw a stationary van in the distance being inspected by a soldier. Jasmin warned him it was the checkpoint and tipped out the contents of one of her bags onto the seat between them.

Aziz banged on the side of his door, relieved to see there were only two soldiers in sight, and that one of them was sleeping in a comfortable old chair on the other side of the road.

When the car came to a halt Scott could hear laughter coming from somewhere. Aziz passed a packet of Rothmans to the guard.

The soldier was just about to wave them through when the other guard stirred from his drowsy slumber like a cat who had been resting for hours on a radiator. He pushed himself up, moved slowly towards the car, and looked over it with admira-tion, as he had done many times before. He began to stroll around it. As he passed the boot he gave it a loving slap with the palm of his hand. It flicked open a few inches. Scott pulled it gently closed as Jasmin dropped a carton of two hundred Rothmans on the ground by her side of the car.

The border guard moved quickly for the first time that day. Jasmin gave him a smile as he retrieved the cigarettes, and whis-pered something in his ear. The soldier looked at Aziz and started laughing, as a large lorry stacked with crates of beer came to a halt behind them.

'Move on, move on,' shouted the first soldier, as the sight of greater rewards caught his eye. Aziz quickly obeyed and lurched forward in second gear, nearly throwing Cohen and the holdall out of the back.

'What did you say to that soldier?' asked Aziz once they were out of earshot.

'I told him you were gay, but I would be returning on my own later.'

'Have you no family pride?' asked Aziz.

'Certainly,' said Jasmin. 'But he is also a cousin.'

On Jasmin's advice, Aziz took the longer southern route around the town. He was unable to avoid all the potholes, and from time to time he heard groans coming from the boot. Jasmin pointed to a junction ahead of them, and told Aziz that that was where he should stop. She gathered up her bags, leaving some fruit on the seat between them. Aziz came to a halt by a road that led back into the centre of the town. Jasmin jumped out, smiled and waved. Aziz waved back, and wondered when he would see his cousin again.

He drove on alone to the far side of the town, still unable to risk letting his colleagues out of the boot while the few locals around could observe what was going on.

Once Khalis was a couple of miles behind him, Aziz came to a halt at a crossroads which displayed two signposts. One read 'Tuz Khurmatoo 120km', and the other 'Tuz Khurmatoo 170km'. He checked in every direction before climbing out of the car, opening the boot and letting the three baggage passengers tumble out onto the road. While they stretched their limbs and took deep breaths of air, Aziz pointed to the signposts. Scott didn't need to look at the map to decide which route they would have to take.

'We must take the longer road,' he said, 'and hope that they still think we're in the truck.' Hannah slammed down the boot with feeling before they all four jumped back into the car.

Aziz averaged forty miles an hour on the winding road, his three passengers ducking out of sight whenever another vehicle appeared on the horizon.

The four of them devoured the fresh fruit Jasmin had left on the front seat.

When they passed a signpost indicating twenty kilometres to Tuz Khurmatoo Scott said to Aziz, 'I want you to stop a little way outside the village and go in alone before we decide if it's safe for us to drive straight through. Don't forget it's only another three miles beyond the village to the highway, so the place could be swarming with soldiers.'

'And to the Kurdish border?' asked Hannah.

'About forty-five miles,' said Scott as he continued to study the map. Aziz drove for another twenty minutes before he came over the brow of a hill and could see the outline of a village nestling in the valley. A few moments later he pulled the car off the road and parked it under a row of citrus trees that sheltered them from the sun and the prying eyes of those in passing vehicles. Aziz listened carefully to Scott's instructions, got out of the car and jogged off in the direction of Tuz Khurmatoo.

General Hamil was too furious to speak when the young Lieutenant informed him that the Cadillac had passed through the Khalis checkpoint less than an hour before, and neither of the soldiers on duty had bothered to check the boot.

After a minimum of torture, one of them had confessed that the terrorists must have been helped by a young girl who regularly passed through the checkpoint.

'She will never pass through it again,' had been the General's only observation.

The only other piece of information they were able to get out of the soldiers was that whoever had been driving the car was the girl's cousin, and a homosexual. Hamil wondered how they could possibly know that.

Once again, the General returned to the map on the wall behind his desk. He had already given orders for an army of helicopters, lorries, tanks and motorcycles to cover every inch of the road between Khalis and the border, but still no one had reported seeing a Cadillac on the highway. He was mystified, knowing they couldn't possibly have turned back or they would have run straight into his troops.

His eyes searched every route between the checkpoint and the border yet again. 'Ah,' he said finally, 'they must have taken the road through the hills.' The General ran his finger along a thin winding red line until it joined the main highway.

'So that's where you are,' he said, before bellowing out some new orders.

It was almost an hour before Cohen announced, 'One Kurd heading towards us, sir.'

As Aziz came running up the slope the grin remained on his face. He had been into Tuz Khurmatoo and he was able to reassure them that the village was going about its business as usual. But the government radio was blasting out a warning to be on the lookout for four terrorists who had attempted to assassinate the Great Leader, so all the main roads were now crawling with soldiers. 'They've got good descriptions of all four of us, but the radio bulletin an hour ago was still saying we were in the truck.'

'Right, Aziz,' said Scott, 'drive us through the village. Hannah, sit in the front with Aziz. The Sergeant and I will lie down in the back. Once we're on the other side of Tuz we'll keep out of sight and only continue on to the border after it's dark.'

Aziz took his place behind the wheel, and the Cadillac began its slow journey into Tuz.

The main road through the village must have been about three hundred yards long and just about wide enough to take two cars. Hannah looked at the little timber shops and the men who were growing old sitting on steps and leaning against walls. A dirty old Cadillac travelling slowly through the village, she thought, would probably be the highlight of their day, until she saw the vehicle at the other end of the road.

'There's a jeep coming towards us,' she said calmly. 'Four men, one of them sitting behind what looks like an anti-aircraft gun mounted on the back.'

'Just keep driving slowly, Aziz,' said Scott. 'And Hannah, keep talking us through it.'

'They're about a hundred yards away from us now and beginning to take an interest.' Cohen pointed to the tool bag and grabbed a wrench. Scott selected a spanner as they both turned over slowly and rested on their knees.

'The jeep has swung across in front of us,' said Hannah. 'We're going to be forced to stop in about ten seconds.'

'Does it still look as if there are four of them?' asked Scott.

'Yes,' said Hannah. 'I can't see any more.'

The Cadillac came to a halt.

'The jeep has stopped only a few yards in front of us. One of the soldiers is getting out and another is following. Two are staying in the jeep. One is behind the mounted gun and the other is still at the wheel. We'll take the first two,' said Hannah. 'You'll have to deal with the two in the jeep.'

'Understood,' said Scott.

The first soldier reached the driver's side as the second passed the bumper on Hannah's right. Both Aziz and Hannah had their outside hands on the armrests, their doors already an inch open.

The second Aziz saw the first soldier glance into the back and go for his gun, he swung his door open so fast that the crack of the soldier's knees sounded like a bullet as he collapsed to the ground. Aziz was out of the car and on top of him long before he had time to recover. The second soldier ran towards Hannah as Scott leaped out of the car. Hannah delivered one blow to his carotid artery and another to the base of his spine as he tried to pull out his gun. A bullet would not have killed him any quicker. The third soldier started firing from the back of the jeep. Cohen dived out into the road, and the fourth soldier jumped from behind the wheel and ran towards him, firing his pistol. Cohen hurled the wrench at him, causing him to step to one side and straight into the firing line of the mounted gun. The bullets stopped immediately, but Cohen was already at his throat. The soldier sank as if he had been hit by a ton of bricks, and his gun flew across the road. Cohen gave him one blow to the jugular vein and another to the back of the neck: he went into spasms and began wriggling on the ground. Cohen quickly turned his attention to the man seated behind the gun, who was lining him up in his sights. At ten yards' distance, Cohen had no hope of reaching him, so he dived for the side of the car as bullets sprayed into the open door, two of them ripping into his left leg. Scott was now running towards the jeep from the other side. As the soldier swung the gun round to face him, Scott propelled himself through the air and onto the top of the jeep.

Bullets flew everywhere as they tumbled clumsily off the back, Scott still clinging onto his spanner. They were both quickly on their feet, and Scott brought the spanner down across the gunner's neck – the soldier raised an arm to fend off the blow, but Scott's left knee jack-knifed into his crotch. The gunner sank to the ground as the second blow from the spanner found its mark and broke the soldier's neck cleanly. He lay splayed out on the road, looking like a breast-stroke swimmer halfway through a stroke. Scott stood over him, mesmerised, until Aziz dived at his legs and knocked him to the ground. Scott couldn't stop shaking.

'It's always hardest the first time,' was the Kurd's only comment.

The four of them were now facing outwards, covering every angle as they waited for the locals to react. Cohen climbed unsteadily up into the jeep, blood pouring from his leg, and took his place behind the mounted gun. 'Don't fire unless I say so,' shouted Scott as he checked up and down the road. There wasn't a person to be seen in either direction.

'On your left!' said Hannah, and Scott turned to see an old man dressed in a long white dishdash with a black-and-white spotted keffiyeh on his head, a thick belt hung loosely around his waist. He was walking slowly towards them, his hands held high in the air.

Scott's eyes never left the old man, who came to a halt a few yards away from the Cadillac.

'I have been sent by the village elders because I am the only one who speaks English,' he said. The man was trembling and the words came stumbling out. 'We believe you are the terrorists who came to kill Saddam.'

Scott said nothing.

'Please go. Leave our village and go quickly. Take the jeep and we will bury the soldiers. Then no one will ever know you were here. If you do not, Saddam will murder us all. Every one of us.'

'Tell your people we wish them no harm,' said Scott.

'I believe you,' said the old man, 'but please, go.'

Scott ran forward and stripped the tallest soldier of his uniform while Cohen kept his gun trained on the old man. Aziz stripped the other three while Hannah grabbed Scott's bag from the Cadillac before jumping into the back of the jeep.

Aziz threw the uniforms into the jeep and then leaped into the driving seat. The engine was still running. He put the vehicle into reverse and swung round in a semi-circle as Scott took his place in the front. Aziz began to move slowly out of Tuz Khurmatoo. Cohen turned the gun round in the direction of the village, at the same time thumping his left leg with his clenched fist.

Scott continued to look behind him as a few of the villagers moved tentatively out into the road and started to drag the soldiers unceremoniously away. Another climbed into the Cadillac and began to reverse it down a side road. A few moments later they had all disappeared from sight. Scott turned to face the road ahead of him.

'It's about another three miles to the highway,' said Aziz. 'What do you want me to do?'

'We've only got one chance of getting across that border,' said Scott, 'so for now pull over into that clump of trees. We can't risk going out onto the highway until it's pitch dark.' He checked the time. It was 7.35.

Hannah felt blood dripping onto her face. She looked up, and saw the deep wounds in Cohen's leg. She immediately tore off the corner of her yashmak and tried to stem the flow of blood.

'You all right, Cohen?' asked Scott anxiously.

'No worse than when I was bitten by a woman in Tangier,' he replied.

Aziz began laughing.

'How can you laugh?' said Hannah, continuing to clean the wound.

'Because he was the reason she bit me,' said Cohen.

After Hannah had completed the bandaging, the four of them changed into the Iraqi uniforms. For an hour they kept their eyes on the road, looking for any sign of more soldiers. A few villagers on donkeys, and more on foot, passed them in both directions, but the only vehicle they saw was an old tractor that chugged by on its way back to the village at the end of a day's service.

As the minutes slipped by, it became obvious that the villagers had kept to their promise and made no contact with any army patrols.

When Scott could no longer see the road in front of them, he went over his plan for the last time. All of them accepted that their options were limited.

The nearest border was forty-five miles away, but Scott now accepted the danger they could bring to any village simply by passing through it. He didn't feel his plan was foolproof, far from it, but they couldn't wait in the hills much longer. It would only be a short time before Iraqi soldiers were swarming all over the area.

Scott checked the uniforms. As long as they kept on the move, it would be hard for anyone to identify them in the dark as anything other than part of an army patrol. But once they reached the highway, he knew they couldn't afford to stay still for more than a few seconds. Everything depended on how close they could get to the border post without being spotted.

When Scott gave the order, Aziz swung the jeep onto the winding road to begin the three-mile journey to the highway. He covered the distance in five minutes, and during that time they didn't come across another vehicle. But once they hit the highway, they found the road was covered with lorries, jeeps, even tanks, travelling in both directions.

None of them saw the two motorcycles, the tank and three lorries that swung off the highway and headed at speed down the little road towards of Tuz Khurmatoo.

Aziz went as fast as he could, while Cohen remained seated on the back behind the gun. Scott watched the road ahead of him, his beret pulled well down. Hannah sat below Cohen, motionless, a gun in her hand. The first road sign indicated that it was sixty kilometres to the border. For a moment Scott was distracted by an oil well that kept pumping away on the far side of the road. Nobody spoke as the distance to Kirkuk descended from fifty-five to forty-six, to thirty-two, but with each sign and each new oil well, the traffic became heavier and their speed began to drop rapidly. The only relief was that none of the passing patrols seemed to show any interest in the jeep.

Within minutes the little village was swarming with soldiers from Saddam's elite guard. Even in the dark, it took only ten bullets and as many minutes for them to find out where the Cadillac was, and another thirty bullets to discover the unfilled graves of the four dead soldiers.

General Hamil listened to the senior officer when he phoned in with the details. All he asked for was the radio frequency of the jeep that had been in Tuz Khurmatoo earlier that evening. The General slammed down the phone, checked his watch, and keyed in the frequency.

The single tone continued for some time.

'They must still be looking for a truck or a pink Cadillac,' Scott was saying when the radio phone began ringing. They all four froze.

'Answer it, Aziz,' said Scott. 'Listen carefully, and find out what you can.'

Aziz picked up the handset, listened to a short message, then said, 'Yes, sir,' in Arabic, and put the handset down.

'They've found the Cadillac, and are ordering all jeeps to report to their nearest army post,' he said.

'It can't be long before they realise it's not one of their men driving this jeep,' said Hannah.

'With luck we might still have twenty minutes,' said Scott. 'How far to the border?'

'Nine miles,' said Aziz.

The General knew it had to be Zeebari, or he would have responded with the elite guards' code number.

So now he knew what vehicle they were in, and which border they were heading for. He picked up the phone and barked another order. Two officers accompanied him as he ran out of the room and into a large yard at the back of the building. The blades of his personal helicopter were already slowly rotating.

It was Aziz who first spotted the end of a long queue of oil tankers waiting to cross the unofficial border. Scott checked the inside track and asked Aziz if he could drive down such a narrow strip.

'Not possible, sir,' the young Kurd told him. 'We'd only end up in the ditch.'

'Then we've no alternative but to go straight down the middle.'

Aziz moved the jeep out into the centre of the road and tried desperately to maintain his speed. To begin with he was able to stay clear of the lorries and avoid the oncoming traffic. The first real trouble came four miles from the border, when an army truck heading towards them refused to move over.

'Shall I blast him off the road?' said Cohen.

'No,' said Scott. 'Aziz, keep going, but prepare to jump and take cover among the tankers, then we'll regroup.' Just as Scott was about to leap, the lorry swerved across the road and ended up in the ditch on the far side.

'Now they all know where we are,' said Scott. 'How many miles to the customs post, Aziz?'

'Three, three and a half at the most.'

'Then step on it,' said Scott, although he realised Aziz was already going as fast as he could. They had managed to cover the next mile in just over a minute when a helicopter swung above them, beaming down a searchlight that lit up the entire road. The radio phone began ringing again.

'Ignore it,' shouted Scott as Aziz tried to keep the jeep on the centre of the road and maintain his speed. They passed the two-mile mark as the helicopter swung back, confident it had spotted its prey, and began to focus its beam directly on them.

'We've got a jeep coming up our backside,' said Cohen, as he swung round to face it.

'Get rid of it,' said Scott.

Cohen obliged, sending the first few shots through the windscreen and the next into the tyres, thankful for the light from above. The pursuing jeep swung across the road, crashing into an oncoming lorry. Another quickly took its place. Hannah reloaded the gun with a magazine of bullets that was lying on the floor while Cohen concentrated on the road behind them.

'One and a half miles to go,' shouted Aziz, nearly crashing into lorries on both sides of the road. The helicopter hovered above them and began to fire indiscriminately, hitting vehicles going in both directions.

'Don't forget that most of them haven't a clue who's chasing what,' said Scott.

'Thanks for sharing that piece of logic with me, Professor,' said Cohen. 'But I've got a feeling that helicopter knows exactly who he's chasing.' Cohen began to pepper the next jeep the moment it came into range. This time it simply slowed to a halt, causing the car behind to run straight into it and creating a concertina effect as one after another the pursuing jeeps crashed into the back of the vehicle in front of them. The road behind was suddenly clear, as if Aziz had been the last car through a green light.

'One mile to go,' shouted Aziz as Cohen swung round to concentrate on what was going on in front of him and Hannah reloaded the automatic gun with the last magazine of bullets. Scott could see the lights of a bridge looming up in front of him: the Kirkuk fortress on the side of the hill that Aziz had told them signalled the customs post was only about half a mile away. As the helicopter swung back and once again sprayed the road with bullets, Aziz felt the front tyre on his side suddenly blow as he drove onto the bridge.

Scott could now see the Kurdish checkpoint ahead of him as the helicopter swung even lower on its final attempt to stop them. A flurry of bullets hit the jeep's bonnet, ricocheted off the bridge and into the windscreen. As the helicopter swung away, Scott looked up and for a second stared into the eyes of General Hamil.

Scott looked back down and punched a hole in the shattered windscreen, only to discover he was faced with two rows of soldiers lined up in front of him, their rifles aiming straight at the jeep.

Behind the row of soldiers were two small exits for those wishing to enter Kurdistan and two entrances on the other side of the road for those driving out of Kirkuk.

The two exits to Kurdistan were blocked with stationary vehicles, while the two entrances had been left clear – although no one at that moment was showing any desire to enter Saddam's Iraq.

Aziz decided that he would have to swing across the road and risk driving the jeep at an acute angle through one of the small entrances, where he might be faced with an oncoming vehicle – in which case they would be trapped. He was still losing speed, and could feel that the rim of the front left-hand wheel was now touching the ground.

Once they were within range, Cohen opened fire on the line of soldiers in front of him. Some fired back, but he managed to hit several before the rest scattered.

With a hundred yards to go and still losing speed, Aziz suddenly swung the jeep across the road and tried to steer it towards the second entrance. The jeep hit the right-hand wall, careered into the short, dark tunnel and bounced onto the left-hand wall before lurching out into no-man's land, between the two customs posts.

'Keep going, keep going!' shouted Scott as they emerged from the little tunnel. Suddenly there were dozens of soldiers pursuing them from the Iraqi side.

Aziz was still losing speed as he steered the jeep back to the left and pointed it in the direction of the border with Kurdistan, a mere four hundred yards away. He pressed his foot flat down on the accelerator but the speedometer didn't rise above two miles per hour. Another row of soldiers, this time from the Kurdish border, was facing them, their rifles pointing at the jeep. But none of them was firing.

Cohen swung around as a stray bullet hit the back of the jeep and another flew past his shoulder. Once again he fired a volley towards the Iraqi border, and those who could quickly retreated behind their checkpoint. The jeep trundled on for a few more yards before it finally whimpered to a halt halfway between the two unofficial barriers that the UN refused to recognise.

Scott looked towards the Kurdish border. A hundred Peshmergas were lined up, their rifles now firing – but not in the direction of the jeep. Scott turned back to see another line of soldiers tentatively advancing from the Iraqi side. He and Hannah began firing their pistols as Cohen let forth another burst which came to a sudden stop. The Iraqi soldiers had started to retreat again, but sensed immediately that their enemy had finally run out of ammunition.

Cohen leaped down off the jeep and quickly took out his pistol. 'Come on, Aziz!' he shouted as he rushed forward and crouched beside the driver's door. 'We'll have to cover them so the Professor can get his bloody Declaration across the border.'

Aziz didn't reply. His body was slumped lifelessly over the wheel, the horn sounding intermittently. The unanswered radio phone was still ringing.

'The bastards have killed my Kurd!' shouted Cohen. Hannah grabbed the canvas bag as Scott lifted Aziz out of the front of the jeep. Together, they began to drag him the last few hundred yards towards the border with Kurdistan.

Another line of Iraqi soldiers started to advance towards the jeep as Scott and Hannah carried the dead body of Aziz nearer and nearer to his Kurdish homeland.

They heard more shots whistle past them, and turned to see Cohen running towards the Iraqis screaming, 'You killed my Kurd, you bastards! You killed my Kurd!' One of the Iraqis fell, another fell, one retreated. Another fell, another retreated, as Cohen went on advancing towards them. Suddenly, he fell to his knees, but somehow he kept crawling forward, until a final volley rang out. The Sergeant collapsed in a pool of blood a few yards from the Iraqi border.

While Scott and Hannah carried the dead Kurd into the land of his people, Saddam's soldiers dragged the body of the Jew back into Iraq.

'Why were my orders disobeyed?' Saddam shouted.

For several moments no one around the table spoke. They knew the chances of all of them returning to their beds alive that night had to be marginal.

General Hamil turned the cover of a thick file, and looked down at the handwritten note in front of him.

'Major Saeed was to blame, Mr President,' stated the General. 'It was he who allowed the infidels to escape with the Declaration, and that is why his body is now hanging in Tohrir Square for your people to witness.'

The General listened intently to the President's next question.

'Yes, Sayedi,' he assured his master. 'Two of the terrorists were killed by guards from my own regiment. They were by far the most important members of the team. They were the two who managed to escape from Major Saeed's custody before I arrived. The other two were an American professor and the girl.'

The President asked another question.

'No, Mr President. Kratz was the commanding officer, and I personally arrested the infamous Zionist leader before questioning him at length. It was during that interrogation that I discovered that the original plan had been to assassinate you, Sayedi, and I made certain that he, like those who came before him, failed.'

The General had no well-rehearsed answer to the President's next question, and he was relieved when the State Prosecutor intervened.

'Perhaps we can turn this whole episode to our advantage, Sayedi.'

'How can that be possible,' shouted the President, 'when two of them have escaped with the Declaration and left us with a useless copy that anyone who can spell "British" will immediately realise is a fake? No, it is I who will be made the laughing stock of the world, not Clinton.'

Everyone's eyes were now fixed on the Prosecutor.

'That may not necessarily be the case, Mr President. I suspect that when the Americans see the state of their cherished treasure, they will not be in a hurry to put it back on display at the National Archives.'

The President did not interrupt this time, so the Prosecutor continued.

'We also know, Mr President, that because of your genius, the parchment currently on display in Washington to an unsuspecting American public is, to quote you, "a useless copy that anyone who can spell 'British' will immediately realise is a fake".'

The President's expression was now one of concentration.

'Perhaps the time has come, Sayedi, to inform the world's press of your triumph.'

'My triumph?' said the President in disbelief.

'Why, yes, Sayedi. Your triumph, not to mention your magnanimity. After all, it was you who gave the order to hand over the battered Declaration to Professor Bradley after the gangster Cavalli had attempted to sell it to you.'

The President's expression turned to one of deep thought.

'They have a saying in the West,' added the Prosecutor, 'about killing two birds with one stone.'

Another long silence followed, during which no one offered an opinion until the President smiled.

PART THREE

'. . . we mutually pledge to each other our Lives, our Fortunes and our sacred Honor.'

35

THE OFFICIAL STATEMENT issued by the Iraqi government on July 2nd was that there was no truth in the report that there had been a shooting incident on the border posts at Kirkuk in which several Iraqi soldiers had been killed and more wounded.

The Kurdish leaders were unable to offer any opinion on the subject, as the only two satellite phones in Iraqi Kurdistan had been permanently engaged with requests for assistance from the State Department in Washington.

When Charles Streator, the American Ambassador in Istanbul, was telephoned and asked by the Reuters Bureau Chief in the Middle East why a US Air Force jet had landed at the American base in Silope on the Turkish border, and then returned to Washington with two unknown passengers as its cargo, His Excellency told his old friend that he had absolutely no idea what he was talking about. The Bureau Chief considered the Ambassador to be an honest man, although he accepted that it was part of the job to lie for his country.

The Ambassador had in fact been up all night following a call from the Secretary of State requesting that one of their helicopters should be despatched to the outskirts of Kirkuk to pick up five passengers, one American, one Arab and three Israelis, who were then to be flown back to the base at Silope.

The Ambassador had called Washington later that morning

JEFFREY ARCHER

to inform Warren Christopher that unfortunately only two people had managed to cross the border alive: an American named Scott Bradley and an Israeli woman, Hannah Kopec. He had no information on the other three.

The American Ambassador was totally thrown by the Secretary of State's final question. Did Professor Bradley have a cardboard tube with him? The Ambassador was only disappointed that the Reuters correspondent hadn't asked him the same thing, because then he would have been telling him the truth when he said, 'I've absolutely no idea what you're talking about.'

Scott and Hannah slept for most of the flight back to America. When they stepped off the plane at Andrews Air Force Base they found Dexter Hutchins at the bottom of the steps waiting to greet them. Neither of them was surprised when customs showed little interest in Scott's canvas bag. A CIA car whisked them off in the direction of Washington.

On the journey into the capital, Dexter warned them that they would be going direct to the White House for a top-level meeting, and briefed them on who else would be present.

They were met at the West Wing reception entrance by the President's Chief of Staff, who conducted them to the Oval Office. Scott couldn't help feeling that, as it was his first meeting with the President, he would have preferred to have shaved at some time during the last two days, and not to have been dressed in the same clothes that he'd worn for the past three days.

Warren Christopher was there to greet them at the door of the Oval Office, and he introduced Scott to President Clinton as if they were old friends. Bill Clinton welcomed Scott home, and thanked Hannah for the part she had played in securing the safe return of the Declaration.

Scott was delighted to meet Calder Marshall for the first time, Mr Mendelssohn for the second time, and to be reunited with Dollar Bill.

Dollar Bill bowed to Hannah. 'Now I understand why the Professor was willing to cross the earth to bring you back,' was all the little Irishman had to say.

The moment the handshakes were over, none of them could hide their impatience to see the Declaration. Scott unzipped his bag and carefully took out a bath towel, from which he extracted the document before handing it over to its rightful custodian, the Secretary of State. Christopher slowly unrolled the parchment. No one in the room was able to hide their dismay at the state the Declaration was in.

The Secretary passed the document over to the Archivist who, accompanied by the Conservator and Dollar Bill, walked across to the large window overlooking the South Lawn. The first word they checked was 'Brittish', and the Archivist smiled.

But it was only a few moments more before Calder Marshall announced their combined judgement. 'It's a fake,' was all he said.

'How can you be so certain?' asked the President.

'*Mea culpa*,' said Dollar Bill, looking a little sheepish.

'So does that mean that Saddam is still in possession of the original?' asked the Secretary of State in disbelief.

'No, sir, he has the copy Scott took to Baghdad,' said Dollar Bill. 'So clearly he was already in possession of a fake before Scott did the exchange.'

'Then who has the original?' the other four asked in unison.

'Alfonso Mario Cavalli would be my guess,' said Dollar Bill.

'And who's he?' asked the President, no wiser.

'The gentleman who paid me to make the copy that is currently in the National Archives,' said Dollar Bill, 'and to whom I released the only other copy, which I am now holding in my hands.'

'But if the word "Brittish" is spelt with two *t*s, how can you be so certain it's a fake?' asked Dexter Hutchins.

'Because, of the fifty-six signatures on the original Declaration, six have the Christian name George. Five of them signed *Geo*, which was the custom of the time. Only George

Wythe of Virginia appended his full name. On the copy I presented to Cavalli I made the mistake of also writing *Geo* for Congressman Wythe, and had to add the letters *rge* later. Although the lettering is perfect, I used a slightly lighter shade of ink. A simple mistake, and discernible only to an expert eye.'

'And even then, only if they knew what they were looking for,' added Mendelssohn.

'I never bothered to tell Cavalli,' continued Dollar Bill, 'because once he had checked the word "Brittish" he seemed quite satisfied.'

'So, at some time Cavalli must have switched his copy with the original, and then passed it on to Al Obaydi?' said Dexter Hutchins.

'Well done, Deputy Director,' said Dollar Bill.

'And Al Obaydi in turn handed the copy on to the Iraqi Ambassador in Geneva, who had it delivered to Saddam in Iraq. And, as Al Obaydi had seen Dollar Bill's copy on display at the National Archives with "British" spelt correctly, he was convinced he was in possession of the original,' said Dexter Hutchins.

'You've finally caught up with the rest of us,' said Dollar Bill. 'Though to be fair, sir, I should have known what Cavalli was capable of doing when I said to you a month ago: "Is there no longer honour among thieves?" '

'So, where is the original now?' demanded the President.

'I suspect it's hanging on a wall in a brownstone house in Manhattan,' said Dollar Bill, 'where it must have been for the past ten weeks.'

The light on the telephone console to the right of the President began flashing. The President's Chief of Staff picked up an extension and listened. The normally unflappable man turned white. He pushed the hold button.

'It's Bernie Shaw at CNN for me, Mr President. He says Saddam is claiming that the copy of the Declaration of Independence on display at the National Archives is a fake, and that anyone who can spell "British" would know it. Do you have any comment to make?'

The President pursed his lips.

'My bet is that CNN have been given an exclusive on this story by Saddam, but probably only until tomorrow,' the Chief of Staff added.

'Whatever you do,' said Hutchins, 'try to keep it off the air for tonight.'

The Chief of Staff hesitated for a moment until he saw the President nodding his agreement. He pressed the button to re-engage the call. 'If you want to go on the air with a story like that, Bernie, it's your reputation on the line, not mine.'

The Chief of Staff listened carefully to Shaw's reply while everyone else in the room waited in silence.

'Be my guest,' were the last words the Chief of Staff offered before putting the phone down.

He turned to the President and told him: 'Shaw says he will have a crew outside the National Archives the moment the doors open at ten tomorrow morning, and, I quote: if the word "British" is spelt correctly, he'll crucify you.'

The President glanced up at the carriage clock that stood on the mantelpiece below the portrait of Abraham Lincoln. It was a few minutes after seven. He swivelled his chair round to face the Deputy Director of the CIA.

'Mr Hutchins,' he said, 'you've got fifteen hours to stop me being crucified. Should you fail, I can assure you there won't be a second coming for me in three years, let alone three days.'

36

THE LEAK STARTED in the early morning of Sunday July 4th, in the basement of number 21, the home of the Prestons, who were on vacation in Malibu.

When their Mexican housekeeper answered the door a few minutes after midnight, she assumed the worst. An illegal immigrant with no Green Card lives in daily fear of a visit from any government official.

The housekeeper was relieved to discover that these particular officials were only from the gas company. Without much prompting, she agreed to accompany them down to the basement of the brownstone and show them where the gas meters were located.

Once they had gained entry it only took a few moments to carry out the job. The loosening of two gas valves ensured a tiny leak which gave off a smell that would have alarmed any layman. The explosives expert assured his boss that there was no real cause for concern, as long as the New York Fire Department arrived within twenty minutes.

The senior official calmly asked the housekeeper to phone the fire department and warn them they had a gas leak in number 21 which, if not dealt with quickly, could cause an explosion. He told her the correct code to give.

The housekeeper dialled 911, and when she was finally put through to the fire department, stammered out the problem, adding that it was 21 East 75th, between Park and Madison.

'Get everyone out of the building,' instructed the Fire Chief, 'and we'll be right over.'

'Yes, sir,' said the housekeeper, not pausing for a moment before fleeing onto the street. The expert quickly repaired the damage he had caused, but the smell still lingered.

To their credit, seven minutes later a New York Fire Department hook and ladder, sirens blasting, sped into 75th Street. Once the Fire Chief had carried out an inspection of the basement of number 21 he agreed with the official – whom he had never met before – that safety checks would also have to be carried out on numbers 17, 19, 23 and 25, especially as the gas pipe ran parallel to the city's sewerage system.

The Deputy Director of the CIA then retired to the far side of the road to watch the Fire Chief go about his work. As the sirens had woken almost everyone in the neighbourhood, it wasn't proving too hard to coax the residents out onto the street.

Dexter Hutchins lit a cigar and waited. As soon as he had left the White House, he had begun rounding up a select team of agents who rendezvoused in a New York hotel two hours later for a briefing, or, to be more accurate, half a briefing. Because once the Deputy Director had explained to them that this was a Level 7 inquiry, the old-timers realised they would be told only half the story, and not the better half.

It had taken another two hours before they got their first break, when one of the agents discovered that the Prestons in number 21 were on vacation. Dexter Hutchins and his explosives expert had arrived on the doorstep of number 21 just after midnight. The Mexican immigrant without a Green Card turned out to be a bonus.

The Deputy Director relit his cigar, his eyes fixed on one particular doorway. He breathed a sigh of relief when Tony Cavalli and his father emerged in their dressing gowns, accompanied by a butler. He decided it would be sensible to wait for another couple of minutes before he asked the Fire Chief's permission to inspect number 23.

401

The whole operation could have been underway a lot earlier if only Calder Marshall hadn't balked at the idea of removing the fake Declaration from the vault of the National Archives and placing it at Dexter Hutchins' disposal. The Archivist made two stipulations before he finally agreed to the Deputy Director's request: should the CIA fail to replace the copy with the original before ten o'clock the following morning, Marshall's resignation statement, dated May 25th, would be released an hour before the President or the Secretary of State made any statement of their own.

'And your second condition, Mr Marshall?' the President had asked.

'That Mr Mendelssohn be allowed to act as custodian of the copy remaining with the Deputy Director at all times, so that he will be present should they locate the original.'

Dexter Hutchins realised he had little choice but to go along with Marshall's conditions. The Deputy Director stared across at the Conservator, who was standing between Scott and the explosives expert, on the pavement opposite number 23. Dexter Hutchins had to admit that Mendelssohn looked more convincing as an official from the gas company than anyone else in his team.

As soon as Hutchins saw two of his agents emerging from number 19 he stubbed out his cigar and strolled across the road in the direction of the Fire Chief. His three colleagues followed a few paces behind.

'All right for us to check on number 23 now?' he asked casually.

'Fine by me,' said the Fire Chief. 'But the owners are insisting the butler sticks with you.'

Hutchins nodded his agreement. The butler led the four of them into the lobby, down to the basement and directly to the cupboard that housed the gas supply. He assured them that there had not been the slightest smell of gas before he went to bed, some time after his master had retired.

The explosives expert carried out his job deftly, and in

moments the basement stank of gas. Hutchins recommended to the butler that for his own safety he should return to the street. With a handkerchief covering his nose and mouth Martin reluctantly agreed, leaving them to try and locate the leak.

While the expert repaired the damage, Scott and Dexter began checking every room in the basement. Scott was the first to enter Cavalli's study and discover the parchment hanging on the wall, exactly where Dollar Bill had promised it would be. Within seconds the other two had joined him. Mendelssohn stared lovingly at the document. He checked the word 'Brittish' before lifting the glass frame gently off the wall and placing it on the boardroom table. Scott unzipped the large tool bag one of the agents had put together earlier in the evening, containing screwdrivers of all sizes, knives of all lengths, chisels of several widths and even a small drill, in fact everything that would be required by a professional picture framer.

The Conservator checked the back of the frame and requested a medium-sized screwdriver. Scott selected one and passed it across to him.

Mendelssohn slowly and methodically removed all eight of the screws that held the two large steel clamps to the back of the frame. Then he turned the glass over on its front. Dexter Hutchins couldn't help thinking that he might have shown a little more sense of urgency.

The Conservator, oblivious to the Deputy Director's impatience, rummaged around in the bag until he had selected an appropriate chisel. He wedged it between the two pieces of laminated glass at the top right-hand corner of the frame. At the same time, Scott extracted from the cylinder supplied by Mendelssohn the copy of the Declaration they had taken from the National Archives earlier that evening.

When the Conservator lifted the top piece of the laminated glass and rested it on the boardroom table, Scott could tell from the smile on his face that he believed he was staring down at the original.

'Come on,' said Dexter, 'or they'll start getting suspicious.'

Mendelssohn didn't seem to hear the Deputy Director's urgings. He once again checked the spelling of 'Brittish' and, satisfied, turned his attention to the five 'Geo's and one 'George' before glancing, first quickly and then slowly, over the rest of the parchment. The smile never left his face.

Without a word, the Conservator slowly rolled up the original, and Scott replaced it with the copy from the National Archives. Once Scott had the sheets of glass back in position he screwed the two steel clamps firmly in place.

Mendelssohn deposited the cylinder in the work bag while Scott hung the copy on the wall.

They both heard Dexter Hutchins' deep sigh of relief.

'Now for Christ's sake let's get out of here,' said the Deputy Director as six cops, guns drawn, burst into the room and surrounded them.

'Freeze!' said one of them. Mendelssohn fainted.

37

ALL FOUR WERE ARRESTED, handcuffed and had their rights read out to them. They were then driven in separate police cars to the Nineteenth Precinct.

When they were questioned, three refused to speak without an attorney present. The fourth pointed out to the Desk Sergeant that if the bag which had been taken from him was opened at any time other than in the presence of his attorney, a writ would be issued and a separate action taken out against the NYPD.

The Desk Sergeant looked at the smartly-dressed, distinguished-looking man and decided not to take any risks. He labelled the bag with a red tag and threw it in the night safe.

The same man insisted on his legal right to make one phone call. The request was granted, but not until another form had been completed and signed. Dexter Hutchins put a collect call through to the Director of the CIA at 2.27 a.m.

The Director confessed to his subordinate that he hadn't been able to sleep. He listened intently to Hutchins' report and praised him for not revealing his name or giving the police any details of the covert assignment. 'We don't need anyone to know who you are,' he added. 'We must be sure at all times not to embarrass the President.' He paused for a moment. 'Or, more important, the CIA.'

When the Deputy Director put the phone down, he and his three colleagues were hustled away to separate cells.

The Director of the CIA put on his dressing gown and went down to his study. After he had written up a short summary of the conversation he had had with his deputy, he checked a number on his desk computer. He slowly dialled the 212 area code.

The Commissioner of the New York City Police Department uttered some choice words when he answered the phone, until he was sufficiently alert to take in who it was sounding so wide awake on the other end of the line. He then switched on the bedside light and began to make some notes on a pad. His wife turned over, but not before she had added a few choice words of her own.

The Director of the CIA ended his part of the conversation with the comment, 'I owe you one.'

'Two,' said the Commissioner. 'One for trying to sort out your problem.'

'And the second?' asked the Director.

'For waking up my wife at three o'clock in the morning.'

The Commissioner remained seated on the edge of the bed while he looked up the home number of the Captain in charge of that particular precinct.

The Captain recognised his chief's voice immediately he picked up the phone, and simply said, 'Good morning, Commissioner,' as if it were a routine mid-morning call.

The chief briefed the Captain without making any mention of a call from the Director of the CIA or giving any clues about who the four men languishing in his night cells were – not that he was absolutely certain himself. The Captain scribbled down the salient facts on the back of his wife's copy of *Good Housekeeping*. He didn't bother to shower or shave, and dressed quickly in the clothes he had worn the previous day. He left his apartment in Queens at 3.21 and drove himself into Manhattan, leaving his car outside the front of the precinct a few minutes before four.

Those officers who were fully awake at that time in the morning were surprised to see their boss running up the steps and into the front hall, especially as he looked dishevelled, unshaven, and was carrying a copy of *Good Housekeeping* under his arm.

He strode into the office of the Duty Lieutenant, who quickly removed his feet from the desk.

The Lieutenant looked mystified when asked about the four men who'd been arrested earlier, as he'd only just finished interrogating a drug pusher.

The Desk Sergeant was called for and joined the Captain in the Duty Lieutenant's office. The veteran policeman, who thought he had seen most things during a long career in the force, admitted to booking the four men, but remained puzzled by the whole incident, because he couldn't think of anything to charge them with – despite the fact that one of the house-holders, a Mr Antonio Cavalli, had called within the last few minutes to ask if the four men were still being held in custody, as a complication had arisen. None of the residents had re-ported anything stolen, so theft did not apply. There could be no charge of breaking and entering, as on each occasion they had been invited into the buildings. There was certainly no assault involved, and trespass couldn't be considered, as they had left the premises the moment they were asked to do so. The only charge the Sergeant could come up with was impersonat-ing city officials.

The Captain didn't show any interest in whether or not the Desk Sergeant could find something to charge them with. All he wanted to know was: 'Has the bag been opened?'

'No, Captain,' said the Sergeant, trying to think where he had put it.

'Then release them on bail, pending further charges,' instructed the Captain. 'I'll deal with the paperwork.'

The paperwork took the Captain some considerable time, and the four men were not released until a few minutes after six.

When they ran down the precinct steps together, the little one with the pebble glasses was clinging firmly on to the unopened bag.

* * *

JEFFREY ARCHER

Antonio Cavalli woke with a start. Had he dreamed that he'd been dragged out of bed and onto the street in the middle of the night?

He flicked on the bedside light and picked up his watch. It was 3.47. He began to recall what had taken place a few hours earlier.

Once they were out on the street, Martin had accompanied the four men back into the house. Too many for a simple gas leak, Cavalli had thought. And what gas company official would smoke cigars and could afford a Saks Fifth Avenue suit? After they had been inside for fifteen minutes, Cavalli had become even more suspicious. He asked the Fire Chief if the men were personally known to him. The Chief admitted that, although they had been able to give him the correct code over the phone, he had never come across them before. He decided Mr Cavalli was right when he suggested that perhaps the time had come to make some checks with Consolidated Edison. Their switchboard informed him that they had no engineers out on call that night on 75th Street. The Fire Chief immediately passed this information on to the police. A few minutes later six police officers had entered number 23 and arrested all four men.

After they had been driven away to the station, his father and Martin had helped Tony check every room in the house, but as far as they could see nothing was missing. They had gone back to bed around 1.45.

Cavalli was now fully awake, though he thought he could hear a noise coming from the ground floor. Was it the same noise that had woken him? Tony checked his watch again. His father and Martin often rose early, but rarely between the hours of three and four.

Cavalli swung out of bed and placed his feet on the ground. He still felt sure he could hear voices.

He slipped on a dressing gown and walked over to the bedroom door. He opened it slowly, went out on to the landing and peered over the balustrade. He could see a light shining from under the door of his father's study.

Cavalli moved swiftly down the one flight of stairs and silently across the carpeted hallway until he came to a halt outside the study. He tried to remember where the nearest gun was.

He listened carefully, but could hear no movement coming from inside. Then, suddenly, a gravelly voice began cursing loudly. Tony flung open the door to find his father, also in his dressing gown, standing in front of the Declaration of Independence and holding a magnifying glass in his right hand. He was studying the word 'British'.

'Are you feeling all right?' Tony asked his father.

'You should have killed Dollar Bill when I told you to,' was his father's only comment.

'But why?' asked Tony.

'Because they've stolen the Declaration of Independence.'

'But you're standing in front of it,' said Tony.

'No I'm not,' said his father. 'Don't you understand what they've done?'

'No, I don't,' admitted Tony.

'They've exchanged the original for that worthless copy you put in the National Archives.'

'But the copy on the wall was the other one made by Dollar Bill,' said Tony. 'I saw him present it to you.'

'No,' said his father. 'Mine was the original, not a copy.'

'I don't understand,' said Tony, now completely baffled. The old man turned and faced his son for the first time.

'Nick Vicente and I switched them when you brought the Declaration back from Washington.' Tony stared at his father in disbelief. 'You didn't think I'd allow part of our national heritage to fall into the hands of Saddam Hussein?'

'But why didn't you tell me?' asked Tony.

'And let you go to Geneva knowing you were in possession of a fake, while the deal still hadn't been closed? No, it was always part of my plan that you would believe the original had been sent to Franchard et cie, because if you believed it, Al Obaydi would believe it.'

Tony said nothing.

'And you certainly wouldn't have put up such a fight over the loss of fifty million if you'd known all along that the document you had in Geneva was a counterfeit.'

'So where the hell is the original now?' asked Tony.

'Somewhere in the offices of the Nineteenth Precinct, would be my bet,' replied his father. 'That is, assuming they haven't already got clean away. And that's what I intend to find out right now,' he added as he walked over to his desk and picked up the phone book.

The chairman dialled seven digits and asked to speak to the duty officer. He checked his watch as he waited to be put through. It was 4.22.

When the Desk Sergeant came on the line, Cavalli explained who he was, and asked two questions. He listened carefully to the replies, then put the phone back on the hook.

Tony raised an eyebrow.

'They're still locked up in the cells, and the bag's been placed in a safe. Have we got anybody on the Nineteenth Precinct payroll?' asked his father.

'Yes, a lieutenant who's done very little for us lately.'

'Then the time has come for him to pay his dues,' said his father as he began walking towards the door.

Tony passed him, taking the stairs three at a time on the way back to his bedroom. He was dressed within minutes, and walked back down the staircase, expecting to have to wait some time for his father to reappear, but he was already standing by the front door.

His father unlocked the door and Tony followed him out on to the pavement, passing him to look up the street in search of a Yellow Cab. But none chose to turn right down 75th Street at that time in the morning.

'We'll have to take the car,' shouted his father, who had already begun to cross the road in the direction of the all-night garage. 'We can't afford to waste another minute.' Tony dashed back into the house and removed the car keys from the drawer of the hall table. He caught up with his father long before he reached their parking space.

As Tony fastened his seatbelt, he turned and asked his father, 'If we do manage to get the Declaration back, what the hell do you intend to do then?'

'To start with, I'm going to kill Dollar Bill myself, so I can be certain that he never makes another copy. And then –' Tony turned the key in the ignition.

The explosion that followed woke the entire neighbourhood for the second time that morning.

The four men came running down the precinct steps. The smallest of them was clinging on to a bag. A car whose engine had been turning over for the past hour swung across the road and came to a halt by their side. One of the men walked off into the half-light of the morning, still not certain why his expertise had been required in the first place.

Dexter Hutchins joined the driver in the front, while Scott and the Conservator climbed quickly into the back.

'La Guardia,' said Dexter and then thanked the agent for sitting up half the night. Scott looked between the two front seats as the digital clock changed from 6:11 to 6:12.

The agent swung on to the outside lane.

'Don't break the speed limit,' ordered Dexter. 'We don't need any more delays at this stage.' The agent edged back into the centre lane.

'What time's the next shuttle?' asked Scott.

'Delta, seven-thirty,' replied the driver. Dexter picked up the phone and punched in ten numbers. When a voice at the other end said, 'Yes,' the Deputy Director simply replied, 'We're on our way, sir. All present and correct.'

Dexter replaced the phone and turned round to assure himself that the silent Conservator was still with them. He was clutching the bag that was now resting on his legs.

'Better take everything out of the bag other than the

cylinder,' said Dexter. 'Otherwise we'll never get past security.'

Mendelssohn unzipped the bag and allowed Scott to remove the screwdrivers, knives, chisels and finally the drill, which he placed on the floor between them. He zipped the bag back up.

At 6.43 the driver pulled off the highway and followed the signs for La Guardia. No one spoke until the car came to a halt at the curb opposite the Marine Air terminal entrance.

As Dexter stepped out of the car, three men in tan Burberrys jumped out of a car that had drawn in immediately behind them, and preceded the Deputy Director into the terminal. Another man in a smart charcoal-grey suit, with a raincoat over his arm, held out an envelope as Dexter passed him. The Deputy Director took the package like a good relay runner, without breaking his stride, as he continued towards the departure lounge, where three more agents were waiting for him.

Once he had checked in, Dexter Hutchins would have liked to pace up and down as he waited to board the aircraft. He stood restlessly one yard away from the Declaration of Independence, surrounded by a circle of agents.

'The shuttle to Washington is now boarding at Gate Number 4,' announced a voice over the intercom. Nine men waited until everyone else had boarded the aircraft. When the agent standing by the gate nodded, Dexter led his team past the ticket collector, down the boarding ramp, and on to the aircraft. They took their seats, 1A–F and 2A–F. 2E was occupied only by the bag, 2D and 2F by two men who weighed five hundred pounds between them.

The pilot welcomed them aboard and warned them there might be a slight delay. Dexter checked his watch: 7.27. He began drumming his fingers on the armrest that divided him from Scott. The flight attendant offered every one of the nine men in the first two rows a copy of *USA Today*. Only Mendelssohn took up her offer.

At 7.39 the aircraft taxied out onto the runway to prepare for take-off. When it stopped, Dexter asked the flight attendant what was holding them up.

'The usual early-morning traffic,' she replied. 'The Captain has just told me that we're seventh in the queue, so we should be airborne in about ten to fifteen minutes.'

Dexter continued drumming his fingers on the armrest, while Scott couldn't take his eyes off the bag. Mendelssohn turned another page of his *USA Today*.

The plane swung round onto the take-off runway at 7.51, its jets revving before it moved slowly forward, then gathered speed. The wheels left the ground at 7.53.

Within moments the flight attendant returned, offering them all breakfast. She didn't get a positive response until she reached row seven. When later she gave the three crew members on the flight deck their usual morning coffee, she asked the Captain why rows three to six were unoccupied, especially as it was Independence Day.

The Captain couldn't think of a reason, and simply said, 'Keep your eye on the passengers in rows one and two.' He became even more curious about the nine men at the front of the aircraft when he was cleared for landing as soon as he announced to air traffic control that he was seventy miles away from Washington.

He began his descent at 8.33, and was at the gate on schedule for the first time in months. When he had turned the engine off, three men immediately blocked the gangway and remained there until the Deputy Director and his party were well inside the terminal. When Dexter Hutchins emerged into the Delta gate area, one agent played John the Baptist, while three others fell in behind, acting as disciples. The Director had obviously taken seriously that fine line between protection and drawing attention. Dexter spotted four more agents as he passed through the terminal, and suspected there were at least another twenty hidden at strategic points on his route to the car.

As Dexter passed under the digital clock, its red numbers clicked to 9:01. The doors slid open and he marched out onto the pavement. Three black limousines were waiting in line with drivers by their doors.

As soon as they saw the Deputy Director, the drivers of the first and third cars jumped behind their wheels and turned on their engines, while the driver of the second car held open the back door to allow Scott and Mendelssohn to climb in. The Deputy Director joined the agent in the front.

The lead car headed out in the direction of the George Washington Parkway, and within minutes the convoy was crossing the 14th Street bridge. As the Jefferson Memorial came into sight Dexter checked his watch yet again. It was 9.12. 'Easily enough time,' he remarked. Less than a minute later, they were caught in a traffic jam.

'Damn!' said Dexter. 'I forgot the streets would be cordoned off for the Independence Day parade.'

When they had moved only another half a mile in the next three minutes, Dexter told his driver they were left with no choice. 'Hit the sirens,' he said.

The driver flashed his lights, turned on his siren at full blast, and watched as the lead car veered into the inside lane and managed a steady forty miles per hour until they came off the freeway.

Dexter was now checking his watch every thirty seconds as the three cars tried to manoeuvre themselves from lane to lane, but some of Washington's citizens, unmoved by sirens and flashing lights, weren't willing to let them through.

The lead car swerved between two police barriers and turned into Constitution Avenue at 9.37. When Dexter saw the floats lining up for the parade, he gave the order to turn the sirens off. The last thing he needed was inquisitive eyes when they finally came to a halt outside the National Archives.

It was Scott who saw them first. He tapped Dexter on the shoulder and pointed ahead of him. A television crew was standing at the head of a long queue outside the front door of the National Archives.

'We'll never get past them,' said Dexter. Turning to Mendelssohn, he asked, 'Are there any alternative routes into the building?'

'There's a delivery entrance on 7th Street,' replied Mendelssohn.

'How appropriate,' said Dexter Hutchins.

'Drive past the front door and then drop me off on the corner,' said the Conservator. 'I'll cross Constitution and go in by the delivery entrance.'

'Drop you off on the corner?' said Dexter in disbelief.

'If I'm surrounded by agents, everyone will...' began Mendelssohn.

'Yes, yes, yes,' said the Deputy Director, trying to think. He picked up the phone and instructed the two other cars to peel off.

'We're going to have to risk it,' said Scott.

'I know,' said Dexter. 'But at least you can go with him. After all, you've never looked like an agent.' Scott wasn't sure whether he should take the remark as a compliment or not.

As they drove slowly past the National Archives, Dexter looked away from the impatient camera crew.

'How many of them?' he asked.

'About six,' said Scott. 'And I think that must be Shaw with his back to us.'

'Show me exactly where you want the car to stop,' said the Deputy Director, turning to face Mendelssohn.

'Another fifty yards,' came back the reply.

'You take the bag, Scott.'

'But...' began Mendelssohn. When he saw the expression on Dexter Hutchins' face, he didn't bother with a second word.

The car drew into the curb and stopped. Scott grabbed the bag, jumped out, and held the door open for Mendelssohn. Eight agents were walking up and down the pavement trying to appear innocent. None of them was looking towards the steps of the National Archives. The two unlikely looking companions quickly crossed Constitution Avenue and began running up 7th Street.

When they reached the delivery entrance, Scott came face to

face with an anxious Calder Marshall, who had been pacing back and forth at the bottom of the ramp.

'Thank God,' was all the Archivist said when he saw Scott and the Conservator running down the ramp. He led them silently into the open freight elevator. They travelled up two floors and then ran along the corridor until they reached the staircase that led down to the vault. Marshall turned to check that the two men were still with him before he began running down the steps, something no member of staff had ever seen him do before. Scott chased after the Archivist, followed by Mendelssohn. None of them stopped until they reached a set of massive steel doors.

Marshall nodded, and a slightly breathless Conservator leaned forward and pressed a code into a little box beside the door. The steel grid opened slowly to allow the three of them to enter the vault. Once they were inside, the Conservator pressed another button, and the door slid back into place.

They paused in front of the great concrete block that had been built to house the Declaration of Independence, just as a priest might in front of an altar. Scott checked his watch. It was 9.51.

Mendelssohn pressed the red button and the familiar clanking and whirling sound began as the concrete blocks parted and the massive empty frame came slowly into sight. He touched the button again when the glass casing had reached chest height.

The Archivist and the Conservator walked forward while Scott unzipped the bag. The Archivist took two keys from his jacket pocket and passed one over to his colleague. They immediately set about unlocking the twelve bolts that were evenly spaced around the thick brass rim. Once they had completed the task they leaned over and heaved across the heavy frame until it came to rest like an open book.

Scott removed the container and passed it over to the Archivist. Marshall eased the cap off the top of the cylinder, allowing Mendelssohn to carefully extract its contents.

Scott watched as the Archivist and the Conservator slowly unpeeled the Declaration of Independence, inch by inch, onto the waiting glass, until the original parchment was finally restored to its rightful place. Scott leaned over and took one last look at the misspelt word before the two men heaved the brass cover back into place.

'My God, the British still have a lot to answer for,' was all the Archivist said.

Calder Marshall and the Conservator quickly tightened up the twelve bolts surrounding the frame and took a pace back from the Declaration.

They paused for only a second while Scott checked his watch again. 9.57. He looked up to find Marshall and Mendelssohn hugging each other and jumping up and down like children who had been given an unexpected gift.

Scott coughed. 'It's 9.58, gentlemen.' The two men immediately reverted to character.

The Archivist walked back over to the concrete block. He paused for a moment and then pressed the red button. The massive frame rose, continuing its slow journey upwards to the gallery to be viewed by the waiting public.

Calder Marshall turned to face Scott. A flicker of a smile showed his relief. He bowed like a Japanese warrior to indicate that he felt honour had been satisfied. The Conservator shook hands with Scott and then walked over to the door, punched a code into the little box and watched the grid slide open.

Marshall accompanied Scott out into the corridor, up the staircase and back down in the freight elevator to the delivery entrance.

'Thank you, Professor,' he said as he shook hands on the loading dock. Scott loped up the ramp and turned to look back once he had reached the pavement. There was no sign of the Archivist.

He jogged across 7th Street and joined Dexter in the waiting car.

'Any problems, Professor?' asked the Deputy Director.

'No. Not unless you count two decent men who look as if they've aged ten years in the past two months.'

The tenth chime struck on the Old Post Office Tower clock. The doors of the National Archives swung open and a television crew charged in.

The Deputy Director's car moved out into the centre of Constitution Avenue, where it got caught up between the floats for Tennessee and Texas. A police officer ran across and ordered the driver to pull over into 7th Street.

When the car came to a halt, Dexter wound down his window, smiled at the officer and said, 'I'm the Deputy Director of the CIA.'

'And I'm Uncle Sam,' the officer replied as he began writing out a ticket.

38

THE DEPUTY DIRECTOR of the CIA phoned the Director at home to tell him that it was business as usual at the National Archives. He didn't mention the traffic ticket.

The Conservator phoned his wife and tried to explain why he hadn't been home the previous night.

A woman holding a carrier bag with a rope handle contacted the Iraqi Ambassador to the UN on her mobile phone and let him know that she had killed two birds with one stone. She gave the Ambassador an account number for a bank in the Bahamas.

The Director of the CIA rang the Secretary of State and assured him that the document was in place. He avoided saying '*back* in place'.

Susan Anderson rang Scott to congratulate him on the part he had played in restoring the document to its rightful home. She also mentioned in passing the sad news that she had decided to break off her engagement.

The Iraqi Ambassador to the UN instructed Monsieur Dummond to transfer the sum of nine hundred thousand dollars to the Royal Bank of Canada in the Bahamas and at the same time to close the Al Obaydi account.

The Secretary of State rang the President at the White House to inform him that the press conference scheduled for eleven o'clock that morning had been cancelled.

A reporter on the *New York Daily News* crime beat filed his first-edition copy from a phone booth in an underground garage on 75th Street. The headline read 'Mafia Slaying in Manhattan'.

Lloyd Adams's phone never stopped ringing, as he was continually being offered parts in everything from endorsements to a feature film.

The Archivist did not return a call from one of the President's Special Assistants at the White House, inviting him to lunch.

A CNN producer called in to the news desk to let them know that it must all have been a hoax. Yes, he had verified the spelling of 'Brittish', and only Dan Quayle could have thought it had two *t*s.

Scott phoned Hannah and told her how he wanted to spend Independence Day.

In CONGRESS, July 4, 1776.

The unanimous Declaration
of the thirteen united
States of America,

When in the Course of human events, it becomes necessary for one people to dissolve the political bands which have connected them with another, and to assume among the powers of the earth, the separate and equal station to which the Laws of Nature and of Nature's God entitle them, a decent respect to the opinions of mankind requires that they should declare the causes which impel them to the separation. — We hold these truths to be self-evident, that all men are created equal, that they are endowed by their Creator with certain unalienable Rights, that among these are Life, Liberty and the pursuit of Happiness. — That to secure these rights, Governments are instituted among Men, deriving their just powers from the consent of the governed, — That whenever any Form of Government becomes destructive of these ends, it is the Right of the People to alter or to abolish it, and to institute new Government, laying its foundation on such principles and organizing its powers in such form, as to them shall seem most likely to effect their Safety and Happiness. Prudence, indeed, will dictate that Governments long established should not be changed for light and transient causes; and accordingly all experience hath shewn, that mankind are more disposed to suffer, while evils are sufferable, than to right themselves by abolishing the forms to which they are accustomed. But when a long train of abuses and usurpations, pursuing invariably the same Object evinces a design to reduce them under absolute Despotism, it is their right, it is their duty, to throw off such Government, and to provide new Guards for their future security. — Such has been the patient sufferance of these Colonies; and such is now the necessity which constrains them to alter their former Systems of Government. The history of the present King of Great Britain is a history of repeated injuries and usurpations, all having in direct object the establishment of an absolute Tyranny over these States. To prove this, let Facts be submitted to a candid world.— He has refused his Assent to Laws, the most wholesome and necessary for the public good. — He has forbidden his Governors to pass Laws of immediate and pressing importance, unless suspended in their operation till his Assent should be obtained; and when so suspended, he has utterly neglected to attend to them. — He has refused to pass other Laws for the accommodation of large districts of people, unless those people would relinquish the right of Representation in the Legislature, a right inestimable to them and formidable to tyrants only. — He has called together legislative bodies at places unusual, uncomfortable, and distant from the depository of their Public Records, for the sole purpose of fatiguing them into compliance with his measures. — He has dissolved Repres/en\tative Houses repeatedly, for opposing with manly firmness his invasions on the rights of the people. — He has refused for a long time, after such dissolutions, to cause others to be elected; whereby the Legislative powers, incapable of Annihilation, have returned to the People at large for their exercise; the State remaining in the mean time exposed to all the dangers of invasion from without, and convulsions within. — He has endeavoured to prevent the population of these States; for that purpose obstructing the Laws for Naturalization of Foreigners; refusing to pass others to encourage their migrations hither, and raising the conditions of new Appropriations of Lands. — He has obstructed the Administration of Justice, by refusing his Assent to Laws for establishing Judiciary powers. — He has made Judges dependent on his Will alone, for the tenure of their offices, and the amount and payment of their salaries. — He has erected a multitude of New Offices, and sent hither swarms of Officers to harass our people, and eat out their substance. — He has kept among us, in times of peace, Standing Armies without the Consent of our legislatures. — He has affected to render the Military independent of and superior to the Civil power. — He has combined with others to subject us to a jurisdiction foreign to our constitution, and unacknowledged by our laws; giving his Assent to their Acts of pretended Legislation: — For quartering large bodies of armed troops among us: — For protecting them, by a mock Trial, from punishment for any Murders which they should commit on the Inhabitants of these States: — For cutting off our Trade with all parts of the world: — For imposing Taxes on us without our Consent: — For depriving us in many cases, of the benefits of Trial by Jury: — For transporting us beyond Seas to be tried for pretended offences: — For abolishing the free System of English Laws in a neighbouring Province, establishing therein an Arbitrary government, and enlarging its Boundaries so as to render it at once an example and fit instrument for introducing the same absolute rule into these Colonies: — For taking away our Charters, abolishing our most valuable Laws, and altering fundamentally the Forms of our Governments: — For suspending our own Legislatures, and declaring themselves invested with power to legislate for us in all cases whatsoever. — He has abdicated Government here, by declaring us out of his Protection and waging War against us. — He has plundered our seas, ravaged our Coasts, burnt our towns, and destroyed the Lives of our people. — He is at this time transporting large Armies of foreign Mercenaries to compleat the works of death, desolation and tyranny, already begun with circum- stances of Cruelty & Perfidy scarcely paralleled in the most barbarous ages, and totally unworthy the Head of a civilized nation. — He has constrained our fellow Citizens taken Captive on the high Seas to bear Arms against their Country, to become the executioners of their friends and Brethren, or to fall themselves by their Hands. — He has excited domestic insurrections amongst us, and has endeavoured to bring on the inhabitants of our frontiers, the merciless Indian Savages, whose known rule of warfare, is an undistinguished destruction of all ages, sexes and conditions. In every stage of these Oppressions We have Petitioned for Redress in the most humble terms: Our repeated Petitions have been answered /only\ by repeated injury. A Prince, whose character is thus marked by every act which may define a Tyrant, is unfit to be the ruler of a free people. Nor have We been wanting in attentions to our Brittish brethren. We have warned them from time to time of attempts by their legislature to extend an unwarrantable jurisdiction over us. We have reminded them of the circumstances of our emigration and settlement here. We have appealed to their native justice and magnanimity, and we have conjured them by the ties of our common kindred to disavow these usurpations, which, would inevitably interrupt our connections and correspondence. They too have been deaf to the voice of justice and of consanguinity. We must, therefore, acquiesce in the necessity, which denounces our Separation, and hold them, as we hold the rest of mankind, Enemies in War, in Peace Friends. —

We, therefore, the Representatives of the united States of America, in General Congress, Assembled, appealing to the Supreme Judge of the world for the rectitude of our intentions, do, in the Name, and by Authority of the good People of these Colonies, solemnly publish and declare, That these United Colonies are, and of Right ought to be Free and Independent States; that they are Absolved from all Allegiance to the British Crown, and that all political connection between them and the State of Great Britain, is and ought to be totally dissolved; and that as Free and Independent States, they have full Power to levy War, conclude Peace, contract Alliances, establish Commerce, and to do all other Acts and Things which Independent States may of right do. — And for the support of this Declaration, with a firm reliance on the protection of divine Providence, we mutually pledge to each other our Lives, our Fortunes and our sacred Honor.

by declaring us out of his Protect

transporting large Armies of fore

ges, and totally unworthy the

their friends and Brethren, or to

dian Savages, whose known ru

umble terms: Our repeated Petitu

Nor have We been wanting in

nded them of the circumstances of

savow these usurpations, which

equiesce in the necessity, which

ntatives of the united Sta

ity of the good People of these Col

Allegiance to the British Crow

ates, they have full Power to levy

nd for the support of this Dec

THE HOLY
CROWN OF HUNGARY
KINGS AND CORONATIONS

ENDRE TÓTH · KÁROLY SZELÉNYI

THE HOLY CROWN OF HUNGARY

KINGS AND CORONATIONS

SECOND EDITION

TABLE OF CONTENTS

owards the end of the year 1000, as Christendom prepared to celebrate the millenary of Christ's birth, the nobles of the Carpathian Basin were looking to the future. They were awaiting leave from the Pope, the highest spiritual and temporal leader in the Christian world, to crown as their king Vajk, son of Géza. He had already received the baptismal name Stephanus, the 'crowned'. Although no record remains of when the coronation took place, the length of his reign—38 years, 7 months and 15 days—and the date of his death, August 15, 1038, are both documented. If these are correct, the coronation was on January 1, 1001, or bearing in mind the variation in the date on which the year began in the 11th century, Christmas Day, 1000. The ceremony may well have been held in the Church of St Stephen the Martyr at Esztergom, the forerunner of the present cathedral.

The coronation, which established Hungary as a Christian kingdom, marked the climax of a process that had lasted for three decades. The initiator was Prince Géza. In 973, shortly after coming to power, Géza sent an embassy of twelve Hungarian chiefs to the Holy Roman Emperor, Otto I. They arrived at Quedlinburg on March 23, where they celebrated Easter with the emperor. What they discussed at their council we do not know, but the upshot was that missionary priests soon arrived in Hungary, and the Prince was baptised. Moreover, his son was granted the hand of the emperor's niece, Princess Gisela of Bavaria. The presence of the German princess in a still semi-pagan country was an unprecedented mark of favour. It was far from the custom to wed imperial princesses to 'barbarian' chieftains, for Hungary still did not have a king in the Western sense. The female members of the Saxon and Salian ruling houses were seldom even married outside the Empire. If no political marriage was arranged, they would end their lives as abbesses of Essen, Quedlinburg or Gandersheim. Gisela herself had prepared for a monastic life. Indeed the husbands of the only two princesses in the 10th and 11th centuries to marry outside the Empire were both from the House of Árpád. Gisela, as second cousin of Emperor Otto III,

married the future King Stephen in 995, while the heir apparent, Solomon, received the daughter of Emperor Henry III in marriage in 1058.

The decades after the Council of Quedlinburg were a decisive period in Hungarian history. Father and son, Prince Géza and King Stephen, were more successful than their neighbours at making a European kingdom out of their people. Hungary was the only country to the east of the Holy Roman Empire that succeeded in becoming an independent kingdom during that period. This kingdom was an enduring one, where the office of king went unquestioned and its existence was not threatened by outside factors. (The hereditary nature of kingship was not established in either Poland or Bohemia in the 11th and 12th centuries. In Croatia, only the Hungarian kings managed to establish continuity on the throne.)

The Hungarian church likewise managed to gain its independence. It was directly subordinate to Rome, whereas the Scandinavian sees were under Bremen until the 12th century. The Bohemian church remained in the province of Mainz until the archbishopric of Prague was established in 1344. This organization of the church under its own archbishop, with subordinate bishoprics, was essential for an independent Christian kingdom. Esztergom became an archbishopric in 1001, which suggests that conversion to Christianity had begun several decades earlier. A church organization could only be established once a sizeable proportion of the population had been converted.

The German chronicler Thietmar of Merseburg recounts the organization of the Hungarian church, the foundation of bishoprics and the coronation establishing kingship as a single act. Vajk, who founded the sees, had received a blessing and his crown by the grace and encouragement of the emperor, according to Thietmar. The crown was the symbol of royal power, while the benediction may refer to the spiritual part of the ceremony, the unction. The Pope at the time was Sylvester II, Gerbert of Aurillac, formerly Archbishop of Reims and Patriarch of Ravenna. He had been the tutor and friend of Otto III, and his

1. The Bamberg horseman. Legend has it that the statue on Bamberg Hill portrays the future King Stephen I of Hungary, in Bavaria for his betrothal

dom could hardly have occurred against opposition from either of them.

The visible sign of the kingdom's establishment was the coronation. This required not only the sanction of the Holy Roman Emperor and the Pope, but acquisition of the most important emblem of royalty, a crown. Stephen naturally turned to the Pope for a crown, because this was to be a Christian kingdom. The rite of coronation counted almost as a sacrament in the 10th and 11th centuries. Bishop Hartvik's 'legend' or biography of St Stephen of Hungary makes it clear that the crown was sent by the Pope, which was equivalent at the time to the emperor sending it. According to the ideas of the period, the power of a ruler was bestowed by God, whose divine intention was conveyed through the Vicar of Christ on earth, the Pope. So it was the Pope who anointed and crowned the Carolingian, and later the Holy Roman Emperor. (Similarly, the Byzantine Emperor was crowned by the Patriarch of Constantinople, who by then was almost independent from the Pope.) Power and the crown that symbolized it could also descend on a ruler through a heavenly mediator, such as Mary, Mother of Christ (especially in the Eastern Empire) or angels. The belief was held in

spiritual partner in 'renovation of the Roman Empire'. The separation of the Hungarian church under its own archbishopric and the establishment of the king-

2. The ruins of the basilica at Székesfehérvár, where many kings of the House of Árpád were crowned and buried

several countries (and sometimes supported by visions) that angels or saints had brought the crown, or other accessories of power. This divine origin of power is clear in contemporary illustrations, which usually depict a heavenly source, and only occasionally a temporal mediator. Numerous scenes in the 10th to 14th-century miniatures, paintings and mosaics of the Eastern and Western empires are there to remind subjects that God places the crown on a ruler's head. Kings ranked next below emperors. Their power, likewise from God, was bestowed not through the Pope, but through the archbishop of the country, as head of the church in its territory.

Although the coronation had temporal aspects as well, the framework was a church ceremony and mass. The texts and acts were laid down in a liturgical book, the *Pontificale Romanum,* containing the rites other than the mass to be performed by bishops. This prescribed the prayers and psalms to be used and the actions to be performed, while the ritual robes and the

4. St Stephen on the throne. An initial in the Picture Chronicle (National Széchényi Library, Budapest)

3. The Legend of Bishop Hartvik relates that Stephen, feeling the approach of death, placed his crown and country under the patronage of the Blessed Virgin Mary (altarpiece by V. Fischer in Székesfehérvár Cathedral. 1775)

insignia to be presented were laid down in a book of ritual (the *ordo*).

The coronation turned Vajk, the heir apparent, into Stephen, the King. The ecclesiastical climax of the ceremony was the anointing of the king, a ritual that dated back to the installation of Old Testament Jewish kings. The custom had reached Western Europe during the Age of Migrations, with the Visigoths, and developed further in the Carolingian Empire. When the Carolingians took over from the Frankish dynasty, Pepin the Short deposed the last Merovingian ruler in 751 by leave of Pope Zacharias, and was anointed king with holy oil. This was applied to his shoulder and right arm, to signify that he had become the Lord's anointed. Accompanying this church ceremony was the presentation of the emblems of secular power: the crown (or possibly a ceremonial helmet), the sword, the sceptre *(baculus* or *sceptrum),* the ring, and the orb *(globus).* The robes worn by the king at the coronation—a long chemise like an alb, a stole and a chasuble—resembled those of a priest.

The coronation of Stephen I of Hungary is described briefly in the greater 'legend' of his life. 'In the fifth year after the death of his father, as the mercy of God ordained, they brought the letter of apostolic blessing, and amidst consonant praises of bishops and priests, lords and people, chose him king, and anointing him with oil, duly crowned him with the diadem of royal office.' These events—acclamation by the people, consecration with holy oil, and coronation—remained the main parts of every later, similar act. Since the description does

5. The stone sarcophagus of St Stephen (originally Roman) in the Garden of Ruins on the site of Székesfehérvár Basilica. The sarcophagus was recarved for the king's burial

not go into detail, there is no way of knowing exactly what rite was used to crown Stephen king. However, in view of the close relations with the Empire, there is good reason to suppose that a ceremony of German origin was employed at the country's first coronation.

No document from which the ceremony could be reconstructed has survived from subsequent centuries. Altogether 36 Hungarian kings were crowned before the Battle of Mohács in 1526, but there are very few documentary references from which conclusions can be drawn about the *ordo*. It is known that Solomon's coronation in 1058, which took place in his father's lifetime, included a prayer containing the words 'be lord over thy brethren.' This, like most coronation prayers, has an Old Testament origin (*Genesis xxvii.29*). It is echoed when Jacob blesses his sons: 'The blessings of thy father ... shall be on the head of Joseph, and on the crown of the head of him that was separate from his brethren' (*Genesis xlix.26*). Since this prayer features in the Old English pontifical of Egbert, Archbishop of York, it is possible that the English rite may have been used at Solomon's coronation. It is not known whether Solomon was exceptional, or whether the other Árpád kings were crowned according to this rite. Caution is called for here. There is no way of telling whether the same liturgy, and the same crown, were used for the coronation of an heir apparent in the king's lifetime as for a coronation after the previous king's death. So unless other arguments can be found, it is unwise to generalize from Solomon's case or say anything conclusive about the forms used for crowning kings of the House of Árpád.

The principle of primogeniture was not always respected by older members of the royal family, often brothers of the king, who advanced claims on the grounds of seniority. It was found prudent on several occasions to crown a future king in his father's lifetime, often while he was still a child. Andrew I's example of crowning Solomon, in 1058, was followed by Béla III, who had his son Emericus crowned in 1182. He in turn had his son, Ladislas III, crowned at the end of his reign. Andrew II nominated his son as 'cadet king' and placed him in charge of part of the country. Béla IV and his son Stephen V were both crowned during their fathers' lives. Nothing is known about these ceremonies or the crown used for them. When Solomon at last succeeded to the throne in 1063, the emperor crowned him again and placed him on his father's throne at Székesfehérvár. The wording of the *Picture Chronicle* could be interpreted to mean that the coronation and enthronement took place by leave of the emperor, in other words that it was a solemn coronation. That, of course, would only suffice to gain the rank of king and govern the country if he was really considered an anointed, crowned monarch. Béla III's son Emericus was crowned twice as well. The first ceremony was performed by Miklós, Archbishop of Esztergom at Whitsun, May 16, 1182, before the king's second marriage. The second occasion came in 1194, when Emericus took over the government of Dalmatia and Croatia, and may in practice have meant his coronation

6. The tomb of the founder, King Andrew I, in the crypt of the Benedictine Abbey of Tihany. This is the sole surviving grave of an Árpád king (1060)

as Croatian king. Béla III died in Holy Week, on April 23, 1196, and yet there is no sign that Emericus was ever crowned again after his father's death. It goes unmentioned in the *Picture Chronicle,* which faithfully records the coronation days of his predecessors and successors. Calculating back from the day of his death and the length of his reign, Emericus took the throne on April 24, the day after his father died. Curiously, the coronation is depicted in the miniature accompanying the account of Emericus's reign. Since the chronicle records all the other coronations, and this illumination may show the earlier occasion, it can be assumed that the 1182 coronation was taken as valid. The same applies to that of his infant son, Ladislas III, ordered by Emericus in the last few months of his life. This was presumably performed by János, Archbishop of Kalocsa, and would probably have been a full-scale coronation. Moreover, it seems to have been conducted with all the jewels usually employed for crowning kings. When Ladislas III and his mother fled to Austria, for fear of Emericus's brother, Andrew, they took the crown with them. This Andrew II retrieved from the Duke of Austria after the boy-king's death, by threatening war. His concern to obtain it again shows that by then the same crown was being used for each coronation. So it seems that heirs apparent were anointed and crowned with full rites. The practice changed in the 13th century, however. Both Béla IV and Stephen V were crowned a second time after their fathers' deaths. Perhaps the first coronation was not a full one. They may not have been anointed, the regular regalia may not have been used, or the enthronement may have been omitted.

Rather more is known about the coronations held after the extinction of the House of Árpád, although a detailed description has only survived of Wladyslaw II's. It is apparent from the account by Antonio Bonfini that the ceremony took place according to the late 13th-century pontifical of Guillaume Durand, Bishop of Mende.

The coronation usually coincided with a feast day. Holy Roman emperors were often crowned at Easter, Whitsun, Epiphany, or on a feast to which the monarch was personally connected. The first factor, of course, was the time of the death and funeral of the previous ruler. In the Holy Roman Empire, where the succession and the historical conditions differed from Hungary's, the coronation of a new ruler as German king often came only months or years after his accession. The imperial coronation, conducted by the Pope in Rome, was even later. Little is known about the day of coronation in Hungary, before the

7. *Esztergom remained a royal town even when Buda became the king's permanent seat after the Mongol incursion of 1241. In the picture: the palace chapel of Esztergom's royal castle*

reign of Béla II, because the chronicles do not include dates. Béla I may have been crowned on the Feast of St Nicholas (December 6). Although there is no Hungarian record of this, it is mentioned in the chronicle of Henrik Mügeln (died after 1369). From Béla II's time, coronations usually fell on a Sunday or feast day. Béla III was crowned on the Octave of Epiphany, and Stephen V as cadet kings on August 20 (the Feast of St Stephen of Hungary). The coronation of Wenceslas fell on the Octave of the same feast, Sigismund's on Palm Sunday, and Ladislas V's at Whitsun. The coronation of Matthias I was set for Palm Sunday, but postponed until Maundy Thursday after the delegations had been held up by bad weather. Coronations only seem to have been held in Lent on the Fourth Sunday (*Laetare,* meaning 'Rejoice') or Palm Sunday, two weeks later. The earlier, Árpád kings were usually crowned on a Sunday. The ceremony might occur just a few days after the predecessor's death. Géza II was crowned on the third day after the death of his father, Béla the Blind (February 13), and Emericus and Stephen V within a week of accession. The haste was understandable. In the cases mentioned, the previous king was buried at Székesfehérvár, where the coronation was due to take place. On other occasions, the coronation was

9

delayed because the old king was buried far away. That was probably why the coronation of Béla II was not held until two months after his nephew, Stephen II, died (if March 1 is the authentic date of his death.) For Stephen was buried at Várad, probably in the Premonstratensian abbey he had founded there, and Béla was not crowned until April 28. Andrew II was buried a month after the death of Ladislas III in Austria. The child's body was then brought to Székesfehérvár for burial, and as mentioned earlier, the crown had to be retrieved. Béla IV was crowned three weeks after the death of

8. After the extinction of the House of Árpád, several kings were crowned in Buda, at the Church of the Assumption of Our Lady. Known today as the Matthias Church, it took its present form at the turn of the 20th c., when the architect was Frigyes Schulek

9. A replica of the Matthias Monument at Bauzen, showing the coronation of Matthias I

his father, Andrew II, who had likewise died far away, and been buried at the Cistercian abbey of Egres.

It was also a habit in Hungary to place the crown ceremoniously on the ruler's head on the great church festivals. This St Gerard refused to do for King Samuel Aba, because 'bloodshed upon bloodshed' had marked his reign: 'When [Samuel Aba] arrived at St Gerard's see of Marosvár to celebrate the holy mysteries of Easter, he sent his chiefs and bishops, on the day of the Lord's Resurrection, to the high priest, and called St Gerard to him, that his hand might place the crown of the land upon the king's head. When St Gerard hesitated and was reluctant to go, the bishops present placed the crown on the king's head ... The man of God thereupon stepped up to the pulpit, filled with the Holy Ghost, clothed in a white stole, and began dauntlessly to berate the king for his savagery.' Solomon was likewise crowned on Easter Sunday by his brother at Pécs: 'They both celebrated the feast of Our Lord's Resurrection, together with their whole courts, at Pécs. There was King Solomon crowned by the hand of Prince Géza on Easter Sunday, in the presence of the nobles of the land,' the *Picture Chronicle* records. The practice of crowning the king on feast days confirmed, as the *Picture Chronicle* tells of Ladislas I, 'that although he had been crowned king against his will, he never placed the crown on his own head.' He aspired instead to a heavenly crown, the crown of the 'living King', not to an earthly one.

The coronations of Hungarian kings had three characteristics. First, they were held at Székesfehérvár, in the Basilica of Our Lady. Secondly, they were conducted by the Archbishop of Esztergom. Finally, the king was crowned with the Holy Crown. They were exceptions, of course, and it is not known when the three criteria began to apply. Székesfehérvár may have been the site from the earliest times, because it was the main church of the Árpád kings, where the royal assizes were held on August 20 each year. The Archbishop of Esztergom conducted the ceremony *ex officio,* as the head of the Hungarian church. His presence was dispensed with only rarely. It was also the practice in other countries for the head of the church to officiate. In the Empire it was the Archbishop of Mainz (or occasionally another prelate, usually the Archbishop of Cologne) who anointed and crowned the German king. From the time of Frederic III, it was always the Pope who placed the imperial crown on the emperor's head. In France coronations were performed by the Archbishop of Reims, and in England by the Archbishop of Canterbury. On occasions like the time when Lukács, Archbishop of Esztergom, refused to crown Béla III, the task was done by the Archbishop of Kalocsa. Charles I of Anjou was crowned for the first time at Esztergom without the Holy Crown, again at the Church of Our Lady in Buda, and for a third time at Székesfehérvár, after the crown had been recovered from László Kán, Voivod of Transylvania. The Archbishop of Esztergom's privilege of crowning the king was confirmed more than once by the Pope. One can only surmise when

11. The crook presented to Károly Hornig, Bishop of Veszprém, by Zita, Hungary's last queen, when he crowned her in 1916 (Archdiocese of Veszprém)

the Holy Crown became essential for a valid coronation, but it cannot have been later than the mid-12th century.

The coronation of the queen was traditionally performed by the Bishop of Veszprém. The custom probably arose because Veszprém had belonged to the ruler's consort, even in the time of Sarolt, mother of St Stephen. The foundation of Veszprém Cathedral is associated with Queen Gisela, who lodged in the building her gold crown, weighing twelve marks. There it remained until Andrew II took it on a crusade to the Holy Land, where he sold it. The right to crown the queen caused a dispute between the bishop and the archbishop. This was resolved in 1216, by two cardinal decisions of the Pope. The Archbishop of Esztergom should crown the king and his consort together, after which the archbishop would anoint the king and the bishop the queen. However, if the coronation was the queen's alone, she was to be anointed by the archbishop and crowned by the bishop.

Let us now see what happened at the medieval coronation about which the most is known. Wladyslaw II was elected king at Buda, at an assembly before St George's Church. A delegation then proceeded to the border of the kingdom to fetch him. On the return to Buda with the king, they were met by another delegation, which accompanied him into the city. On August 29, Osvát, Bishop of Zagreb,

10. The Great Legend of St Stephen the King states that St Michael's Cathedral in Veszprém was built and richly endowed by his consort, Queen Gisela

12. A victim of the 14th-c, disputes over the succession: Charles II, king for only a few weeks in 1385–6 (19th-c. engraving, Hungarian National Museum)

brought the Holy Crown from Visegrád to Buda, where it was kept in the Church of the Assumption of Our Lady until the coronation. The sheriffs of the counties, the military commanders, and the nobles dressed in ceremonial robes processed in a long line to Székesfehérvár. The ceremony was postponed because the Archbishop of Kalocsa and Prince László Újlaki had not arrived, but eventually they did not come at all. The king fasted on every other day in the week before the coronation. The ceremony took place on Saturday, September 18 in the Basilica of Our Lady. The king entered the church flanked by two bishops. Before them went János Corvin bearing the Holy Crown, István Bátori the sceptre, and Count János Szentgyörgyi the orb. István, Bishop of Szerém, carried the tablet of the kiss of peace and the Provost of the Knights of St John at Vrána the cross. Pál Kinizsi bore a naked sword and Mátyás Geréb a sword in a gold sheath. They led the king's horse, while László Losonczi bore the king's standard. The master of ceremonies was János Filipecz, Bishop of Várad, who took suitable pains that all should go correctly. His ornate liturgical book, with miniatures similar to the ones found in the codices of the Corvina library, was copied from manuscripts of texts already used for the coronation of Louis the Great.

The mass was celebrated by Osvát Laki Túz, Bishop of Zagreb, who also performed the coronation, standing in for Hippolit Estei, Archbishop of Esztergom, who was still a minor.

When the procession arrived in the basilica, the regalia were placed on the altar. Responding to a question from one of the bishops, the congregation agreed that the ceremony should proceed. The bishop conducting the ceremony made the king swear on oath to foster justice, the law, religion and peace. Wladyslaw swore on the Gospels and bowed down at the bishop's feet. After a prayer, they anointed the king's bare arm and shoulder with chrism and led him back to the throne. While the bishop began to say mass, the king changed his robes in the vestry: 'Taking off his cloak, they placed on him the robe of the heavenly Stephen and put golden boots on his feet. The velvet mantle was sky blue, and on his robe of triumph chased with palm fronds had been sewn in shining gold the throne of God and the Apostles.' The celebrant bishop, handing the king the naked sword, called upon him to keep the Christian commandments. Then he buckled on the sword, which the king unsheathed and sheathed again. The bishops placed the crown on Wladyslaw's head and placed the sceptre in his hand. Then the king, having unbuckled the sword, was seated on the throne with the crown on his head and the sceptre in his hand. The crowning bishop greeted Wladyslaw as king, after which the choir sang the *Te Deum*. The conclusion of the mass brought the spiritual part of the coronation to an end. Then Wladyslaw, like his predecessors, processed into St Peter's Church with his entourage, where he held an assize. Afterwards, on a platform on a hill outside the town, he swore to uphold the laws and kissed the cross. Returning to the town, he stood on a prominence and made a cut with his sword in all four directions, to signify his defence of the country.

What happened to the coronation insignia during the first half of the Árpád period? Was there a designated crown after the reign of Stephen I? There are no records of a crown of special importance being kept at Székesfehérvár until the middle of the 12th century, although that does not mean no such crown existed. It is not that the documents fail to mention such a crown, simply that we have no documents. How many crowns did the kings have? Without specific evidence, there is scope for the view that the acquisition of new crowns implies the want of a crown. In 1044, after the Battle of Ménfő, Emperor Henry III sent the gilt lance and crown of Samuel Aba to Rome, according to a letter he wrote to Pope Gregory VII in 1074. That is apparently why Andrew I had to request a new crown from Byzantium. Known as the Monomachus Crown, this was later hidden and lost, until it was found again in the last century, buried in the ground at Nyitraivánka. So Géza I had to seek a new crown again, and this may be the lower, Greek part of the composite Holy Crown. These suppositions, however, cannot be supported. After all, we do not know how the Monomachus Crown arrived in Hungary, and it is questionable whether it is the crown of a male ruler at all. The crown of Michael Ducas is a typical female crown, so that the queen, not Géza, must have received it.

So what happened to the crown with which Stephen I was crowned? We do not know. It can hardly have been placed in the ruler's grave, because that was not the custom. It would be still less likely in the case of a coronation crown of special importance as the first of its kind. From the general practice at the time, the likeliest theory is that Stephen presented it to a church. Emperor Otto II presented his crown to the monastery of Bergen, and Otto III his cloak to the monastery of St Alexis in Rome. Emperor Henry II presented Cluny Abbey with his coronation orb and a crown studded with precious stones. The same practice may have been followed by Stephen, whose queen, Gisela, presented her crown to Veszprém Cathedral.

The earliest information about the coronation regalia refers to the year 1167, when Székesfehérvár

13. The coronation sword play of Leopold II (detail of an engraving, Hungarian National Museum)

14. The coronation procession of Maria Theresa in Pozsony, where she was crowned on June 25, 1741, after giving the noble estates a written assurance of their privileges (Hungarian National Museum)

15. *The Monomachus Crown, with enamel pictures of the Byzantine Emperor Constantine IX Monomachus and the Empresses Zoë and Theodora*

is already known in the Eastern Empire as the place where the main insignia of kingship are kept. In 1198, Pope Innocent III refers, in a letter to the Provost of Székesfehérvár, to the canons as being guardians of the kings' crown, as if it were an established custom. In 1205, Andrew II threatened the Duke of Austria

16. *Roman and Byzantine imperial helmets*

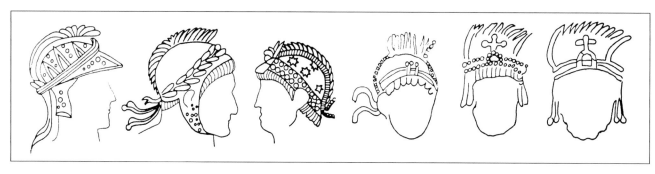

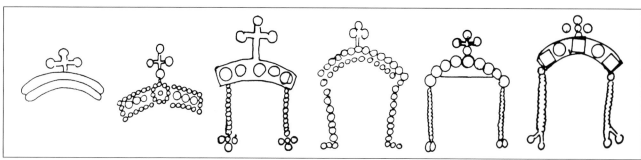

with war unless he returned the crown. In 1256, Béla IV in a document called it the Holy Crown, this being the earliest surviving reference to the *Sacra corona*. Andrew III referred to it as the crown of St Stephen, the saint-king. The evidence suggests that the coronation insignia became clearly distinct from the royal treasury and the other crown jewels by the mid-12th century at the latest, and was kept at Székesfehérvár.

Several scholars investigating the Holy Crown have tried to draw conclusions about the shape of the coronation ensign from surviving illustrations. The search for analogous items runs into difficulties, however. Authentic representation of such objects was not customary in the Árpád period or later, in Hungary or elsewhere. Investigations suggest that the Eastern Empire was the first place where attempts were made at least to make the shape of the crown realistic, if not the details of it. The best source of information about the crowns of Byzantine emperors, empresses and dowagers is the coinage. Coins show how the various crowns developed out of the insignia of the Roman Empire. The crown worn also depended on the emperor's dress. If he appeared as *imperator,* the commander-in-chief of the army, he would be in armour with a lance, and a helmet on his head, although the diadem was still placed on top of it. If he was shown in formal civilian dress – an ornate, late Roman form of toga – the diadem would be the head decoration. These two basic versions were developed and modified over the centuries. On the other hand, the goldsmiths of the mint may have shaped the crown arbitrarily, in which case it would not be the crown that changed but the way it was represented. There are certainly some recognizable types in the 10th and 11th centuries. The same process can be observed only later in the Western Empire. Far fewer coins have survived in far fewer versions, and there are no sets equivalent to those in the East. It becomes hard to draw conclusions, from these simplified, idealized or schematic representations, about the shape of crown worn. The issue is clouded further

17. A mosaic of Emperor Theodora in San Vitale, Ravenna (AD 547)

because no crown of the 10th to 12th centuries has survived from the Eastern Empire, and only one or two from the Western. There is no way in which the depictions can be checked against originals.

The same points apply to the Hungarian insignia. On the coronation mantle, the saints and King Stephen all wear the same shape of crown, which shows that the shape is schematic. The Hungarian orb provides an example of how far the depictions differ from the

18. Crowns of Byzantine empresses

19. The Hungarian coat of arms surmounted by a crown, from a map by Wolfgang Lazius (1552–6, Vienna)

21. Matthias II in coronation robes (copper engraving by L. Kilian, 1610)

actual coronation insignia, so that even the most characteristic features of them cannot be discerned. This ensign dating from the Angevin period is surmounted by a double cross. Although we do not know what the earlier one was like, it is certain that double cross has been among the symbols of Hungarian kingship ever since the reign of Emericus. Yet right up to the coronation of 1867, the orb with a double cross was visible on only one coin, from the reign of Wenceslas!

So far as we know, the closed form found in the Holy Crown first appears on seals in the reign of Matthias I. It is possible that attempts were made to portray it true to life after its return in 1463. This is suggested by the presence of slightly pointed crests on the edge of the band, instead of the customary stylized leaves or lilies. The first clearly authentic depiction of the crown dates from a hundred years later. The Fugger Chronicle, preserved in Munich, tells the history of the Habsburg dynasty. The section on the reign of Emperor Frederic III, recounting the return of the crown, includes an almost entirely realistic picture of the Holy Crown. It shows the pictorial plates, the semi-precious stones, the frame of

20. Drawing of the Holy Crown in the Fugger Chronicle (latter half of the 14th c., Bayerische Staatsbibliothek, Munich)

stones on the upper part, the crest decorations, and the cross surmounting the crown, still standing straight at the time. The pendants are also shown faithfully, although there are only three chains hanging on each side instead of four. An engraving was made in 1610 showing Matthias II in his coronation robes. The crown, coronation mantle, orb and sceptre all appear with great realism. The cross on the top of the crown is shown crooked, although this may be a consequence of how the king is holding his head. The Holy Crown also appears accurately on thalers of Matthias II, struck at Körmöcbánya in 1609, 1610 and 1611, and on coins of other denominations. The obverse bears the head of the sovereign, while the arms on the reverse are surmounted by the crown, on which the cross is not only slightly crooked, but inclined correctly, to the left. So the cross may have been bent before the reign of Matthias II. Another hundred years pass before realistic pictures of the crown appear on coins again: the *poltura* of Charles III in 1713 and the copper *denarius* of Maria Theresa faithfully portray the Hungarian crown above the coat of arms. On the ducats and thalers of Joseph II and Leopold II, the crown is lifted above the Hungarian shield by angels. On the latter, the crown is slightly stylized and not shown crooked. With the coronation of Francis Joseph in 1867, the coat of arms surmounted by the crown with a crooked cross became general on the coinage.

16

THE HOLY CROWN

The crown has two main parts: an upper part consisting of crossed bands, with Latin inscriptions and plates depicting apostles, and a lower band with four pendant chains with precious stones *(pendilia)* on each side and one at the back. The cross surmounting the crown was affixed later, by piercing the uppermost enamel plate. The parts are made of gold of different qualities, the upper part, which has no supporting function, being of finer, softer, yellower metal. The lower band has a higher silver content, so that the gold is lighter in shade. The lower part of the crown, known as the *corona graeca,* is a separate, integral object in its own right. It was a crown whose form suggests it was worn by empresses in the Byzantine Empire. The upper part *(corona latina)* is not a separate piece, and cannot be considered a royal ensign or a liturgical object in its own right. The upper and lower parts differ materially in style and technique. The upper part has filigree decoration, with alternate pearls and almandines on a mounting. The frame of this mounting has been folded onto the enamel plates. The enamelling covers the whole surface of the plates, which bear inscriptions in Latin. The Greek crown has no filigree. The

22. The Holy Crown

rows of pearls have been strung on wire, and the enamel plates fit behind the inner grooves of the frame. They are not enamelled right up to the edge. Finally, the crest decorations and the rim of the band on the Greek crown are framed with the same beaded gold wire. The work on this differs from the way the beaded wire of the bands on the Latin crown has been made. There is no doubt, therefore, that the Holy Crown was assembled out of two main parts.

In its present form, of course, it constitutes an integral object, but it has been so only since the parts, made in different workshops at different times, were married together.

The Greek crown (corona graeca)

The frames of the 5.1 cm-wide band and the triangular and semicircular crest decorations were cut from a single plate of gold, which was folded together into a slightly elliptical circle. The larger circumference is 20.9 cm and the smaller 19.8 cm. Two rings on each side were welded onto the lower edge of the band, with a fifth ring at the back. These held the original pendant chains. Later, probably in Hungary, the chains were exchanged for four pairs. These chains each end in a three-lobed cluster of oval almandines. The upper and lower edges of the band are framed with rows of true pearls strung on gold wire. Precious stones and enamel pictures alternate on the rest of the surface.

Between the crest decorations on the upper edge of the band, over the temples, there is a framed enamel picture of Christ Enthroned. In the same position at the back is a smaller enamel showing the Byzantine Emperor Michael Ducas. Both of these have the shape of a semicircular arch. The front picture shows Christ seated on a typical Byzantine throne without a back, resembling a chest, with a red cushion. Over a light-blue under-garment, he wears a dark-blue cloak with an ornate border. He holds a book in his left hand, and has the right hand raised in blessing. The heavenly scene is intimated by a cypress tree on each side of the throne. Level with the figure's shoulders, there are round monograms on each side, bearing the Greek initials of Christ's name. The figure on the rear plate is shown in the ceremonial imperial mantle of a ruler *(loros)*, a sword in his left hand and the *labarum* or imperial standard in his right. The Greek inscription on the enamel plate reads, 'Michael, the Emperor of the Romans and Believer in Christ, the Ducas.' The band bears pictures of saints whom it was customary to present in pairs, so that they could be arranged symmetrically. These enamels alternate with precious stones. On either side of the Pantocrator are the Archangels Michael and Gabriel, with bands in their hair and the staffs of messengers in their hands. Each is turned slightly towards Jesus. George and Demetrius, the military saints and great martyrs of the Greek church, wear armour and each hold a shield and spear. They were particularly revered as saints and patrons of the Byzantine Empire. The row concludes with busts of Cosmas and Damian, the physicians and martyrs, who guard over the ruler's physical health. On the rear, under the picture of the emperor, are three-quarter views of Constantine Porphyrogennetos and of Géza I, King of Hungary. The emperor is young, hardly more than a child. He wears a crown similar in shape to Emperor Michael's, from which strings of pearls hang on each side. His left hand holds a document tied with red cord, and his right hand the *labarum*. The inscription in Greek reads 'Con[stantine], Emperor of the Romans, Born to the Purple.' Identifying the figure is made more difficult because the abbreviation could be interpreted as either Constantine or Constantius. While the saints and the emperors, after Byzantine custom, have been given a round nimbus, green in colour, Géza has not. He wears a mantle, and carries a sword in his left hand, and in his right a typically Byzantine sceptre with a cross. He is looking towards the emperor. The inscription reads 'Geobidzas, faithful king of Turkia' (Hungary).

The imperial court of Byzantium still lived according to the ceremonial rules laid down in late Roman times by Diocletian and Constantine the Great. The imperial court reflected the hierarchy of Heaven, with the ruler, Christ's representative on earth, enthroned at the peak. The emperor was considered and revered as the highest, and one true ruler on earth. Everyone else, whatever country they might rule, could only come after the emperor in rank. This difference in rank is also expressed in the pictures on the Greek crown. The inscriptions on the plates of Michael and Constantine are in the red or purple colour mete for an emperor. The one for King Géza is dark blue. The Byzantine rulers were broad, ornate crowns. Géza has a narrower diadem and no nimbus.

The small, almost square pictures were made by the accustomed techniques of the Eastern Empire, using cloisonné. They portray the busts of the saints and rulers in bright, sparkling colours. The silhouettes of the figures were sunk into the gold plate. The inside details were picked out with thin gold strands. The panels were then filled with coloured glass powder. Finally, the plates were fired, which left them slightly curved. The letters of the inscriptions were sunk into the gold plate and likewise filled with enamel. The enamelling technique used was excellent, giving splendid blue, green, red, white, black and yellow colours. They are products of workshops where several hundred years of tradition and expertise lay behind the final phase in a golden age for Byzantine enamel.

The crest decorations of triangular and semicircular plates, arranged symmetrically at the front of the crown on the upper edge, diminish in size towards the sides. The enamel pieces inside the frames of these were made by a highly extravagant technique. Because there is no backing plate, this rare translucent enamel (known as *à jour*) gleams enigmatically in shades of blue and green when lit from behind. This kind of work is extremely fragile, so that hardly any examples have survived. The pieces are arranged in the kind of overlapping, imbricate patterns common on the altar rails and mosaic floors of churches in late Roman times. These spread later to gold and silverware and miniatures in Eastern and Western Europe.

The direct antecedents of the design could be Byzantine glass vessels made about the turn of the millennium, on which the same scale pattern was painted. Since the glasses are transparent, the idea for this decoration, requiring so difficult a technique, could well have come from glassware. The pinnacles have been adorned with amethysts.

Some idea of when the *corona graeca* may have arrived in Hungary may be had from the dates of the rulers it portrays. Byzantine Emperor Michael VII Ducas reigned from 1071 to 1078, and King Géza I of Hungary from 1074 to 1077.

The most important outcome of examining the goldsmith's work on the crown was to establish that the plate depicting Emperor Michael had been fixed on in an unusual way. The enamel is slightly larger than its mounting, but the decisive difference is that instead of the frame being folded, the plate has been superimposed and then attached with rivets. The problem was not the size, for it could easily have been trimmed slightly. The trouble is on the reverse, where a semicircle of gold thread about 3 mm thick has been welded on, which prevents the plate from fitting flat against the mounting. This meant the frame had to be folded outwards, and the picture of the emperor attached to the edge with rivets. So there can be no doubt that Michael's was not the original picture on the mounting.

Various ideas have been put forward to explain this. It has been suggested that it replaced another plate depicting the Virgin Mary, or that the crown originally bore no pictures of historical figures at all. There is no basis for these suppositions, however. There could be no motive for making the change in Hungary. Why would they remove a picture of Our

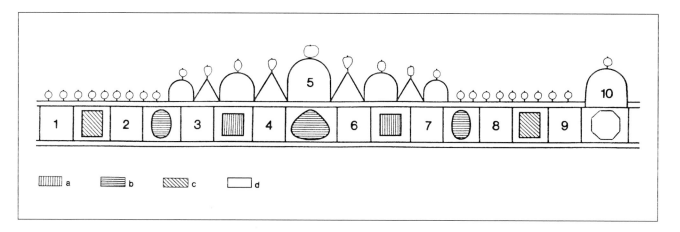

23. Drawing of the Greek crown extended flat.
Stones: a. almandine, b. sapphire, c. green glass, d. aquamarine.
Enamels: 1. Géza I of Hungary (1074–1077), 2. St Cosmas, 3. St George, 4. St Michael the Archangel, 5. Christ, 6. Archangel Gabriel, 7. St Demetrius, 8. St Damian, 9. Constantius or Emperor Constantine X of Byzantium, 10. Emperor Michael VII Ducas of Byzantium (1071–1078)

19

24. The back of the crown

Lady, who had offered the realm to Stephen I and was the country's heavenly patroness, least of all in favour of a Byzantine emperor, of whom nothing was known in Hungary some decades after this death? In principle the reverse would be more likely: to substitute Mary for the emperor. There is one solution that may also help to explain some other changes. The plate could have been exchanged most easily at the imperial court in Constantinople, where a suitable picture of the emperor would have been available. Michael may have wanted to send a gift on Géza's accession to the Hungarian throne, to a man whom he liked and to his Greek wife. Rather than making a new crown, they took an existing female crown from the treasury and altered it slightly. The style of the crown suggests it cannot have dated from much earlier than that, probably from the reign of Constantine X Ducas (1059–1067), Eudocia (1067) or Romanus IV (1068–1071). Michael's son Constantine may have been born by the time the gift was made, so that the picture was applied to him, which the abbreviated name allowed. Originally the

25. King Géza I of Hungary

26. Front view of the pendant at the back of the crown

27. Emperor Constantine

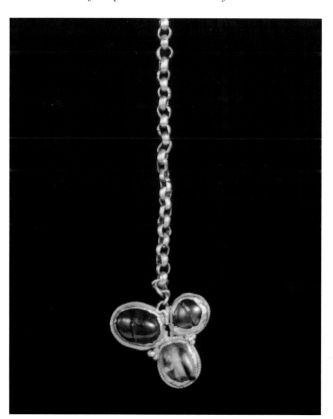

picture may have represented Michael's brother, Constantius.

There is no way of telling exactly when the gift was made. Géza I became king after the Battle of Mogyoród on March 14, 1074, when the vanquished King Solomon fled to the Western marches. Géza was probably crowned in 1075. He had the following written in the deed of foundation of Garamszentbenedek Abbey: 'I, Magnus, known also as Géza, king in the beginning of the Hungarian princes, later consecrated king by the grace of God ...' There is no way to tell whether Emperor Michael sent the crown for Géza's coronation or for his wedding.

Certainly the crown did not arrive for the personal use of Géza I, King of Hungary. The *corona graeca* can be shown to be female, not a male crown, typical of the kind of crested crown worn for centuries by empresses. It can be seen exclusively on the heads of consort and reigning empresses on countless coins, miniatures and enamels. Alternately pointed and semicircular pinnacles can also be found on the crowns of empresses (and of female saints such as St Helen). Similar crowns appear in the 11th century worn by the co-empresses Zoë and Theodora on coins, by the consort of Michael VII Ducas in the Khakhuli diptych, or by the Empress Irene (*alias* Piroska, daughter of St Ladislas) in the mosaics of the Hagia Sophia (Ayasofya). It used to be thought that the crown sent to Géza had later been altered, the crest decorations being added. This would imply that the crown had been made ready for the queen in Hungary. That cannot be so, however, because the gold plate of the crown and the frames of the crest decorations were cut from the same sheet of gold. The style of the band of the crown conforms well with the characteristics of Byzantine work in the 11th century. According to Byzantine custom, only the ruler's wife and possibly some other privileged persons might wear a likeness of the emperor, and he would never wear such a picture on his own crown or dress. It would have been even less appropriate for King Géza I of Hungary to have the likeness of the emperor on his crown. For according to Byzantine ceremonial and ideas, this would imply acknowledgement at least of a nominal allegiance. His consort, on the other hand, might have done so, for she was of Byzantine descent, from the Synadenos family. (Her name is not known.) It was almost undoubtedly she who received the crown, on Géza I's accession or soon after.

It is not known whether the side pendants (two on each side and one at the back) were attached to the crown on its arrival from Byzantium. Certainly the two further pendants on each side were added in Hungary, perhaps when the crown was assembled in its final form.

28. Depiction of the Holy Crown in Péter Révay's book 'De sacrae coronae Regni Hungariae ortu ...' (Augsburg, 1613)

The Latin crown (corona latina)

The upper part of the crown consists of bands in the form of a cross. These bear a square enamel at the junction between them and oblong enamels along them. The four gold bands have been welded to the central, square panel, while the base of each is attached to the band of the Greek crown with rivets. The use of these two different methods is further confirmation that the Holy Crown consists of two combined parts. The enamel plates on the cross bands have a filigree surround studded alternately with true pearls and almandine stones. The number of these is significant. There are twelve pearls and twelve almandines round the plate of the Pantocrator, and with the cross bands altogether 72 stones. So there are twelves and a multiple of twelve. The number of stones round the plate showing Christ recalls the number of apostles and the number of minor prophets, while 72 is the number of Christ's disciples.

The mountings of the bands contain full-length standing pictures of eight apostles. The order of these originally conformed with the one given in the *Acts:* Peter, Paul, James and John, and on the lower plates, Andrew, Philip, Bartholomew and Thomas. The order has been changed, however, during the stormy history of the crown: Bartholomew and Thomas have changed places. The reason may be that the plate of Bartholomew has been severely truncated, so that only the uppermost part and some of the inscription remains. This is hidden by the picture of Christ on the front of the Greek crown.

Only eight of the twelve apostles appear on the bands. Many people have therefore assumed that the upper part of the crown originally bore twelve apostles in some form, and that four were removed when the two parts of the crown were joined. On examining the crown, however, it can be seen that the filigree, studded pattern is concluded at the lower ends of the cross bands, and there is no continuation of the pattern. There can be no question of the bands having been shortened. The ends cannot have been cut off, which means there were places for only eight apostles in the first place. (There is no rule to say that all must be represented. Indeed there are many works of art in which the number is incomplete. All twelve need only be shown in scenes at which they were all present, such as the Last Supper or the descent of the Holy Ghost at Pentecost.)

The central plate, over the junction of the cross bands, shows Christ Enthroned, on a gold surface.

Level with his head are the sun and the moon, symbolizing rule over the world, and on each side there is a cypress tree, signifying Heaven. The plates of the apostles differ from the plate showing Christ in their style and technique. So it is possible they were not made in the same workshop, or at least that they are not by the same artist. The technique used is cloisonné enamel. The figures and the inscriptions are separated from the frame the surrounding ornamentation by a band of gold, but the whole surface of each plate has been covered with enamel. The portrayal of Christ has also been done using the recessed cloisonné technique typical of Byzantine enamel work. However, only the centre of the panel has been recessed, round the edge of the figure, and this area filled with cloisonné. Thus Christ sits against a shining background. (The portrayals of Christ and of the apostles also differ in their treatment of the panels. Christ does not present a convergent view, and there is no spiral lining on the apostle panels.)

On the apostle panels, the figures are accompanied by decoration in the broad band of gold, at shoulder height. Peter and James have the same stepped pattern of tendrils, and Andrew and Paul of rows of circles. Thomas and Philip are also depicted as a pair. Whether John and Bartholomew also made

29. *Drawing of the Latin crown extended flat.*
Apostles: 1. Peter, 2. Paul, 3. James, 4. John, 5. Andrew, 6. Philip, 7. Bartholomew, 8. Thomas

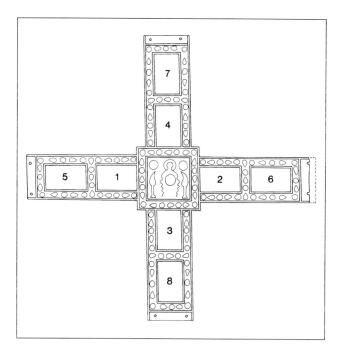

30. The names of Paul and Thomas as inscribed on the crown

a pair cannot be established because of the damage to the latter.

The apostle depictions are akin to Western European Romanesque in their style. On the other hand, their technique and their details also betray influence from the art of the Eastern Empire. These characteristics include the thin band of gold separating the figure from the surrounding ornamentation. Then there are the decorations themselves: the steps, fronds and rows of circles, depiction of the apostles without arcades, the key hanging from St Peter's wrist, the fine technique of the enamels and the shaping of the panels, the clover-leaf pattern of the noses, and the way the eyes are shown. All these attributes suggest that the panels of the apostles were done in a place where the influence of Byzantine art was strong. A candidate area in the Romanesque period was Italy. The southern part belonged to Byzantium, and artistic relations with the Eastern Empire remained strong in the 11th century, in spite of the Great Schism of 1054.

The influence of Byzantine goldsmiths is also apparent in the inscriptions of the apostles, which are given in 11th-century capital letters. Two of the letters, however, betray a Byzantine influence, and help incidentally to date the plates: the initial T of 'Thomas' and the second U of 'Paulus'. Both of these are known from Byzantine coins. The inscriptions usually appeared until the mid-11th century in Latin letters, including these unusual forms of T and U, which had been present for centuries. When the

31. Thomas the Apostle and the clasp of the enamel showing Emperor Michael

language of the coin inscriptions eventually changed to Greek, these forms disappeared. So the depictions of the apostles on the Latin crown cannot have been made later than the mid-11th century.

This does not mean that the bands themselves are of the same age. All that can be said at present is that the object which the apostles adorned was made in Italy before the mid-11th century. Only further research can decide whether this object was a crown or some liturgical item.

32–3. Side views of the Holy Crown ➤

34–5. Front and back views of the Holy Crown ➤ ➤

24

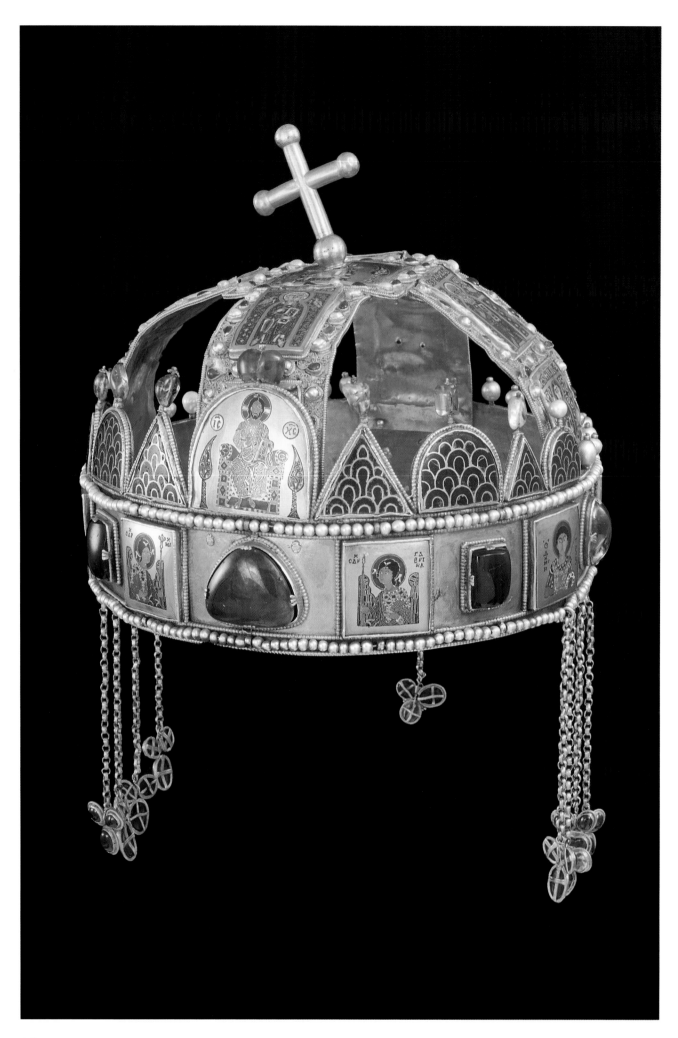

38–41. Enamel pictures on the Greek crown: Archangels Michael and Gabriel (above) and St George and St Demetrius (below)

◀ *36–7. The front of the crown with the picture of Christ*

42–3. *Pictures of St Cosmas and St Damian on the Greek crown*

Assembly of the Holy Crown

No written record has remained of how the Greek crown came to be merged with the bands carrying panels showing apostles. Conclusions about the date can only be drawn from the resulting shape. The Holy Crown has two attributes of significance in this respect. It has broad in the shape of a cross, and these bear pictures. There is only one surviving pictorial crown in Western Europe: the German imperial crown made at the beginning of the 11th century, which is adorned with depictions of Christ and Old Testament figures. There was another, Italian crown with pictures of Christ and the apostles, but it was destroyed at the beginning of the 19th century, and its date is uncertain, although it was probably centuries older than the Holy Crown. However, female crowns and diadems bearing pictures have survived from Byzantium and the area of Byzantine cultural influence. One such may have been the crown made of Greek enamel plates that was cut up by the Holy

Roman Emperor Henry II, and used to decorate the covers of books. These 'pictorial' crowns seem to have made and worn mainly under the Neapolitan Byzantine emperors. High, closed crowns were worn for the first time in Byzantium when the Comnenian dynasty took the throne. These were made in the reign of Emperor Alexius I (1081–1118), and used thereafter. The closed crowns of the Western empire, which became more common in the 12th century, are known only from depictions dating from the 11th to 13th centuries. Without a thorough examination, there is no way of telling whether this form of crown was an influence when the Holy Crown was turned into a closed one. It is even questionable whether the Eastern or the Western empire was the decisive influence on the Hungarian crown. If the form of the Byzantine crown is taken to be the pattern, the assembly of the Holy Crown is likely to have taken place in the reign of Béla III (1172–1196),

44–5. *The extreme crest decorations on the Greek crown*

who was brought up in Byzantium. This would have involved surmounting the bands with pictures of apostles onto the Greek crown and riveting these to the main band. Perhaps future investigations may help to decide whether the cross bands were made out of an earlier object in precious metal that was connected with the traditions of St Stephen and bore pictures of apostles, or whether the Greek crown was added to an earlier crown or part of a crown.

There are several debated questions about the cross on top of the crown. The junction of the cross bands has an enamel plate bearing a figure of Christ Enthroned. This figure was pierced through the stomach to attach the cross. It is unlikely that such a crude, iconoclastic act would have been committed in the Árpád period, when the crown was assembled. However, before Queen Isabella handed the crown over to Ferdinand I in 1551, she is known to have removed a cross or lily-shaped element from it. The question is whether a causal link can be assumed between these two events. The cross was missing from the crown, and *therefore* the present

cross was mounted on it. The life-like picture of the crown, found in the Fugger Chronicle of several decades later, shows it surmounted by the present-day cross. Since there is no earlier authentic representation of the Holy Crown, the most that can be said is that the cross probably found its way onto the crown after the Árpád period.

The crookedness of the cross is a marked characteristic of the crown. There are no grounds for assuming any deliberate intention behind this. The cross that symbolizes Christ is erect and vertical. The cross on the Holy Crown is crooked because it has been damaged. Evidently there was serious damage at some point, as the breaks in the upper cross bands of the crown show. A force was applied that caused the top to cave in, and three of the cross bands to break. The little ball on the upper end of the cross was also deformed. The band and the enamel plate under the cross could not be made erect again either, and the unevenness of the plate enhances the crookedness of the cross. The cross was certainly bent over when this great injury was sustained. It is not known when the accident took place.

31

46–50. Jewels on the Greek crown

Research into the Crown

I am was able to spend several weeks examining the crown in 1995. This allowed me to confirm some earlier observations, the features in dispute, and the techniques employed by the goldsmiths. I was concerned especially to check the observations and conclusions made by József Deér, whose monograph on the crown appeared in 1966. Its author was an outstanding Hungarian historian, who after 1948, became an authority in the West on the history of monarchical symbolism and emblems. These he examined more thoroughly and in greater detail than ever before. There were question marks over many of Deér's conclusions, first of all because he was never able to see the crown. Having demolished the earlier theories, he reconstructed the history of the crown's development in a radically new way. According to Deér, the crown, having arrived from Byzantium about 1074, was altered at the beginning of the 12th century, when it was mounted on a new band, and the crest decorations typical of female crowns were augmented. He considered that the plates showing apostles had been made at the very beginning of the 13th century, under Byzantine influence, in a workshop associated with Venetian and North Italian goldsmiths. The crown was then assembled in its present form in the 1270s, because after Béla IV's death, his daughter, Anne of Macsó, had taken several items from the royal treasury, including the original coronation crown, to her father-in-law in Prague. That crown was never returned, and a new one had to be found. Deér refuted several earlier theories about the artistic provenance and history of the Holy Crown, drawing conclusions mainly from the stylistic resemblances of the object and details of it. Ultimately, it was Anne of Macsó's theft from the treasury that influenced his views most strongly. He used that date as the basis for his chronology. This was possible because, on examining the Holy Crown, one faces the problem that it cannot be identified with any of the coronation insignia mentioned in historical sources, at least from the Árpád period. There are no literal depictions of it before the second half of the 16th century. The most important point in Deér's conclusions—that the coronation crown was stolen from Hungary in 1270 along with the other items from the treasury—has been rebutted. However, the observations published in reviews of his book and criticisms of his opinions do not yield a single firm date in the history of the crown either. A typical example was the sterile debate on the curvature of the apostle plates on the Latin crown. Differing opinions were expressed even when an autopsy had been held, and far-reaching conclusions reached from these opinions. The fine, thin sheets of gold necessarily bend during the enamelling process, as can also be seen with the smaller, square enamels on the Greek crown. After the Holy Crown was returned from the United States in 1978, there were chances of making personal observations. These have changed the views and conclusions on some aspects of the crown's history fundamentally.

There have been several books and accounts of the coronation jewels. In this book I have focused primarily on some details about the coronations and insignia of the Árpád period, about which little has been said before. These confirm earlier assumptions in some places and conflict with them in others. I completed an examination of the inscriptions on the Latin crown, which had not been done before, and I have used the results here. However, this book is not extensive enough to include an account of the examinations of the crown and the other insignia, or of the various opinions and criticisms of them. My own researches have not been completed, although I have been able to reach firm conclusions on some points. My purpose is to present a more realistic account that is nearer to the truth, while acknowledging that we can never know every event in the history of the crown.

51. An amethyst on the crest decoration

52. Pearls on the Greek crown

34

53–6. The four cross bands of the Latin crown, with pictures of Peter, Paul, James and John

57–8. The figures of Peter and Paul on the Latin crown ➤

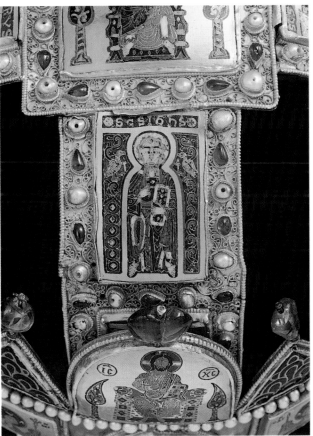

37

59–59/a. Where the bands of the Latin crown meet the Greek crown: the apostles Andrew and Philip

60. Top of the Latin crown

61–4. Front and back views of the side pendants

65–6. *The inside of the crown, showing the marks of assembly and repair work*

40

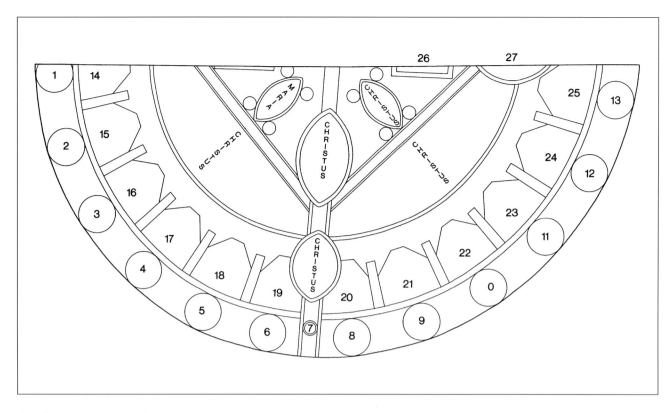

68. *The coronation mantle:*

S a i n t s :
1. *Unidentified*
2. *Cosmas*
3. *Damian*
4. *George*
5. *Vincent*
9. *Stephen the Protomartyr*
10. *Unidentified*
11. *Sixtus*
12. *Cornelius*
13. *Laurence*

6. *Queen Gisela*
7. *Prince Emericus*
8. *King Stephen I*

A p o s t l e s
14. *Peter*
15. *Paul*
16. *John the Evangelist*
17. *Thomas*
18. *James*
19. *Philip*
20. *Bartholomew*
21. *Matthew the Evangelist*
22. *Jude Thaddaeus*
23. *Simon*
24. *Thaddaeus*
25. *Andrew*

26. *Christ on the Cross*
27. *Transfiguration of Christ*

The coronation mantle is the only survivor from the coronation robes, which would have consisted of several garments. It is a semicircular garment in a bluish lilac colour, densely embroidered in gold. Its original function is clear from the semicircular inscription on the cloth, done by the same technique as the rest of the mantle: 'ANNO INCARNACIONIS XPI : MXXXI : INDICCIONE XIIII A STEPHANO REGE ET GISLA REGINA CASULA HEC OPERATA ET DATA [EST] ECCLESIAE SANCTAE MARIAE SITAE IN CIVITATE ALBA.' All the most important

pieces of information are imparted: 'This chasuble was caused to be made and presented to the Church of St Mary in the city of Alba [Fehérvár] by King Stephen and Queen Gisela, in the 1031st year of the incarnation of Christ, and in the 14th indiction.' So the mantle was originally the chasuble of a priest, which in the 11th century had a closed, conical shape. Three circumstances made it possible for this vestment to be turned into a coronation mantle, at some time towards the end of the 12th century. It had a connection with the first Hungarian king, it was unmatched in its embroidery, and it was already kept in the church where the coronations took place. This was probably when the collar was added. Taken from

◄ *67. The central part of the coronation mantle*

another vestment, it carries embroidered foliage and animal figures contained in an arcade pattern, and also a large number of pearls.

The gold embroidery almost covers the surface of the mantle, so that only traces can be seen of the thin, parti-coloured base material of silk, which is of Byzantine origin. In the 17th century and again in the 19th, meticulous work went into mounting the remaining silk and the patterns onto a new base textile. The figures of people and animals, and the decorations, were laid on the textile in a different direction for each piece of pattern, and sewn in gold thread, while the contours were marked with silk thread as well.

Like the chasubles of the time, the back of the mantle shows a large forked cross in the shape of a Y. There are 61 larger and smaller figures, and 52 small busts, birds and four-legged animals on the garment, in four distinct bands. The varied solutions employed in this complex, but still clear set of pictures, the dense decoration, hardly leaving a free area of the surface, and the masterly way it has been executed single this garment out from similar relics of its period and kind, which are all too easily destroyed. The inscriptions it carries, along with those on Stephen's coins, are among the earliest pieces of writing from the Hungarian area: a dedication recording the gift, and a verse interpretation of the pictures can be found. It includes the first written mention of Székesfehérvár, as the king's main church. It also contains the only contemporary representations of Stephen, Gisela and Emericus.

Beneath the hands of blessing at the very top, which symbolize God the Father, Jesus stands on the right-hand side, clasped by two angels. The inscription round the vesica reads 'DAT SUMMO REGI FAMULATUM CONCIO CELI' (The host of Heaven renders service to the king of the highest), which might serve to describe the subject of the whole composition. The figures in the descending rows present the hierarchy of heaven, the assembly of saints who serve Christ, the heavenly king. The left-hand vesica, also held by angels, contains Mary: 'EMICAT IN CELO SANCTAE GENITRICIS IMAGO' (The image of the Holy Mother shines in Heaven). This represents Mary, patroness of the Székesfehérvár church, who according to Catholic doctrine was 'assumed', body and soul, into Heaven. Between these two images is another vesica holding a picture of Christ with his feet on a dragon and a lion, representing his triumph over his enemies: 'HOSTIBUS EN CHRISTUS PROSTRATIS EMICAT ALTUS' (Christ shines sublime, his enemies laid low).

Under the fork of the cross, the prophets stand in symmetrical rows, six on each side, in the canonical order sanctioned by the church. They hold open scrolls to represent their prophecies of Christ's coming, and their names have been embroidered on their breasts, as have those of the apostles and martyrs. Under the strip with the dedication, the apostles are seated in the gates of the towered city wall. Those whose books appear in the New Testament are shown writing. Their order of appearance follows the Canon of the Mass. In the midst of them, on the back panel of the chasuble, appears Christ in a vesica, enthroned as judge over the world. This ties in with the inscription: 'SESSIO REGNANTEM NOTAT ET CHRISTUM DOMINANTEM' (A throne befits Christ regnant and governing).

The band below the apostles has three-quarter figures embroidered in medallions. To the right of the axis down the back of the garment is St Stephen of Hungary. Then comes his patron saint, St Stephen the Protomartyr, followed by Clement, Sixtus (Xystus), Cornelius and Laurence. On the other side (from the left) are an unidentified saint (the fragments of the name are illegible), Cosmas, Damian (previously misread as Pantaleon), George, Vincent, and Queen Gisela. On a smaller medallion between the royal couple is the bust of a youth, without an inscription. This must surely be the heir apparent, Prince Emericus. Except for Gisela, the figures are shown in the same way, in a symmetrical stance with the opposite pair, holding a lance and orb, and wearing a crown. All the saints selected were martyred, and the order in which they appear corresponds with lists found in the Litany of the Saints and the Canon of the Mass.

The breast of the chasuble has been cut down during alteration. The upper, oblong panel shows Christ on the cross, with the inscription 'SIGNUM CRUCIS O SPES CERTA SALUTIS' (The sign of the cross is the sure hope of salvation). The subject of the picture below this is disputed. It presumably shows the transfiguration of Christ, in which case the inscription can be completed accordingly. A thin strip was probably cut off the chasuble when it was altered. This presumably bore medallion pictures of the confessors.

The intricate composition of the chasuble, with its many figures and scenes, was designed on the basis of liturgical texts. That is how the rows of prophets,

69. The coronation mantle ➤

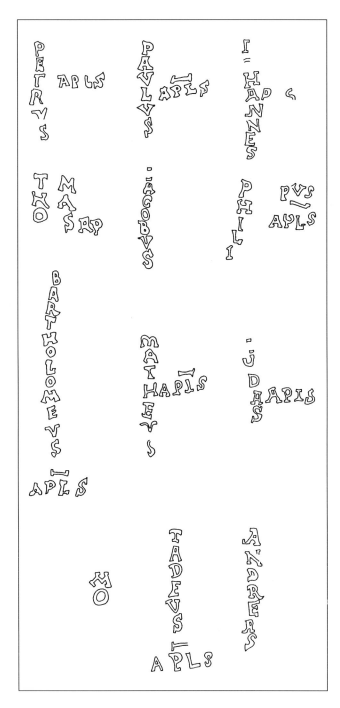

70. The inscriptions to the apostle pictures

apostles and martyrs were compiled. The pictures are grouped in bands, one beneath the other, on the cone-shaped surface. At the top is God the Father (in the form of hands making a blessing before the cross), then come Christ and Mary with the angels, and then the rows of prophets, apostles and martyrs. The grouping as a whole corresponds with the heavenly hierarchy, with the orders of saints praising God. This order for the heavenly Jerusalem, the assembly of saints, is known from late Roman times onwards. It corresponds with the list in the Litany of the Saints, which is followed by many other church texts: hymns, benedictions, and salutations to rulers *(laudes)*. This is the fullest and most detailed and fitting text for a composition showing the assembly of saints. The litanies sometimes list the prophets by name, and always mention the apostles and many saints and confessors. The groups of saints follow in the same order as on the chasuble. The size of the vestment meant that a selection had to be made from the martyrs. This was done in accordance with the Canon of the Mass and the *laudes,* so that the saints early in the lists were included. The exceptions are St George and St Vincent, who do not feature in the Canon of the Mass. George was especially revered in 11th-century Hungary. Stephen I's standard showed St George when he did battle with the pretender Koppány, and he obtained relics of the saint during his campaign against the Bulgars. Veszprém Castle had a chapel dedicated to him at the beginning of the 11th century. Since Stephen is placed next to his patron saint, St Stephen the Protomartyr, Gisela may have had a special relationship with St Vincent. Her name was not a Christian one, and so she may have followed the contemporary custom of taking as a patron the saint on whose day she was born. This would mean Gisela's birthday was on January 22.

The royal couple appear at the bottom of the composition, on either side of the axis. They are not depicted in a kneeling posture of self-abasement, as was the custom at the time, but in the same style and scale as the martyrs. This is in line with the texts of the *laudes,* whose influence on the design of the chasuble can be shown. The ruler is shown in similar splendour in the illuminations of German liturgical manuscripts around the turn of the millennium.

It was also customary for rulers to make gifts to churches. Stephen had passed a law decreeing that the newly established Christian churches in his realm be supplied with liturgical objects, and legend has it that Gisela herself was active in making church textiles. The chasuble converted later into the coronation mantle was not just a simple gift, however. Its pictorial scale and complexity, and the careful planning of every detail and the whole composition, place it far above other vestments of the period. Moreover, the church to which it was presented was still being built at the time. It includes an unusually precise double dating, reminiscent of a document; this, according to the dating methods of that time, would refer to the period December 25, 1030, to September 1 or 24, 1031. Stephen was celebrating the 30th anniversary of his coronation at the time, which coincided with his 35th wedding anniversary. The chasuble was an act of thanksgiving to God, for the victory over the Germans in 1030, and for Stephen's earlier success in establishing the country and the church. Thanksgiving for

71–2. Queen Gisela and St Stephen the King on the mantle

the heavenly aid and patronage received was an act worthy of a ruler. The chasuble also constitutes a plea for further help from God in the future.

It is questionable whether the tradition that the Hungarian queen does some sewing on the mantle before each coronation can be traced back as far as Queen Gisela. Making a chasuble requires great expertise. The liturgical objects for the nascent Hungarian church had to be made in the absence of any local tradition. Workshops where vestments were made must have developed at the main centres: at Esztergom, Veszprém, or even Székesfehérvár.

Although the designer of this complicated composition cannot be identified personally, the cultivation that went into it is clear. The decoration of the chasuble, and especially some of the details, point to a close relationship with the Reichenau school of miniature painting in South Germany.

It is just possible that Stephen and Gisela may have presented the chasuble on August 15, 1031, to the priests of the still incomplete Royal Church of the Assumption. That was the dedication festival of the church, which would have been an appropriate occasion for such a festive gesture.

73. The picture of Prince Emericus on the axis of the mantle

*76. The picture of Christ triumphant over his enemies
on the axis of the mantle* ➤

77. Christ at the head of the heavenly host ➤

78. The right hand of Christ in Picture ➤

*74. Queen Gisela with a representation of Székesfehérvár
Cathedral*

75. King Stephen with his crown, lance and orb

82. Bust of an angel on the shoulder of the mantle

83. Scroll decoration depicting a bird

84. Detail of the architectural frame for the row of apostles

85. Pair of birds on the hem of the mantle

◄ *79. Christ, Judge of the Earth, among apostles*

◄ *80–1. Details of the row of prophets*

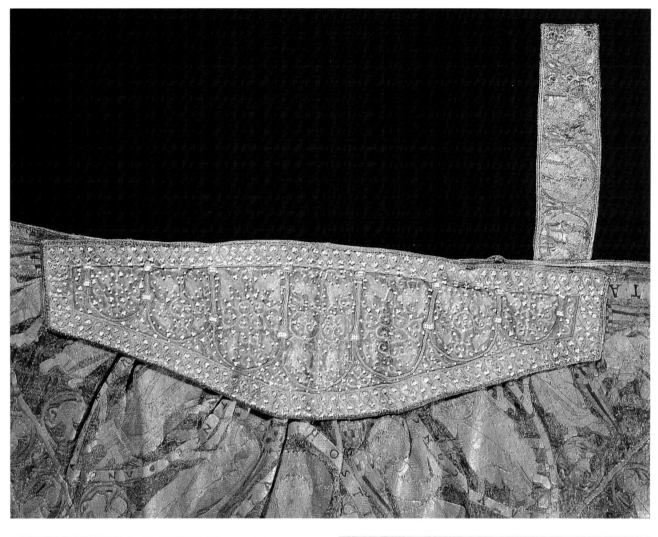

86. The collar of the coronation mantle

87. Detail of a picture of a building

88. Detail of a picture of an angel

THE SCEPTRE

The coronation sceptre consists of a rock-crystal sphere on a cylindrical staff 29.5 cm long. Three figures of animals resembling lions have been carved on the surface of the globe, which has a vertical diameter of 65 cm and a horizontal diameter of 73 cm. The sphere was made in Egypt in the 10th century, under the Fatimid dynasty, out of rock-crystal. Vessels and objects of this material spread from 10th-century Egypt, where crystal from Madagascar was used, to the courts of Europe, especially the Holy Roman Empire. The sphere is held by three pairs of bands of gold, which run from the head to the flower-shaped plates decorating the base. The plates, which divide into ten petals, and the surfaces of the bands are densely covered in filigree. The centre of each plate shows a Solomon's knot pattern augmented by a square. There are 26 little gold balls hanging from the head on thin chains: one from each band and ten from each plate.

The gilt silver of the shaft contrasts strongly with the delicate golden setting of the crystal sphere. The plate covering the hazel-wood shaft is divided lengthways into six strips, bearing lines of heart-shaped filigree pattern similar to the strap design on the sphere.

The sceptre is certainly the oldest piece in the coronation insignia to survive more or less in its original form. The 10th-century carving of the crystal and the date of the first coronation place it around the turn of the millennium. The filigree work cannot be dated exactly because the patterns were used frequently for an extended period (11th-13th centuries). The best starting point for dating the sceptre is the shape. No similar mace-shaped sceptre has survived. It may be of Eastern origin, because staffs with a round head have been found among the Avars and on a site near Kiev. However, there are some depictions of sceptres almost identical with the

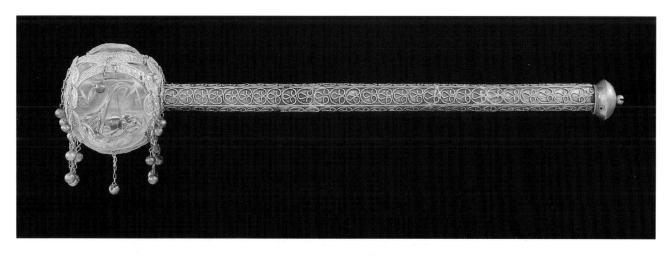

89. A full picture of the sceptre

53

90. *The top of the globe of the sceptre*

91. *The filigree mounting of the globe of the sceptre* ➤

54

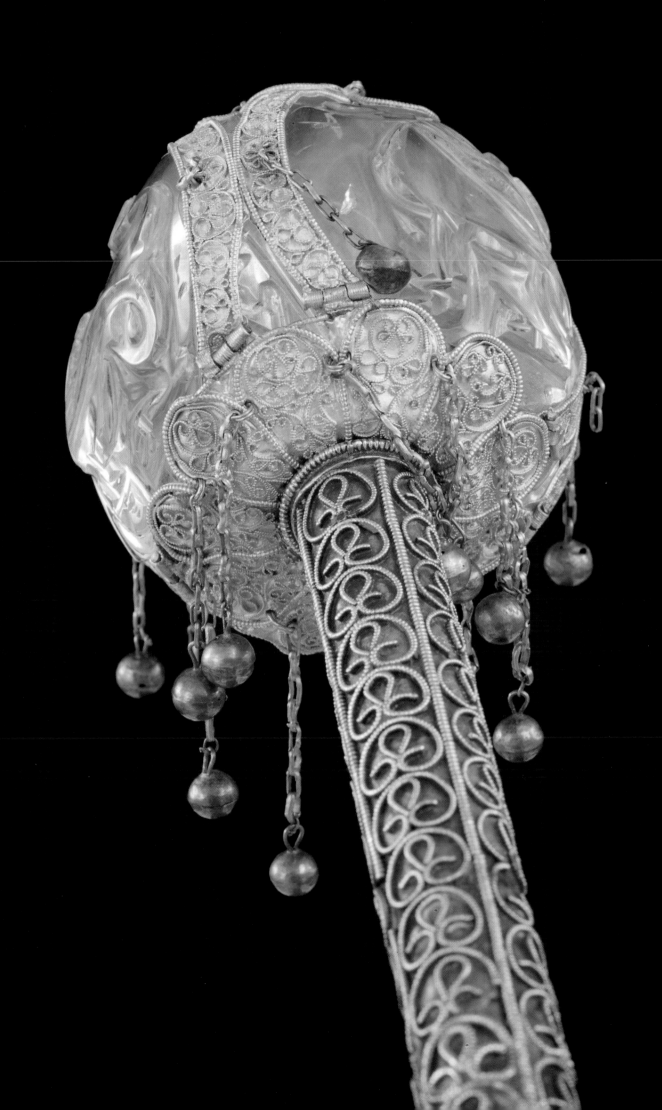

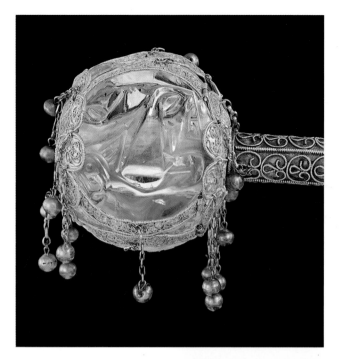 

92–4. The three carvings of lions on the crystal globe of the sceptre

Hungarian one. Holy Roman emperors are shown in 10th-century miniatures holding long staffs with spherical heads.

A sceptre similar to the Hungarian one was used by 11th-century German rulers until the end of the century, when it suddenly ceased to feature among the ensigns of power. Henry II, brother-in-law of Hungary's Stephen I, was fond of objects in rock-crystal. (The church treasury of Bamberg contains a similar sphere, and there is also one in the treasury of Essen Cathedral. This suggests that the royal Hungarian sceptre may have been a gift from the emperor to St Stephen.) Indeed Henry II holds a sceptre identical to the Hungarian one, with a short shaft and a spherical head, on a papal bull of 1003. Another sceptre of similar form appears in the hand of a maternal relative of the emperor's, Rudolf III, King of Burgundy, on a seal dating from 1017. This strongly suggests that the sceptre dates from the first half of the 11th century, during the reign of Stephen I. The crystal sphere or the whole sceptre may have been a gift from Henry II.

THE ORB

The orb has been a symbol of power since ancient times. Byzantine emperors are depicted holding a globe surmounted by a cross, and so are Carolingian rulers. However, no such ensign as an orb existed until the 11th century; the depiction was symbolic. The first orb was presented by Pope Benedict VIII to Emperor Henry II in 1014, for the imperial coronation. Henry presented it afterwards to the Benedictine Abbey of Cluny, but the orb features among the insignia of power belonging to his successors.

The orb first appears in Hungary on the coronation mantle, where it is seen in the hand of King Stephen. The martyrs also hold similar objects. It is not known whether the orb seen in the king's hand existed as an object by then. It features on 11th-century royal seals (in the hands of Peter, Solomon and Coloman), but it remains unclear which Árpád king first possessed such an object. (None was placed in the grave of Béla III.) The Hungarian orb, 16 cm high, is made of gilded silver. The sphere has a horizontal diameter of 8.9 cm and a height of 7.9 cm. It consists of two hemispheres joined together, surmounted by a patriarchal cross. On the side of the

96. The coronation orb

95. Hand of a saint holding an orb on the coronation mantle

globe is a small inlaid shield that quarters the red and silver bars of the Árpád rulers with the lily device of the House of Anjou. So the orb can be associated with the Angevin kings. It was probably made at the beginning of the reign of Charles I (1310–1342), although it is possible that the orb itself is older than the shield it bears.

The double, patriarchal cross is common in illustrations from the Eastern Roman Empire, but first appears in Hungary on coins of Béla III, who was brought up in Byzantium. If there were an earlier orb belonging to the House of Árpád, it would have borne a single, Latin cross. The first depiction of an orb with a patriarchal cross appears on a seal of Emericus (1196–1204), son of Béla III. However, the only coins of Hungarian kings to bear the Hungarian orb with a patriarchal cross were minted by Wenceslas in 1301. Otherwise, the coinage continued to show an orb with a simple, Latin cross for several more centuries.

97. Orb with a patriarchal cross, on a seal of King Emericus (1202)

98. A denarius of King Wenceslas (1301): the king on his throne holds a sceptre and an orb with a patriarchal cross

THE CORONATION SWORD

The sword, the most recent addition to the coronation regalia, was made in the second half of the 15th century. The floral motifs on the large pommel can scarcely be seen any more. The likeness of a pair of turbaned Turks and (presumably) a pair of Hussars has been etched into each side of the blade, next to the hilt. The type of the sword points to an origin in North Italy, perhaps in the mid-15th century. Sometime later, this simple weapon became one of the coronation insignia. The length is 98 cm, and the width of the blade 6.5 cm.

This sword has nothing to do with the House of Árpád. However, two other swords connected with the early history of the ruling house have survived. One is a Scandinavian piece of the 10th century, which has been lodged at the Cathedral of St Vitus in Prague since the mid-14th century. Even the first record of this sword describes it as St Stephen's. This Western-type sword with a carved, ivory cross-piece was not a ceremonial weapon, and has become worn with use. The style, period, and early appearance of the tradition leave hardly any doubt that it belonged to St Stephen. However, there is no way of telling whether there was a role at Hungarian coronations for this sword, which is thought to have arrive in Bohemia in the 1270s. The other notable relic is a sabre adorned with gilt studs, known variously as Charlemagne's and as Attila's Sword. This came from the treasury of the Holy Roman Empire, and is now kept in Vienna. Its form and style of decoration suggest it was made in the 10th century. This was probably the ceremonial sword with which Anastasia, daughter of the Russian Grand Duke Yaroslav I and widow of King Béla I of Hungary, presented to Otto of Nordheim, Duke of Bavaria, in 1063, for having helped her son Solomon to gain the Hungarian throne.

The question of the swords that belonged to the Árpád kings ties in with the coronation ceremonies, and the changes in the 11th-century in the institution of the princedom and the order of coronation. The princedom had been introduced to resolve disputes over the succession, and was directed by the king's brother, an elder relative, not the king's children who would succeed. Its insignia, at least in the 1050s and 1060s, was a sword. The events at the end of the reign of Andrew I relate to this. Andrew I had designated his son Solomon as his successor, as opposed to his brother, Béla, and the infant Solomon had even been crowned in 1058. Andrew I gave his brother a choice, at Tiszavárkony, between the crown (the kingdom) and the sword (the princedom), where Béla chose the sword of princedom. This story draws a clear distinction between the crown and the sword, the kingdom and the princedom, which is significant. The German coronation ceremony of Mainz included the presentation of a sword, but the Old English *ordo* of Egbert did not. It is not impossible that this change in the ceremony in the mid-11th century ties in with the temporary loss of the sword from the insignia marking royal power and from the coronation. This was precisely the time when the ceremonial sabre left the Árpád treasury for the West. The presentation of the gift presumably occurred during the period in the mid-11th century when the sword had no function as an emblem of power, because the ritual of Egbert was being used.

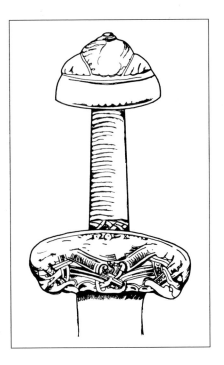

99. Drawing of the hilt of St Stephen's Sword, now in Prague

There is an interesting explanation as to how this ritual found its way to Hungary. The English king, Edmund Ironside, died on November 30, 1016, shortly after coming to the throne. He had been murdered by order of the king who succeeded him, Canute the Great. The rest of the story would be worthy of a Shakespeare play. Edmund's sons, who were one or two years old (and probably twins) were exiled to Sweden, where they lived from 1017 to 1028. They then fled to the court of the Swedish king's son-in-law, Yaroslav the Wise, Prince of Kiev. From there, at about the age of thirty, they went to Hungary in 1046, probably with the Hungarian princes Andrew and Levente, who had also been at the Kiev court. They returned to England in 1057, when summoned to do so by their father's brother, Edward the Confessor, who had no heir. So the princes spent about ten years in Hungary.

The connection was not broken afterwards either, because the name of a later Hungarian king, Solomon, also appears in the English chronicles. So there are grounds for assuming a connection between the presence of the princes and the adoption of the English rite of Egbert. This also sheds light on subsequent events that would otherwise be difficult to explain. While Andrew I's son, Solomon, had been crowned according to the English ritual in 1058, it was the prince, Béla I, who succeeded his brother when Andrew died in 1060. After Béla died in the autumn of 1063, Solomon became king with the help of the emperor and Prince Otto, and was crowned a second time at Székesfehérvár. This was when Solomon's mother presented Prince Otto with 'Attila's Sword', for which there was no use at the time. So for a time, the coronation regalia did not include a sword.

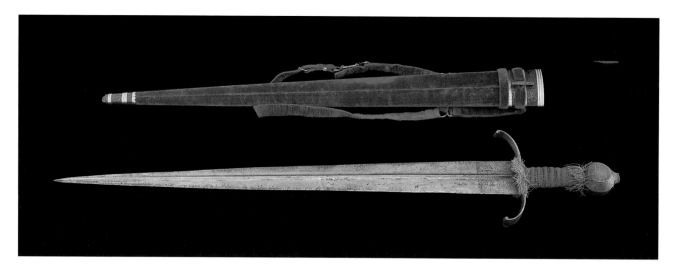

100. The coronation sword and its sheath

OTHER CORONATION ITEMS

The coronation was a church ceremony performed according to Catholic liturgy during a Mass. Francis Joseph I and Charles IV, crowned King of Hungary in 1867 and 1916, were the last monarchs to receive the traditional church rite. Alongside the regal emblems of temporal power, several liturgical objects and vestments also became features of the coronation. The church was responsible for the safekeeping of these. The task was shared until the 16th century by the Chapter and canons of the Coronation Church at Székesfehérvár and the Archbishop's Treasury at Esztergom. After the 17th century, they were kept in the Treasury of Esztergom Chapter.

Other robes that went with the Hungarian coronation insignia and the mantle were mislaid or deteriorated. None of these simple cloth and leather garments has survived. However, when the insignia returned from Vienna to Buda and Pozsony in 1792,

Sámuel Decsy (doctor of philosophy and medicine, and a member of the Royal Society of Scholars in Frankfurt/Oder) wrote a book about them, with coloured engravings depicting the insignia and the surviving objects kept by the church.

Péter Révay, a coronation guard, simply mentions the robes worn by the monarch. Decsy gives a brief description of these, which tradition associated with St Stephen. The same applied to 'the famous banner of St Stephen', which caught in the door jamb of Székesfehérvár Basilica during the coronation of Charles II (the Less), 1385, and was torn to shreds. Since the cloth items have not survived, there is no way to tell their age, although the history of the coronation insignia indicates the second half of the 16th century. Thereafter they were guarded by the crown guards. After Hungary's defeat in the 1848–9 war of independence, Interior Minister Bertalan Szemere, before fleeing the country, had a

101. An 18th-c. replica of the coronation mantle, a gift of Queen Maria Theresa (Archabbey of Pannonhalma)

102. *A colour engraving of the Holy Crown, from Sámuel Decsy's book (1792)*
(University Library, Budapest)

103. *A colour engraving of the sceptre, sword, orb and processional cross, from Sámuel Decsy's book (1792)*
(University Library, Budapest)

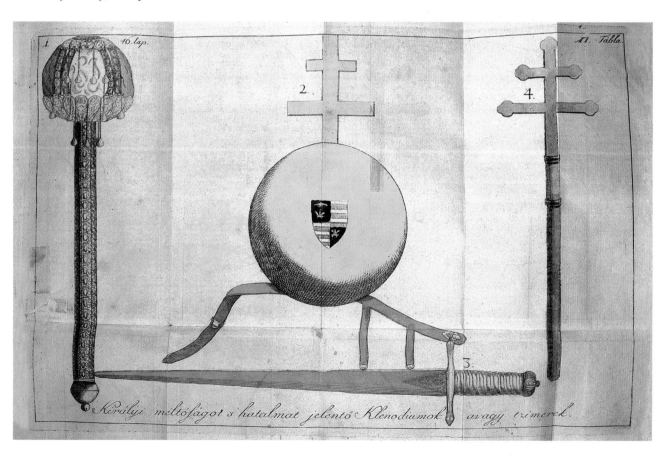

box containing the regalia buried at Orsova by the Danube. However, the box was flooded and this caused the coronation garments to perish irrevocably, although the jewels were unscathed. Indeed when found and opened on September 8, 1853, it contained the sorry remains of several perishable items, according to a minute by Johann Kempen von Fichtenstamm, the Austrian police minister: 'There were also several sodden silk coronation cloths bearing a seal, a bundle of partly rotten documents, a pair of shoes and sandals, all rotten. In the bottom of the box was a third velvet cushion, and in a side compartment with a separate lock, two old-fashioned stirrups with their straps. The case of each piece had been turned into pulp by the wet; this filled the spaces between the insignia.' Kempen's account is confirmed by minutes taken by the coronation guard before the coronation ceremony of 1867.

The dress included not just the mantle but 'gloves and sandals', according to Révay, a coronation guard. Decsy wrote more fully: 'The garments of Stephen, King and Saint, are only handed on the coronation day to the king to be installed, and then kept with the Holy Crown locked up under heavy guard.'

Notes on the items of clothing and liturgical equipment are very terse. Most confine themselves to the most notable piece, the coronation mantle of St Stephen. It can only be surmised that the other garments were mainly ecclesiastical in character, corresponding to or resembling the vestments of a bishop. Not until the 19th century did military uniform become customary. The records of coronations mention only the major events, with hardly a word about details or otherwise familiar aspects of the mass.

The long gauntlets, up to the elbow, were made of thick yellow deerskin, without decoration. The footwear, traditionally called sandals, bore no resemblance to the boots worn at the end of the 18th century, Decsy reported. They were made of finely worked yellow Spanish leather. 'St Stephen's sandals have short uppers reaching the calf, split at the front from foot to knee, in precisely the shape of the sandals worn today by Hungarian infantrymen, and laced to the king's feet with cord of red silk. The heels are likewise yellow and very high, without spurs of any kind.' Antonio Bonfini noted at the coronation of Wladyslaw II in 1490 how 'they put St Stephen's clothing on him and slipped on golden boots.' Matthias II's is the only coronation from which an account survives of the king's attire: a red

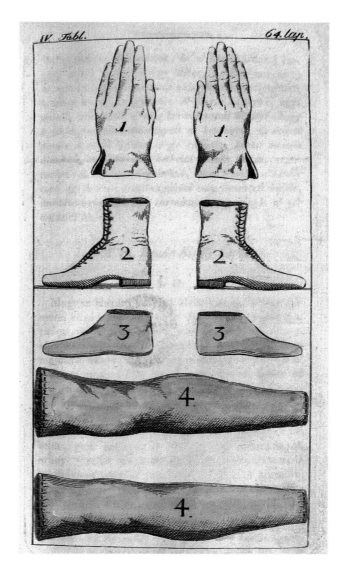

104. A colour engraving of the surviving fragments of coronation dress, from Sámuel Decsy's book, 1792 (University Library, Budapest)

gown with a white one over it, then St Stephen's mantle. Also worn were 'leggings of red Spanish leather, reaching the knee, and a pair of stockings up to the thigh, in dark-red silk.' Decsy thought only the sandals belonged to the attire of the first Hungarian king, and the other two items were later. Their age is not apparent from his drawings, but they could hardly be from the Árpád period. So it is not known what clothes were worn at medieval Hungarian coronations. Kings were dressed for their coronation in clothes similar to the vestments of a bishop. However, the liturgical vestments of the church, including shoes, stockings and gloves, were not made of leather. So the leather attire worn at later coronations can hardly have been medieval, although the red silk stocking may have been early.

The church items, by their nature, could not be assumed traditionally to have belonged to St Stephen. Nor was there a stipulation that these items alone should be used at coronations. Only

105. *The royal cross of the kiss, from the 17th c.*
(Cathedral Treasury, Esztergom)

106. *The 15th-c. apostolic cross*
(Cathedral Treasury, Esztergom)

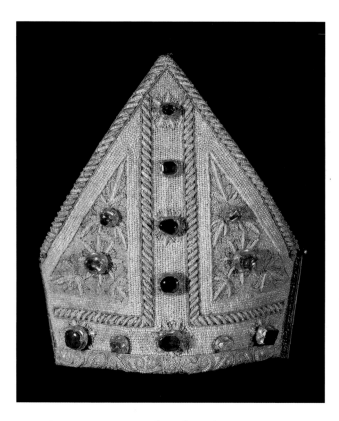

107. *The coronation mitre, from the 15th c.*
(Cathedral Treasury, Esztergom)

after the storms of history, in the 16th and 17th centuries, did their use become regular. A partial exception is the cross of the coronation oath. The crowned king swore by this to observe the constitution, independence, laws and customs of the country and preserve its territorial integrity. The coronation invested the new king with the power of a ruler, while the royal oath safeguarded the country's legal order and constitution. From the 15th century, the text was, 'We swear that we shall protect Hungary and all its several inhabitants by our laws and freedoms, and that we shall not alienate the borders of the country, but protect them, and to the extent of our ability, retrieve that which has been lost.' Joseph II did not have himself crowned precisely to avoid taking the coronation oath and issuing the coronation diploma, in which the same terms were confirmed in writing. This was known as the lay oath. During the mass, the ruler also swore the church oath. The rulers of the Holy Roman Empire swore this by the gospel. According to Bonfini, Wladyslaw did so too. Ursius Velius noted the same at the coronation of Ferdinand I in 1527: 'I will keep

108. The 13th-c. cross of the coronation oath, on a 17th-c. base (Cathedral Treasury, Esztergom)

109. The 17th-c. coronation chasuble (Cathedral Treasury, Esztergom)

the law, justice and the peace for the church of God for my people, as I am able with the help and advice of my followers; I will respect the priesthood and protect the estates of the churches. I will persuade my officials and vassals to do likewise,' ran the oath, according to the liturgy.

The king took the lay oath at the end of the service, not in church, but before the people outside. Francis Joseph did this in 1867 outside Pest's Inner City parish church in Eskü tér (Oath Square), and Charles IV outside Matthias Church in Buda Castle, beneath the Holy Trinity Statue.

The significance of the coronation oath could be why the cross of the oath is the oldest piece of liturgical equipment connected with the coronation–earlier than the coronation sword or orb. The 40-cm-high cross, made of gold, including its base, is kept in the Cathedral Treasury at Esztergom. The cross itself, 27.5 cm high, was made in the 13th century. Its finial and base recall the generosity of Archbishop Péter Pázmány (1616-1637). Both sides of the cross, the ends of whose arms are lobed, bear dense filigree work studded with pearls and gems. A relic of the cross is embedded at the junction. Pázmány had the base repaired in 1634. It was adorned with amethysts and emeralds in 1790 by Primate József Batthyány (1776–1799). It features in the Treasury registry in 1551, and may have come from Székesfehérvár Basilica, before the city was taken by the Turks in 1543.

The 29.5-cm pure-gold cross of the kiss was made in Prague between 1612 and 1622. Primate György Szelepchényi (1666–1685) later inserted an enamel shield. The arms are adorned with sapphires and pearls, and the body of Christ is covered with enamel. The priests held this to greet the king, who kissed the cross at the door. János Liszty noted that at Maximilian's coronation, priests met him at the door of St Martin's in Pozsony, while the archbishop waited at the altar. At Rudolf's coronation in 1572 in Pozsony, the king is said to have been offered the cross of the kiss on arrival by Archbishop Antal Verancsics (1569–1573).

Two long-armed crosses were borne in the coronation procession. Bonfini recalls that at Wladyslaw's coronation in 1490, Stephen, bishop of Szerém, bore the gold cross and the prior of Vrána the simpler cross. When the procession moved the place where the oath was to be sworn, the bishop seated on the horse in front of the crowned king bore the silver apostolic cross. Mrs János Kottanner wrote of the coronation of Ladislas V: 'They also bore an apostolic cross before the noble king, for no king of Hungary has made Hungary a vassal of the Holy Roman Empire.' The gold and silver cross, now in the Cathedral Treasury at Esztergom, was made in Italy about 1480 and decorated with enamel, niello and relief work. On the obverse, four-lobed fields of dark-blue enamel, at the ends of the cross, show a pelican, with Mary Magdalene below, and three-quarter relief figures of the Blessed Virgin Mary and St John the Evangelist on the horizontal ends. There are figures of the four evangelists on the reverse. The stem of the 32-cm cross was added by Prince-Primate János Simor (1867–1891) in Vienna.

110. The 15th-c. crosier used at coronations (Cathedral Treasury, Esztergom)

The most recent liturgical object associated with the coronation was made in gold and silver in Neo-Gothic style, for the coronation of 1867. The vessel with a domed cover, 31 cm high, has the arms of Hungary on the base and a Latin inscription saying where and why it was made: it held the unction used to anoint the king.

The coronation chasuble and oath-taking mantle were made for the 1867 coronation, using earlier ornate church textiles. The chasuble was worn by the officiating primate, along with other vestments (stole, maniple *etc.*) The back and breast bear three vertical panels of embroidered tulips, pomegranates, rosettes and pinks. The Hungarian beadwork embroidery of a chasuble made for Primate György

111. The Holy Crown, with the sceptre, orb and coronation sword, being placed in the Domed Hall of Parliament on January 1, 2000

Szelepchényi was mounted on new gold brocade. The original chasuble had been used at coronations since the end of the 17th century. The archbishop donned the cope or pluvial after the mass, for the king's oath. The 17th-century gold embroidery was mounted on new material in 1867 for Prince-Primate János Simor.

The coronation mitre, the oldest coronation vestment, was made for Primate György Pálóczy (1423–1439) about 1430. The pointed mitre of white silk is covered on each side with beadwork embroidery. This and the ribbons are adorned with gems.

The archbishop used a gilded silver crosier made in the 15th century, later owned by Archbishop Miklós Oláh (1553–1568). At the top, the crook and knop are late Gothic work; the stem was made in the 16th century. The crook is adorned with gems. There is a relief of Our Lady of Hungary seated on a crescent moon at the end. The knop depicts a round chapel with Gothic niches. The height of the Gothic part is 37 cm, and the full length 188 cm.

In the procession to the king's oath-taking, the bishop riding before the crowned king carried a double cross of silver.

A Chronology
of Hungarian Kings and Coronations

This chronology includes the known coronations of Hungary's kings and their heirs, and the places of custody where the Holy Crown was kept. Kings were crowned in Székesfehérvár until 1527, and usually in Pozsony after 1563. The place of coronation is given only if it was held elsewhere.
The dates of reigns are given where they do not coincide with the coronations.

The coronation of Matthias II in Pozsony (Meteranus Novus, Amsterdam, 1633, tinted engraving).
Ráday Collection, Budapest

Golden coin of Stephen I

A denarius of Solomon's reign

The accession of Ladislas I (illumination in the Picture Chronicle)

The seal of Kálmán

Christmas, 1000	♔	STEPHEN I (ISTVÁN) is crowned in Esztergom. (The year was 1001 according to the date on which the year began at that time.)
September 2, 1031		The heir apparent, Prince Emericus (Imre) dies, and is buried in the Church of Our Lady, Székesfehérvár.
August 15, 1038		Stephen I dies and is buried in the Church of Our Lady, Székesfehérvár.
August, 1038	♔	PETER's coronation. First period of rule: 1038–1041.
Second half of 1041		Samuel Aba on the throne.
April 22, 1044		Samuel Aba's coronation takes place at Csanád (Cenad).
July 5, 1044		Battle of Ménfő, followed by the death of Samuel Aba, who is buried at Abasár Monastery.
July, 1044		Peter resumes the throne (1044–1046).
1046		Peter dies and is buried in Pécs Cathedral.
September, 1046	♔	ANDREW I (ANDRÁS, 1044–1060) is crowned .
1058	♔	SOLOMON is crowned as a child in his father's lifetime.
Autumn, 1060		Battle between Andrew I and his brother, Béla. Andrew is wounded at Moson and dies at Zirc. He is buried at the Benedictine Abbey of Tihany.
December 6, 1060	♔	BÉLA I is crowned on the Feast of St Nicholas.
After September 11, 1063		Béla I dies and is buried at the Benedictine Abbey of Szekszárd
September, 1063		Solomon (Salamon) takes the throne (1063–1074) with German help. His mother, Queen Anastasia, presents Otto of Nordheim, Duke of Bavaria, with 'Attila's Sword'.
April 11, 1064		Géza ceremonially places the crown on Solomon's head at Pécs, as a sign of peace.
March 14, 1074		Battle of Mogyoród. Solomon flees to Moson.
1075	♔	GÉZA I (1074–1077) is crowned.
April 24, 1077		Géza I dies and is buried in Vác Cathedral
April or May, 1077	♔	LADISLAS I (LÁSZLÓ) is crowned.
July 29, 1095		Ladislas I dies, and is buried in Nagyvárad Cathedral.
August, 1095	♔	COLOMON (KÁLMÁN) is crowned, probably by Szerafin, Archbishop of Esztergom.
February 3, 1116		Death of Colomon, who is buried at Székesfehérvár.
February, 1116	♔	STEPHEN II (ISTVÁN) is crowned by Lőrinc, Archbishop of Esztergom.
March or April, 1131		Death of Stephen II, who is buried at Nagyvárad, probably at the Premonstratensian Priory of Váradelőhegy.
April 28, 1131	♔	BÉLA II is crowned by Felicián, Archbishop of Esztergom.
1137		Béla II brings home from Byzantium the body of his father, Prince Álmos, and has him buried at Székesfehérvár.

February 13, 1141		Béla II dies and is buried at Székesfehérvár.
February 16, 1141		GÉZA II is crowned on a Sunday.
May 31, 1162		Death of Géza II, who is buried at Székesfehérvár.
Early June, 1162		STEPHEN III (ISTVÁN) is crowned by Lukács, Archbishop of Esztergom.

Grave goods of Béla III and Queen Anne of Antioch

June or July, 1162		LADISLAS II (LÁSZLÓ) is crowned by Mikó, Archbishop of Kalocsa.
January 14, 1163		Death of Ladislas II, who is buried at Székesfehérvár.
January 27, 1163		STEPHEN IV (ISTVÁN) is crowned on a Sunday by Mikó, Archbishop of Kalocsa.
April 11, 1165		Stephen IV dies at Zimony (Zemun). He is first buried there, in the Church of the Protomartyr, and later reburied at Székesfehérvár.
1167		The crown is held at the Church of Our Lady in Székesfehérvár.
March 4, 1172		Stephen III dies in Esztergom and is buried there.
March, 1172		Béla III is chosen king.

Copper coin of Béla III

January 13, 1173		BÉLA III is crowned on the Octave of Epiphany by the Archbishop of Kalocsa.
May 16, 1182		EMERICUS (IMRE) is crowned on Whit Sunday, in his father's lifetime by Miklós, Archbishop of Esztergom.
April 23, 1196		Béla III dies and is buried at Székesfehérvár.
August 26, 1204		LADISLAS III (LÁSZLÓ) is crowned on a Thursday by János, Archbishop of Kalocsa, at the desire of his father, Emericus, and with the authority of the pope.
September (?), 1204		Emericus dies and is buried in Eger Cathedral.
May 3, 1205 q		Ladislas III dies in Austria. The Bishop of Győr brings his body back to Székesfehérvár, where he is buried with the ceremony due to a king.

The seal of the Golden Bull of Andrew II

Spring, 1205		Andrew II obliges the Duke of Austria to return the crown.
May 29, 1205		ANDREW II (ANDRÁS) is crowned on Whit Sunday by János, Archbishop of Esztergom.
1214		Béla, son of Andrew II, is crowned at his father's behest.
1217		Andrew II sells the crown of Queen Gisela for 140 silver marks while on a crusade in the Holy Land.
1220		MARIA LASCARIS, wife of Béla, is anointed and crowned.
September 21, 1235		Andrew II dies and is buried at the Cistercian Monastery of Egres.
October 14, 1235		BÉLA IV is crowned on a Sunday by Róbert, Archbishop of Esztergom.
1241–1304		The Holy Crown is kept at Székesfehérvár.

Béla IV (illustration in the Augsburg Turóczi Chronicle)

Seal of the Latinists of Esztergom. 13th c.

A denarius of Andrew III

The first known illustration of Buda Castle (H. Schedel's World Chronicle, Nuremberg, 1493, in the Ráday Collection, Budapest)

August 20, 1245		STEPHEN (ISTVÁN) is crowned at the behest of his father, Béla IV.
1254		Béla IV refers in a deed to Székesfehérvár as the place where the royal throne and crown are held, where kings are anointed, and where his ancestors are laid to rest.
December 16, 1256		The first mention is made of the Holy Crown.
May 3, 1270		Death of Béla IV, who is buried with the Franciscans at Esztergom.
After May 13, 1270		STEPHEN V (ISTVÁN) is crowned king.
August 6, 1272		Stephen V dies and is buried on Margaret Island (now part of Budapest).
Before September 3, 1272		LADISLAS IV (LÁSZLÓ) is crowned by Fülöp, Archbishop of Esztergom.
July 10, 1290		Ladislas IV is murdered, and buried at Csanád.
July 23, 1290		ANDREW III is crowned on a Sunday by Ladomér, Archbishop of Esztergom.
January 14, 1301		The House of Árpád becomes extinct with the death of Andrew III.
Before May 13, 1301		CHARLES I (KÁROLY) of Anjou is crowned in Esztergom by Gergely Bicskei, Archbishop of Esztergom, with a crown made specially for the occasion.
August 27, 1301		WENCESLAS (VENCEL, 1301–1305), Prince of Bohemia, is crowned on a Sunday, the Octave of the Feast of St Stephen of Hungary, by János, Archbishop of Kalocsa.
1304		King Wenceslas has the Holy Crown in Bohemia.
1305		Otto, Prince of Bavaria, brings the crown back to Hungary. It is lost on the way, but recovered again.
December 6, 1305		OTTO OF WITTELSBACH, Prince of Bavaria, is crowned king on the Feast of St Nicholas, by Benedek Rád, Bishop of Veszprém, and Antal, Bishop of Csanád.

1305–10		The Holy Crown is in the custody of Voivod László Kán in Transylvania.
June 15, 1309		Charles I is crowned for the second time, at the Church of Our Lady in Buda, by Tamás, Archbishop of Esztergom, with a crown made for the occasion and blessed by the papal legate, Cardinal Nicholas Boccasino.
August 27, 1310	♔	CHARLES I is crowned for the third time, at Székesfehérvár, with the Holy Crown.
December 19, 1317		Queen Mary, consort of Charles I, dies at Temesvár.
1323–1403		The Holy Crown is kept in Visegrád Castle.
July 16, 1342		Charles I dies and is buried at Székesfehérvár.
July 21, 1342	♔	LOUIS I (LAJOS) the Great is crowned on a Sunday by Csanád Telegdi, Archbishop of Esztergom.
September 10, 1382		Louis I dies and is buried at Székesfehérvár.
September 17, 1382	♔	MARY (MÁRIA), daughter of Louis the Great, is crowned on a Saturday by Demeter, Archbishop of Esztergom.
December 24, 1385		Mary abdicates.
December, 1385	♔	CHARLES II (KÁROLY) the Less is crowned on a Sunday by Demeter, Archbishop of Esztergom.
February 7, 1386		Charles II is mortally wounded by an assailant. Mary resumes the government.
February 24, 1386		Charles II dies, but because he has been excommunicated, he is buried only in 1390, at the Benedictine Abbey of St Andrew, near Visegrád.

Queen Mary

March 31, 1387	♔	SIGISMUND (ZSIGMOND) of Luxemburg (1387–1437) is crowned on Palm Sunday, by Benedek Himházy, Bishop of Veszprém.
May 17, 1395		Queen Mary dies and is buried at Nagyvárad.
1401		While Sigismund is in captivity, a state 'Seal of the Holy Crown of Hungary' is made.
1403–1434		The crown is kept in the treasury at the Royal Castle of Buda, in Prince Stephen's Tower.
1434		Sigismund ordains that the crown and the accompanying jewels shall be in the custody of György Pálóczy, Archbishop of Esztergom, and Mátyás Pálóczy, Lord Chief Justice.
1434–9		The crown is kept in the Archbishop's Palace at Esztergom.
December 9, 1437		Sigismund dies at Znaim (Znojmo) in Moravia. He is buried in Nagyvárad Cathedral.
January 1, 1438	♔	ALBERT OF HABSBURG is crowned on a Tuesday by György Pálóczy, Archbishop of Esztergom.
1438		After the death of Archbishop Pálóczy, Albert removes the crown to Visegrád Castle.
October 27, 1439		Albert dies at Neszmély, Komárom County, and is buried at Székesfehérvár.

A gold forint of Sigismund's reign, depicting Ladislas I

1439–40		The crown is kept in Visegrád Castle.
February 1440		Ilona Kottanner obtains the crown from Visegrád for her infant son, Ladislas V.
May 15, 1440	♛	LADISLAS V (LÁSZLÓ, 1452–1457) is crowned king on Whit Sunday by Dénes Szécsi, Archbishop of Esztergom, with the Holy Crown. (The other coronation insignia were absent.)
July 17, 1440	♛	WLADYSLAW I (ULÁSZLÓ, 1440-1444) is crowned on a Sunday by Dénes Szécsi, Archbishop of Esztergom, with the crown of the reliquary of St Stephen.
1440–64		The Holy Crown is at Wiener Neustadt, in the keeping of Emperor Frederic III.
November 10, 1444		Wladislaw dies in the Battle of Varna.
November 23, 1457		Ladislas dies in Prague.
July 24, 1463		The Hungarians redeem the crown at Sopron from representatives of Frederic III, for 80,000 forints.
March 29, 1464	♛	MATTHIAS I (MÁTYÁS) HUNYADI (1458–1490) is crowned with the Holy Crown by Dénes Szécsi, Archbishop of Esztergom.
1464		An act is passed on custody of the Holy Crown.
April 6, 1490		Matthias dies in Vienna.
April 24, 1490		Matthias is buried at Székesfehérvár.
September 18, 1490	♛	WLADYSLAW II (ULÁSZLÓ) JAGELLO is crowned by Osvát Laki Túz, Bishop of Zagreb, in place of the Archbishop of Esztergom, who is still a minor.
1492		Act (XII) on the episcopal and baronial crown guards.
1500		Act (XXXI) on the lay crown guards.
July 26, 1506		Queen Anne (Foix-Grailly, Countess Candale) dies and is buried at Székesfehérvár.
June 4, 1508		Louis II (1516–1526) is crowned at the behest of his father by Tamás Bakócz, Archbishop of Esztergom.
March 13, 1516		Wladyslaw II dies at Buda.
March 19, 1516		Wladyslaw II is buried at Székesfehérvár.
August 29, 1526		Louis II drowns in the Csele Brook while fleeing from the Battle of Mohács.
November 10, 1526		Louis II is buried at Székesfehérvár.
November 11, 1526	♛	JOHN (JÁNOS) OF SZAPOLYA is crowned on a Sunday, St Martin's Day, by István Podmaniczky, Bishop of Nyitra.
November 3, 1527	♛	FERDINAND I OF HABSBURG (1526–1564) is crowned by István Podmaniczky, Bishop of Nyitra. This is the last coronation to be held in Székesfehérvár.
November 4, 1527		ANNE, the Hungarian princess, daughter of Wladyslaw II and consort of Ferdinand I, is crowned.
1527–1529		The Holy Crown is kept at Visegrád.

The seal of the Golden Bull of Matthias I

The seal of John of Szapolya

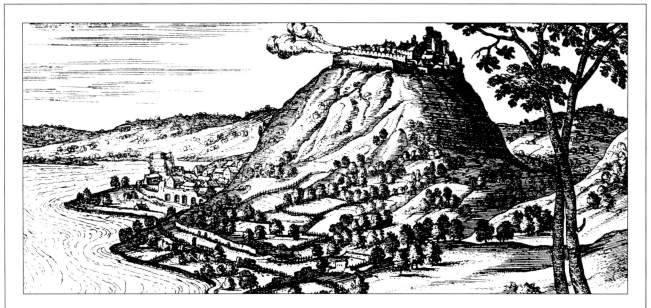

Detail of a view of Visegrád (copper engraving after a drawing by Jakob Hufnagel, 1597–8, Cologne)

1529		The crown is in the possession of Sultan Suleiman (at Pest and Rákosmező), and then of King John of Szapolya.
1529–51		The crown is kept in Transylvania.
July 22, 1540		John of Szapolya dies and is buried in Székesfehérvár Basilica. In 1543, Sultan Suleiman orders that the body be removed and reburied in the Church of St Michael.
July 21, 1551		Queen Isabella hands the crown to Ferdinand I.
1551–2		The crown is kept at Tokaj, and then in the castle at Pozsony.
1552–1608		The crown is kept at Pozsony, or sometimes in Vienna or Prague.

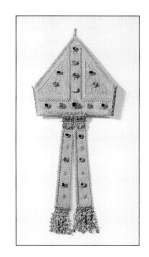

A coronation mitre

September 8, 1563 ♔ MAXIMILIAN (MIKSA, 1564–1576), son of Ferdinand I, Emperor and King, is crowned at his father's behest, on the Feast of the Nativity of the Blessed Virgin Mary, in St Martin's Church, Pozsony. The ceremony is performed by Miklós Oláh, Archbishop of Esztergom.

September 9, 1563 MARY, daughter of King Charles V of Spain, is crowned queen with a crown made for the occasion. She is touched on the shoulder with the Holy Crown, in a manner repeated at the coronations of later queens consort. The ceremony is performed by Miklós Oláh, Archbishop of Esztergom.

September 25, 1572 ♔ RUDOLF I (1576–1608) is crowned at Pozsony by Antal Verancsics, Archbishop of Esztergom.

November 19, 1608 ♔ MATTHIAS II (MÁTYÁS) is crowned on the Feast of St Elizabeth at Pozsony, by Ferenc Forgách, Archbishop of Esztergom. This is the first coronation in which the national colours of red, white and green feature on the hangings.

1608–18 The crown is kept at Pozsony Castle.

March 25, 1613 ANNE OF HABSBURG, Duchess of Tyrol and wife of Matthias II, is crowned queen at Pozsony on the Feast of the Annunciation. Anne was the founder of the Capuchin Monastery in Vienna, the Habsburgs' place of burial.

Antal Verancsics, Archbishop of Esztergom

75

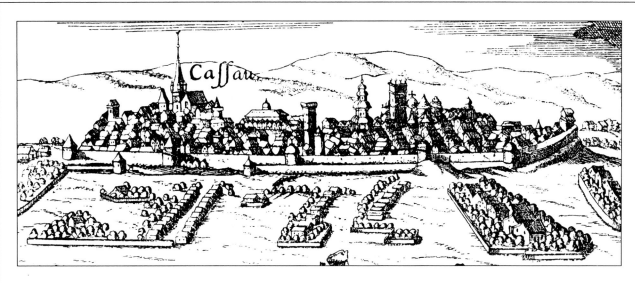

Kassa in the 18th c. (contemporary engraving)

The Franciscan Church at Sopron

July 1, 1618	♛	FERDINAND II (1619–1637) is crowned on a Sunday by Péter Pázmány, Archbishop of Esztergom.
1619–22		The crown is taken to Zólyom, Kassa, Eperjes, and then Ecséd Castle, by Péter Révay, the Crown Guard, accompanying Gábor Bethlen, Prince of Transylvania.
May, 1622		ANNA ELEONORA GONZAGA, Duchess of Mantua and wife of Ferdinand II, is crowned queen at Sopron.
December 31, 1622		Gábor Bethlen returns the crown, which is taken to Pozsony by way of Kassa and Trencsén (Trencin).
November 27, 1625	♛	The heir apparent Ferdinánd (who later became FERDINAND III, 1637–1657) is crowned in the Franciscan (Goat) Church at Sopron by Péter Pázmány, Archbishop of Esztergom.
February 14, 1638		MARY OF HABSBURG, the Spanish Infanta and first wife of Ferdinand III, is crowned on a Sunday at Pozsony by Imre Lósy, Archbishop of Esztergom.
1638		Threatened by the campaign of Kara Mustafa, the crown is taken to Vienna, Linz and Passau, and then returned to Pozsony.
June 16, 1647	♛	FERDINAND IV (d. 1654) is crowned king in his father's lifetime by György Lippay, Archbishop of Esztergom. The coronation has had to be postponed because of the fire in Pozsony.
June 6, 1655		MARIA ELEONORA GONZAGA, princess and third wife of Ferdinand III, is crowned queen in Pozsony.
June 27, 1655	♛	LEOPOLD I (LIPÓT) is crowned king in his father's lifetime on a Sunday, Feast of St Louis, King of Hungary, by György Lippay, Archbishop of Esztergom.
November 9, 1681		ELEONORA MAGDALENA, the Rhenish Countess Palatine, third wife of Leopold I, and a member of the Wittelsbach family, is crowned queen on a Sunday in Sopron. The Holy Crown is placed on her shoulder by the Primate (Archbishop of Esztergom) and the Palatine (king's lieutenant) jointly. The Bishop of Veszprém places the domestic crown on her head, and the Primate anoints her.

December 9, 1687	👑	JOSEPH I (JÓZSEF), (1705–1711) is crowned in his father's lifetime on a Tuesday, by György Széchényi, Archbishop of Esztergom.
1703–11		The crown is kept in Vienna.
1711–40		The crown is kept in Pozsony.
May 22, 1712	👑	CHARLES III (KÁROLY) and his wife Princess ELIZABETH CHRISTINA OF BRAUNSCHWEIG-WOLFSBÜTTEL are crowned on Trinity Sunday by Ágost Keresztély, Saxon Prince and Primate.
1740–48		The crown is kept at Komárom Castle during the War of the Austrian Succession.
June 25, 1741	👑	MARIA THERESA (MÁRIA TERÉZIA, 1735–1780) is crowned queen on a Sunday at Pozsony, by Imre Esterházy, Archbishop of Esztergom.
1748–84		The crown is kept at Pozsony.
1784–90		The crown is kept by Joseph II in the imperial treasury in Vienna.
February 17–21, 1790		The Holy Crown returns to Hungary, where it is taken to Köpcsény, to the Bishop's Palace at Győr, to the Archbishop's Palace at Esztergom, and to Buda.
November 15, 1790	👑	LEOPOLD II (LIPÓT) is crowned on a Monday in Pozsony by József Batthyány, Archbishop of Esztergom.
1791–1849		The Holy Crown is kept in Buda Castle.
June 6, 1792	👑	FRANCIS I (FERENC) is crowned on the vigil of the Lord's Day in the Guards Church of St Mary Magdalene in Buda.
June 10, 1792		MARIA THERESA OF BOURBON (d. 1807), Princess of Naples and Sicily and second wife of Francis I, is crowned on a Sunday in Buda.

Queen Maria Theresa

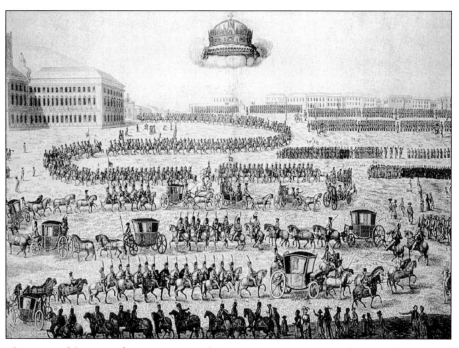

The Return of the Crown from Vienna to Buda in 1790. Hungarian National Museum

December, 1805	During the Napoleonic Wars, the Coronation Regalia are taken from Buda to the Bishop's Palace in Ungvár.
1808	MARIA LUDOVICA OF HABSBURG (d. 1816), third wife of Francis I, is crowned queen in Pozsony.
1809	The Holy Crown is hidden successfully in the Pest house of the Crown Guard Pál Almásy, in the cathedral treasury and then the county hall at Eger, and in Almásy's house at Gyöngyös. It is returned to Buda in November.
1825	CAROLINA AUGUSTA, Bavarian Princess and fourth wife of Francis I, is crowned in Pozsony.
September 27, 1830 ♛	FERDINAND V (1835–1848) is crowned on a Sunday. This is the last coronation to take place in Pozsony.
1849	During the Hungarian War of Independence, the crown is taken successively to Debrecen, Szeged, the Bishop's Palace in Nagyvárad, Arad, Lugos (Lugoj), Karánsebes (Caransebe), and Orsova (Orova).
August, 1849	Bertalan Szemere buries the crown at Orsova.
September 8, 1853	The crown is discovered at Orsova, taken to Buda and Vienna, and then returned to Buda.
1853–1944	The Holy Crown is kept in Buda Castle.
June 8, 1867 ♛	FRANCIS JOSEPH I (FERENC JÓZSEF) and his consort, ELIZABETH (ERZSÉBET) OF WITTELSBACH, Bavarian Princess, are crowned on the eve of Whit Sunday in the Church of Our Lady in Buda.
December 30, 1916 ♛	CHARLES IV (KÁROLY) and his consort, ZITA OF BOURBON-PARMA, are crowned on a Saturday in the Church of Our Lady in Buda. The crown is placed on the king's head by János Csernoch, Archbishop of Esztergom, and Count István Tisza, the Prime Minister. This is the last coronation of a king or queen in Budapest.
1944	The Holy Crown is known to have been in Veszprém at the end of October and in Kőszeg on December 6.
1945	The crown, held in Velem in January, is taken in March to Kőszeg, then to Mariazell, Austria, and then to Mattsee, where it is buried. It is discovered again in July, taken to Augsburg, and finally to Frankfurt.
1951–78	The crown is in Fort Knox, Texas.
January 6, 1978	The Holy Crown and regalia are returned to Hungary by the Carter administration and placed in the Hungarian National Museum in Budapest.
December 21, 1999	The Hungarian Parliament passes an act on the commemoration of St Stephen's foundation of the Hungarian state and on the Holy Crown.
January 1, 2000	The Holy Crown, the sceptre, the orb and the sword are solemnly transferred to the Parliament building, where Prime Minister Viktor Orbán opens the Millennium Year.

A ducat of Ferdinand V

Francis Joseph I and Elizabeth on a commemorative card for the 1896 millenary celebrations

Select Bibliography

This list is confined to works in the main Western European languages. A full bibliography, including works in Hungarian, appears in the Hungarian edition of this book.

Bak, J.M.: 'Sankt Stefans Armreliquie im Ornat König Wenzels von Ungarn', in: *Festschrift P. R. Schramm*, Volume I, Wiesbaden, 1964.

Balassa, Fr.: *Casulae S. Stephani regis Hungariae*, Vienna, 1754.

Bárány-Oberschall, M. von: *Die Sankt Stephans-Krone und die Insignien des Königreiches Ungarn*, Vol. 3 of *Die Kronen des Hauses Österreich*, Vienna and Munich, 1961.

Benda, K. and E. Fügedi: *Tausend Jahre Stephanskrone*, Budapest, 1988.

Bogyay, Th. von: 'Ungarns Heilige Krone', in: *Ungarn-Jahrbuch 9*, 1978.

Deér, J.: *Die Heilige Krone Ungarns*, 'Denkschrifte der österreichischen Akademie d. Wiss. Phil-hist.' series No. 91, Vienna, 1966.

Fodor, I.: *Die große Wanderung der Ungarn vom Ural nach Pannonien*, Budapest, 1982.

Fügedi, E.: 'Medieval Coronations in Hungary', *Studies in Medieval and Renaissance History*, No. 3, 1981.

Kelleher, P.: *The Holy Crown of Hungary*, Rome, 1951.

Kovács, É.: 'Casula St. Stephani Regis', *Acta Historiae Artium*, No. 5, 1958, pp. 181–222.

Kovács, É.: 'Iconismus Casulae Sancti Stephani Regis', in: F. Glatz and J. Kardos (eds.): *Szent István és kora* (St Stephen and His Age), pp. 133–44.

Kovács, É. and Zs. Lovag: *The Hungarian Crown and the Coronation Regalia*, Budapest, 1980.

Kovács, É. and Zs. Lovag: *Die ungarische Krone und Krönungsinsignien*, Budapest, 1980.

Lovag, Zs. (ed.): *Studien zur Machtsymbolik des mittelalterlichen Ungarn*, Vol. 1 of *Insignia Regni Hungariae*, Budapest, 1983.

Révay, P.: *De sacrae coronae Regni Hungariae ortu, virtute, victoria, fortuna. Commentarius cum icone*, Vienna, 1652.

Tóth, E.: 'Zur Ikonographie des ungarischen Krönungsmantels', *Fol. Arch.*, Vol. 24, 1973, pp. 219–40.

Uhlirz, M.: *Die Krone des heiligen Stephan, des ersten Königs von Ungarn*, Graz, Cologne and Munich, 1951.

Vajay, Sz.: 'La relique stéphanoise de la Sainte Couronne de Hongrie', *Acta Historiae Artium*, Vol. 22, 1976, pp. 3–20.

Vajay, Sz.: 'Corona Regia—Corona Regni—Sacra Corona. Königskronen und Kronensymbolik im mittelalterlichen Ungarn', *Ungarn-Jahrbuch 7*, 1976, pp. 37–64.

Váczy, P.: 'Helm und Diadem (Numismatische Beiträge zur Entstehung der byzantinischen Kaiserkrone)', *Acta Antiqua*, Vol. 20, 1972, pp. 169–208.

Veszprémy, L. (ed.): *Die 'Gesta Hungarorum' des anonymen Notars. Die älteste Darstellung der ungarischen Geschichte*, Sigmaringen, 1991.

Places Formerly in Hungary Mentioned in This Book

Arad – Arad, Romania
Csanád – Cenad, Romania
Egres – Igriş, Romania
Eperjes – Prešov, Slovakia
Garamszentbenedek – Hronský Beňadik, Slovakia
Karánsebes – Caransebeş, Romania
Kassa – Košice, Slovakia
Komárom – Komárno, Slovakia
Köpcsény – Kittsee, Austria
Körmöcbánya – Kremnica, Slovakia
Lugos – Lugoj, Romania
Marosvár, Marosújvár – Ocna Mures, Romania
Nagyvárad – Oradea, Romania

Nyitra – Nitra, Slovakia
Nyitraivánka – Ivanka pri Nitre, Slovakia
Orsova – Orşova, Romania
Pozsony – Bratislava, Slovakia
Szerém – Srem, Croatia and Serbia
Temesvár – Timişoara, Romania
Torda – Turda, Romania
Trencsén – Trenčin, Slovakia
Ungvár – Ushgorod, Ukraine
Várad – Oradea, Romania
Zimony – Zemun, Serbia
Zólyom – Zvolen, Slovakia

Text by Endre Tóth

Photographs by Károly Szelényi

The photographs No 101, 105, 106, 107, 108, 109, 110 were made by Attila Mudrák

Expert advisers: Balázs Dercsényi, István Éri, Dr Zsuzsa Lovag and Dr József Török

Drawings by Katalin Nagy, Katalin Pintér and Ágnes Vári

Editor: József Vadas
Co-editor: Aranka Sz. Farkas

Translated by Brian McLean

The publisher would like to express gratitude to Dr Tibor Kovács, Director of Hungarian National Museum,
Dr Géza Érszegi, Dr Éva Kovács †, and Dr Gábor Zongor

The illustrations in this book are reproduced by kind permission of the
Archabbey of Pannonhalma
Cathedral Treasury, Esztergom
the National Archives, Budapest
the National Széchényi Library, Budapest
the Ráday Collection, Budapest
and the University Library, Budapest

Colour processing by Révai Repro Kft., Budapest
Printed by Prospektus Nyomda Kft., Veszprém
Bound by Egyetemi Nyomda, Budapest

Frontispiece: Top of the Holy Crown
Page 3: The marble king's head of Kalocsa (early 13th c.)

Publisher responsible: András Sándor Kocsis,
Chairman and Managing Director, Kossuth Publishing Corp., Budapest

ISBN 963 09 41708